THE WEIGHT OF A
THOUSAND OCEANS

THE FORGOTTEN ONES BOOK ONE

JILLIAN WEBSTER

ALSO BY JILLIAN WEBSTER

Scared to Life: A Memoir

For my husband, with all my heart.

PROLOGUE

It's happening again.

Her nightmares have been occurring more and more. No matter how hard she tries, she can't seem to escape them. They chase her into the deepest recesses of her mind, smashing through locked doors and hidden rooms, mercilessly dragging out everything she's fought her entire life to forget.

She recognizes this wild and foreboding trail where she now stands—knows every detail of it with every cell of her being. She's familiar with every green vein of each fluttering leaf and every knotted and twisted branch snaking deep across the path. She's walked this passageway thousands of times throughout her twenty years of life. Each night, when it greets her in her dreams, she knows her mother will be waiting for her on the other side.

And she knows what she'll be expecting.

Closing her eyes, Maia holds out a single trembling hand. With one sweeping motion, she commands the branches of the overgrown trees to swoop to the ground, clearing the once obstructed trail leading to the beach. She wanders along the path, careful to avoid the huddled branches on the ground, now quivering from the fear of being crushed.

Stepping from the forest onto the warm sand, Maia is immediately enveloped into her mother's welcoming embrace. "Good, darling. *Very good*," her mother whispers with a smile. She grasps Maia's hands and leads her farther onto the beach. "Now," her mother says with an even bigger smile. "Do the same with *all* the bush."

Maia turns to the woods behind them. Swiping her hand across the landscape, she gasps as every tree and bush bows to the ground.

"*Shhh*, be careful—*don't hurt them*. They are all your children," her mother says. She grabs Maia's shoulders and steps behind her. "Look how they bow to you. Look how much they *love* you."

Alarmed, Maia retracts her hand. The trees uncoil upwards, sending leaves seesawing to the ground.

"I don't know ... I don't understand," Maia breathes with alarm.

Her mother stands proudly behind her but says nothing.

Maia turns to face her. "Mum, I miss you so much."

"I'm right here, darling. I've always been with you, right here in your dreams."

"What is happening to me?"

Maia's mother gazes down at her with a discouraged look across her face. "Come," she says with a sigh. Wading into the ocean, her fingertips skim the glassy surface and her white gown flows behind her.

Maia stands reluctantly on the shore with the rolling hills of the tranquil New Zealand coastline sitting behind her. The sky a placid dome of blue, a light breeze sends newly fallen leaves tumbling across the beach.

Scanning the shoreline, Maia watches as the coast on either side of her slowly wraps around until it connects across the ocean, transforming the body of water into an immense lake.

Maia's mother stands in the middle, reaching out to her. "Come, my darling," she says with a smile.

Behind her mother, a foreign city now looms, murky and vague. Countless dark towers shoot into the sky, disappearing into a rolling layer of black clouds.

Maia stands frozen on the beach, consumed with fear. The water is just a step away. She peers over the edge to find the shore has morphed into a sudden drop into a bottomless watery abyss. "Mum, I can't jump!" She shakes her head, frantic as her mother's body begins to dissolve into the sea. "Please, don't do this."

Her mother's hands clench in fists at her sides. "Stop being so *afraid*, Maia. I'm trying to help you!" Her voice fades into a whisper. The details of the mysterious city behind her are now illuminated through her gown. "Hurry!" Her mother reaches out to her.

The once placid ocean is now furious, sending countless massive crests of water hurling towards Maia. Her mother continues to call to her, and then she stops, mesmerized by something along the shore. Her eyes narrow and her hands drape to her sides, placated like a rag doll. A smile curves up from her lips, and then she disappears completely.

Maia cries out but her screams are immediately silenced. The ocean is still heaving swells at her feet, sending white explosions of water scattering into the wind, but the surges make no sound. There is no rustling in the trees, no birds chirping along the shore. Maia's gasps remain mute despite her adrenaline stealing the breath from her lungs. It's as if the air itself is being sucked into a void.

Soft laughter travels in waves across the barren expanse. Chills race up Maia's spine as she recognizes the laughter as her own. She turns to face a fierce young woman standing alone along the shore, her delicate white gown rippling softly behind her.

Maia remains frozen, captivated ... *terrified*, as the reflection of herself glares at her with two different-colored eyes faintly glimmering like crystal. Her skin is like porcelain, and her long red ringlets of hair spill down her back.

Maia pulls frantically at her hair; her long auburn waves have been replaced by a full head of red spirals. Wrapping her arms around herself, she trembles in her white gown.

The two stand across from each other—mirror images, motionless and silent. Then the ghost reaches for Maia as a peculiar grin spreads wide across her face and Maia unleashes an earth-shattering wail.

Sitting up in bed, Maia's screams still pour from her lungs. Her clothing is soaked with sweat, her face streaked with tears. She clutches at the sheets, gasping for air as her grandfather rushes to her side.

ONE

A match strikes a fire. His old hands tremble as they cup the delicate flame. Its flickering light dances across the dark cabin high up in the mountains as he carries it to a half-melted candle sitting on the table between them. The glow casts wavering shadows across his weathered face, the deep lines and crevices of his skin tracing like road maps on scorched land.

She looks at him in earnest, the fluttering candle bouncing waves of light off her porcelain skin. They sit for a moment—too afraid to speak yet terrified of their silence.

"Grandpa?"

His body trembles and she fights the urge to hold him. His tired eyes cast down upon the flame as an entire world flashes before him.

"Grandpa, tell me."

He looks up with glassy, bloodshot eyes, holding her motionless in his gaze. "How could I possibly—" He takes a deep breath and his head collapses into his hands.

She drops to her knees, wrapping her arms around his frail body. "I'm sorry. It's okay." She holds the side of his face.

"We don't have to talk about it." She kneels before him and he grabs her hands.

"The earth used to be such a *beautiful* place." His eyes are wide—afraid—searching the darkness from beneath a deeply furrowed brow. "Like the wheels of a clock, everything clicked together. Life had evolved that way for billions of years." Hesitating, he looks up at her. "We were so arrogant. We had been playing the hand of God for too long." His voice cracks. "We controlled everything back then, or at least we lived in the illusion that we did, and life was really good for a while. We had control over sicknesses, aging, and death. We controlled the production of our crops, our livestock, even our genes and the genes of our children. Life was engineered and modified to fit our needs and our population grew at warp speed. The earth groaned under the weight of our actions but we couldn't hear it. Like supercomputers, we defied the laws of nature. Our technology, *my God*, the things we could do. We were unstoppable."

A gust of wind rattles the windows of their cabin. Maia quickly pulls a few pieces of wood from a large wicker basket and stacks them in the living room fireplace. Pulling out a small reed, she lights it from the candle and places it under the stack. She leans close to blow the embers, and the delicate flames stretch like arms around the timber.

"From the beginning of time, life on Earth has experienced numerous *massive* extinctions," her grandfather continues. "And from those extinctions, beautiful things have evolved, things that would have never existed before. Life as a whole tends to work like this. Some of the most beautiful things in this world have been born from disaster."

He looks at her with a fondness in his eyes and he softly cups her chin. "Darling, *you* are a beautiful thing born from this disaster. Life is still here. If there is one thing we all have in common, from the smallest, most insignificant creature to the largest, it would be that nothing wants to die." He quickly moves away. Holding his breath, he searches his pockets and pulls out a small cloth.

The fire hisses and pops, spitting sparks into the darkness. Maia sits on a tattered old rug, anxiously watching her grandfather as he hunches over and coughs violently into his cloth. He shoves it into his pocket and leans back in his chair, his rattled lungs wheezing as he catches his breath.

"I still can't figure it out," he gasps. "I can't seem to wrap my head around it—how we could have done better, where exactly we went wrong. We could have never imagined, Maia. But that all seems like so long ago now."

"Grandpa? What *happened*?"

Exhausted, he rests his head back in his chair and moans as he winces in pain.

Maia grabs his pipe. "Take it."

His knotted fingers clutch the briar pipe and he repositions himself forward as she lights the bowl. He leans back, gazing into the fire, and a heavy flow of smoke streams from his nose.

A low rumble barrels from a distance.

"Quake," Maia says. Jumping to her feet, she crouches beside him and wraps her arms around his hunched body.

They close their eyes and brace themselves as the ground beneath them begins to shake. The cabin moans and creaks at the seams as it wavers from the unstable ground. The earth jolts forward again and a picture drops from the wall. Maia whimpers and her grandfather holds her tight. Another jolt.

"Grandpa?!" Maia looks at him in panic.

Dust and dirt hiding between the tightly packed rafters fall in streams from the ceiling. She grabs his arms and lifts him to his feet. The earth jolts back again and they tumble to the ground.

"Grandpa!"

He holds her face next to his. "Maia? *You are my sunshine...*"

She smiles. "*My only sunshine.*"

"*You make me happy, when skies are gray.*"

"Is it still going?"

"A little bit. *You'll never know, dear...*" He sits back and lifts her chin. "*How much I love you.*"

The earth calms beneath them and Maia sighs.

"That was a good one," he says as he surveys the cabin. "I thought we bolted down everything, but looks like there was a straggler."

Maia stands and grabs the picture frame, a photo of a young child on a swing. Her auburn hair is up around her face as gravity pulls her away from the photographer. Her one foot higher than the other, she is kicking to the sky and smiling ... or is she laughing? Her two front teeth are missing. Grandpa says she was about six when this photo was taken. That was *before*. Before what, though, he still has not been able to talk about.

"Your mother was such a happy child." He reaches out and Maia hands him the photo. "You look just like her. Have I ever told you that?" he asks, gazing at the glass. "You even have the same eyes."

"Many times, Grandpa."

"It's very unusual to have two different-colored eyes, Maia. Beautiful really. One blue and one green, like the colors of the earth. Here, help an old man up."

She takes the photo and sets it aside, then helps him maneuver to his feet. He rests back in his chair. A high-pitched whine sounds from the porch.

Her grandfather looks up at her. "No."

"Grandpa, *please*. You know how much he hates earthquakes, the poor thing."

"That dog is not stupid. He's putting on a show just to make you feel bad."

"Well, it's working." She walks to the front door and cracks it open.

A large black dog barrels his way through and heads straight for the rug. He circles twice and then he's down, resting his head on the ground as he looks up at them.

Maia smiles. "You are *such* a baby."

She hangs the photo back on the wall, making a mental note to secure it later, then stands back and surveys the collection of pictures hanging before her. "Would you like some hot water?" she asks without turning around.

"That would be great."

After bringing her grandfather a mug filled from the kettle on the wood burner, she sits down on the ottoman next to him. She sighs, feeling defeated. "So, another time, then?"

"Yes, darling."

"You promise?"

He hesitates.

"Grandpa?"

"Your life is better not knowing."

"Grandpa!"

He winks at her. "I promise."

They stare into the fire. Another gust of wind berates the side of the cabin. Maia runs her hands through the dog's thick fur, listening to the burning wood crackle and pop next to her.

"Darling."

She looks back to her old grandfather, startled to see tears in his eyes.

"You haven't experienced much adversity in your twenty years on this earth, but you will. This is a fact of which no one human is exempt. Throughout your life, you may hear or meet people who are capable of doing terrible things." He leans forward and she meets him, grabbing his fragile hands once more. "You, my darling, may do terrible things. Every human has the potential to do great things—earth-shattering things—both good and evil. Don't let this harden you. Don't ever commit the crime of believing one person cannot make a difference. Every change has stemmed from a single thought, a single action, a single person. One person can change the world."

TWO

Racing along the ancient trail, Maia braces herself against the countless branches of ferns stretching awkwardly into the path. The long waves of her auburn hair swoosh behind her as she ducks and winces against the imposing limbs. She curses herself for not bringing her machete.

Her heart pounds as he gasps in spurts behind her, knowing any minute he could inch close enough to pounce. She jumps over another tree's tangled, mossy roots, then dives under a large branch drooping stubbornly across the trail. "I'll never hand it over!" she screams as she jumps over another fallen trunk.

The brush clears ahead and Maia knows what she must do. Breaking out from the thick covering of branches, the hot sun sweeps over her. She stops in her tracks and whips around.

He nervously watches her, his brown eyes twitching. She slowly steps back, holding it high above her head. He inches closer.

She flips around. Running to the edge of the cliff, she

dives headfirst and plunges into the sparkling water below. Reaching the surface, her laughs echo off the rocky cliffs above.

His head peeks over the edge for a brief moment, then disappears, leaving nothing but a furry black tail waving against the stark blue sky.

"Come on, Huck, don't be such a baby!"

His tail waves faster and he lets out a pitiful bark.

"Silly dog. If you want this stick, you're going to have to come and get it!" She holds it above the water and his head peeks over the edge.

He disappears again, and an outpour of barking echoes off the cliff. She giggles as she treads the surface. He whimpers and paces the trail above, pausing every few steps to glance down at her and his precious stick.

"If you don't come down here, I'll come up there and throw you in!"

He disappears.

"Huck!" She begins her swim to the rocks, gliding through the warm salty water as she giggles to herself.

A large, circular blob floats in front of her and she stops. Holding her breath, she ducks her head beneath the water, watching as the massive jellyfish's striated cap opens and closes, slowly propelling it along as its elongated tentacles flow delicately behind it.

What is that doing here? She lifts her head above the water. This space is netted off—she has spent years securing the area so she and Huck could swim in the ocean without fear of being stung. Another jellyfish catches her eye just beneath the surface, followed by two more below it.

There must be a tear.

Whipping around in the water, Maia eyes her surroundings. She ducks her head above and below the surface, searching for more. And that's when she sees it.

A bloom.

Thousands of jellyfish encircle the thick nets, their sheer weight permitting them to slowly bulldoze through the massive netting as if the tightly braided enclosure were merely a suggestion.

Moving in a zigzag motion, Maia attempts to swim to shore, stopping every few strokes to dip her head below the surface and check her surroundings.

Eventually reaching land, she crawls on top of the large boulders lining the shore. Her knees knock together and her arms give out. The salty ocean water drips off the tip of her nose as she catches her breath, watching as hundreds of jellyfish slowly trickle in through the loose and broken netting.

This is not the first time this has happened and it won't be the last. Jellyfish rule the ocean now. With limited predators, warm seas, and over 700 million years of evolution, they've become sly at adapting to the elements. She'll have to wait for them to clear out to fix the netting ... *again.*

She trails her way back up to the platform but by the time she reaches the top, her beloved pup is gone. Shaking her head, she peers over the once crystal blue waters, crushed by the severity of the situation below. Thousands of translucent, balloon-like creatures mindlessly stack on top of each other as they swarm the nets, slowly invading her once pristine swimming area.

She gazes past the nets to the horizon and lets out a disheartened sigh. Out there. She wonders what sort of worlds lie out there? A smile slides across her lips then fades just as quickly. Years of early morning prodding and late-night pleadings with her grandfather drum the banks of her memory like a migraine. Pounding, pounding, pounding.

"*What if...*"

"*No, darling.*"

"*But maybe...*"

"*No, darling.*"

"*But—*"

"*No, no, NO.*"

There's nothing out there. The world is deserted, just like the oceans. She takes another deep breath and starts the trek home.

Back on the path, she brushes her hands along the broad flax leaves curving like explosions along the increasingly overburdened trail. Her ancestors used the long hardy leaves to make anything from woven baskets to rope to footwear. Centuries later, they are still invaluable to daily life. She'll have to collect some again to fix her netting.

So familiar with these leaves and this land, Maia's walked it thousands of times, from adventures as a child to even more repetitive adventures as an adult. She gazes around, loving this familiar bush as much as she loathes it.

Far off, a figure catches her eye. She looks up in shock as a strange man races down another trail. The fabric of his peculiar, one-piece suit swishes together as he runs. A long zipper stretches from his left ankle up to his dark beard, peeking out from the black netting sewn around his wide-brimmed hat. The netting has been tucked beneath his collar, hiding his face. Despite his obscurity, she knows he's not from around here. There are only a handful of people around these parts and she has known them her entire life.

Distracted, Maia unknowingly hooks her foot beneath a tree root stretching across the path. She falls forward and the tree's branch whips across the trail, slamming across her waist. She grunts as she doubles over the knotted arm and the limb lifts her back to her feet.

Maia stumbles back as the branch slowly moves above the path to its original position. Bewildered, her eyes dart between the dirt track and the branch. Back, forth, and back again. A few glistening streams of light flicker across the tree. She shakes her head.

A twig cracks in the distance, grabbing her attention once more. The stranger is far away now—she can't lose him. *What is he doing here?* She trails behind him as quietly as she can, but not without stealing a few uncertain glances back at the branch sitting innocently above the trail.

The man comes to a clearing, slowing his pace as he breaks from beneath the line of trees. Maia watches from behind a row of bushes. A lone woman with a baby stands in the middle of the field. She is also wearing a wide-brimmed hat and the same simple clothing. The fabric isn't something Maia has come across when rummaging through abandoned shops and homes. It appears light but protective, with an uninterrupted material stretching from the woman's boots to her collar. Her netting has been folded back and now drapes across the top of her hat.

The woman smiles when she sees him. She looks relieved. He pulls the netting out from under his suit and removes his hat. She hands him the baby and he holds it against his chest.

"So?" the woman asks as she strokes the baby's head.

"Nothing, just an old man living with his granddaughter. That's all that's up here."

"Right." A look of disappointment hangs heavy across her face.

"So, I guess we'll have to stick closer to shore for now." He rubs the side of her arm. "Maybe next to the boat graveyard we passed, outside of that flooded town? There are a few others that have set up there as well—plenty of abandoned homes to choose from."

She grimaces.

"You don't like that idea."

"It's just so *eerie*. Back in Australia, we had our family's house; this is a new concept for me. It's like the world has become one enormous ghost town full of abandoned homes, skeletons from a world that no longer exists. It's haunting."

"I know, but we're here now. We've found a better life for ourselves."

"I hope so."

"You should see the setup that old man and his granddaughter have up there. It's brilliant. I want to make us something like that."

"That could take years. What will we do until then? This is exhausting."

He pulls her to him and wraps his arms around her, kissing the top of her head. "We'll figure it out. It will be okay, I promise."

Back from behind the bushes, Maia plans her escape. Hunched over, she delicately guides each foot into the leaf-littered ground. Just a few more steps and she can sneak off along the trail.

"Hello?"

Maia winces, stopping in her tracks.

"Excuse me?"

She stands and forces a smile. "Hello."

"Hi." The young man is now facing her. He hands the baby back to the woman and steps towards her. "I'm Collin. This is Sarah, and our boy, Henry."

Maia walks towards them, extending her hand. "I'm

16

Maia."

"Maia. Hello! You live with your grandfather?" Collin cups her hand between his with an enthusiastic shake. Up close, the details of his burns stretch across the lower part of his face and neck. The scar tissue has caused the skin to pucker and crease in rumpled swirls.

"Yes." She averts her eyes. "Welcome to New Zealand. I assume you've traveled here from somewhere else? I haven't seen you around."

"Yes, we're from Australia. We've come with a few others. Conditions over there are pretty deadly. The droughts and fires are out of control ... we've lost everything."

"I'm so sorry to hear that." She scratches the back of her head. "*Others*? You've come with others?"

"Yes, my parents."

"Right."

"We don't mean to bother you. We were just trying to figure out our next step. It seems pretty nice here, a bit cooler too ... and *abandoned*. Where is everyone?"

"Everyone? What do you mean? Are there many where you are?"

"Not many, but more than this."

"Our population has always been relatively small from what I've heard. There are people left here, not many, but they're here," Maia says.

"Right."

"I think your best bet would be to find an abandoned place. There are a ton farther down the coast."

"Yeah, that's what I think we may have to do for now ... not a whole lot up here," Collin says.

"There is a small tribe in the closest Northern Island—"

"No. Not north. Not on this side of the equator, at least. We are trying to get as far south as possible. We thought it might be a bit cooler still on your Southern Islands, especially up here in the mountains."

"Oh, it's still cool, especially since we're in the middle of winter. The evenings are a bit chilly but the days can heat up quickly if the sun is out."

"Snow?"

"No. Not in my lifetime—not anymore." Maia shrugs.

"*Hmm*, disappointing." Collin flashes a sympathetic look towards Sarah. "I've done quite a bit of research and thought for sure all the way up here you'd still have snow, at least in the winter, but things just keep heating up, so I guess I should have known."

"Yeah, you can see the remnants of some rusty ski lifts and lodgings around the area but those all closed down years before my grandfather bought the land to build up here, and that was when he was a young man."

Sarah tugs at Collin's sleeve. "Maybe we should keep moving?" she whispers. "I thought our goal was to find snow. The heat here will be quite intense by the time we're old—"

Maia brushes the side of the cooing baby's cheek. "I haven't seen one of these for a while."

"Are there not many young ones here?"

"Not many. The few that were here have grown and left."

"Left? And gone where?"

"I'm not sure. Out there. To find other life, start over. I guess exactly what you've done."

"Yes, but we didn't have a choice."

Maia fidgets with the waist-high weeds at her side.

Oblivious, Collin smiles at Sarah. "This place seems perfect—albeit secluded."

"*Hmm*." Maia kicks the stones beneath her feet. "Yeah, I suppose it is."

"Well, those young ones are brave." Sarah puts Henry on the ground and he crawls forward, grabbing at the long grass around him. "I wouldn't dare head out there yet. What if it's terrible?"

Maia looks up at her. "Sure..." she says. "But what if it's not?"

THREE

Maia enters a small grassy clearing where a modest log cabin sits tucked back in the corner. Ancient pines and ferns surround the home, forming a wall-like labyrinth of green. Thick smoke pours from the home's brick chimney, half-devoured by moss. The smell of cooking onions and garlic fill the air. The front doors have been left open to a small covered porch, where Huck sits waiting between wooden rockers on an outdoor rug. His tail wags as he watches her approach from the corner of his eye, too lazy to lift his head.

A little black bird sits on the fence just outside the cabin and starts squeaking when he sees her.

"Well, hello there. Back again?" Maia asks.

The bird hops along the mossy wood, tipping his body forward and back while spreading his black and white tail in a beautiful, fanlike display. The white markings on his face resemble a pair of bushy white eyebrows and a beard. His rounded brown chest could pass as a vest under a black dinner jacket, giving him the look of a distinguished old man. He squeaks repeatedly, sounding more like a pet's chew toy than a bird.

Maia walks past, shaking her head at Huck as she approaches the stairs. "Traitor." She pats his head and walks inside.

She smiles as she enters their home. The living room fireplace roars inside the large, blackened hearth, and an array of homemade candles have been lit, making their one-room cabin feel warm and inviting. Large mats cover the worn wooden floor, and a few sheepskin rugs have been placed between the fire and their two faded leather recliners. Countless framed photographs of her mother and deceased family and friends blanket the cabin walls. Two beds sit tucked in separate corners, their heavy privacy drapes pulled back and tied around the large wooden posts. Her grandfather's pride and joy, an antique mahogany grandfather clock, is nestled in the corner by his bed, chiming four o'clock.

Maia's grandfather stands next to the wood stove in the kitchen with a large pot of vegetable stew steaming on top. He turns around and smiles, his spectacles fogged from the steam. "Hello, darling."

She laughs.

"How was the hunt?" With a quivering hand, he wipes his glasses on his flannel. "Find anything today?"

"Nothing."

"You look a little wet." He sets his glasses back on his face, eyeing her suspiciously through his cracked frames. "I know you didn't fish in the ocean, nothing but jellies in there."

"The nets broke again."

"You didn't go in and fix them, did you? You know you need a spotter for that."

"No, I was already in when I noticed." She hesitates and then adds, "There was a bloom."

"And you were in there?"

"It happened out of nowhere! Anyway, I'll wait for it to clear and maybe you could spot me again?"

"Sure. In the meantime, please be more careful, aye?"

"Of course, Grandpa."

"There's a bowl of potatoes sitting on the table. Could you cut them into cubes for me?"

Maia takes a seat at the table and grabs a knife. A large painting of a tiger hangs on the wall across from her. Not the whole tiger—just his head, off-center, with the image cutting off at the tear duct of his second eye. When she sits at the table, she'll often drift into a daze, mesmerized by the mirroring black lines painted across his face and his furry, rust-colored nose. It looks so soft. What would it be like to touch it? To run her finger down its broad, flattened surface and then back up the opposite direction between his eyes to his forehead. It's always been Huck's favorite spot. She can almost always lull him to sleep this way.

This leads her back to the tiger's eye. Always back to his eye, the color of limes, haloed with yellow. So detailed … she can nearly count the individual striations that lead into his pupil before abruptly disappearing into a black hole. There's a whole universe located inside that pupil. So focused. *So sad.*

His face is like an old friend Maia has known her entire life. The painting has always transfixed her, not only because her mother painted it, but for some other reason … maybe it was the way he looked at her. It was like he *knew.* And when she looked at him, she knew too.

That same familiar squeak interrupts her thoughts, this time just outside the dining room window. "That fantail has been here quite a bit lately, hasn't he?" Maia asks as she watches the bird flitter about, catching countless microscopic bugs.

"*Ah*, the pīwakawaka. My favorite." Her grandfather chimes in from the kitchen. "He must have something to tell us."

"As long as he doesn't come inside, he can talk all he wants."

"Maia, a fantail coming in the house doesn't mean anything."

"You taught me quite the opposite, Grandpa. Can't take it back now."

"Excuse me? I taught you the traditions of our land— which include a belief that fantails are spiritual messengers and an old *superstition* that there may be a death in the family if they come into your home. I also taught you the myth that before the North Islands flooded, they were one main island that was plucked out of the sea by the God, Māui, while fishing. So please keep that in mind."

Maia watches the bird from the corner of her eye as she reaches for another potato. "Like I said, I'm happy as long as he doesn't come inside."

The fire crackles and the table's candles flicker. As the sun begins to slip into sleep for the night, countless chirping birds scatter among the woods beyond the window. Maia watches the glow from the fireplace, then looks at her grandfather and smiles.

He brings the steaming pot of stew over to the table. "Potatoes."

She grabs a handful and throws them in.

"Maia, what do you wish for your life?"

She shrugs her shoulders. "I'll stay here."

"By yourself?"

"What choice do I have?"

"Maia, come sit down."

They walk over to the living room. He groans as he lowers himself into his favorite chair and she sits on the ottoman in front of him.

"Honey, what do you want from this life?" her grandfather asks.

"I want to stay here—with you."

"You and I both know that's not entirely true."

She anxiously repositions herself on the seat.

"I see the longing in your eyes, the boredom, the restlessness. I'm an old man now. We've traveled these islands extensively over the last handful of years and you've seen your options. There are a few. There *are* people here, Maia, small communities. Why don't we plan another visit to the Northern Tribe? They said we were welcome back anytime."

Maia stares into the fire.

"I'm not going to be around forever, Maia."

"Don't you think I know that?"

"So, what will become of you, darling? I have to know that you won't be left all alone."

"I don't want to join that community."

"And why not?"

She hesitates, her heart suddenly pounding. She can't tell him the truth. She won't. Not now—not ever.

"Maia?"

"They're boring." Lies. "*Old.* I'll just grow old and be boring with them."

"Better than the alternative. You can't stay up here alone, Maia. Maybe you could stay up north a while until you meet someone and then come back here. Start a family? That sounds nice, doesn't it?"

"Maybe for some people."

"But not you."

"I don't want to live with the Northern Tribe with all those old men and 'procreate.' Where are all the young men anyway?"

"They'll come."

"That's not the point. I don't want to sit around and make babies. I want to be a *part* of something."

"Darling, that *is* being part of something."

"But I want more than that. I'm afraid I may spend my entire life waiting to live." She looks up at him. "I don't want to escape through books anymore, Grandpa."

He lights his pipe. Swirls of smoke plume above his head, painting the air in alternating streaks of gray. "You have the same spirit as your mother." He leans back into his chair and smiles. "Sometimes I look at you, and it's like you are the same person. She lives in you, Maia. I've always felt this."

Maia inches her seat closer. "Grandpa, I keep thinking ... I feel very strongly that there might be something more out there for me."

"What—as in, outside of these islands?"

"Yes, Grandpa. I feel it every day. Every night I have these dreams—"

"Don't be a fool, child. You don't know how bad it is out there, how lucky you are to be here. The communities here are small, but there *are* communities. And they have given you an open invitation up in the Northern Islands. The few people possibly left out there would give anything to have what you have. Don't be silly."

Her eyes well up and she looks away. "Yes, Grandpa."

"Don't do that. I don't understand! I've worked my entire life to give you everything you could ever need. Look at this place! Go north for a few years, meet some people and come back here. Start your own community. *That's* being part of something. You'll never need or want for anything."

"But what if I do? What if I need *more*?"

"The adventures you've spent your childhood reading about are fiction, Maia. *Fiction*. Do you think there are adventures out there? Because there aren't. There is famine and death. It's a bleak, decaying world out there. How could you desire that?"

"You don't understand."

"What don't I understand? Explain it to me."

"I want to love it here, and in a way I do." She turns and looks at him, tears spilling from her eyes. "But, Grandpa, these trees ... these trees I've grown up with have become like bars in a jail cell. The fire we keep going is like the burn I feel in my heart every day I don't pursue what it's been telling me for years. I could go north and *settle* and wait to find someone to partner with, but every night I will wonder. I don't want that, Grandpa. I want life—*my life*. And I know it's out there, I know it."

"Baby, you don't. The only things you know have come from books and a very secluded section of a remote island. You don't know what you want yet. You're young. You've got your whole life ahead of you. It's beautiful up north. And people are trickling in from Australia and the other islands. I don't doubt for a second that some young man will be on one of those boats. You could be happy here. And it could be *really* bad out there."

"I know ... it could." She bites her lip as years of stagnant, unspoken frustrations swirl inside her gut like poison. "So, what ... I'm just supposed to sit up north and what ... *wait*? Wait for some guy, who may or may not ever come, to make *babies*? Like some sort of hog in an incubator?!" Her voice now bordering on shrill, she suddenly becomes quite aware she may ruin her validity with hysterics.

Her grandfather rolls his eyes and chuckles. She hates when he laughs at her, especially when she's serious. She glares at him until he finally looks up at her with a silly grin on his face, making it nearly impossible for her not to smile.

"Don't say it." She crosses her arms.

"You're so *dramatic.*"

"Grandpa!"

He puts his hands up in surrender. "I know, I know. I'm sorry."

"I'm serious. I know it could be bad ... but, it could also be *magical.* I could meet people, and I can defend myself. You've taught me that. I can shoot an arrow, work a gun and throw a spear like the best of them. I can hunt and fish, make a fire and find food. You've spent my entire life teaching me everything I know. I could find life, Grandpa. And if people are out there rebuilding, I want to be a part of that. I want to make a difference."

"Darling." His face becomes very serious. "It is more likely that you'll find that up north than out there."

"You don't know that."

"Neither do you." Her grandfather grunts as he hoists himself out of his chair and walks back to the table where he'd left the pot of stew. After returning it to the kitchen, he tosses a few more logs under the stove. He grabs the counter and hangs his head.

Maia stands and watches him. "I know it sounds crazy. *I know.* But I feel strongly about this. I feel it in my bones." She sits back down on the ottoman and bites her nail. This isn't going well.

"Maia." Her grandfather's voice sounds quietly from the kitchen.

She turns to look at him.

He smiles tenderly. "I hear you, okay? I do."

"I just don't feel I have a choice. It's like a pull ... a *yearning*." Her clenched fist clutches at her top.

"And where is it pulling you?"

She gazes at the fire, its flames dancing in her eyes. "*Out there.*"

FOUR

S lowly raising her arrow, Maia aims for a fat wood pigeon weighing down a scrawny branch above. He stares blankly at her, cocking his head to one side.

"Stupid pigeon, it's a wonder you're not extinct." She squints and closes one eye, aiming for his chest.

Panting sounds from below and a stick drops at her feet.

"*No*," she hisses.

Huck barks, startling both Maia and the pigeon. The bird lifts off the twig and flies away. She lowers her head in defeat.

Huck's face peers up at her, his tongue swinging from his mouth from his wagging tail. He barks again and picks up the stick, impatiently dropping it once more before backing up in anticipation.

"I don't see you for days and *this* is when you show up? Nope. You owe me dinner." She starts walking and Huck picks up his stick and follows.

Trudging along the familiar path, Maia enters a clearing where a small platform overlooks the rolling countryside with the ocean horizon nestled between the mountains in the distance. A broken road weaves along scattered farm-house roofs peeking above a thick carpet of green, swiftly choking out any last remnants of man-made structures left to rot.

Maia sits down to dangle her feet off the side of the cliff. Huck stands next to her, sniffing into the air.

"What's up, boy? I've missed you." She strokes his thick black coat. His large tongue hangs haphazardly from the side of his mouth, its curve like a smile. No matter how hard Maia tries, she can't stay mad at him for long. "You silly mutt, dinner is on you tonight."

She looks back out to the horizon. "What do you think, Huck? Anyone out there?" She squints her eye and raises her thumb. Sliding it back and forth, she covers and uncovers the slice of ocean between the mountains. "There has to be."

When Maia was a child, her grandfather would take her out into the bush every day. Hours and hours they would spend in the wilderness as he taught her about the world.

"Do you think this is the most beautiful land in the world, Grandpa?"

"Could be. The world is a massive place, child. The mind could never imagine how beautiful some of these places used to be. Mountains so high, oceans so blue..."

"Sounds magical. Can we see it?"

"See what? The world?"

She smiles bashfully. "Yes, Grandpa, I want to see the whole world."

"You are just like your mother."

. . .

"What do you think? What if there's more out there? A city perhaps, full of people. A new generation of souls re-creating a new world? I want to be a part of it." Her heart sinks. "But then again, what if there isn't? Then I leave all this, all I have—for *nothing*."

Huck whimpers and rests his head on her lap. She wraps her arms around him, her heart aching. "I know ... me too."

She lifts herself to her feet. "Come on, let's check the traps."

One trap, two traps, three traps later, she is still empty-handed. Now closer to sea level, she hesitates at a fork in the trail. To the left is the way home, and to the right—an old, abandoned sea town.

She turns right.

Together, Maia and Huck follow the winding trail until they reach the remnants of a crumpled road consumed by clusters of large, floppy weeds. Lifting her chin in defiance, she steps out onto the cracked asphalt.

Huck whines nervously, cowering behind her in the bush with his tail between his legs. After all these years living on a mostly abandoned island, Maia's grandfather has still maintained that she never travel the open roads. *Too dangerous.* Huck whimpers again from the bush.

"*Huck.*" She snaps her fingers.

Walking down the battered road, Maia constantly scans her surroundings as Huck trails nervously behind her. They approach a mountain of rubble from a collapsed overpass. She considers turning around as the thick brush encasing the pile would be all but impossible to work through, but her curiosity overpowers her.

Carefully scaling the ragged boulders and broken steel to the top, she peers over the edge to find the abandoned village on the other side. She cautiously descends, and after much coercion, Huck follows.

They wander along the deserted street. Smeared signs of once-loved cafés hang from rusted chains and sinking, dilapidated awnings. Thick moss engulfs the rotted wood while gnarled cobwebs shroud the buildings' shattered windows. Rubbish and shoes and clothing litter the streets, covered in layers of dirt and dust and rot. Downed utility poles slump across the road, hanging neglected and useless like the signs and village themselves.

Now she remembers why she doesn't come to these places anymore. This village, this remnant of an expired world, only serves as a painful reminder of her complete isolation. Everyone is gone, and she is left with the mire.

She steps over an old car tire onto a crumbling curb, approaching what used to be a clothing shop. The large display window has been busted open, and a fallen mannequin with an outstretched hand reaches through the broken glass. Maia crouches down, delicately touching the tips of the model's cracked fingers. She slowly wipes the dirt from the mannequin's cheeks and nose. Then with a swipe of her thumb, she rubs the dust from its open eyes. They stare blankly ahead—vacant, numb, forgotten.

Left behind.

A baby's cry echoes in the distance, jolting Maia from her daze. Huck sits panting in the middle of the road. His ears perk as he looks in the direction of the cries.

They follow the sound to a house near the edge of the town. Maia sneaks behind to watch from behind the trees. Sarah is sitting with Henry on a blanket on the lawn while Collin cooks something over a fire. He looks over at his wife, smiling while she coos to their baby and kisses his head.

Lost in her own world, Maia remains motionless. Huck

paces the ground, sniffing under dead leaves and branches. He lifts his nose into the air, then darts towards the couple.

"No, *Huck*!" Maia hisses.

At first, Collin and Sarah are startled by the large creature running towards them. Sarah plucks Henry from the ground and cradles him in her arms.

"It's okay. I think he's friendly," Collin says as Huck runs up to him with his tail whipping back and forth. Shielding his eyes from the sun, Collin gazes in Maia's direction. She shrinks down. "Maia?" he calls out.

Damn. "Hello." She smiles as she steps from the tree line. "I'm sorry, I didn't mean to spy. I was exploring the town when I heard Henry crying. It's not a sound you hear very often."

"Well, don't be shy. Come on over."

"Don't worry, he's harmless," Maia says as Huck licks Collin's hand.

"He's very handsome." Sarah laughs as she tousles the long fur on Huck's head. He rolls onto his back and she rubs his belly.

"He doesn't normally take to strangers like this," Maia says. "He must really like you."

"Well, he's welcome anytime. We both grew up with dogs—we love them." Collin bends over and joins his wife in petting the big black dog.

"Be careful what you wish for," Maia says, chuckling as Huck's tongue flops from the side of his mouth.

Collin returns to his fire and flips a small piece of meat. Maia hasn't had meat on the grill in ages. The smell of the small, charred scrap causes her mouth to water.

"Are you hungry? We've got some canned beans and a bit of seagull. Nothing but the best for our guests," Collin jokes from the fire.

Maia recognizes that the bird will provide very little meat even for one person, so despite her hunger, she politely declines. "How are you settling in?" Maia asks.

"Well, it's a lovely house, but not anywhere we'll stay for long," Sarah says as she dabs a bubble of spit from Henry's mouth. "This neighborhood is a ghost town."

"We're actually looking to make a set-up like what you and your grandfather have," Collin adds. "I think we'll just stay here until we find a good place to settle and start building."

"That's a good idea. This town is depressing anyway. I think there are only a few elderly people and a town drunk around." Maia shrugs.

"They still have those?"

"Apparently. And your parents? How are they doing?"

"They're all right. They're inside resting at the moment. Would you like to meet them?" Sarah asks.

"Oh, thank you—maybe next time, I shouldn't stay long."

"Maia, I don't mean to be forward, but—your *eyes*." Sarah tilts her head to the side.

Maia looks away, sweeping her hand over the long grass. "Yes, I know. Pretty weird, isn't it?"

"No, no I wasn't going to say that at all. You're *stunning*." Sarah gently lifts Maia's chin. "You really are. One blue eye and one green, they're striking really—*unique*. You're a beautiful young lady." Sarah smiles. "Your mum must be a beautiful woman."

"Thank you ... she *was*."

"Oh, right. I'm sorry."

"It's okay. Happened a long time ago."

Sarah changes the subject. "So, I know you're young ... but what's your story? You're planning on staying here?"

Maia stares at them for a moment before answering. "I..." She shakes her head. "I don't know."

"That's okay." Sarah waves it off. "You have plenty of time."

Maia flashes her an uncertain smile. "Well, I better head off. Will be getting dark soon. I don't want my grandpa to worry."

"Of course." Collin walks up behind Sarah and rests his hand on her shoulder. "You know where we are. Stop by anytime. We'd love the company."

Waving the couple goodbye, the familiar weight of disappointment once again settles over Maia's heart. She shakes it off and begins the long trek back, completely unaware of a little black fantail following her home.

FIVE

Maia lifts her lantern high above her head, casting a small orb of golden light across the misty, early morning trail.

"What are you thinking about?" Maia's grandfather calls from behind, gripping his walking stick as he struggles to keep up.

Maia turns to face him, and her bow and arrows fastened to her overstuffed pack catch on a dead branch.

"Here, let me help." Her grandfather sets down his stick and breaks the tree limb from between her bow and strings.

"Grandpa, you dragged me out of bed at the crack of dawn to check traps. The only thing I'm thinking about right now is *bacon*." A smile spreads across her lips.

He chuckles. "Honey, if there's a hog in one of those traps, the last thing we'll be doing this morning is eating bacon."

"Well, at least when I'm working my butt off preparing it, I'll know there'll be bacon someday in my future. *Lots* of it."

"True. Let's pray for bacon, then."

"*Amen.*"

A light breeze ruffles the canopy leaves and a few tūī birds swoop along the trail.

"And you, Grandpa? What are you thinking about?"

"Nothing really."

There's a short silence. She waits for it.

"*You*. Your future."

"God, Grandpa. Can we not? It's early."

"Yeah, okay." He groans behind her.

She turns around. "Are you okay?"

"Yeah," he says while rubbing his back. "Just an aching back. Don't ever get old."

She smiles at him. "You've told me this before."

"Well, don't do it." He wags his stick in her direction.

"I'll try my best." She leads him by his scrawny arm in front of her. "You go first. I need to keep an eye on you."

As he walks ahead of her, she can't help wondering when he suddenly got so old.

Two out of the four traps are empty.

"Damn," her grandfather sighs. "I honestly don't think I can eat another rabbit."

"Did you know you can die if you only eat rabbit?"

He eyes her suspiciously. "Where did you read that?"

"I read it in our shed library last week. You have to eat it with lots of vegetables, otherwise eating it alone will leach your body of vital nutrients and you'll die."

"Well, that sounds a tad dramatic. Haven't you read every book in there at least twice? How are you still getting new information?"

"At least twice—more like six times. I'm an encyclopedia of useless information."

"I wouldn't say useless. And that's great, that's why I stole them from the university where I worked so long ago. One day I hoped *someone* would read them. Let's head to the next trap."

"Haven't you read them, Grandpa?"

"Some. Not as much as you, darling. Too much building, farming, and hunting. It's taken my entire life to create this home and land we have now."

A pang of guilt clenches her chest.

"Look at this leaf." Her grandfather stops on the trail. "What do you see?"

Maia shakes her head. "I'm not sure I follow. I see a leaf, Grandpa."

They are surrounded by early morning light. The scent of deep wet earth fills the air. Maia and her grandfather stop and watch a tūī sitting in the branches above. The bird fluffs out his brown chest. Then, extending his deeply turquoise wings, he cocks his head, displaying a prominent ball of fluffy white feathers dangling from beneath his chin.

"New Zealand," her grandfather whispers with pride. "It's always been a bird's paradise."

The tūī straightens his neck as far as it will go, performing his signature jumbled mix of chirps, squawks, and clicking noises.

"Maia."

She glances back at her grandfather, humoring him. "Yes, I'm listening."

"We don't have many of these bush teachings anymore. I feel like we've spent your entire life out here in the forest, learning about the earth and the world ... history, life."

"We have." She faces him, meeting his gaze. "They're some of my fondest memories."

"This leaf is *life*," he says very seriously. "It is the one and only link between the earth and the sun; every second it is taking light and creating the nutrients our bodies need to survive. It takes toxins from the air to give us clean oxygen to breathe. It supplies us with medicine to heal our bodies. Even when humans numbered in the tens of billions, this leaf—our plant life—made up over ninety-nine percent of the earth's living creatures. All of life depends on them. They were here long before us and they will be here long after we're gone."

He pulls down a vine. "This will wrap itself around everything we've ever created and will consume it whole, as something as simple as water breaks it down into nothing. Worms, slowly over time, will bury it deep under the earth. And it will be like we were never here."

"Nice, Grandpa. Uplifting."

"Maia, this earth is alive in much the same way we are alive. From the smallest insect to the largest tree, this earth and everything on it is *living consciousness*—life striving to thrive. This tree can see, sleep, smell, taste, touch, and hear. Not in the same way we can, but don't you ever discredit something living because it is different from you. From our atmosphere to our oceans, our dividing cells to our beating hearts ... life is so brilliant in such a quiet way that we often take it for granted."

"Grandpa," Maia smiles and shakes her head. "We've discussed this."

"I just don't want you to forget. I keep thinking about where we went wrong, and I think this may be part of the answer. *We forgot*. We forgot who we really are and our place in this immense and complex community of life. We have a responsibility to protect this earth, to protect each other. Animals, plants—we are all in this together.

"The basic elements that make up this tree, the ant below you, the beating heart within you, were created in a star above you, billions of years ago." He pauses, then turns to look at her. "Maia, everything that lives will one day fall into the earth and become one with it. *We are all one.* Never forget that.

"Hold your hand against this tree—can you feel it?"

She hesitates, gazing up at the gentle giant.

"Maia?"

She takes a deep breath. Slowly raising her hand to the wet bark, she spreads her fingertips wide as she hovers next to it. A few spark-like balls flicker between her and the tree. Horrified, she looks at her grandfather.

His smile fades. "Are you okay?"

A glimmering stream of energy rolls up and down the tree in waves. Maia squeezes her eyes shut, fighting the visions in her head. It has been nearly ten years since she last allowed this inexplicable force to take her over, and she never wants to endure it again.

The last time she did, she accidentally wiped out an entire colony of bees.

A hive was still such a rare sighting. They were so close to extinction for so long. She and Huck had followed their sound, amazed by the intensity of their quiet hum. But then Huck ran off, as he often did. He'd always been such an independent dog. She was standing in awe just a few feet away when Huck ran back to her, whimpering. He had been stung as he dug around too close to the hive. She tried to calm him but he was so young, yelping and rubbing his nose into the dirt.

Maia's temper flared. Next thing she knew, she stood gasping as hundreds of bees fell to the ground around her, curling into themselves and writhing in pain. They were so *loud.* She tried covering her ears but she couldn't escape it.

She could hear every last one of them dying.

· · ·

Looking down at her feet, the waves of crystalline light now emanate from her body in ripples. "Grandpa ... can you see this?" she whispers.

"See what, darling?"

Her eyes fixate on the glistening rays.

"Honey, are you okay?" He places his hand on her shoulder, startling her, and the glimmer disappears in a flash.

Astounded, she backs up from the tree.

"Okay, let's go home," he says with alarm and picks up his walking stick.

"No." She walks back to the tree and presses her hand hard against it. Nothing happens. She closes her eyes, placing her other hand against the rough bark and pushes harder. Nothing. She bangs her fists against the tree.

"Maia!"

She drops her hands, exhaling deeply. "Yes, Grandpa."

"What's going on with you?" He pulls her hair off her face, tilting his head into her view.

She looks up at him. "It's fine. I'm fine. What were you saying?"

He stares at her with ambivalence.

"Grandpa—*the tree*. What am I supposed to ... feel?" She eyes it suspiciously.

"What's going on? *Talk* to me."

"Grandpa, *please*, just forget about it. Please continue."

"I just ... I just don't want you to forget. That's all."

She holds the side of his face, feeling his cheekbone protruding from his delicate skin. "I know, darling. I won't forget."

"*Darling*. You're *my* darling." He smiles and places his hand on top of hers. "I know you have some big decisions in your life right now. *Big* decisions." His smile fades. "I know you're afraid, child, and I don't blame you. I'm afraid too."

41

"Grandpa?"

"The answers you seek are within you. When you find yourself searching for God, as we all do at some point in our lives, look deeply into your own eyes and see, *God is within you.* God is in this vine stretching across the forest canopy. He is in the chirping birds above us and in the sweet, tangy explosion of a blackberry. God is *everywhere*, Maia. I want you to know this above all else. Because when you truly know this, you won't be afraid anymore."

SIX

Maia pushes aside the low-hanging branches and steps cautiously onto the warm sand. Her mother runs up to her and grabs her hands, leading her onto the beach. Smiling, they embrace.

"Mum, I miss you so much. Promise me you'll never leave me. Please? Never leave me."

Her mum leans her forehead against Maia's, staring deep into her eyes. "I'll never leave you, Maia." Her long white gown flows behind her in the breeze. She squeezes Maia's hands. "Come," she says as she steps into the water's edge.

Maia shakes her head, once again standing alone on the shore. "No..."

The edges of the ocean wrap around until they meet on the other side. Behind her mother, the foreign city still looms in a murky fog. Bigger. *Darker*. New lights now blaze from deep inside the windows.

"Come, my darling." Her mother reaches out to her.

Maia stands frozen, the endless abyss just a step away.

"Mum, I can't." She shakes her head, panicking as her mother stands farther and farther away from her.

"You don't have to be afraid, Maia. It's okay. I'm right here with you."

"You're not. You're far away now!" Maia cries out into the wind, her toes now tottering on the edge.

Both Maia and her mother reach out to one another, her mother seemingly at peace while tears stream down Maia's face.

"You said you would never leave me!" Maia screams from the shore. "You *left* me." She watches in horror as her mother slowly disappears, the mysterious city behind her now visible through her gown.

"Darling, hurry." Her mother's voice continues to fade.

Maia peers into the water, now an endless chasm opening into the depths of the earth, and panic sets in. When she looks up again, her mother's silhouette is barely visible. Maia takes a deep breath. Closing her eyes, she falls forward into the abyss.

The water closes in on her with the weight of a thousand oceans. Despite kicking with all her strength, her body plummets as if being pulled by some great unknowable force. The sun pierces the water above in flickering streaks of light. Her mother still stands along the surface, gazing down at her with a callous scowl across her face.

The dark ocean morphs into an underwater city. Highrises of glass and metal now tower above her. Rusted cars line the street below. Maia spins beneath the water. Struggling for air, she sinks deeper as the gloomy city closes in. The sun dwindles to a pinprick of light in the vast ocean above. She screams as she is swallowed up in darkness.

Maia's hand shatters the surface of the water like a pane

of glass. Gasping and coughing up seawater, she finds herself stranded in the middle of an endless ocean.

And her mother is gone.

"*No*. No, no, NO!"

This can't be real. The cool water laps across her shoulders and a delicate breeze flows across her wet skin. Her breathing is now the only sound breaking the deafening silence. *This is a nightmare—this can't be real!*

A white gown floods Maia's vision. She twists within the water. The ghost of herself stands before her, looking down upon her with a distant, vacant face and shimmering eyes. Maia clutches at the image's feet, desperate to find something to hold on to, but her hands slice through as if grasping at a mirage.

"Help me!" Maia screams breathlessly.

The reflection of herself does not react. She is stoic, indifferent ... almost enchanting.

Maia's limbs begin to tire. Thrashing against the water, she chokes on the harsh salty ocean. The mirage tilts her head to one side, and then a single tear tumbles down her cheek as thousands of bees spew from her mouth, engulfing Maia in a deafening, black cloud.

Maia screams as she shoots up in bed, soaked in sweat and gasping for air. But this time, her grandfather is nowhere to be found.

SEVEN

Garden tools crash to the floor.

"Maia?" Her grandfather limps towards her from across the backyard.

"Where is my speargun?" Maia searches through the equipment stacked in the corner of the shed.

"Maia, we have to talk about this. You've been sleeping all day and now you just up and leave? Where are you going?"

"I need to be by myself. We should have fish tonight. I'll go spear us a fish."

"A *fish*? When is the last time you saw a fish?"

"There are some. I saw one last week. He was small, but ... maybe he's grown up now."

"Maia."

"I don't want to talk about it!"

He puts his hand on her shoulder. She shrugs it off.

"What are you dreaming about that so distressful? Your nightmares, are you dreaming about your mother again?"

"Yes."

"Do you want—"

"*No*! I don't want to talk about it." She turns towards him with her speargun in hand and he cowers back. Horrified, she lowers her spear.

"Maia, what is happening?"

"Where were you in the middle of the night?"

He stares at her but says nothing.

She shoves past him and races across the lawn. "You said you wouldn't leave me."

"I said what?" Her grandfather stumbles out of the shed.

"Never mind." She runs towards the trail.

Down by the ocean, Maia grabs a heavy rope and pulls a floating dock to shore. There are a few jellyfish floating about. Picking up her paddles left under a bush, she climbs aboard and pushes out the dock, paddling until the rope is taut.

She stands tall while gripping her spear and stares into the water. She tries to see past her reflection into the ocean, but all she can see is the woman from her dreams. It was *Maia*. But with wild, deeply red hair. And those eyes ... so similar in color, yet surely her eyes have never emanated like that. Or *have* they? She certainly has never witnessed it, but her vision does change whenever the energy has revealed itself.

Her thoughts race. What is her reflection trying to tell her? Maia can't stay here anymore. She has to get out of here. There's something out there ... something is waiting for her. A life. Something. She knows it.

A handful of jellyfish float just beneath the surface. *Jellies.* Nothing to worry about but each other, just like humans when they used to rule the world. Well, it can't last forever. Enjoy it while you can, jellies.

She sits cross-legged on the dock and leans over the edge, poking the top of a jellyfish. It bobs down and back up again. No fish in sight. She focuses on her reflection. Her wavy auburn hair is pulled into a large bun wrapped on top of her head. A few strands have fallen out and now kiss the side of her face. She sweeps her fingers across the freckles scattered across her cheeks. Her blue and green eyes almost glow against the ocean.

You look just like your mother.

She sighs and glances back to the shore. Huck has wandered in after a full day of excursions on his own. He lifts one paw as he watches her, his tail wagging.

She looks back to her reflection, longingly drawn to her necklace, the only thing she owns from her mother. She reaches around her neck and unclasps the back, holding the small circular charm in her hand—a small jade koru. Shaped like the unfurling of a fern, the delicate spiral carving sits flat in her palm. In the old tradition of the land, it's meant to symbolize new life and growth. Her mother carved it for Maia while she was pregnant with her. It's tiny, perfect for a baby. It now sits on a fine flax cord her grandfather made. She carefully wraps it back around her neck and clasps it shut, patting it against her chest for reassurance.

She waits until the sun begins to set. Straining her eyes, she stares into the water. Nothing. Not one damn fish. She could spear a jellyfish—make fritters. She pulls herself to her feet and stands strong along the edge of the dock, bracing her arm to spear. She has been doing this for years. It's too hard to fish with a pole and line when there's so little fish and so many jellyfish. She's discovered her best option is to sit with her spear on a makeshift dock. Much more stable than a boat.

She spears a jellyfish out of boredom and lets it hang off the side as she grabs the rope and pulls herself back to the beach. Now they *have* to eat it. As she approaches the shore, Huck lifts himself off the sand and greets her.

"Hey, boy," she says as she jumps off the dock.

She leaves the jellyfish on the sand and uses a stick to hold down its tentacles as she cuts them off. Huck sniffs around her head. She scrunches her face as his wet nose traces along her cheek. Grabbing a large leaf, she scoops up the tentacles and tosses them beneath some bushes off the track.

A familiar squeak sounds from the branches above. The little black fantail rocks forward and back, flashing his tail.

"*You* again."

Squeak squeak squeak!

"Yeah, yeah, yeah. I've heard it all before. Let's go, Huck. Grandpa's going to *hate* this jelly."

EIGHT

Assorted glass jars are spread across the table. Maia's grandfather is reading in his favorite chair in front of the fire.

Maia stares at the back of his head as she absently pours melted wax into another jar. "Aren't you hot sitting so close to that fire?"

Her grandfather chuckles from behind his chair. "Nah. Good reading light. How are the candles coming?"

"Fine. Where were you this morning?"

He closes his book and turns to look at her. "Another question? How about you answer some of mine and then maybe I'll answer some of yours."

"I can't. I'm not ready to talk about it—not yet."

"But you will."

"I will."

"Soon?"

"Yes, Grandpa. And what about you? Where were you in the middle of the night?"

"No. I'm not ready to talk about it. Not yet."

"But you will?" she asks.

"I will."

"Fine."

He turns around in his chair and flips open his book. Maia slowly pours more melted wax into another jar, relieved his omission has temporarily allowed hers.

After a while, her grandfather sets his book down and stares at the fire. Maia watches him from the corner of her eye, quickly looking away when he stands. He shuffles over to her without speaking.

"You're hovering," she mumbles.

"Have I ever told you the story behind your mother's tiger painting?"

"Is there more to it? She was sixteen when she painted it; she adored tigers."

"Yes, there's more." He steps closer to it and runs his rheumatic fingers over the protective glass. Just beneath it, the uneven oils form miniature ridges and valleys. "Your mother was going to be a scientist. She wanted to save the tigers."

This makes Maia look up. "But I thought tigers went extinct ages ago."

"They went extinct right before your mother painted this. She was so passionate about them. She really felt she'd be able to save them somehow. When the news was broadcast that the last tiger had died of complications at a zoo, your mother locked herself in her room for days. When she finally came out, she had painted this. She had an even bigger resolution to save whatever was left. Nothing would stop her."

"Well, I guess the whole world stopped her, didn't it?" Maia grumbles.

Her grandfather grasps the bookshelf below the painting and drops his head. "Every time I look at this painting, I see the young woman your mother was, how strongly she dreamed and how hopeful she was. Every time I look at that tiger, I make an even bigger resolution in my heart that what happened to her won't happen to you."

"What happened to her ... you mean dying from childbirth?"

"No, that's not what I mean. Have you thought any more about what you want for your life, Maia? Your dreams, northern adventures maybe?" He still doesn't turn around.

"I think about it all the time."

"And?" He turns around to face her, his eyes glassy.

"And what?" She immediately turns away, twirling the small jars between her fingers to check for air bubbles. "What does it matter what I want? I'll just stay here."

"Alone."

"Not alone. I have you."

"I won't be around forever, Maia, you know that. We've *talked* about this."

"I have Huck."

"Maia, he's a wild dog. Why is he still here anyway? You're not feeding him, are you?"

"Of *course* not." She suppresses a smile. "And he's not wild—look at him."

Huck lays sprawled on his back across the porch rug. His feet are in the air with his tail lazily wagging from side to side.

"Maia."

"*What*? What am I supposed to say?"

Her grandfather grabs a chair and sits across from her. "I understand you need more than this. We both know that. But you have got to *choose* your life, Maia. You'll never be happy sitting up in these mountains by yourself. Your 'adventures' have grown old, and your only friend is that nomadic mutt."

"Grandpa, seriously. Huck—don't listen to him."

"I can't leave you alone like this. Let me help you."

"Who said anything about you leaving? And really? Because last I checked, there wasn't much life left around here."

"There's life, Maia. Not necessarily the sort of life you crave, but there's life here. I know you'll love it up north, if you just give it another chance. You could have a little adventure, meet your own tribe of friends and hopefully a partner, and bring them back here. You'll never want for anything up here; you just need some family with you. You could find that up north."

Maia shakes her head, trying to calm her temper.

"Don't make me say it again. Maia, what do you want?"

"I want what any single, twenty-year-old woman wants. I want to live in a big city, like the ones in my books. I want to go to a university and travel around and meet men and have sex!"

Her grandfather tips his head. "*Maia.*"

"But I don't really have that option, do I? I don't want to go to the Northern Tribe. I'd rather be up here alone than go back there. Or..."

"Or what?"

An awkward silence hangs over them. Maia bites her lip, resolving to keep her mouth shut.

Her grandfather looks back to the tiger painting hanging on the wall. "Your mother was a teenager when I took her high up into these mountains as the world crumbled around us. After a handful of years, she was ready to leave, but I wouldn't give her my blessing. I knew it was too soon and too dangerous. I don't think I was far off from reality, but I scared her. I told her there was nothing left."

"Sounds familiar," Maia says from under her breath.

"I'm pretty sure, even in my old age and deep regrets, that I was correct in my assumptions. The way things happened was so severe and bleak, your mother and I were all we had. I swore I would protect her, and that's exactly what I did.

"But sometimes I wonder." He pauses. "Day after day, I watched her anger eat her alive. I still don't believe it could have been any other way, but I can't help but think maybe I should've gone with her, traveled the islands to find other civilization. The way I have with you. Maybe things could have been different."

"So, where did she want to go?"

"What does it matter? She met your father and everything changed. She didn't love him. She settled. I knew it wasn't right and so did she. They stopped coming around, started drinking a lot. A year passed where we didn't speak. And then she came over to the house one afternoon. *Pregnant.*"

"With me?"

"With you, darling. She was different—full of life. She was excited and hopeful for the first time since The End. We embraced each other back into our lives without a second's hesitation. We sat together the entire day and talked. You gave her life again, a reason to hope. She named you Maia because, here in New Zealand, it means 'brave warrior.' She said you were going to change the world. She knew it. You were going to be different—special. She spoke with such conviction. It was like she had already met you. I'll never forget the smile on her face as she rubbed her belly with you inside. I've never seen her so assured and happy.

"Your father came over that night for dinner and he was different too. He was so in love with your mother. He had stopped drinking, and they seemed happy. There wasn't much medical help but your father found a woman who had some experience and could assist with the birth. They figured out a rough due date and she had planned to be there for the month around then. Your father was working around the clock to make room for you and store enough food. The three of us stayed up all night talking. It felt like real life again; it was so nice having your mother back at home.

"That was the last time I saw her."

"Because of me..."

"No, you gave her life. You gave *all of us* life. What happened couldn't be helped. Childbirth is a complicated and dangerous endeavor. Women all over the world from the beginning of time have given their lives to give life. Your mother wouldn't have had it any other way."

"Why are you telling me this, Grandpa?"

"One night I dreamed about her, after she died. She came into the cabin and talked to me, clear as day. Told me everything was going to be all right and that she was happy and safe. She smiled that same big smile and told me you were going to do great things. And then, just as quickly, she grabbed my hand and told me to go to you. '*Immediately. Do not hesitate.*'

"And then I woke up. It was morning, and I quickly grabbed my things and made the journey to the other side of the island. I arrived that evening and found your father living in his boatshed. He was drunk, almost incoherently so. And angry. You were in a crib in the corner, crying in dirty clothes. And I knew. I threw my bag down and grabbed you."

"What did he do?

"He yelled a bit, stumbled off his chair. Grabbed his gun but I was faster and had already pointed mine at him. I told him not to follow me and that I would take care of you from now on."

"Did he put up a fight?"

"No."

"How nice of him."

"He knew it had to be done. He yelled a lot as I packed up your belongings, but he didn't stop me. He was scared and bitter and angry. He couldn't take care of himself, let alone take care of you."

"Was that the last time you saw him?"

"No. I've seen him a few times over the years when I've gone hunting for supplies, but we've never acknowledged each other. Too much unspoken that we'd rather bury."

"Grandpa, I think the same thing is happening to me now. My dreams ... I want more."

"I know. I see that. Let me take you back up north again—"

"I don't want up north! Why won't you *listen* to me? I need to be a part of something. There aren't many of us; you always said one person could make a difference. I want to make a difference. The world back then was a different place but no less dangerous—"

"YES! Yes! Less dangerous!"

"But we overcome. We adapt! That's what humans do! I don't want to sit here and rot and *procreate*. Surely people are rebuilding out there. They must!"

"But Maia, that's what they are doing in the Northern Islands. You could start something in the Southern Islands."

"No—it's not right. I'm made for something bigger than this. I'd rather live a short life and die out there trying than live a long life with all those creepy old men, already dead inside."

"*Creepy*? They weren't creepy. They would take care of you. You need community—you don't know what you're saying. There's *nothing* out there beyond these islands. It's not safe!"

"And it's safe here? You think just because we have a huge greenhouse and a library and water tanks that I'm *safe*?"

"Much safer than out there, don't be foolish."

"I'm dying inside, Grandpa! This life isn't for me."

"*Argh*, you're so *dramatic*!"

"You said it yourself, that you saw Mum die inside. You *just* said that. Can you not see me doing the same thing right before your eyes?"

"YES! I can! So, go up north, *goddammit*!"

"I don't understand why you are pushing this so hard on me, Grandpa, after everything you just said about Mum."

He sighs as he bows his head. "I would give my life over and over again to protect you. I want what's best for you, I do. I don't understand why you think the Northern Tribe is ... *creepy*. It was and always has been the best possible option for you."

Maia holds her head in her hands as silence overtakes them.

"I've ... I've made a deal with one of the elders to come for you."

Anger surges through her veins and she rises from the table. "*What*?!" Her fists slam against the wood, clanking the glass jars together.

He holds his hand towards her. "Now, calm down..."

"Why would you *do* that?!"

"I ... I just thought we'd give you some time after our last meeting. You weren't ready then, but I thought you'd be ready after a few years. I needed to know that, no matter what, someone would look after you and make sure you were all right..."

"No matter what? What does that mean? Are you leaving me?"

"NO! No, I—"

"When? When are they coming?"

"I'm ... I'm not sure..." His voice is shaking.

Somewhere deep inside, her heart breaks at the thought that she is scaring him. She sits down. "When?"

He doesn't respond.

"Grandpa."

"Soon. The next six months."

Another surge of anger. "No." She shakes her head, tightly gripping her hands as she feels the cabin closing in on her. "I won't. No. I'm leaving. I'm leaving New Zealand. I'm leaving this crowded shithole of a cabin." She pushes herself up from the table and grabs her pack.

"*Shithole*..." His face looks pained. "But I thought—"

"No, you didn't think. You didn't think with Mum and you're not thinking with me. You're the one killing me by forcing me to stay here. And those men..." She bites her tongue. "No, I'm leaving. I can't take this anymore." Her heart breaks as she says it, but she pushes it down and shoves her things inside her pack.

"Honey—" Her grandfather starts to cough. He pulls himself up from the table and stumbles towards her. "Darling, let's talk."

"I think you've said enough." She ties the pack closed and throws it on her back, pushing past him and out the front door. It slams behind her as her grandfather calls out from an empty room.

NINE

A single drop of water splats against Maia's nose as she sits silently in the black of night. Her head falls back against an ancient pōhutukawa tree and another drop breaks against her cheek. Heavy pellets of rain collide into the leaves above, snapping and bursting and breaking like the broken heart beneath her chest. Endless tears run in streams down her cheeks and her body shakes as she weeps, but she doesn't make a sound.

She's been running through the dark forest for hours now, desperate to escape the ghosts that have harassed her for years. She was reckless in her attempts. Overcome with madness, she flung herself through the tangled weeds, falling over countless tree stumps as the forest gnawed away at her layer by layer. Now her body lies covered in mud, her hands and knees throbbing from a cruel accumulation of cuts and bruises.

Lost. How did she become so lost and in so many ways? Seems like just a few days ago she was ... *happy*. But that was a lie as well. The lies seemed easier then. Now it seems hopeless. Grandpa pulls so tenaciously from one direction while her dreams pull from the other.

He's probably right. He knows much more than she does —it's probably really bad out there. And she's alone. Maybe she should go up north when they come for her. Maybe she'll meet someone her age ... someone who will come back here with her. Maybe she should stop being so foolish. Foolish. Her grandfather has never called her that before. Now it seems like that's all he says. Foolish. Foolish. Foolish.

Let it be over now.

Adventures are for books. This is real life. Go up north and find a partner. Grandpa says with the small number of humans left, they could still go extinct. So, it is her duty to procreate. There's dignity in that! Besides, it's the only life that's left for her. That's all there is.

She gathers her legs against her chest, shivering as the rain trickles down her cheeks and off the tip of her nose. Her eyes flicker against the drizzle as she strains to see through the blackness. She lays her head on her crossed arms, praying for it to be over, but the rain continues on, unbroken and merciless. It covers her body and soaks her to the bone. It falls on the pōhutukawa and the tūī and the ferns.

And then the heavens open up. The rain crashes in waves across the swaying trees above, pouring a deluge upon her.

It's as if the entire heavens are in mourning.

———

The smell of smoke fills Maia's nostrils, pulling her out of a deep sleep. Her eyes flicker open to a little black fantail sitting quietly on a branch above.

A thick awning of leaves and branches are wrapped tight and tangled around Maia like a cave. She breaks her hand through the dense weave, cracking off enough branches to create an opening. Pushing herself through, she shuffles backward on her hands and feet along the soppy mud and drops in the sludge. Dumbfounded, she examines the canopy she had slept beneath.

This wasn't here last night. She collapsed against a tree and cowered under the open skies. There was nothing here. She shakes her head as she touches the knotted twigs. Was she delusional? Is she delusional now? She pokes at the hard weave.

Shivering from the early morning cold, she slowly lifts herself from the damp ground. Her body is coated in layers of dried, cracked mud, and her legs and hands are covered in small nicks and cuts.

Smoke. From a fireplace? Where is that coming from? She doesn't recognize anything about this area. She can't remember how long she had been walking last night or when she finally fell asleep. Climbing to her feet, she clumsily stumbles forward, following the scent like a hound. It must be from a fireplace. *So cold.* She wraps her arms around herself and scans the forest floor. Somewhere in her frenzied delirium last night she lost her pack. She has nothing.

The rising sun has filled the clouds with swirls of a deep tangerine. A white glint of light flickers off the roof of a large metal shed in the distance. She lurches forward. Smoke wafts from the shed's chimney. Someone is in there. She creeps up to the thick bushes surrounding the shed's overgrown yard and hunches behind them.

After a few minutes, Maia tiptoes across to the closest window. Pushing the snarled cobwebs aside, she peers inside to find a man motionless on a chair next to a wood burner. She pulls her sleeve over her fist and wipes away the window's thick layers of mold and dirt.

The inside of the shed looks like a half-attempted effort to serve as a home. A sad excuse for a kitchen sits sagging and burdened with pots and garbage in the corner of the large room, alongside an old couch topped with a pile of rumpled blankets and a pillow. The walls are lined with countless stacked boxes, some of which are labeled with barely legible faded writing.

She looks back to the man, who still hasn't moved. It's too dangerous to wake him, especially by herself. She backs away from the window and decides to keep moving.

As Maia heads across the lawn, she spots what appears to be an abandoned cottage in front of the shed. She briefly glances back to the window.

No. *Run!*

She hesitates, then despite herself, sprints across the yard to the cottage.

Standing in the dense, overgrown weeds just outside the front door, Maia grapples with an overwhelming feeling of nostalgia. The cottage's faded yellow paint hangs off in curved, ragged sheets. The entire house is blanketed in a film of black grime and moss. Thick cobwebs and forest debris fill the dark entryway. She reaches through the tangled webs and grabs the knob—*locked*.

Piles of rusted tools sit propped against the building. She digs through them until she finds a blade. She's become good at picking locks from years of rummaging through abandoned homes and shops for whatever may be left this long after The End.

Maia works the old rusted handle, peering every so often at the shed to make sure she hasn't awakened the man.

Jimmying the blade between the door and its frame, she works the lock until the door swings open with a drawn-out creak. She quickly steps inside, quietly closing the door behind her.

This house ... something so familiar about this house.

She stands in the entryway of a large living room where dust has coated its contents in thick layers of muted grays. A whisper of a baby's laughter echoes across the room, sending chills down her spine.

Wandering over to a large bookshelf, she absently runs her fingers along its contents, leaving a trail of parted dust in their wake. She comes across a glass tiger figurine. Picking it up, she examines it with a peculiar curiosity before setting it back down and continuing further.

Picture frames line the shelves, along with books and other various objects she's never seen outside of magazines. Objects like what her grandfather said were used before The End, objects that contained a power within that she has never quite been able to understand. A power that had connected the entire world together but has long since died without the electricity and the humans who created it.

She picks up a novel, blowing the dust away as she flips through its pages, then sets it down next to a frame where a glint of glass catches her eye. She slowly pulls the frame from the shelf, breaking the grasp of a knotted cobweb. Gently wiping the layers of dust from the glass, her breath catches in her chest as she finds her mother staring back at her.

She frantically rubs off the rest, uncovering her mother smiling at the camera, her dark auburn hair blowing across her face. Her smile is radiant, happy—*in love*. A handsome young man stands with his arms wrapped around her. His eyes are closed and his face is buried into the side of hers.

Dad.

"What the—"

Startled, Maia looks up as a wobbling drunken man stands at the door, half-propped against the frame with a handgun swinging at his side. It's the same man from the photos. He's a much older version than the man she holds in her hands. His beard lies crooked across his sunken face and his clothing hangs from his bony frame.

Still grasping the photo, Maia turns towards him, absently brushing the dirt from her clothes. Gathering what little dignity she has left, she lifts her chin.

He looks shocked—*horrified*. "*Ghost*," he mumbles with glassy, terrified eyes.

"No." Her voice sends him stumbling against the wall. "Not a ghost, although I bet you wish I was."

He points his gun at her while reaching for the door. "*No*, stay away from me!" His face panic-stricken, he frantically searches the air behind him.

Maia holds out her hands, tears filling her eyes. "I'm not a ghost! I'm your *daughter*."

He lowers his gun. "What did you say?" He steps towards her with a trembling, outstretched hand. "That *necklace*..."

She grasps her mother's carving and backs into the shelf, knocking the tiger figurine to the floor.

"*Ah!*" Her father lunges and Maia jumps to the side, shielding her face. The tiger tumbles across the floor.

Picking up the figurine, he grasps it between his palms and sighs relief. He examines it for damage, then wipes it off and returns it to the only spot on the shelf not buried in dust.

He turns to look at her, his hazy eyes darting between the photo in her hands and the woman standing before him. He stares at the jade carving on her chest. "*Maia?*"

She softens her gaze.

"No..." Her father shakes his head. "You left. You went to The Old Arctic Circle with your grandfather."

"*The Old Arctic Circle*? What? No, I didn't."

"Your grandfather said he was taking you there," he says as he shakes his head. "Twenty years ago."

"He didn't. We didn't. The Old Arctic ... you mean North? Like the Northern Islands?"

"NO!" His voice booms across the deserted room. "No. The Old Arctic Circle. The place *we* were going to go before your mother got *pregnant!*" He snatches the photo from her and wipes the rest of the glass with his tattered shirt, then carefully places it back on the shelf. His body swaying, he scans the room for any more discrepancies, then turns back to gawk at Maia. "You ... you look just like her." He shakes his head. "What are you doing here?"

"I don't know." She gazes at her feet and folds her arms across her muddy shirt. "I got lost ... I was looking for a change of clothes."

"Your *mother's* clothes? How long have you known I was here?"

"No—I didn't know ... I had no idea what this place was. I followed the smoke. I was cold ... and hungry."

"I have food. I have food! I can..." He points towards the open front door and motions her forward. "Come. I can give you some food in the *other* house." His smile is awkward and twitchy.

Maia looks around. "I don't know."

He lowers his arm, and his body wavers as he struggles to focus on her. The smell of liquor from his fetid breath is overwhelming.

This may be her only chance to talk to him, so she takes a deep breath and agrees. "Okay. Food, yes."

"Okay!" He quickly walks out the front door then immediately back in again, shuffling her out with his fingers in her back. Slamming the door behind him, he pauses as he surveys the broken lock.

"I'm sorry. I didn't know. I was just—"

"I know. *Looking for food*," he says without turning around.

"I can fix—"

"Never mind!" He shoves past her. "Let's get you some food."

She trails nervously behind him.

The inside of the shed smells worse than it looks. Maia's father bangs around the kitchen, pulling out old pots, rattraps, and a few odd shoes from the cupboards. She eyes the old boxes stacked against the walls. Sagging and molding, they appear as if they haven't been touched in decades.

He staggers around. "*Ah*, here!" he proclaims as he pulls out a small bag from a pile of garbage on the table. "This is the best jerky you'll ever have."

She eyes the meat suspiciously.

"Go on, it's safe. I just ate some tonight."

"Tonight? It's morning."

"Whatever." He tears a bit off with his few remaining back teeth and tosses the rest on the table. "It's there if you want it, but don't complain about being hungry." He stumbles back to his chair and picks up a large bottle of hazy liquid. Swigging it back, he grimaces as he swallows. "I made it myself. Want some?"

Maia shakes her head.

"Sit down ... if you want."

Reluctant, she keeps her arms wrapped around her body.

"Sit!" He startles her. "Or leave. But wipe that smug look off your face. You don't know anything about me."

"You're right, I don't. And whose fault is that?"

He jumps out of his chair with his hand in the air and Maia cowers to cover her face. Horrified, he lowers his hand. "I'm sorry ... I'm—I would never hit you. Please," he begs, shoving the blankets and garbage off the couch. "Please, sit down? I'm sorry. I'm sorry. I'm sorry," he whispers as he rocks back and forth. He takes another swig of his liquor.

Maia gazes down at him, his sadness palpable. She quietly sits along the edge of the couch and flashes him an awkward smile.

"It's like ... you're a ghost. I can barely look at you," he says, averting his eyes to the floor. "Your grandfather—is he still alive?"

"He is. Better than ever." She lies.

"That's great," he slurs. "I know you probably won't believe me, but I was always comforted in my omission from your life because I knew you were with him. Well, I *assumed* you were still with him, off in some faraway land like The Old Arctic Circle."

"The Old Arctic Circle ... I'm sorry, I'm trying to wrap my brain around ... where is this?"

He belches. "It's exactly like it sounds, *dear*," he sneers. "*THE OLD ARCTIC CIRCLE*. The ... Old ... Arctic ... how many times I gotta repeat this?"

"I just ... I don't think—you're slurring. You mean to tell me people, including my grandfather at one point, were traveling to this Old Arctic Circle?"

He looks confused. "Your grandfather—"

"Yes, but he didn't. And I don't know what you're talking about."

He sighs. "I wouldn't even know where to begin."

"Anything. I'll take anything."

His eyes dart to the ground, nervously drumming his fingers together.

"Please," she whispers.

He looks up at her and a flash of kindness crosses his face. "Okay," he says. "Right before The End—"

The rubbish on the table shifts and a small rat peeks its head out from underneath. It sniffs into the air, then crawls into the bag of jerky. Maia's stomach churns. Her father watches with a resentful look in his eyes.

"You were say—" she starts but her father lifts his hand.

The rat sticks its head out once again. Her father chucks an old leather boot at the table. It slides across the mess, pushing the bag of jerky onto the ground. The rat scurries under a closed door.

"Right!" Her father looks pleased with himself. "Where was I?"

"The End..." Maia mumbles, not taking her eyes off the door.

"Yes. Before The End, there was a lot of talk about this anomaly, this place on earth that for thousands of years had been covered in ice. A wasteland—no man's land. Once the glaciers melted, there were these massive uninhabited pieces of earth at the beginning stages of what they were like millions of years ago. Eventually, they knew the area would become sub-tropical and full of life. Of course, it wasn't like that yet, but it was starting. The oceans were much cooler up there than they had become everywhere else, so they still supported sea life.

"They called the area 'The Old Arctic Circle.' People tried traveling there to claim a bit of land, but the world powers began a war over it, so there was a tight restriction on travel. No one wanted anyone populating it until they

knew who would own it. And then everything ... fell apart."
He shakes his head. "Falling apart is an understatement."

"I think I've read about that place ... in old magazine articles and newspapers my grandfather had collected, but that was so long ago. You were going to go there?"

"Yes."

"People are still going there?"

"Yes. Well, that's what I've heard."

"And my grandfather said he was taking me there?"

"Yes."

"But instead, no one went?"

"Guess so." He takes another swig.

Her mother's face suddenly flashes before her, with the massive city rising behind her every night in her dreams. "The dream."

"What?"

"Oh my God."

"What?"

"And you and my mother wanted to go there?"

"Where? The Old Arctic Circle?" He shrugs. "Sure, once upon a time."

"How?"

"How were we going to go there? With a boat. We were building one."

Maia jumps from her seat. "You have a boat?!"

Her father flinches, spilling liquor on his lap. He hugs his bottle and looks up at her with a disgruntled look on his face.

"Can you help me? Please! I have to go there. I have to ... where? Where is the boat now?"

His jaw clenches and he glares at the ground. "I burned it." He grips the glass bottle.

"What? Why?"

"Because it was all *ruined*!" He stands from his chair and whips the bottle across the room. Maia ducks and the glass shatters across the back wall. "Every plan I've ever made with the love of my life was *ruined*! She was everything and you took her from me! Everything is gone! GONE!" He falls to his knees, his bellow filling the room.

She races towards the open front door.

"Maia! No please, wait!"

But she does not wait. She sprints as fast as she can back into the forest. Her father screams out her name in the distance. She runs even faster.

TEN

Two days have passed since his darling girl had left
in the dark, cold night. She needed to talk and he
wouldn't listen. *Foolish*. He had called her foolish
just as he called her mother foolish, and now he has lost
them both.

The old man sits quietly on the porch, trembling from
the cool night air. A glass of carefully rationed whisky sits
next to him while a very nervous Huck paces across the
sagging wooden deck. The fireplace inside is dark and
barren. A cold uneaten pot of soup with a thick layer of haze
growing along the top still sits on the lifeless wood burner
in the corner of the kitchen. He coughs violently, gasping for
air, then pulls his blanket tighter around him.

He'll die out here waiting. He will not go back inside
that empty cabin, not without her.

Please come home. Oh, my darling, please come home.

ELEVEN

"**G**randpa?"

Her shaking hand hovers over his, sticking out from beneath his tattered wool blanket. Terrified, her breath leaks out in spurts as she lightly brushes the top of his pale skin for warmth. He doesn't move. His face is drained into the color of ash. She leans over and listens for breathing. When she hears it—short and shallow—she lets out her breath.

His eyes scrunch and peel open. A low mumble rolls from between his cracked lips.

"Oh my God, Grandpa." She opens the porch door and rushes back to his side. "Come on, let's get you inside."

"Darl ... darling."

"Yes, Grandpa. I'm here. What have you done?" She peels open his wool blanket and wraps her arms around his hollow frame. He groans as she lifts him from his chair. "I know, Grandpa. Come on, help me out here, lift. *Lift!*" She pulls her grandfather to his feet as his trembling body doubles over, coughing and gasping for air. "Let's get you inside."

He struggles to place one foot in front of the other as they shuffle back inside the dark cabin. Maia piles his frail body into his chair and grabs every blanket she can to layer on top of him.

"Hold on, Grandpa." She holds the sides of this ghostly face with shaking hands. "What have you done?"

She races around to the outside of the cabin and frantically fills a basket of wood from their storehouse. Grandpa has always been so prepared. Always something—there is always something that can be done. Every day has a schedule to be followed; check the calendar if unsure. Every day should be spent chopping wood, weeding, hunting, collecting, building, cleaning. Wood, there is so much wood in this shed. But they can never have enough, Grandpa would say. It's not like they won't use it.

After building a fire, Maia shoves his chair as close to the heat as she can, then unwraps his feet and places them on a pile of wool blankets. She runs to the kitchen and lights the wood oven, setting the molding soup aside and placing the kettle on top.

"Darling," her grandfather's voice cracks from the living room.

"I'm right here, Grandpa." She runs back to him and unwraps his blankets, the fire now roaring behind her. "Let's get you some more heat."

He lays his head against his chair and she holds his icy hand against her cheek as he drifts off to sleep. Feeling hopeless and overwhelmingly guilty, Maia glances around the dark cabin in search of something to do. She fixates on the stacks of newspapers in the corner of the living room, glaring at them like unwanted houseguests. What a waste of space. She can only be grateful that her grandfather has finally agreed to use them for kindling.

There are scores of periodicals filling countless boxes in the library, the corners of the house, even the woodshed—a musty, dust-covered accumulation of papers with one glaring, painfully obvious subject in common.

The weather.

The changes were so small, so gradual, over such a long period of time. It only took a few degrees to change the world—but change the world they did.

Maia wanders to the sagging pile and grabs the top paper to feed the fire. She quickly glances through it. Sometimes the most tragic headlines were placed in the smallest spaces in the very back of the paper, like an afterthought added to fill an empty slot. Not this one. She unfolds the crinkled periodical. Ominous black lettering sprawls across the cover: *Super Tsunami NYC: Millions Flee Inland After World's Last Superdam Toppled.* She rips the paper in half and tosses it into the flames, watching as the title is quickly incinerated: *World Mourns as Ocean Claims Another Coastal City.*

She grabs a few more papers and without looking, shoves them under the logs, watching as the flames devour the past. The quicker the fire burns these the better—no point dwelling in someone else's hell.

The roaring fire quickly nips the chill in the air but she tucks her grandfather's hands and feet beneath the blanket anyway. She spends the evening in the kitchen, making a fresh batch of vegetable soup as her grandfather sleeps. Every so often, she sneaks back to his chair and listens to his breathing, relieved to see the color of his face slowly returning to normal.

Maia's grandpa wakes the next morning to a smoldering fire and Maia's head resting on his lap. He gently sweeps back her hair and her eyes flutter open.

She looks up at him and smiles. "Hi, Grandpa."

"Hi, darling."

She lifts herself up and stacks new logs on the fire.

"You came back," her grandfather says as he coughs into his towel.

"Grandpa, what were you doing out there? You could've died."

"I know."

"Was that your intention?"

"God, no. I was waiting for you ... I was thinking."

"You were *drinking*. You pulled out your whisky reserves?"

"Yes, I do that from time to time."

She sits on the ottoman and sighs. "Are you feeling warm?"

"Yes, thank you for taking care of me."

"Thank you for taking care of *me*, Grandpa."

He shakes his head and gazes back at the fire. "I don't know about that."

"What are you talking about?"

"I've had a lot of time to think these last couple days. *A lot*." He looks up at her, his tender eyes pleading. "I was wrong. And I'm sorry."

She shakes her head. "Wrong ... about what?"

He sighs. "Life. It's so different now from when I was young. We had the whole world available to us and we took advantage of that. People, education, food, big cities, travel. Life was expansive and the opportunities were endless. I know what it's like to feel restless, and I went out and saw the world. I can imagine what you're feeling now, what you have been feeling for years when I force you to stay here." He closes his eyes and massages his forehead.

"I see the way you look to the horizon," he says without looking up. "The restlessness in your soul. I saw the way you looked when the few available men up north stumbled over you. Your face ... you were horrified." His voice catches and he looks up at her. "I can't get that look out of my head."

"You saw that." Anger surges from within her. "So why push it on me!?" she yells.

He reaches for her hand and she snatches it away, glaring at him through the haze of her tears.

"Because I thought ... I still think the situation could change. People will keep coming in from other places. The people up there now are not the official be-all-and-end-all of the tribe. It will keep growing. Just because you go up there, it doesn't mean you have to procreate with those old men."

She turns away, feeling as if her head is being shoved under water.

"But—"

Surprised, she looks back at him.

"The only thing worse than the thought of me dying and leaving you up here alone is the thought of you settling up north in a life you resent. You'd be alive, but my darling granddaughter would die." A tear falls down his crinkled face. "You would end up like your mother, and your mother ... she died anyway."

"Because of me."

"Stop saying that, child! Your mother died long before she got pregnant with you. You—you gave her hope. And now, here you are ... you're still alive. We've made it through the hardest years. You're a full-grown woman now. There were so many nights I was sure we'd never make it. I've never worked so tirelessly, worried myself sick, or sacrificed every fraction of my being as much as I have in raising you. All I've ever wanted is for you to be safe, to be content, and maybe create a family of your own. But I can't force you to stay here, Maia. I know you dream about your mother. I know you feel a pull to go out and find a new life. And I know you're capable. But you could die out there, Maia."

"I know."

"You simply can't imagine what it's like out there. And what—you'd go *alone*? The atrocities that people are capable of are what got us in this mess in the first place. The danger awaiting you out there surely would be..."

She leans her head back and closes her eyes as his words slice through her like blades. His voice raises, asking her if she's listening. She's heard it all before. Over and over and over again.

"But," he continues, "I'm not so naïve to deny that you could also find life."

This is a trick.

"Maia, please look at me."

Her head flops forward and she looks in his direction, but not in his eyes. Not his eyes. She can't.

"Darling, please."

She inhales and finally looks at him, preparing herself for a lecture.

"Your mother's spirit lives within you. She wanted to go out and find a better life and I stopped her. I won't die making that same mistake again. If you want to find another life, then I have no choice but to help you. We can take our time and make a plan. I don't love the idea, but I will help you in every way I can."

"How much weed did you put in that pipe?"

He snorts.

"Grandpa—are you serious?"

"I have to be. Your life is not mine to dictate. I won't lose you, Maia, not like this. Not again."

"So ... you'll help me. You're going to *help* me? *Leave*?"

"Baby steps, Maia. There's a lot to do. This could take years."

She glares at him, lost for words.

"You can trust me. I wouldn't tease you about this."

She studies his face—the tired, loving look in his eyes. This man, this man has been her whole life, her best friend, her mentor. "You support this?"

"I support *you*, Maia. You are my baby. You are the only thing in the world that matters. I will not clip your wings, even if that means losing you. Eventually, I knew I'd have to let you go. I guess I just hoped you wouldn't go ... so far." He smiles. "I support *you*."

With that, Maia drops her head in her hands and sobs. After all this time, so much fighting and tension between them. Can this really be happening?

She looks up at him. "Grandpa, I'm terrified. Every day I'm terrified. What if I leave everything behind to find nothing?"

"Then, my darling, you've left everything behind to find nothing. I suppose you come back. But Maia, that's generally not the way things work. You may not ever be able to come home again—not to the home you left. Things change, people change, you'll change. I may not be here anymore. That's the deal you make."

Dissatisfied, she grabs a rod and pokes at the fire. "Tell me about The Old Arctic Circle."

"I was going to talk to you about that—"

Maia rolls her eyes. More lies. "When?" She turns to look at him. "Honestly? When were you going to tell me?

When were you going to tell me that my parents were planning to go there ... that you wanted to go there, with me? How could you..." She pauses, swallowing back her tears. "How could you *lie* to me for so long?"

His face is horrified. "Oh, darling, I ..." He looks down. "I don't even know where to begin."

"I'm getting a little sick of hearing that."

"You found your father."

She stabs the logs, sending sparks into the air.

"I was only trying to protect you."

"You can't protect me anymore, Grandpa. I'm a grown woman now."

"You'll always be my baby."

"Stop it! Can't you see that you protecting me is only hurting me more?"

Her grandfather looks stunned. "You're right. Okay," he says after a while. He pulls himself upright in his chair. "So, here it is. I didn't tell you about your father because he is a coward and a drunk and I thought it would be dangerous if he knew about you. He can't be trusted. He was bad news before your mother, but after he lost her, he became a bit of a loose cannon."

"And The Old Arctic Circle?"

"I didn't tell you about The Old Arctic Circle because ... hell, who really knows about that place. It's a great story—a myth even—about this place that used to exist, but no one knows for sure anymore. And now it's been so long that there's no way of telling. I've heard rumors around the islands over the years about people traveling there. But when they leave, they don't come back. We never hear from them again. For all we know, it could be an old legend. So, I hope you could understand if I was going to support you doing anything, *of course* I was going to try to keep you here."

"But ... Mum was going to go there? *You* were going to go there? My father said you told him you were."

"I did. Yes..." He nods. "I did. But that was when you were a baby. I thought maybe we would go once you were a bit older ... five or six even. It would have given me time to prepare. I'd heard the rumors, had a few friends who had packed up and made the journey there. I got excited. But as I started getting older, my health wasn't the greatest, and the journey required to get us there was more than I was willing to risk.

"And I didn't see what was so wrong with this life anyway. I've worked really hard to make something really great up here. In the end, I didn't *want* to leave. And you seemed happy." He pulls his cloth from his shirt pocket and wipes the tears from his eyes. "Maia ... it wasn't so bad, was it? I mean, I didn't do so wrong by you, did I?"

"Of course not, Grandpa."

"You're my family. So, I was selfish, and I'm sorry for that. I pushed the Northern Islands on you more and more because it *is* the safest option. Sailing out into the world ... I can't imagine how we'd do it. But I can't leave you here alone. I can't leave you with no plan, no help, no family. I'm no dummy. I know you won't do something you don't want to do. Demanding you go to the Northern Tribe is not only hurting you *and* hurting me, but it's a waste of precious time. I see that now." He looks up at her with heavy eyes.

"Those dreams I've had for years, about Mum..." Maia begins.

"Yes."

"Those are also my nightmares. The longer I ignore them, the worse they get. They used to be full of laughter on the beach, but now she drifts out into this endless abyss of ocean, calling out to me to come. And now ... now there is this massive city behind her, looming in the distance. And there's a city below her, in the water. Like the cities you say exist all over the world now. This entire time, she's been calling me to The Old Arctic Circle."

He sighs and reaches out to her. "I don't know what else to say. If you really feel that strongly about it, then I will help you in any way that I can."

"But you said you can't imagine how I'd make it over there."

"I can't. I honestly can't. But we will take our time and we'll figure it out. We'll make a plan for every situation. We'll train you and run exercises. We'll build a goddamn boat if we have to. Or we can travel the islands and barter for someone else to. We've got a lot to offer. Besides, life up here is getting a little boring." He winks. "If it takes us five years, then at least in five years, you can think about it again and if you still want to go, you will be prepared."

"Thank you, Grandpa. *Thank you.*"

"And if you change your mind, that's fine too. Maybe before you leave, you could visit the North—"

"Stop."

He chuckles. "Okay." He plasters a sarcastic smile across his face and she can't help but laugh. "So, what do you say? Are we doing this? Because I'm ready, I'll start tomorrow."

She glances back at the tiger painting, then at her grandfather. She smiles, feeling like a million butterflies may burst out from within her. "Yes, let's do this."

He pulls himself up from his chair and wipes his eyes. "Well, all right. Come here."

She wraps her arms around him.

"My baby. *My baby,*" he repeats as she rests her head on

his chest. "Did I ever tell you when I first picked you up, this is right where you put your head? Right here." He pauses, patting the side of her face. "Right where you belong."

"Yes, a few hundred times now, Grandpa."

"My baby." He holds her tight. "We're going to make this right. We're going to make a plan for your life."

TWELVE

The next morning, Maia awakens with a deep sense of peace. Smiling, she stretches her arms high above her head, then rips open her privacy curtains to find the early morning sun flooding beneath the front door. She runs across the room towards her sleeping grandfather and jerks open his curtains. "Rise and shine!"

He shields his eyes from the light. Moaning, he sits up. "I already regret this decision."

Maia heads to the kitchen. Latching open the stove door, she throws in a few bricks of wood. "Let's do this!"

Her grandfather smiles. "It's nice seeing some life in you again."

Maia walks to the kitchen table and pulls out a chair. "Where shall we begin?"

Her grandfather grunts as he pulls himself out of bed. He hobbles towards the table. "So ... that wasn't just a nightmare I had last night?" he jokes as he plops down into a chair.

"I'm going to pretend I didn't hear that," Maia says as she pours him a cup of water.

He looks up at her over his spectacles. "So ... The Old Arctic Circle it is, then?"

She nods, waiting for him to change his mind.

"Okay, then. The Old Arctic Circle." He stares blankly ahead, clearly trying to prepare himself for something he isn't ready for.

Maia holds her breath.

"Okay," he says again. "We're going to need a *serious* plan. And for that—"

"We'll need paper," Maia says with a sigh.

"Lots of it, I'm afraid," he adds.

"There's none around the local towns," Maia says. "I know that for sure; I cleaned those out years ago. I could always go on a mission."

He looks up at her and smiles. "I have something for you ... in the shed library."

Standing below the towering stacks of books, her grandfather raises a single shaking finger. "Up there."

"You want me to get something from all the way up there?"

"There's a ladder in the garden shed."

She shoots him a dubious look.

"You'll probably want some sort of rake, too, to pull it down. It's a little higher than any ladder will go."

"How did you even—"

"Off you go." He shoos her.

Maia runs across the yard to the garden shed and pulls out the longest metal ladder she can find. Back in the library, she places it against the shelving and climbs up the rungs. Her grandfather hands her the rake and she hooks it across the top of a box. "This one, right?"

"You got it."

"How am I supposed to—"

"Just knock it down ... nothing in there that will break."

She slides the box off the top shelf. With no lid, the contents spill out as it falls. Scores of papers scatter across the room, along with pencils, pens, and crayons. Maia hurries down the ladder and picks up a faded box of Crayola crayons.

"Where did you..."

"I've been saving it for you. For the day you have children of your own. No child should live a life without crayons and paper."

"*Grandpa.*"

He shrugs as he looks around, then wipes a tear from his eye. "I saved more than I thought. Guess I got a little excited."

Maia's shoulders slump and the crayons slip from her hand, hitting the ground with a loud *thud*. "What is this..." she whispers. "*A guilt trip*?"

"No, darling," he says softly. He picks up a piece of paper from the ground and walks over to her. Grabbing her hand, he flips it open and places the paper on top, and then places his hand on top of the paper. "I saved this box of supplies as an act of faith. Faith that someday, when you were grown, you would use it in a way that celebrated *life*. This box of paper is a celebration. The fact that we stand here today, about to use them, is a dream come true. I hid them away when you were a child, knowing if you found them, you would have used every last one." He chuckles. "It was a significant act of faith for me, to save something for a future I feared may never come.

"Maia, these papers were always meant to be filled by you. They were always meant for this moment. I just didn't know it until now. Take them. Fill them up with your plans."

She pulls her hand from between his and the paper falls to the ground. He looks at her, unsure.

She smiles at him through her tears. "Okay, Grandpa."

He beams. "Okay."

———

Over the course of a few hours, the kitchen table becomes a disarray of papers, pencils, and stacks of books. Plans, plans for plans, and backup plans are all initiated and placed in binders.

"What do we do about a boat?" Maia asks while flipping through another survival book.

"Probably have to barter for one. Maia?"

She dog-ears a page before looking up at him.

"I hate to ruin this moment, but the elders of the Northern Tribe are still coming."

She looks back to her book. "I know."

"It's actually a good thing," he says, ignoring her growl. "Saves us a trip up there. They're our best option for bartering. Maybe we could start a list of what we can offer in exchange for a boat. Or help in learning to sail. It's been ages since you and I have navigated our way around a ship; I'm sure you could use a refresher course."

"I don't need them for a boat. I could have a look again for one around here, there's got to be something."

"*Nah*, I reckon most have been taken. There have been a few decades of people coming and going."

"There'll be something."

"Okay, just don't count it out. You may need to go up

there and work for a while in exchange for one. Just brainstorming here—"

"*Ugh*—no. I'd rather build one. Or die."

"Okay, okay, let's just see what happens, shall we? Anyway, add those options to our boat brainstorm. Every idea, good or bad, needs to be added."

"*Mm-hmm*," she grumbles as she slides the binder out from a stack of papers. She flips it open and starts a list:

Mission islands for a boat.

Build a boat with **will take years* next to it.

Look for good skeletons of boats to build back up.

She looks up, checking to see if her grandfather is watching. He is. She begrudgingly adds *Northern Tribe work for barter.*

"Good girl." He slides his chair from the table. "Tea?"

"Sounds great."

As he heads towards the wood burner, she aggressively scratches out the last option.

Life around the cabin completely changes. Maia's grandfather, despite himself, accepts his new duty with unexpected vigor. As a retired university professor, he doesn't waste any time before making up a rubric, lists, and topics for study. A new daily schedule is made. Mornings begin at the crack of dawn and are for intense study and brainstorming. Afternoons are for chores and boot camp.

"Boot camp?"

"Yes, ma'am! You're going to be strong, Maia, and you're going to learn self-defense as well."

She is delighted. This is good for him. Not only has their plan and subsequent new schedule breathed life back into her days, but they've brought him a little more vigor as well.

Not only that, but her nightmares have stopped. It's like a weight has been lifted. There are no more bad dreams, no more staring off into the horizon, no more feeling like she's been left behind. Whatever has been nagging at her soul has been silenced. And what's left is nothing short of a reprieve.

Running across the yard, Maia touches her grandfather's toes, then runs back in the direction she came. She taps the edge of the fence and races back towards him. Huck sits on the sidelines, panting. He rolls onto his back with his feet in the air.

Maia starts to laugh and nearly trips over herself. "Okay, I'm done now," she gasps.

"*Whaddarya* ... gettin' tired?" her grandfather yells.

She stops. Placing her hands on her knees, she looks up at him as sweat drips off her nose. "Is that an old American accent? Who *are* you?"

"I didn't say you were done. *Git! Git!* No stopping! I didn't raise no sissy!" He claps his hands.

"Oh my God."

Morning sunlight peeks through the cabin's closed window shutters, highlighting a brume of dust particles as they dance in and out of the beams of light. Birds chirp incessantly around their home. Huck's paws click against the wooden porch steps outside. He stops to sniff under the front door before plopping down onto the rug.

The whole world seems to be awake and ready for the day. Four weeks have passed since Maia's grandfather agreed to help her, and life has been really good.

But sleeping through the sunrise has never happened. Not once.

Maia pulls back her privacy curtains enough to see her grandfather's bed in the other corner of the room. His curtain has been left open and he is still under the covers. This isn't like him; he never leaves his curtains open.

She slides her feet into her wool slippers and climbs out of bed. "Grandpa?"

He doesn't move.

She rushes to his bed, startling him awake. "Grandpa?"

"What, child?" His voice cracks.

She takes in the sight of her sickly grandfather, his face a pale green with dark circles under his eyes. "You're sick again."

"Yes, today is not a good day."

Her heart sinks.

"Get my pipe, over by my chair."

She grabs it and hands it to him. "I'll get the fire started."

"Quickly, darling."

After getting the fire going, Maia excuses herself outside. Her grandfather has been smoking his pipe a lot more lately. The cannabis inside it makes him feel better—takes away his aches and nausea. He hasn't let on that he wasn't well, not until today. Or has she been too distracted to notice?

Huck waits for her on the porch.

"Come on, boy, let's check the traps."

A few more days pass and Grandpa still isn't well. He sleeps all day, smokes his pipe, and makes frequent runs to the bathroom. Maia knows the routine when this occurs: lots of water, plain vegetable broth soup, and cannabis for his pipe.

She stays home and tries to work on the plan but can't get too far without him. She escapes by re-reading the stolen books stacked in countless columns from the library out back. She has read every one at least a dozen times about the magical world that used to exist.

Her grandfather told her that as a child she would look at picture books of the Old World the way children used to look at picture books of dinosaurs. She'd flip through page after page of plants and animals now forever wiped off the face of the earth: elephants, pandas, orangutans ... rain forests and coral reefs ... What she wouldn't give to see a living coral reef. She has swum across a few dead ones while searching for fish, desperate to find something to eat. Each time she would try to envision the vibrant colors they used to hold. Now they are only graveyards—frail skeletons covered in layers of black slime. Stubs speckling the ocean floor, they have been smashed into shreds of what once was.

She re-reads one of her favorite books about a young woman living in Hong Kong. It all sounds so unbelievable: the electricity, the endless food in shop aisles just for the picking, the lightning-fast transportation that could take you anywhere in the world.

But then there was the other stuff: terrorists and war; people divided over religion, skin color, sex, and oil. There was widespread disease and never enough food and water. A few people had more wealth than they knew what to do with, while billions slowly died from starvation. And the rich people, despite having everything, were still so sad.

Maia has always been obsessed with the past, trying to

imagine what it must have been like with equal strokes of envy and anger, wonder and horror. The most anger she feels, though, an anger that wells up deep inside her, is from how quickly this earth and its living things were destroyed. Not because humans were evil, but because they were unstoppable. Like a virus. A force to be reckoned with.

She thinks about these things as she sits at the kitchen table, staring once again at the oil painting of her mother's tiger. So sad she'll never see one. They look *magnificent*.

Squeak, squeak, squeak!

Maia smiles. Turning towards the open windows, she looks for her little black fantail sitting on the railing, but he's not there.

Squeak! The bird is sitting on the back of her grandfather's chair.

He's in the house.

"NO!"

Her grandfather screams from his bed. "*What*!?"

Maia runs to the corner of the kitchen. Grabbing a broom, she whips it across the room at the bird. "NO! Get out, get OUT!"

The fantail flies out of the window and swirls high into the sky, leaving both Maia and her grandfather gasping for air.

"What the hell was that?!" her grandfather yells from behind his privacy drapes.

Maia stands in the kitchen, lost for words.

"Well?" Her grandfather pulls back his curtain.

For a brief moment, Maia doesn't recognize his pale face. He's never looked so sick. Her heart sinks to the bottom of her chest as grief falls upon her. "Fantail."

"A *bird*. Maia, what the hell?"

"Grandpa, it was a *fantail*."

"Get me my pipe. How dare you scare an old man like that. I think my heart just stopped."

Maia falls to her knees and drops her head to the ground.

"What on earth?"

"You're dying, aren't you?" she yells into the floor.

Her grandfather grabs his pipe and shuffles to his chair. "Come here."

Maia climbs to her feet and swipes a blanket from her bed. She covers her grandfather before sitting on his ottoman. They stare at each other for a long while before she finally says, "You're really sick, aren't you?"

He takes a deep breath and lets it out slowly as his head tips back against his chair. He winces in pain as he repositions himself. Finally, when he opens his eyes, they are heavy and broken. "Yes, honey, I'm really sick."

Her head falls into her hands. "You can't leave me, Grandpa."

His voice trembles. "I'm so sorry..."

"We just went hunting ... it wasn't that long ago. You've been sick a lot the past few years but you always get better again."

"Yes, darling, I do." He coughs into his hands—deep and desperate. He looks at them, then quickly wipes the blood away with his cloth.

Maia stares at him, horrified.

He looks at her apologetically and then shakes his head. "I'm not sure I have much time left."

"NO, no please, stop."

"The herbs I keep in my pipe have made life much easier on me, the symptoms less consuming. But they aren't working as well as they used to."

"Grandpa, please," she sobs and drapes herself

across him.

"I'm so sorry, sweetheart." He hugs her tight, holding his breath to stop himself from crying out in pain.

The fire crackles next to them, illuminating the room in an orange glow as the sun sets behind the trees. Maia pulls herself away from him and clutches his blanket. "I can't do this without you."

He wipes his eyes and forces a smile. "You can, sweet girl. You can and you must."

She sits back on the ottoman in disbelief, glaring at a small black feather resting on the back of his chair. "That's why you've been spending so much time in the woodshed, isn't it? Sometimes in the middle of the night? I snuck in there. I can see that you're building something."

Her grandfather starts to cough. His entire body shakes as a deep rattling sounds from his broken lungs. After he composes himself, he lights his pipe, the flame illuminating his sunken cheeks.

"What is it?" she asks.

"A pyre."

"*A pyre*?! No. For who?"

"Don't make me answer that."

"No, absolutely not."

"Maia."

"You want me to *burn* your *body*?"

"Remember what we talked about? I'll never leave you. I'll always be right here beside you."

"Stop *saying* that! No, you won't. You'll be dead and I'll be alone."

He looks wounded by her words. "Hopefully you won't need to use it for a long time, but I've finished all the preparations, and I need you to go out there and take a look at it."

"I won't."

"Maia, *please*. There is a cot with a rope attached."

"*Stop!*"

"You can roll me onto the cot and use the rope and pulley from a tree branch." He winces again and repositions himself in the chair. "The pyre is easy to pull out. This is the best way. It's this or burial."

"No, I can't."

"Honey, we're just talking about it now. Maybe I'll get better again. But there'll come a time when I won't. I've set aside a jar and have left it next to the photos on the fireplace mantel. I want you to collect my ashes with it and spread them everywhere you go."

Maia holds her head in her hands and sobs. Her grandfather pulls her into him and wraps his arms around her. He holds her for a long time, softly humming as tears flow down his weathered cheeks. "I'll be in the wildflowers covering the mountainsides. I'll be in the wind, dancing through the trees. I'll be in the twinkling starlight, lighting your path no matter where you go. I'll always be with you."

Maia crawls next to him in his chair, resting her head on his chest.

He pulls his blanket over them both. "My baby." He holds her and she closes her eyes. "I'll love you forever. Don't ever forget that, my darling. And when forever is over, I'll still keep loving you."

THIRTEEN

The next day, Maia wakes before dawn and opens up the cabin on her own—just as she has every morning for the last week, and how she always has when her grandfather gets sick.

But this time feels different.

She gets the fire going again in the living room and below the stove in the kitchen for tea. Then she sits at their table and bites her nail, focusing on the drawn curtains around his bed. She knows he's not getting up, but she waits anyway.

A low, raspy cough echoes from his dark corner, then crescendos into a violent, gasping attack. *Cough. Gasp. Wheeze. Cough, cough.*

Maia stands from the table, unsure of what to do. His coughing has increased in intensity and frequency, keeping her on high alert all hours of the day and night, ready to jump up and help him in some way if it sounds like he is suffering too much. Even if it's just to distract him, or hold his hand, or grab the bucket when he coughs so hard that he vomits.

There is silence. She knows what's happening behind that curtain. Hunched over with a red face, he has coughed so hard he can't breathe. She holds her own breath. Finally, when it comes, his gasp is loud and desperate.

She takes a step forward. He doesn't like to be bothered when he is ill. "Grandpa?"

"I'm fine, darling," he says quickly before hacking into his handkerchief, clearing another mound of bloody mucus from his lungs.

She sits down again on the edge of her seat and resumes biting her nail. Staring at his curtain. He moans.

Cough. Gasp. Cough gasp. Gasp. Gasp. Cough.

She can't just sit here.

Stepping out onto the front porch, she softly closes the front door behind her. The intense, early morning sun pours through the yard's surrounding trees in beams. The air is crisp, cool. Refreshing, actually. She reminds herself to crack open the windows when she goes back in.

Huck is curled up on the rug next to their rocking chairs —the chairs she and her grandfather had made together when she was a child. Okay, it was mostly him, but she helped. They were so proud of them. She didn't do anything but keep him company or tell him where to whittle another carving into the wood, but she was proud. When her grandfather placed the rockers on their empty front porch, they sat on them side-by-side for hours every night, just beaming at each other. It was the first thing they made together. They've sat on them almost every night since.

Maia gazes around the yard. Everything is the same, yet it all looks so different now. What would this place be like without him? Empty. A gaping void.

She sneaks down the creaking wooden steps and heads for the greenhouse. Pausing in the middle of the backyard, the grass is crisp below her feet. Frosts are a rare occasion now, which is shocking for an area of the mountain that used to be covered in snow most of the year. Shivering, she rubs the sides of her arms.

The bathhouse and outhouse are nestled alongside the cabin, while three large sheds line the far back border of the yard. There's a small garden shed with nearly every tool one could ever wish for. Next to it, Grandpa's woodshed, where he has built or repaired nearly everything they own. Next to that, the library, covered in vines and surrounded by forest. It looks like a fairytale. It has always been her space. Her escape.

Just inside the library's front door, now hidden behind layers of musty, dust-laden books, lies a whole wall Grandpa allowed her to paint as a child. Layers upon layers. She had been using up all the paper, so he put her on to this. Whenever she had a new idea, she would paint the wall white again and start from scratch.

The library is where she hid to escape, just as her grandfather used the woodshed. When one was in his or her shed, they had an unspoken rule to leave that person alone—unless the door was left open. It was their only reprieve, especially during her early teenage years when they wanted to rip off each other's heads.

At the farthest corner of the yard sits the glass greenhouse. The glass is covered in so much moss the building nearly blends into the background. The metal is deeply rusted at the seams. She's an old girl now but still sturdy. Maia always meant to give it a good clean—as a surprise. Her grandfather would have loved it.

Stepping inside, she breathes in the rich scent of dirt. Grandpa had taught Maia everything one could possibly know about food: growing it, foraging for it, hunting it, cooking it. He had found solace in the sense of control working in the greenhouse had given him. It was his mother who had taught him. Having grown up during the worst food shortage in the history of mankind, being able to forage, hunt, and grow your own food was what gave you a fighting chance to live when everyone around you was starving. Grandpa never let go of his tenacity for food. And he was good at growing it.

They've spent nearly every day of her life in this greenhouse. Even if it were just short spurts to pick a few things for dinner, or to snip cannabis buds to dry for his pipe. Most days it was longer. Rotating the crops, fertilizing, weeding, watering ... this greenhouse has been their lifeline. When hunting proved fruitless, at the very least they knew they'd have food. Good food.

She pulls up her grandfather's wobbly wooden stool and sits in front of the tomatoes. His "babies." She absently taps one of the green leaves. The only thing in this world that had more pet names than her. She sighs and looks around. This place *is* her grandfather. This land, this home, this set-up in this safe and secluded area—he had created a kingdom, and just for her.

Now he is helping her leave it all behind. How it must be killing him.

He's dying, and there is nothing she can do about it. She knew this day would come ... of course she did. She just assumed it would be much farther down the road. He isn't that old. This can't be his time. Not yet. Oh, please, not yet.

Things were supposed to be different when he left her. She was supposed to be prepared. Older. And now? She gazes through the green spotted glass back to her library. That wasn't her escape. No, she hasn't been back to her real escape in years.

She slides back the stool and heads to the woodshed to grab her rusty bike. It's practically useless with all the over-grown trails but will come in handy today. She drops it by the front porch and peeks her head inside. Her grandfather is snoring. *Asleep at last.* She grabs a bright red rock from a basket near the front door and places it in the middle of the kitchen table. *Be back soon* is painted across its face.

Maia stands before the decaying old mansion, now devoured by weeds and vines. It certainly has aged dramatically over the years. The paint has started chipping away, and the once bright white porch is covered in moss. Grandpa was right. It will only be a matter of years before this earth swallows up every last trace of them.

She walks to the side of the house first, checking for any signs of life. All appears empty.

She had found this place as a young girl, and it was such a find. In a land where nearly everything had been picked over and left to rot, this was a real score. Unlike most of the homes on the island, this one was pristine. No skeletons or half-rotted corpses inside. No red X painted on the door. The furniture was still covered in sheets. There was gold cutlery in the drawers and intricately designed dishes. And tea cups. She even found a brand-new dog bed for Huck.

Maia was ecstatic. After surveying the lot from top to bottom, Grandpa agreed to let her play there on her own. It was close enough to home and was nicely tucked away in the mountains. Kind of like them—all secluded and hidden and locked.

But she had to do her chores first. And check in often.

Hours, days, years were spent at this house. She took

care of it as if it were her own. And then she imagined an entirely different life inside. She had a mother and a father … siblings too. She'd pretend to come home from a long day at school and her "family" would be there, waiting for her with open arms. She would tell her mother about soccer practice and the bully she stood up to in gym class. Her "friends" would come over for sleepovers and her mother would bake them cookies. And make sweet tea. And fried chicken. Whatever that tasted like, they sure did love it *back in the day*, as Grandpa would say. And then her mother would sneak into her bedroom while Maia slept and kiss her on the forehead. That's what mothers did, right? That's what her books say.

It gave Maia comfort. She didn't know why it did, but that didn't matter. In this house, an entire world came alive where Maia didn't have to be alone. Where the future possibilities were endless. Where she had a family. And friends. And as a child, that was enough.

That was back when she thought her adult years were forever away. Back when she thought that by the time she grew up, the Southern Islands would have lots of people on them again. That it would only take a *few more years*. Back when she believed she would have options, and she wouldn't end up like the other lonely souls she's come across while exploring—all alone in their homes, decaying and filled with maggots.

That was back when she thought her grandfather would live forever. That she wasn't wasting precious time escaping from the only human she's ever known. And she could live here, in this gorgeous mansion with her family—close to him, but not *too* close. In her dream house. With the porch swing. And the ornate front gate with the giant golden *M* in the middle. Of course, Maia knew it wasn't after her own name, but it made for a lovely coincidence that fit nicely within the walls of her make-believe world.

It was enough to live in a world that didn't actually exist because that world was going to come again. Someday, when she was all grown up. Until then, she had this house all to herself. And she would pretend.

Maia hesitantly climbs the sagging porch steps to find the rusted lock she had kept around the front door handles broken. Left snapped in two on top of a pile of red decomposing chains. Her heart sinks. She takes a deep breath and cautiously nudges the unlatched front door with a single finger. It opens with a loud creak.

The inside of the entrance is littered with leaves and dirt. She prepares herself, knowing that what is about to greet her is not at all what she left behind. She takes another deep breath and steps inside, her hand resting on her knife tucked in its holster.

Wrecked. The entire place is wrecked. Her drawn-out sigh echoes in the foyer, and a few birds fly across the cathedral ceiling and out a shattered window. All her beautiful things—the elaborate wall hangings, the tables and chairs and blankets—have been burned in an enormous heap in the middle of the great room. Whoever did this behaved like cavemen. Even the rungs of the banisters up the steps. Whole sections of the banisters—gone. Those were the banisters she would slide down in a grand display every time her "friends" came to the front door.

"*Maia? Your friends are here!*"

Like a beloved princess, she'd greet her adoring tribe by sliding down the railings into the grand, sun-lit foyer. *Ta-da!*

Maia falls to her knees, too numb to cry. Doesn't this

figure? Her one precious thing that was all her own, and some apes have destroyed it.

Pulling a small joint from her pocket, she twists the end and lights up. Smoking pot has always been a rare occurrence for her, but she's not opposed to it when in need of an escape. She inhales deeply and holds her breath, gazing up at the black mold sprawling across the ceiling. Back in the day, this place would have cost someone a fortune. That's what Grandpa said. Not that it means a whole lot to her, being the first generation to rise after The End.

But now ... firewood. It's as good as firewood.

Maia wanders the halls, stopping just as the kitchen comes into view. The cabinets have been ripped off the walls, her precious teacups shattered across the tiles. The paintings she plastered over the fridge after her grandfather showed her what magnets were for ... all gone.

Fuck you.

Lifting her bike from the gravel and weeds, she turns to take one last look at her old mansion. Her childhood. The four walls that held her dreams, comforted her during a time she naïvely thought everything would turn out to be okay. Now, her grandfather is dying. Her dreams of sailing to The Old Arctic Circle are perishing alongside him. And her home, her getaway—destroyed. This was the only place on this godforsaken island that was normal. There wasn't a single sign of the apocalypse. She used to really cherish that.

Anger burns within. More than anger, pain.

Maia searches her pockets for her box of the few remaining matches she owns. Indignant, she lights the match and holds it up, the silhouette of the house blurring behind its flame. She could just drop it. Let the place burn. She stands frozen, willing herself to release her grip. The flame slowly works down the wooden stick until the heat begins to singe the tip of her fingers. She blows it out.

She looks up at the house. Nothing left but a shell. Just let it burn. She slides open her little box and doesn't hesitate to remove her last precious match. She strikes it against the side. Nothing. She strikes again. And again.

A dud. Her head tips back and she drops the match. What a waste. She turns to leave and that's when she sees it. She stands frozen in the driveway. The ornate gate with the immense golden *M*, now hanging by a single hinge. Run through, smashed, and crooked on its side. She takes a step towards it, her fists clenched.

She spins back around to the house. This pathetic, dilapidated waste of space. What she wouldn't give for a match. She picks up a large rock and hurls it at the front door. A perfect shot—the glass shatters across the welcome mat. She picks up another, and another, tears streaming down her face. She breaks every window, and when that is done, she continues to hit the house with every last stone she can find. Hurling her anger, hurling her pain, her disappointment, her shame.

Foolish. Foolish. Foolish.

She falls to her knees and holds her head in her hands. Huck wanders up next to her and reassuringly licks her arm. She wraps herself around him, resting her head upon his shoulder as she sobs.

FOURTEEN

Days pass and the nights continue on, but Maia's grandfather does not get better. She hovers over him, carefully wrapping cold cloths across his feverish forehead as he sleeps more and more. He does not drink his broth or his water. She pleads with him, but often he does not wake to her whispers. So, she moves her chair next to his bed and curls into a ball, watching in horror when he coughs and gasps for air.

Maia doesn't sleep much, although sometimes her body takes over and she passes out with her head on his bed. When she wakes, she rushes to check his breathing, hovering her ear next to his mouth. Sometimes he wakes, reaching out for something she cannot see. Sometimes he smiles and speaks to her mother. But most of the time he sleeps, leaving Maia to hover around him in a constant state of fear.

She paces around the cabin, running her fingers over their things, their memories, their books, and candles. The blanket she made him. His beloved bottle of whisky, the last of the bottles he had so diligently stockpiled before The

End. The plans and maps and lists they have made for her journey sitting in piles around the kitchen table.

After her daily inventory of their life together, Maia will often collapse into a heap and cry until her tears have run out. She is resentful. She knows there is nothing she can do. There is no one who can help. She is completely alone.

She continues to mind the house, hoping her grandfather will come out of his sickness and knowing when he does, he'll ask if the veggies have been pruned, the water replenished, the wood chopped. She wakes up all hours of the night to keep the fire going, making the cabin uncomfortably warm for her ailing grandpa.

Finally, he wakes. She helps him to the outhouse toilet, an overwhelming affair as his once strong body is nearly too weak to walk. Then he wants to sit in his chair. She moves it close to the fire and wraps his frail body in every blanket she can find. He speaks to her between gasps and moaning in pain. She feeds him water and reassures him in whispers.

"You're doing great, Grandpa."

"I'm right here, Grandpa."

"Just a little more sleep and you'll be okay."

"Please be okay."

"Please be okay."

"Please be okay."

"*Please don't leave me.*"

She pulls herself away from him long enough to close up the house and tries the entire time not to notice the dog out on the porch, staring through the window. She keeps her eyes fixated on her grandfather as she climbs into bed.

"Dear God," she pleads as her exhaustion pulls her into a deep sleep. "If you're up there, please bring him back. Bring him back to me. Please bring him back."

She stands on the familiar shore of her dreams, but this time her mother is nowhere to be found. There are no trees, no city in the distance. There is only sand, and then, only water. She stands in the middle of a vast ocean. Off in the far distance, her grandfather stands alone. Confused, he looks around, calling out to her.

"Grandpa! I've been so worried about you!" She tries to run, but the water only slides beneath her feet. She tries harder, reaching her hands out to him. "Grandpa! Help me!"

Despite running faster and faster, Maia remains stationary as her feet glide across the water like ice. She slips and falls, breaking the surface and sinking beneath it. She kicks back to the top but remains trapped underneath. Her grandfather stands above, still searching and calling out for her.

"Grandpa!" She pounds the underside of the water.

He sees her. Placing his hands on the surface, he mirrors hers. His voice is muffled; he's saying something she cannot understand. What is he saying? He repeats it a few times ... *her mother's name.*

"No! *Maia!* It's *Maia*, help me!"

He says it again and again, pounding the surface.

Maia's scream startles her awake. She glances over to check her grandfather. The fire is down to embers. He groans and moves his head, and then he is silent. She wants to get up but her weary eyes close once again.

Still dark, moments later, she opens them. Or has it been longer? The fire still smolders, but its embers tell her time has passed. It lays a soft glow over the silhouette of her grandfather's body.

She peels back the covers, keeping her focus on her grandfather. He doesn't move. She takes each step as if walking on fractured glass ... as if any moment she could break through and sink into nothing.

"*Grandpa?*" she whispers.

There's a glass of whisky in his hand, resting in his lap. *How did he get this?* She places her hand on his shoulder and stares at his chest. It does not move.

"Grandpa?"

Blood lines the edge of his lips. She shakes his shoulder and his head falls forward. She jumps back, her hand over her mouth. Stepping forward, she touches his ghostly skin, now clammy and cool.

"*Grandpa!*" She falls to her knees as a wail she's never heard pours out from her lungs.

Lifting his head, she places her ear next to his mouth. Nothing. She stares at him, flooded with horror. She places her head next to his mouth once again, then against his chest, pressing hard, harder, desperate to hear a beat.

Nothing.

"NO! No please, *please*! I'll do anything!" Tears blur her vision and she shakes him once more. "Grandpa?" She smiles. "It's okay. You're going to be okay. This is just a dream. I'm just dreaming."

She climbs to her feet and gently releases his head. It hangs from his body. She holds her breath ... listening, waiting. Cries fly from her mouth. "How *DARE* you leave me! Please, come back? Come back, Grandpa! *Please!*"

She looks around the house and screams with all her might as the wind outside the cabin beats against the windows. Screaming, moaning, can't breathe. *Can't breathe!*

Tears coat her face as she paces the cabin floors. Huck howls from the front porch and more dogs howl from a distance.

Gasping, gasping, *gasping* for air as her grief swallows her whole. Lightheaded, she falls to the ground and beats her fists against the floor. For a moment, it seems the world shakes in response. Her mother's painting falls to the ground and the glass cracks across the tiger's face.

Maia curls into a heap in the middle of the floor. The fire embers glow and the wind calms to nothing. Her tears puddle in a pool beneath her head and she presses her cheek into the ground, grasping the wood with both hands as if any moment she may slide into the fire.

"Grandpa? *Please.*"

She stares at the painting sitting up against the wall. The fractured glass cuts between the tiger's eyes, slicing across the floor, tearing apart her and the only love she has ever known.

She closes her eyes, and then she shatters completely.

FIFTEEN

A glass of whisky sits in the middle of the table. *The glass of whisky.* The glass he had somehow lifted himself up to retrieve and pour. All while Maia slept. Could've seen him, could've talked to him, could've hugged him one last time. But instead, she *slept.*

She's been staring at it for about an hour now, glancing between it and the pyre holding her grandfather, sitting in the far corner of their yard.

After lying in the middle of their cabin and crying herself into hysteria, Maia stumbled out to the shed to find the most intricate pyre she's ever seen.

He was right; he thought of everything. The pyre was on a smooth, glossy plastic sheet with ropes woven along its edges for handles, making it easy to glide across the ground and drag where she needed. Then there was the cot, the one she lifted his frail, lifeless body onto, all while moaning and crying and at one point becoming physically ill. The whole process seemed to go on forever as she stopped between each stage to cry until her body could no longer release another tear. She would then pick herself up and move on to the next step. Moving, dragging, crying, groaning, pulling. And all the while, the whole world became unbearably empty. Like a gaping void.

He was much lighter than he used to be. She knows this from the past when he was so sick that she had to help him back and forth between the house and the toilet. But she'll never wrap her arms around him again. No more bush walks, no more cooking together, or reading by the fire. Never again will she see his smiling face when she walks through the front door, no more deep hugs or *goodnight darlings*. Just like that, *he's gone.*

Huck hasn't left her side. Even now, as she sits at the kitchen table and stares outside, he remains right next to her, his head on her lap.

She grabs the glass, slowly raising it to her mouth. The smell burns her nose; the taste burns her mouth. It burns her throat all the way down to her stomach. She loathes everything about it, but it tastes like memories and the burn numbs the pain. So, she sips. She sips and she stares.

I have to burn his body.

I have to burn his body.

Another sip.

And another.

The tears flow once again, but this time Maia does not make a sound.

She leaves a small amount left in his glass, a bit of whisky that a man who no longer exists had poured.

Where did you go?

"I am always with you."

Are you here now? Are you really in the trees and the stars or living inside me?

I feel nothing.

She stands, a bit wobbly as the liquor courses through

her, and slowly walks out to the pyre. A ladder lies against it, leading up to him. She places his glass in the grass and stands before him. His body is wrapped up to his neck in his favorite blanket. Her hand flies against her mouth and her body trembles as she sobs.

Placing one hand on a rung, she grips the cool wood and screams. Huck jumps up from the porch. She reluctantly climbs each rung until she is next to her grandfather and places her hand on his. It sits resting beneath the blanket, so that the last time she touches him, she doesn't remember cold.

"I am so sad, Grandpa." Her voice cracks. "I am *so sad*. I feel broken. I wasn't ready ... but I know you were very sick. I know that. You were in pain, and now you won't be anymore." She rubs his arm. "But I'm really going to miss you."

She gazes around the cot and the wood placed beneath his body, ready to burn. "I really wish I didn't have to do this ... I would give *anything* not to do this." She reaches her hand out to his chest. Waiting. Climbing up onto the cot, she kneels beside him and places her ear next to his mouth. Her tears fall onto his pale skin.

She holds the sides of his face. "Please come back, Grandpa. *Please*?" She listens for a while and then pulls back, staring at him ... *willing* him to breathe. "I guess this is it."

Turning towards the ladder, she hesitates. She turns around and lays her head against his chest, wrapping her arms around him for the last time. "I'll love you forever, Grandpa. And when forever is over, I'll still keep loving you."

After setting the pyre alight, Maia steps back as the fire begins to rage, holding onto his glass of whisky. The smoke is thick, black. The smell overwhelming. She forces herself not to cover her mouth.

Then the ashes begin to fall like snow. They cover the ground and the roof of their cabin. Large flakes coat her hair as the blaze devours the pyre.

She takes one last sip from his glass and then walks as close to the fire as she can. Shielding her face, she tosses it in. "For you—one last drink." She backs away and collapses to the ground.

Huck walks up next to her with his head down, his fur now covered in ash.

She kneels in front of the pyre, watching as her grandfather, the only person she's ever loved, disappears. And she does not move.

So the fire burns.

And the ashes fall.

SIXTEEN

L ying on her back, a single strand of a spider's web floats above her. Its silk glitters in waves as it dances in the bright sunlight streaming across the cabin. Maia stares at it until her vision blurs.

She lifts her grandfather's pipe and takes another long, slow drag. A heavy barrage of smoke swirls from her parched mouth. She curls her tongue, puffing repeated rings of smoke.

Her head is pounding. Huck wanders over and sniffs her face. She lies unmoving, gazing up at the ceiling. He whimpers, then spins in a few circles before curling up next to her.

A few decaying vegetables sit soft and sunken on the table next to a pot of molding soup—another unsuccessful half-attempt to eat.

She rolls her head to the side and stares at the tiger. The tiger stares back. She rolls her head away.

A few flies buzz in circles above her. She's in the same clothing she wore when she burned him, her messy hair still half-wrapped in a loose bun. Dark ash is smeared down her face, with tear lines etched in the layers of gray tracing from her eyes into her hairline.

Her hair, her clothing, her floors, her yard—all sit buried in ash. It has been days. His bed is still unmade. His whisky still sits at the table. She closes her eyes and sucks in another drag, *willing* her heart to stop.

But it beats on.

She curls into a fetal position and stares at the broken tiger on the ground. His face spins left to right, left to right. This is what she has been doing for days. She stares at the tiger and the tiger stares back ... calling out to her, reminding her that her mother was brave, that she was a fighter. And Maia is not. She looks away.

Flashbacks play like movies across the ceiling. She smiles and a tear follows its designated path into her hair. Her grandfather smiles back at her.

Hello, my darling.

She watches as she and her grandfather dance in the living room. He smiles as she lays her head against his chest. He kisses her forehead. They walk through the trails and he looks back at her and winks. He places her hand on a tree and then sweeps his hand across the sky. Together, they look at the stars. He reads her a book by the fire. She cuts his hair on the front porch with Huck sleeping peacefully by the door.

His face. His smiling face ... his worried face. Scared. The color of his skin drains and his cheeks sink. Blood lines his lips and then drips from his mouth. Fire, flames, ash. Ash. ASH.

She lights the pipe again, her world continuing to spin. Her stomach churns and she rolls onto her belly, lifting herself onto all fours. She sways and buckles to the ground. Her stomach twists. She moans and tries again, pulling herself up on her hands and knees. Her body is heavy, burdened with gravity. As she slowly crawls towards the porch, her hands slap against the floor and her knees dig into the hard wood.

Out on the porch, she inches towards the railing, an arduous affair as her head hangs like a block of cement. Falling to the ground, she repositions her face along the edge and vomits over the side. Huck paces behind her. She stays on the deck and stares at her grandfather's charred remains until her eyes glaze over, and then she slips into a deep sleep.

Squeak!

Maia's eyes peel open. She reaches out in a desperate attempt to shield herself from the late afternoon sun. Somehow, she has made her way back inside the cabin and is lying on the floor. Her head is still pounding.

Squeak!

She sits up, grimacing. "*No.*"

Sitting on the railing just outside the open door sits a little black fantail.

"NO!" She pulls herself to her feet. Lightheaded and disorientated, she grabs the bottle of whisky from the table as the little bird continues to chirp. "NO! Get *out* of here!" she screams and chucks the bottle as hard as she can.

It flies over the bird and lands in the blackened grass. Surprisingly, the fantail does not move.

"*Aaaaarghh*! This is all your *FAULT! GO AWAY!*" She

grabs the fractured tiger painting off the floor. Without thinking, she whips it towards the little bird.

He soars into the sky, while the painting does not make it out of the doorway. Hitting the wall, the glass shatters across the floor.

Maia stands, gasping. Her mother's painting lies face-down in a pile of its own broken glass, like a body in a murder scene. Its frame has cracked in half at the seams. She steps forward, oblivious to the shards of glass strewn across the floor. She bends over and lifts the canvas. The pieces slide off the tiger and onto the ground. "Shattered," she says quietly. "Everything I love has fallen apart."

She sighs and looks around the empty cabin. Her stomach grumbles. Dusk is soon approaching, but the fire does not roar in the living room. There is no food being prepared. There is no one else here, and there is no hope of anyone ever being here again.

She places the tiger on the table, slowly running her fingertips over the oils ... his whiskers, his eye, his fur. What was the point? Such a beautiful creature and now ... *everything's dead.*

She backs away from the table. Rubbing her arms for warmth, she surveys the gloomy cabin. Her grandfather's unmade bed in the corner. His worn leather chair in front of the barren hearth. His pipe lying on the floor. Empty. Empty. *Empty.* Sober for the first time in days, she steps forward, then steps back again, unsure of what to do.

She wanders to the old mirror by the front door and her breath catches in her chest as she takes in her reflection. A concerned, wretched version of herself stares back at her. Skinny, pale, and covered in ash—covered in the remains of her grandfather. She slowly reaches up to her cheek, tracing the tear lines carved into the layers of gray. The light in the cabin continues to fade.

Shivering, she loads their fireplace full of wood. Within a few minutes, a comforting roar blazes from inside the hearth. She does the same with the wood-burning stove and heats several buckets of water for a bath.

The empty glass jar still sits on the mantel from their last conversation. She walks over to it and holds it with both hands.

Place my remains in this. Take me everywhere, Maia. Spread my ashes over this land, the only land I've ever loved, and know that I am no longer contained inside a body. I am floating on the wind. I am swaying with the wildflower. Whenever you look at the stars, remember how even though many have burned out, their light still reaches us. This is like my love for you. Even though my body is gone, my love will never fade. I am always with you.

She steps outside and briefly pauses along the edge of the porch, staring at the scorched remains of the pyre. She is overwhelmed as she walks to the site ... *so many ashes.* There's no way to tell between her grandfather and the burned wood. But funerals aren't for the dead, they're for the living. She drags the jar into the ashes, scooping up as much as she can from the spot where he was laid, and replaces the lid. Then she heads to the bathhouse behind the cabin, grabbing his bottle of whisky from the yard on her way.

She places the jar and the whisky next to a few lit candles on the bathhouse's wooden bench and slides the entire thing closer to the large ceramic bath. She leaves the door unlatched for Huck, knowing he loves to come in and soak up the heat given off during bath time.

The glow from the candles highlights the heavy steam

twisting and curling from the water. Maia peels off her soiled layers of clothing one by one and drops each piece into a pile she vows to burn, knowing she'll never be able to look at the clothes again.

Testing the water's temperature, she lightly dips one toe. Perfect. As she steps inside the bath, pleasure from the water's heat floods through her. The black ash coating her legs melts off in ripples as she lowers herself down. Huck nudges his way through the door and plops next to the tub.

Grandpa loved this antique claw-foot bathtub. He built a bathhouse almost nicer than the cabin just to house it. Maia rests her head along the curved ledge of the bath and gazes through the skylight in the cathedral ceiling. She can barely make out a single twinkling star. What a place this is. He was right; she would never want for anything here.

She can't help wondering now how much he really supported her leaving. Maybe he knew his time was limited … he *had* to know. He would have known that he could appease her childish dreams and have peace in his last days by "agreeing" to let her go. By letting her figure out how limited her options really were. By hashing out every last idea and seeing once and for all how deeply dangerous and flawed they were. How could she ever leave this place on her own? They hadn't even gotten that far in their plans anyway. Options. They had only discussed *options* of "what" could get her there. Not "how." Never "how."

But then, he always seemed so genuine. After all that time just the two of them, wouldn't she be able to tell?

"Huck?" She leans over the ledge of the bath and reaches out to him. Water trickles along the underside of her arm and drips onto the ground. Huck tenderly licks the tip of her finger. "This is it. And that's fine, isn't it? Grandpa had given me his blessing, but I can't do it without him."

She leans back again and watches as the single star flickers through the skylight. "I can't. I can't do it without him." She repeats this to herself as she closes her eyes, knowing with each passing *can't*, not only that she *can*—but she must.

SEVENTEEN

Countless iridescent blue specks illuminate the expansive forest like stars. Maia sits cross-legged in the dark on an old mossy bridge still standing from when her ancestors built it. A full moon shines between the canopy of branches. Beneath her, a shallow creek glides gently over a jumble of rocks.

She faces a large waterfall. Roaring, white, intense. She can barely make it out in the black of night but its sound is unmistakable. Comforting. The white noise helps drown out the voices in her head.

This is her favorite spot, a place of peace where she can just be. She has been coming here her entire life, whenever she's craved solitude. The best part about this place is visiting at night. All across the ancient forest, little blue lights shine forth as thousands of glowworms nest on trees, cliffs, and between rocks. Everywhere she looks, constellations of blue shimmer back at her.

It is nothing short of magical.

She pulls the jar of ashes from her pack and slowly unscrews the lid. With tears in her eyes she whispers, "I'm not sure where you are now, Grandpa, how it must feel? Do you still feel pain?" She looks around, almost expecting an answer. "I'll just leave a bit of you here, so that you may always feel peace." She tilts the jar and scatters her grandfather's ashes softly into the creek.

This is not the first place she has taken him today. She awoke before the sun and searched his workshop for a sturdy piece of wood, then spent all morning in his chair carving a headstone. As the morning light filled the sky, she dug a grave in the corner of their yard and filled it with the ashes left from what remained of the pyre. And then she knelt on the ground before it and sobbed.

Her eyes swollen, she wandered into the cabin and stuffed a pack full of food and a few jars of water, her light sleeping bag, a small lantern, and her bow and arrow. Then she grabbed her grandfather's ashes and locked up the cabin to begin her tour of the island.

She took him along their favorite path, where they had taken countless walks throughout their twenty years of life together. It was the first time she'd been on this specific trail alone. It had always been *their* trail. She followed the same route for hours as it snaked through misty forests covered in layers of moss. She hiked up along the mountain's edge, where she stopped as they often did for a rest and enjoyed the breathtaking views across the endless green expanse. Then she headed back down again, past rivers and streams that lead to the ocean.

"Come on, Grandpa. Hurry! Hurry!"

Her bare feet jump from boulder to boulder along the river's edge. Her grandfather's much younger voice chuckles from behind her. "I'm coming. Don't you worry, child, I'll catch up!"

She picks up the pace, thrilled at the slightly cooler summer breeze compared to the recent string of stinging hot days. Behind her, a sweet-faced black puppy nips at her heels.

"Huck! Ow! No, Huck!" She picks him up and giggles as he licks her face. "This is the best birthday present ever, Grandpa, thank you!"

"He's not your birthday—we're not keeping him!" her grand-father yells from a distance.

"But I'm ten now. I'll take good care of him." She sets the puppy on the boulder next to her where a brown sludge coating the surface of the river laps around its base. Huck stares up at her with large eyes and a wagging tail.

"Young lady..." Her grandfather joins her along the shore of the winding creek where large mounds of rubbish has stacked on top of itself for miles. He steps over a half-buried white plastic chair. His younger skin is still furrowed with lines from the sun, but his middle-aged face is much more filled in—his hair only a salt and pepper version of where it ended up years later. "It's not up for discussion."

She puts her hands on her hips and pouts. Huck whimpers until she picks him up again. She kisses the top of his head as he squirms in her arms.

"Young lady."

She turns and grins at her grandfather standing along the creek's shore. His arms hang at his sides and he drops his head in defeat. He peers up at her and smiles.

Maia knelt along the shore and dragged her fingertips along the mostly clear creek. She and her grandfather spent two years cleaning the rubbish out of those waters so they could flow again. Two years of pulling and digging and hauling load after load of old, slimy garbage from those waters, and not without giving her grandfather plenty of grief.

"What difference is this going to make? Why are we doing this anyway? No one is even around to notice it."

"Trust me, child. Every little effort you make matters. It makes a difference. One day you will come back and there will be new life here."

"When, in like a million *years?"*

"Mark my words, young lady, it matters. Every little bit matters."

A small frog hopped from his spot in the sun into the sparkling water. "It matters," she whispered as she smiled. She poured a line of ash into the dampened sand. "So that you may forever feel my gratitude."

Exhaustion setting in, Maia then wandered up to her favorite cliff. Scooping up another handful of ash, she tossed it over the edge. Caught on the wind, it swirled before her. She squinted through the bright sun, extending her hand. For a moment, she could almost see him reaching out to her from within the ashes. Then the wind carried him away, leaving her gazing out into a vacant sky.

Despite her consuming weariness, Maia pushed on, stopping by her and Huck's favorite swimming hole. "So that you may forever feel joy." The field where she and her grandfather loved to picnic. "So that you may always feel fulfilled." Finally, after spending the night curled up in the glowworm forest, she returned in the very early morning hours the next day, ending her quest right back in front of their cabin. Maia reached into the jar and gently spread some ashes across the footpath leading to the front porch.

"So that you may always feel love."

Now standing in front of the dark cabin, her lantern casts strange shadows across its face. There's no smoke coming from the chimney. The only time it has ever stood empty was when she and her grandfather were out for the day. Even when he was ill, she would keep the fires going—in their fireplace, their stove in the kitchen, even the small rocket stove in the corner, often boiling water or soup or broth. Life was always happening.

With Huck trailing behind her, she walks up the front steps and into the cabin. The inside is cold, damp. Shivering, she places the lantern in the living room and gets the fireplace going, then the kitchen oven. She starts to boil water for tea but finds herself pouring a glass of whisky instead.

Her grandfather's jar sits on the table, a small portion of his ashes remaining. Maia finds a tiny bag. Prying it open where it's cinched, she pours in the last of the ashes. She closes the sack with a knot and then another. After she is fully convinced that it is sealed tight, she places her grandfather in her pocket.

The fire is roaring now. With her glass of whisky, she sits in her grandfather's chair, watching Huck's stomach rise and fall as he sleeps. She absently takes another sip as her thoughts race.

This is fine. It is. Just give it time. Life will find a new normal. This is fine.

I can't live like this!

What am I going to do?

Her grandfather's smiling face flashes from her memory. His chuckle, his knotted-up old hands. She pulls up her legs and curls into a ball.

Where did you go, Grandpa?

She walks over to his bed and ties back the privacy curtains. Slowly moving her hand along the blankets, she smooths out the wrinkles before falling on top, grabbing the pillow and breathing in the fading scent of her grandfather.

Her hand presses against something hard between the pillow and its cover. She reaches in and pulls out a notebook. Her heart skips. *A notebook.* She flips through it, finding pages filled with notes he'd written to himself, quotes from his favorite books, and checklists. In the very back, there is a letter to her. Sloppy, the handwriting does not look like the rest. He must've written it toward the end of his life. She devours its contents immediately.

My darling Maia,

What I wouldn't give to have another lifetime with you, to not leave you alone up here like this. I've worked so hard to make sure you could have everything you could ever need, but looking back, I didn't work hard enough. I should have traveled with you more, tried harder to find a community where you felt safe. I would give anything for more time. Anything. But that's life, and life never asks for our permission. I am so sorry. Please know that even when my body is absent, I am still here.

In the chaos of The End, people said it was Hell on Earth, the apocalypse, Armageddon. They said it was the end for us, that humans and this earth were finished. But we're not, Maia. We're not finished because you're still here. It's not over. You are proof that miracles do exist.

There is no greater travesty in this world than for a soul to waste his or her life merely existing. This one life we have is not to be taken lightly. It is a gift and a privilege now denied to billions. So, you are going to choose life, Maia. Whether you stay on this island, go to the next, or sail across the world, you are going to find the life written in the stars for you. I know this. You'll find a way.

As a recipient of this life, it is not only your responsibility—it is your duty. You are a child of the universe. Your heart was created from galaxies of stardust billions of years old. In your genes, you carry the souls of generations passed—you carry the soul of the world. Never forget what I've told you, Maia. You are not alone. Every step you take, you take while holding the hand of God.

Go. Now. Be diligent. Be sound in mind and steadfast. Formulate a plan and if that plan fails, try again. The path you must take will make itself known to you. The law of the universe has always been, if there is a will, there is a way.

Just don't give up.

Finish the plans we have made.

Find a way.

You have universal backing. Make your mother proud. Above all else, make yourself proud. I will be with you every step of the way.

Maia scans his messy writing as he rambles and repeats himself, until she arrives at his final message.

Our species has been plunged back into the Stone Age. There are no guarantees—there's only life and death.

Choose life, Maia.

EIGHTEEN

Huck sits panting in the middle of the living room, watching Maia as she circles the inside of the cabin, lost in thought. She absently walks past her grandfather's empty bed in the corner, running her fingers along the tucked-in blankets. She passes the fireplace mantel, layered with family photos and memorabilia. As she circles past his chair, she does not take her eyes off the letter.

That letter.

She wanders past the front door, now closed and locked, then past her messy bed in the opposite corner. She finishes the loop as she passes the dusty and neglected kitchen. She circles the house all night, always under the watchful eyes of her mother's painting sitting crooked on the dining room wall, its glassless frame now nailed back together. Each time she walks by the painting, she keeps her eyes to the ground, unable to face the eyes of a creature long gone, painted by a woman long gone.

Her grandfather's words repeat themselves in ripples.

Choose life, Maia.

Go.

Now.

Be diligent.

She stands in front of the stacks of books and plans she and her grandfather had been working on, now lost and forgotten in a dark corner of the kitchen. Grabbing an armful, she spreads the maps across the table as a few moldy apples roll off and hit the ground with a green, dusty *splat.*

She paces before the papers while biting her nails and scanning the layers of lists, diagrams, maps, and drawings. Grabbing the table, she leans over the lists, *willing* a solution to present itself.

A flicker of light catches Maia's eye.

Her head snaps up to the painting. The tiger stares back at her. She grabs the jade carving resting on her chest and walks over to the canvas. The tiger's one eye briefly reflects hers, flashing pale blue for a moment before returning back to the bright green and yellow paint. She jumps back, glancing around.

Reaching out to the painting, Maia's fingertips hover over the corrugated canvas. Electricity surges between the picture and her hand, then up through her veins. Bright blue sparks ripple from her skin in waves. As the current courses through her body, her vision becomes clear as crystal and her auburn hair curls into red ringlets.

The sensation is familiar, but one she's always resisted— pushed down, wrangled into submission. She never wanted her grandfather to see or to fully see for herself. She's never understood what *it* was or why it would happen, loathing the phenomenon as much as she's loved it.

But now she no longer has to worry about being seen. Tilting back her head, she closes her eyes as an intense, overwhelming force bubbles up from the ground through her feet, slowly flooding her entire body. Gratifying. Satisfying. Despite the continuous stream of current burning her from within, she smiles.

A vision appears. No longer in her cabin, Maia watches as the tiger, *alive*, pads across an immense open room like a great hall of a castle. Tall windows stretch high into the vaulted ceiling and a gentle breeze sweeps clusters of leaves across the intricately tiled floors.

In the middle of the room, Maia's mother sits upon a throne made of ornately twisted tree branches that break through the ceiling, towering into the sky. The tiger approaches the throne as her mother extends her hand to him. He curls up at her feet and rests his head upon his paws.

Maia's mother stands to face her. Her mother? No ... it's *Maia*. It's the same version of herself that she's seen in her dreams. The same crystalline eyes. The same wild red hair with ringlets sweeping across her shoulders. The same long white gown.

Looking down, it's the white gown Maia also wears. The deep red of her hair hangs in her vision. She fingers a curl before looking at the reflection of herself, now standing directly before her. Maia holds out her hand and the mirrored version reaches hers in response. Electricity sparks between them as they lock eyes and a peculiar grin spreads wide across both their faces.

Maia falls back, slamming her head against the kitchen table on her way down. The palm of her hand burns. Deep red ringlets of hair fall across her face. She sits up with eyes wide, wrapping a curl around her finger.

The painting appears untouched on the wall. Huck is still sleeping soundly next to the fire. Maia's ringlets slowly unravel into waves and she falls onto her back. Exhaustion falls over her like a black cloud. She succumbs to the pull of sleep as the early morning light seeps in from behind the curtains.

Whimpers penetrate the blackness. Maia opens her eyes to Huck nervously pacing in front of the door. He whines as he watches her rub her eyes, then barks, jolting her awake. She peels herself off the ground and stumbles to the door, unlocking all three bolts and sweeping it open. Huck races to the blackened grass to relieve himself. Maia squints into the sky as the sun begins its descent. It must be close to six o'clock by now.

Stealing glances at the canvas, she holds her mother's carving around her neck. Was it a dream? Drawn back to the painting, she takes a deep breath and braces herself as she slowly raises her hand to the tiger. One finger brushes the rough paint. *Nothing.* She presses her whole hand against it. *Nothing.* She grabs her wavy hair and frantically pulls it forward. Auburn—no ringlets. It must've been a dream. She sweeps her hair back and looks around the empty cabin.

Grandpa's letter still sits on his chair.

Just don't give up. Finish the plans we have made. Find a way.

Find a way. She must find a way. After building a fire, she glances over the lists on the table, most of which were things to figure out and work on ... answers that still needed to be found versus solutions that could help her now. It was such a big task. They were still only researching.

The biggest point of discussion was finding a boat—or

building one. They were going to possibly barter with the Northern Tri—*the Northern Tribe.* Her heart sinks.

The deal.

They are still coming for her.

She rushes to the front door and slams it closed, bolting all three locks. Huck cocks his head as he watches from the living room. She yanks the curtains together, closing out the day's remaining light. The fires are still going in both the living room hearth and the kitchen stoves. *Life is always happening.* Lock or no lock, it will be blatantly obvious she is here. And now her grandfather's new grave sits in the corner of the yard. She slides down the wall with her head in her hands.

She doesn't have much time. Who does she know who can help? The only people she really knows on this island are Collin and Sarah ... and her father, but that's certainly not going to happen.

Collin—*boat graveyard.* When she spied on them on the trail, he had mentioned a boat graveyard outside one of the flooded towns. She knows the one, although she hasn't seen it since she was a child. She flips through the stack of papers on the table and pulls out an old map of New Zealand, back when it had only two main islands. The perimeter will be off but she can still gather where the town is. She negotiates a route and packs a bag.

She'll pick a boat and sail it back here. She'll bring her boating books. Worst case scenario, she can always abandon ship and come back home. There must be a way. There's always a way. It'll work ... it has to.

It is her only option.

NINETEEN

Two days.

It has taken Maia two days trekking through the dense bush to get here. It has not stopped raining. Her feet are soaked, clothes are soaked, pack is soaked. It's okay. It'll be worth it. She will find shelter on a boat. It will work. It *has* to work.

She drops her pack at her feet and mud splatters up her leg. The ocean air snaps at her face and blows her hair from her slumped shoulders as she overlooks the boat graveyard, too exhausted to cry.

Only a handful of ships remain—skeletons tipped on their sides in the shallow, muddy water. Rusted, flooded ... *destroyed*, they lie defeated. Smeared in green slime and ravaged by vines, the boats have been slowly swallowed by the mud. Planks and panels drift through the sludge. The only color outside of *rot* is the hint of an orange life preserver peeking out from the mire like an SOS.

Another drop of rain hits the top of Maia's head and with that, it begins to pour. She stands in the deluge, watching from the cliff as the dense rain obscures the scraps from view. Huck walks up behind her, whimpering as he nudges her hand.

"Come on, boy," she mumbles as she picks up her muddy pack and flings it across her back. She takes one last look as the rain soaks into her hair and runs down the tip of her nose, then starts the long trek back home.

Night falls quickly in the densely shrouded bush. Maia lays the small tarp she's brought with her across a few low-hanging branches and finds warmth next to Huck, who hasn't left her side.

For two days, Maia travels back home in silence, her mind endlessly reeling with options that one by one she determines impossible. The path is littered with ideas, falling to the ground like leaves in her wake. Her despair grows with each failed possibility until she finally arrives at her doorstep—drenched and depleted.

So, she sleeps. She sleeps both in search of an escape and to find her mother again, but her mother never comes. Weeks pass but her dreams remain dark, endless, lost. No closure, no answers to be found. Just Maia, falling into a black abyss.

Chores are still done—at a minimum. She makes sure she still has water to drink and food to eat. She checks the traps a few times, but with dwindling bait to lure anything, they remain empty.

She does keep the fire going, mainly to keep warm on the long, lonely nights. She sits curled in her grandfather's chair, watching the flames while she smokes his pipe. A machete lies next to her on the ground—it comes with her everywhere she goes. That and her grandfather's gun.

After weeks of jumping at every bump in the night, Maia has resolved herself to her new future. The Northern Tribe is coming for her and she will not go down without a fight.

She'll die before she goes back up there. She pushes the memories from her mind. Her grandfather passed away never knowing what really happened and she's proud of herself for letting him die in peace.

Her food normally consists of something small—a bird or rodent or rabbit, whatever she can hunt. She cooks her meat over the open fire. It's harder this way, more time-consuming, but the kitchen contains too many memories, so it remains dark. Her grandfather spent so much time making sure they kept to the traditions of his time, and now here she is, swiftly moving back into the Stone Age. Just like the rest of the world.

The last of her grandfather's whisky sits in a glass next to her. She holds it in her hands for a moment before tilting it back and swallowing the last swig whole. She throws it against the back of the hearth and the glass shatters into the fire.

Pulling the letter out from beneath her cushion, Maia reads it for the hundredth time. There's just no way. No way will she settle up north in that crummy little village with some crummy old man. And there's no way she can get off this island alone. So, there's no point in considering it anymore.

She holds the letter out to the flames and leans closer to the fire. Her grandfather's handwriting glows through the paper.

Choose life, Maia.

Her hand shaking, she cannot stop staring at his sentence. What was he thinking? He knew he was dying. He knew he wouldn't be here to help her. Maybe he was delirious. He must've been.

Choose life.

The fire pops before her, its flames dancing behind the paper.

Just burn it. Let it be over now.

Huck lifts his head from the rug. He jumps up and growls as he creeps towards the cabin's locked front door.

Maia pulls back from the fire and twists in her chair, watching the black fur on his back slowly lift. "Huck? What is it?"

His growling intensifies. He lowers his head and snarls.

"Huck—"

The wooden porch creaks.

Someone is out there.

Maia abandons the letter on the chair and crouches down. This is it—they have come for her. Huck continues to growl, then barks as three knocks bang from the other side of the door. Her heart pounding, Maia pulls out her grandfather's handgun.

More knocking, answered with more barking from Huck. Maia runs behind the kitchen table and crouches down as she flips back the gun's safety mechanism.

"Maia? You there?"

She grips the table and stands up, recognizing his voice immediately.

You.

She rushes to the door and unlocks it with a fury, pointing her gun at his face. Her father jumps back, horrified. Huck continues to bark.

"*Whoa.* Maia, it's ... it's me. Remember?"

"*What* are you doing here?"

Her father cowers behind his hands. "Please, lower your gun. And get that dog under control. I haven't come all this way to die."

Maia continues to point the gun as she catches her breath.

He peeks out from behind his hands. "Maia. *Please.*"

Reluctantly, Maia clicks on the safety and lowers her gun. She bends down to reassure Huck, never once taking her eyes off her father. "Good boy. *Shhh.*"

Huck grumbles, sniffing in her father's direction.

"Well?" She shakes her head.

"Maia ... you don't look good."

"*What* are you doing here?"

"I see there's a new grave in the yard ... I'm so *sorry.*"

"What do you *want*!?" she screeches.

He stares at her in shock.

"Have you come to tell me more about how I've ruined your life?"

Her father lowers his head. "I'm sorry," he says. "I can't believe I said that. I ... I never thought I'd ... I was drunk. I'm sorry."

Maia's jaw clenches as tears brim her eyes. "You were *drunk*? *That's* your excuse?"

"Can I come in?"

"No."

Huck begins to growl again.

"*Huck.*" She snaps her fingers.

"Listen, I didn't come here to hurt you. Not any more than I already have. No amount of apologies will rectify that, I know. I came here to let you know a boat has arrived. A huge boat. They come every five years or so from around the world to barter."

"And?"

"And ... one of the sailors is an old man named Davies. He's a known people smuggler. He ... he isn't friendly—*at all*. But I've made a deal with him, and he'll take you on."

"*What?*"

"Listen, you need to really think about this. You would be *smuggled* on board. The crew members are rumored to be criminals but they won't know about you. It's a dangerous decision but it may be your only decision. If you want to get to The Old Arctic Circle, this is your best bet. And ... Davies says it does exist, Maia, that something is up there."

"Wait..." She shakes her head. "*What?*"

"The boat is huge," he continues. "The smuggler has given me his word that you would be taken care of, albeit with bare basics but you'll have a pretty fair shot of getting to North America. That's as far as they go. The Old Arctic Circle isn't very close to where they dock but at least it's on the same continent."

"I know where it is."

"Once there, he's made it *very clear* you are to get off without being seen, and then you'll be on your own. If you are caught, you will be killed—or worse."

"Worse?"

He shakes his head. "Just ... don't get caught."

"Why are you doing this?"

He doesn't speak for a while. Standing motionless on the porch, the glow from the fire flashes over his skinny body. His beard somehow looks even more crooked than before. "You have twenty-four hours," he says.

"*Twenty-four—*"

"That's the best I could do. The men don't stay for long and I had to do a lot of negotiating. Listen, the men dock in the old town harbor for restocking and rest. They will be leaving before sunrise the day after tomorrow. Davies will be waiting for you at three, just a few hours before they wake to leave. You need to stay in the dark bush. He will let out three loud whistles when it's safe for you to come out.

Don't show your face until he does, and don't be late. I've done a lot so you can go; you won't have this opportunity again." He hesitates, then looks at her tenderly. "God be with you." He turns and walks off the porch.

Maia walks out to the edge of the stairs. "Dad?"

Her father stops and turns around, looking up at her with yellow, broken eyes. She stares at him for a moment. There are so many things she wants to say, so many questions she needs to ask, but watching him stand in the cold night, she realizes the answers could never be good enough to rectify a life without him.

So instead, she only thanks him.

He turns and walks away, and she does the same. As she closes the door, he calls out to her from the bottom of the stairs. She steps back out.

"Losing your mother wasn't the worst thing to happen to me, Maia. Losing *you* was. I don't drink because I lost your mother—that couldn't be helped. I drink because I've lost you."

He walks away, leaving her speechless in the doorway.

TWENTY

Huck whimpers as he paces the front porch, watching Maia. Her body shivers from the cold but she does not move. The only sound breaking the silence is her shattered breathing and a ruru owl's call off in the distance. Her father's words hang in the crisp air like daggers.

Twenty-four hours.

If you get caught, you will be killed.

It's a dangerous decision but it may be your only decision.

And then, *I drink because I've lost you.*

Stunned, Maia slowly closes the door before dropping her head against it. She sighs and looks around. The fireplace is still holding a blaze. Huck has returned to his spot on the rug. Her mother still smiles from her frame on the mantel. Everything is exactly as it was just a few moments ago, and yet, everything has changed.

You have twenty-four hours.

Something moves by the fire. Her grandfather's letter slides off the corner of the chair and into the hearth. Maia bolts towards the flames and pulls the corner out as the paper is engulfed in racing lines of red embers. Throwing it to the ground, she stomps on it in a frenzy to save what she can.

She falls to her knees in disbelief. Just like that, his letter is gone. She holds up the remnant of the page. Just a few words remain: *choose life*. She holds it higher, watching the fireplace flames through the gaping holes of the charred letter.

She can imagine her entire life up in this cabin alone. And that's only if she is lucky enough to escape the tenacious claws of the Northern Tribe. Eventually, she'd bury Huck next to her grandfather. And then she'd bury all her hopes and dreams alongside them. Her life would disappear into a meaningless shuffle of empty days filling empty years that would pass by without her even realizing it. She would become just like her father. Drinking, smoking, wasting away until something besides old age took her life. She would fall, or run out of food, or become ill. Even just a small cut could become infected. And who would go out into the mountains for more medicine from the bark? There would be no one. She would settle into a life unlived until she slipped away into nothing. With no one to bury her, no one to remember her, no one to mourn her death.

Choose life.

This is it. Her father's offer is the solution she has been praying for. For months she's been racking her brain trying to find an answer and this is it. She's barely been keeping herself alive in this cabin alone ... that's all she'd have to do on the ship. That, and not get caught.

It's a dangerous decision but it may be your only decision.

Maia's eyes dart to the grandfather clock in the corner. Stopped. She looks to the dusty clock on the mantel.

Stopped. In her depression, she hasn't wound a single clock. Time didn't seem to matter anymore.

Maia races to her grandfather's bedside table and rummages through the drawers. Did he have his watch on when he died? He loved that antique watch; it was wound by the movements of his wrist. If that has stopped as well, she'll have no way of knowing the time. Where is it? There is nothing in the drawer. She anxiously looks around, scanning the contents of their home until she stops on the window ledge by the sink. He always took off his watch when washing dishes. She runs to the kitchen and spots the silver band lying across the ledge. Snagging it from the windowsill, relief showers over her as the second hand still ticks away.

1:35 a.m.

You have twenty-four hours.

She grabs her pack, mud-flecked from her previous trek, and tosses it onto her bed. Then she picks up the checklists and preparation books stacked in heaps next to the fire—ready to burn—and spreads them out across the kitchen table. They had piles of books from their library to study. She thought they had *years*. They were building the whole endeavor from the ground up. And now she has slightly more than twenty-four hours with her only belongings being those she can carry on her back. She scans the lists and works tirelessly through the night, packing only the most basic essentials.

Maia finishes just before dawn. She sinks into her grandfather's chair with her last cup of tea in the home where she has spent her entire life. Her hands brush the cracked leather of the armrests, the same armrests she has sat on countless times with her grandfather as they talked about life into the wee hours of the morning. She rises from the chair, tracing the cabin's four faded walls, filled with photos of faces she'll never see again, vases she'll never fill again, candles she'll never light again. She stops in front of her mother's painting, delicately outlining the tiger's face with the tip of her finger, memorizing it for the last time.

With her steaming cup of tea in hand, she stands in the middle of the cabin and closes her eyes. Willing the bravery to come to her, she whispers prayers to her mother to help her stay strong, to her grandfather to help her stay safe. The burned remnants of his letter now rest folded in her pocket, next to the small pouch of his ashes.

Maia has kept the front door open all morning, waiting for her precious pup to return. She let him out soon after she started packing, and despite her repeated breaks standing on the porch whistling for him to come home, he is still missing.

It is now midmorning. It will take all day to get to town and she'll need to arrive before dark. Her stuffed pack is sitting on the steps of the front porch next to a letter for Collin and Sarah, which she'll drop, along with the keys to her home, against their door on her way. The only thing she asks for in return is that they take care of Huck. He has spent his entire life at this cabin and will be sure to return.

Taking Huck with her is not an option, a factor that has made her question this entire endeavor repeatedly throughout the evening. But he is an old dog and has also really taken to Collin, Sarah, and Henry. This alone has given Maia the strength to carry on. She knows they will all be very happy in the life she could never belong to.

Maia stands at the edge of the porch, desperately scanning the surrounding forest for any sign of Huck. "Oh please, buddy, I have to go. Please come back," she whispers.

Placing her fingers in her mouth, she blows the loudest whistle she can muster and screams out his name.

Nothing.

Wiping the tears from her eyes, she closes the front door to her home, dropping her head against it. Her insides screaming, she feels frozen in place. "Thank you, Grandpa, for this beautiful home and all the memories it's held," she whispers into the wood. "For everything you've done for me and for creating this sanctuary. For all the ways you tried to secure my future. And then, for forgiving me when I told you it could never be enough. I will forever be grateful to you and this life that you built. In the very worst of times, it gave me a life most could only dream of."

Maia takes a step back and lets her hands fall to her sides. After another moment of silence, she finds the strength to take her first step. She hauls her bloated pack onto her back and begins the long journey down the side of the mountain, knowing with every step she takes, she is one step closer to her destiny.

TWENTY-ONE

Clouds of breath swirl in the cool haze of darkness before her. In and out, in and out, appearing and disappearing in repeated puffs as she stares out in complete disbelief. The harbor lies like a blanket of glass, bar the occasional lap of water against the skirt of the massive ship. Thousands of stars puncture the black sky alongside an almost completely full moon, illuminating the sharp lines of the immense boat in hints of blue. The ship is docked at the edge of town in a somewhat obscure place. Had Maia not come before dusk, she would have missed it completely.

A dim sphere of light blooms through a small window of the murky ship. Maia buries her face in the ground and a billow of dirt wafts from her exaggerated breath. Her heart pounding, she lifts her head and peers through the branches of the wind-blown, crooked bush. The lantern slowly moves in and out of each window frame as it makes its way across the vast structure.

Eventually, the light reaches the outside deck facing the brush-dotted hill Maia now cowers on. The lantern is the first to cross the threshold, then a large, hunched figure holding the light follows behind it. He latches the door behind him.

The figure is a stocky old man with a dark coat and wide-brimmed hat. He moves over to the railing and holds the lantern high, illuminating his wretchedly weathered face. Maia flinches at the sight. His large knotted nose seems to pull at his rumpled skin, and his mouth is melted into a permanently dissatisfied grimace. He pulls a cigarette out of his pocket and lights up, exhaling a long stream of smoke while scanning the shore.

Maia lowers herself even farther behind the bush, her heart pounding as another wave of nausea swims about her empty stomach. She stays as close to the ground as she can. Closing her eyes, she takes repeated deep breaths.

She has spent hours in this spot, flipping from panic to elation in the prospect of her newfound future. More than once, she gazed along the shoreline and considered picking up her things and returning home. The only thing keeping her here is the thought that she can still turn back. She doesn't have to leave. She can still go home.

The man with the lantern moves down a plank leading onto the docks.

What was she thinking? She spied on those men earlier in the night when they came back from town. Dark, light, tall, short ... rough, dirty, *drunk*. Just looking at them made her feel overwhelmingly uncomfortable. If she gets caught, her father said her fate could be worse than death. How could she be so foolish? Boarding this ship is a death sentence.

With that, Maia decides to return home. Lifting her head from the dirt, she rises to her hands and knees. Crawling out from her hiding spot, twigs snap beneath her.

The old man stops. Lifting his lantern, he looks in her direction. He puts his fingers to his mouth and blows three loud whistles. Maia drops to the ground. He cocks his head to the side, then glances back at the ship. He looks back at her and puts his hand on his hip.

She lays her head on the ground. If she stays in this position, he'll leave. She doesn't have to go. She can stay here and head straight back home where it's safe and warm. She listens to her heart pound.

No. All that's left for her is a dark cabin and a vacant spot up north with a bunch of old men. This is all she's ever wanted. If she lets this go, she may never have another opportunity again.

The man blows another three whistles.

Just get up, Maia. Get up!

She lifts her head off the ground. Her legs trembling, she stands to her feet and collects her pack. She takes a deep breath, then hastily makes her way down to the boat.

The man is even bigger as she approaches. He crosses his arms in irritation and lets out an exaggerated sigh. A sour stench fills Maia's nostrils, both of body odor and booze. Her stomach churns again.

"Maia?"

"Yes," her voice cracks.

"Davies," he grunts, looking her up and down with equal tones of annoyance and disgust. "Listen..." He hesitates in his displeasure and then lowers his face down to hers. "These are the rules. You do not *exist.*" Spit flies from his mouth. "You will spend all your days in the room I place you in. You do not move. You do not leave. You do not speak. *Ever.* Food will be given to you twice a day. It won't be much, but it'll be something. You are not to use the toilet until after the evening meal is left for you. That's when the men's work is done until dusk, so no one should be going down there."

"I understand."

"No one should find you as long as you follow these rules."

"Okay."

"If you break them and get caught, I will look away and I will not feel bad. I will not claim responsibility. Some of these men are animals. I'd rather shoot you dead and put you out of your misery before letting them find you. Do you understand?"

She swallows the bile rising up her throat.

"Speak when you're spoken to, woman! Do you understand?"

"Yes ... yes, I understand ... sir."

"*Sir*," he grunts. "Far from it." He lets out a long sigh and shakes his head once more. "Okay then, let's do this. But that thing can't come with you."

Thing? She follows his gaze behind her to find Huck with a stick in his mouth, eagerly wagging his tail.

"Oh my God, *Huck*!" She kneels down and he drops his stick, licking her face between whimpers. "Where have you been?" she whispers. She grabs his thick black fur between her fingers. Kissing his face, tears sting her eyes.

"Get on with it, girl!" Davies hisses.

"Huck." She wraps her arms around her dog and he rests his head on her back. "I have to go now."

He whimpers again.

"I am so sorry. I don't know how I'm going to do this without you. You're my best friend," she sobs as he licks her cheek. "There will never be a day that I won't miss you."

Maia stands tall. Closing her eyes, her tears fall to the cold earth. Taking a deep breath, she reaches for his stick.

He backs up with his tail wagging. She whips the stick as far as she can and he races into the blackness. She stands for a moment, gazing into the dark as her heart fractures beneath her chest.

She turns towards the man.

"There's no crying," he says dryly.

"I'm not—" Maia wipes her face. "I'm not crying."

She picks her bag off the ground and follows him to the ship. The water gently laps against the creaking old structure with rust running like tears from its circular windows. The air sits cool and stagnant, allowing a misty fog to gather in bloated patches along the sea. She follows the old man up a wide plank onto the deck. Shaking, nauseated, and light-headed, she fights back tears and wills her heart to calm.

Out of the corner of her eye, a dark figure races across the land towards the docks. Huck runs as fast as he can as Davies pulls the plank up and off the ground, sliding the long wooden board across the ship's deck. Huck drops his stick and stands on the dock, anxiously whimpering as he surveys the gap between him and the ship where Maia now stands.

Oh God, Huck. I am so sorry.

His tail drops between his legs and he paces back and forth, barking loudly.

"You shut that thing up or I'll do it for you!" Davies spits in her direction.

Huck barks again. A look of panic flashes across Davies's face and he reaches into his pocket. The moonlight glints off his pistol.

"NO!" Maia lurches for his arm.

"Hands off me, woman!" He shoves her onto the ground

and points his pistol at her. "You watch yourself or you'll join that thing at the bottom of the sea."

Huck continues to bark. Davies pivots towards him.

Maia throws herself between them. "*Please!* Please, I'll tell him." Without hesitating, she turns towards Huck. "Huck!" she calls as quietly as she can. She holds her hand up toward the dog. Tears stream down her face as she puts her trembling finger to her mouth. "*Shh.*"

Huck stops barking. He softly whimpers, then lowers himself down along the edge of the dock.

Both Maia's hands drop to her sides. "Good boy," she whispers.

Huck lays his head on his outstretched legs and gazes up at her. Maia knows this is where he'll stay, waiting for her to return. She turns away and faces Davies.

He looks annoyed. "Don't make me regret this."

Maia says nothing. He leads her across the deck and unlatches a heavy, wooden door. Exhausted and numb, she forces herself not to steal one last glance at Huck looking up at her from the docks.

Maia and Davies tread down the uneven stairs to a small room in the back corner of the basement. It appears to be a storage closet, filled to the ceiling with rows of wooden crates.

"There's no food in here, so don't bother searching." A look of pity crosses Davies's face. "You'll have less visitors that way. You can't be found, Maia. I made a deal with your father and I am a man of my word."

He leads her into the farthest corner of the room, between the last two rows of crates. There, a few wooden boards have been placed across the lowest crates against the wall. A blanket hangs over the opening like a curtain, forming a small hidden nook underneath. He walks over to it and pulls the curtain back, revealing two folded blankets next to a small bowl of water. Just like a dog.

"I'm not sure how long this trip will take, it's different every time," Davies mumbles as he shakes his head. "At least a month. I hope you're hardier than you look." He walks towards the door and then hesitates without turning around. "There's a bucket there if you need to be sick. It can get rough out there. And use the toilet before dawn." He closes the door, enveloping her in darkness.

The boat rocks from side to side. Maia listens for any barking outside, praying her beloved pup remains quiet. Then she crouches down and shoves her pack inside her nook.

The basement air feels dank, the smell of mold burning her nose. A chill bites at her bones. She pulls out her grandfather's ashes and holds them in her hands, then crawls into her new home and curls into a ball in the corner. Gripping her little sack of ashes, she stares into the suffocating black around her.

Back on land, blanketed in darkness under a tall pōhutukawa tree, a man with a crooked beard stands watching. And, sitting high up in the branches, a little black fantail.

TWENTY-TWO

Maia's body rolls from side to side, waking her to a chorus of muffled yelling and heavy footsteps pounding the floor above. She slowly peels back the blanket, squinting against the sunlight flooding through a small window located near the ceiling of the room. Exhausted, she pulls herself upright and rubs her eyes. Water splashes against the glass of the window and her body rocks forward. Moving. *They are moving.*

Her heart sinks. She quickly jumps to her feet and peers behind the half-dozen rows of crates that stand between her and the door. It's latched shut. Keeping her eye on the door, she crouches down and runs across to the window, immediately breaking Davies's number one rule.

She climbs up the shelving to peer out of the glass. New Zealand sits tranquilly in the distance, a hazy crown of clouds resting above it. She reaches her hand to the glass as tears fill her eyes.

She searches for her grandfather's ashes back inside her pocket.

No matter where you go, I am always with you.

This is it—no turning back now. She stays on the crates and grips the slivered wood as New Zealand slowly slips from the horizon.

Shaking, she lowers herself down and surveys her surroundings. Wooden crates fill the small room to the ceiling where large spider webs have claimed their territory. Her spot in the corner is surrounded by crates, mostly hidden by anyone who may enter the room. A cockroach scurries across a few rat droppings along the wall. *Rats.* If there is anything she hates more than cockroaches, it would be *rats.*

A small plate with a cooked potato and some vegetables has been placed just around the corner from her hiding spot. She grabs it and crawls back to her blankets, slowly forcing down the food. She hasn't eaten since her father showed up a few nights ago, her adrenaline and fear chasing away any hope of an appetite. She slurps down the large bowl of water and curls back into a ball, pulling the blankets over her head as she shivers—more from shock than from cold.

The next few days come and go in a dismal blur. In her deep state of exhaustion, Maia spends more time passed out than awake, often crying herself to sleep after being sick in her bucket from the rolling sea. Everything rocks, everything creaks, and footsteps constantly pound the ceiling above her. At times she can hear the men's muffled voices, sometimes laughing, oftentimes yelling. If they get too close to her door, she pulls her blanket high above her head and trembles until they pass.

In the middle of the night, she lies wide awake as the ship's rats scurry around her, repeatedly praying they don't come too close. She passes out for what seems like brief stints, waking up time and again to tears streaming from her eyes.

In the darkness, she cannot escape the images of everything she's loved—everything she's lost. Her visions play out across the black screen before her. She walks around their cabin deep in the quiet woods, turning to see her grandfather's smiling face and outstretched arms. And then, like a nightmare, his pyre engulfed in flames flashes before her.

She and Huck run through the woods. She tilts her head back laughing as he kisses her face. Then his tail drops between his legs as he whimpers at the shore with Davies's gun pointed at him.

And then there's her mother. Maia searches her dreams to see her again, for some sort of confirmation that she is doing the right thing and she didn't just give up everything for an illusion. But her mother doesn't come.

There is only blackness and teardrops.

TWENTY-THREE

L ying on her back, Maia stares idly out of the small window at a thick covering of clouds stretched across the sky. She breathes deeply, gently rocking with the ship.

After nearly a week of sleeping with the ghosts of her past, she has grown tired of waking to a black room, desperately holding on to a life she no longer owns. She had allowed herself to slip into a muddy amalgam of depression and exhaustion, but can now no longer tolerate her own weariness.

A few sporadic footsteps pound the floors above her and a muffled voice vibrates through the ceiling, but overall, the ship is quiet—a stark contrast to the previous days. Today must be Sunday. Davies had mentioned Sundays were mostly a day of rest for the men.

"I'm not sure how long this trip will take ... at least a month."

Maia reaches into her pocket and pulls out her knife, then twists to the nearest crate to carve a large *S* over a tally of six markings.

Grandpa said the most important thing you can do at

sea is have a purpose. She pulls back her curtain and glances around. A dead cockroach lies on its back with its legs in the air next to her empty bowl. *Damn.* She has quickly learned that mornings are a race between who can get to the food first—Maia or the rats. After waking more than once to creatures devouring her limited food for the day, Maia has started getting up before dawn.

Now, when Davies comes in, he slides a small bowl of food across the floor and waits as she slides the last empty one back. Neither one says a word, and he leaves as quickly as he comes. Her bowl usually has some sort of dried meat and preserved fruit or vegetable, sometimes a crumbling biscuit or boiled, soggy potato. Except today. Today she has nothing. She stares at the empty bowl as her stomach growls.

The floorboards creak just outside her door. She drops her face to the ground and rips her curtain closed.

"Lucas! Grab some netting while you're in there!"

She peeks out from under the blanket, watching as a shadow appears in the space beneath the door.

"Yes, okay," he yells back.

Lucas. She has heard the men calling down to him before. He must be the sailor in charge of stock in the basement. She often hears him moving around, whistling and sometimes mumbling to himself. His voice is deep, his words foreign. When he speaks English, he uses an accent she has never heard before.

The door swings open. He is wearing brown leather sandals today. He stands for a while at the entrance of the room, then walks around the corner from her and pulls a few crates down, setting them on the floor while rummaging through another. After a while, he re-stacks the crates, grunting from the weight.

Then he stops.

He walks over to Maia's empty bowl and picks it up, mumbling something in a foreign tongue. She holds her breath. After a moment, he sets the bowl back down and exits the room, slamming the door behind him.

Exhaling, Maia remains frozen. He couldn't see her nook from where he was standing. She knows this—she's tested it out. But the bowl? Her mind races. Does she pick it up? Or leave it now that it has been seen? "*Worse than death.*" That's what awaits her if she's found. Petrified, she keeps her head to the cold ground, focusing on the space beneath the door. She stays like this all day until the light from her window fades into evening.

Maia floats in the space between sleeping and awake when the floorboards creak outside her room. Her heart skips a beat and she grips her knife beneath the blanket. The door swings open, flooding her room with light. She recognizes Davies's feet right away. A new bowl slides across the floor and she crawls out from beneath her blanket to slide the old one back. He picks it up and quietly closes the door behind him.

She breathes a sigh of relief.

Blindly searching the dusty floor for her scraps, she grabs hold of her bowl, then crawls on her knees back under her nook. Her fingers softly prod around the contents of the dish, meeting a cold boiled potato and what feels like green beans. No meat this time. She sits hunched in the pitch black, shoveling the food into her mouth like an animal. The ship groans around her. She licks the bowl clean.

TWENTY-FOUR

Twenty-one more notches have been carved into the wooden crate next to Maia's head. She has now memorized the ship's routines, sounds, and creaks, giving her a sense of familiarity deep within the dismal basement.

Assuming the days of the week, she has started her own routine to pass the time. Every morning while she waits for Davies, she starts her day with prayers of gratitude to keep her spirits high. She finds the smallest thing—anything—to count her blessings. A bowl of water. This ratty blanket. The small window high on the wall, letting in sunlight to warm her weary soul.

This alone has helped her crawl out of the hell in which she has found herself, seeing her new undertaking hiding in the murky bowels of a ship as her destiny towards a new and better life versus a risky and possibly fatal decision to escape a lonely existence in New Zealand. She holds on tightly to her father's words and repeats them like a prayer:

"*Davies says it does exist, Maia, that something is up there.*"

Closing her eyes, she relives the life she left behind. She

talks to her grandfather next to the fire and places her head on his chest. He calls her *darling* and she can nearly hear his voice echo in the cobwebs. She smiles alone in her nook.

After breakfast, Maia performs a short round of stationary exercises to avoid losing too much muscle yet conserve as much energy as she can. She still sleeps as much as possible throughout the day—mostly out of boredom.

After dinner, she drags herself out from under the curtain to stretch her cramped and knotted muscles, allowing her blood to flow freely once again. It also proves to be a valuable warning to the ship's nocturnal creatures that she is not just another lifeless fixture in the room.

A few storms have passed through, whipping the ship across the ocean's angry waves. Maia holds tight to the tied and netted crates, jumping up and kicking her feet as rats race back and forth with the rocking of the ship. She wraps her arms around the wood and hums childhood songs through the night until the storms pass. Then she wearily pulls down her things and places them back inside her nook, fixing any fallen crates close by to avoid too many visitors the next day.

Maia stares anxiously out her window, biting her nail down to a stub. The sunlight unravels extended shadows across the room, painfully reminding her of time. She checks her grandfather's watch for the hundredth time: three p.m.—far from dusk when she can run to the toilet. She slept past her opening this morning and is now excruciatingly full—and bordering on the brink of insanity. Normally, she could relieve herself in her bucket but that was confiscated during the cleanup from the last storm.

She crawls on her hands and knees down her aisle of crates and peers around the corner towards the closed door. The ship is mostly silent, which is normal for a Sunday. The men have been drinking since morning. They've already had lunch and must be deep into their afternoon naps by now. She listens for a few more minutes to the placid, creaking boat. She has no choice but to risk it.

She slowly unlatches the handle of her door, cringing as the metal lock noisily clicks open. This is her first time seeing the basement in daylight—it's much bigger than she thought. The large open space is filled with more boxes and crates. A few storage rooms sit tucked in the corners. Many of their doors are latched open, making her journey to the toilet even more risky, but a puddle of urine will most certainly lead to discovery.

She curses herself for her neglect.

After listening for any noises, she pulls the door all the way open and slides out, letting it softly latch behind her. And then she *runs*.

When she finishes, she cracks open the bathroom door and peers out from its slivered opening. A breeze flows down the back steps, leading up to what appears to be a small deck. The stairs are drowned in a deluge of sunlight. She opens the door a bit more, closing her eyes as she inhales the salty ocean air.

She *pines* for those sundrenched stairs. Only a few steps separate her from the sun's heat. She glances at the door to her room, then back to the stairs. She hasn't felt the sun in nearly a month, and that ocean ... what she wouldn't give for just a moment out there. Her bones ache for it. She looks up at the ceiling and listens for movement. Surely no one would be doing chores at a time like this. She glances back to the stairs.

Just a peek—just for a moment.

Her foot slides out from behind the door, drawn to the bright and inviting staircase. She slowly tiptoes across the floor to the stairwell, lured by the flood of sunlight radiating down. As she reaches out her hand, her fingertips are bathed in the glow. She takes another deep breath and smiles.

How I've missed you.

Maia creeps up the stairs, glancing back with every step. She knows it's risky—deadly even—but after spending week after week alone in a damp, dark room filled with roaches and rats, her desperation for the airy, sun-drenched deck surpasses any logic that may stop her.

At the top of the staircase, she grips the railings with both hands, overwhelmed with gratitude. The ocean looks just like her dreams—endless, calm. A few downy puffs of cloud float serenely in the middle of the infinite sky. She looks around the back of the boat; she must be in the loading area. She inches towards the end of the deck and holds the warm metal railing.

Not so long ago, she was lying on her living room floor covered in ash. Alone. Hopeless. She would spend the rest of her life up there. She had locked the library, given up on her dreams. And now? Now she stands on the back of a boat in the middle of the Pacific Ocean, on her way to The Old Arctic Circle ... on her way to *something*. Either way, she made a choice for her life, and she won't stop until she finds it.

She grips her grandfather's ashes in her pocket. "Grandpa," she whispers as a smile spreads across her face. "I'm really doing it." She pulls out the sack and pours a pile into her hand. A few ashes float away in the breeze. She casts the rest into the sky. "So that you may taste freedom."

Feeling a deep sense of relief, Maia steals one last moment to breathe in her new life. She no longer has to end each day staring at the horizon in wonder, no longer awaken every morning to a life she does not belong to. She smiles.

Instead of staring at the horizon, *she is part of it.*

She backs up and tiptoes softly, slowly, down each step. A large crash sounds from inside one of the open rooms. Lucas's voice yells out a chorus of foreign words.

Maia stops and looks around, quietly rushing back up the stairs. A loud creak sounds from her weight and she nearly loses her footing in panic. The breeze sweeps her hair across her face. She frantically wipes it away. *Where to hide?* A large stack of netted crates sits tucked in the corner. She squeezes between it and the back of the ship and crouches down.

After a moment, Lucas walks up the steps onto the platform. Maia slides farther behind and watches him from between the wooden slats. In the unhindered light of day, she can see him clearly for the first time. He stands at the railing, gazing out across the water. The wind tousles his dark curly hair, falling in short ringlets framing his face.

Besides Davies bringing rations of food, Lucas has been Maia's only visitor over the last month. It must be his duty to monitor the stored stocks and replenish supplies for the sailors above. He generally visits on a daily basis, each time causing terror to flood her veins. Unmoving, her sharp bones often dig into the ground sending a throbbing pain through her joints. The sound of her breath is amplified in her meager nook, so she holds it in and lets it out in controlled and restricted bouts. Even the most short-lived visit from Lucas leaves Maia exhausted for hours.

He shifts towards her and she drops to the floor, scrunching her eyes closed like a child. She sits frozen for a few moments, holding her breath as she strains to listen to his movement. It is silent. She keeps her head towards the ground and peers out.

Lucas is still standing at the railing with his back towards her, gazing across the horizon. He is tall, his shoulders broad. He is younger than she thought, possibly in his thirties. A few deep lines curve out from the skin around his eyes. His chiseled jawline is speckled with a dark shadow of facial hair. A green, yellow, and blue braided bracelet is tied around his tanned wrist.

He turns towards her and she flinches back. His elongated shadow slides from the ground up the wall as he moves closer to the crates. His feet shuffle around the side and then he stops. She holds her breath. A few steps closer and he will find her, cowering in a ball on the ground.

After a while, his shadow slips from the wall and the basement stairs creak under his weight. Maia lets out her breath. She does not move again until nightfall.

Hours later, Maia slides back up the wall. Gripping the dewed netting, she grimaces from her aching back. Her knees throb as new blood courses through her joints. The ship has been silent for hours. She glances around the corner down the dark steps, a gaping mouth into the basement.

She feels her way down the stairs, horrified when she reaches the creaking step once again. Fourth step down, fifth step up. Not that she'll ever come out here again. She tiptoes blindly across the basement with her hands in front of her, slowly sliding and tapping each foot before her like a cane. She has memorized the steps required to get to the toilet, but this is new territory.

When she reaches the outside wall of her room, relief showers over her. She latches the door behind her as slowly as possible and then crawls back to her nook under the blanket. Her heart pounding, she keeps her head to the ground and strains her eyes against the blackness. Her dinner bowl sits empty once more, or is it still her old bowl?

Lucas. Could he see her? It seems he was searching for something out there. She feels for her crate in the darkness and carves another tally into the wood, fervently praying that it won't be her last.

TWENTY-FIVE

Maia spends the next few days on high alert. Every thud reverberating across the floorboards sends a shiver up her spine. Every visit from Davies bringing her food and water, every creak outside her door, every bang or commotion in the slightest sends her body to the ground as she focuses her gaze on the space beneath the door.

Lucas continues to come and go from the storage room and each time she shakes violently under her nook, gripping her knife with both hands. She stares at the curtain, waiting for it to open at any time. She'll swing her knife at him. She'll lunge. If they drag her out, she'll fight to the death.

I'd rather shoot you dead and put you out of your misery before letting them find you.

She won't let them take her. She didn't come all this way … no, she won't allow it. Once again, she prepares herself for the fight of her life, the same way she prepared for the elders of the Northern Tribe. Not that there is anything she can do besides hide alone in this nook.

She curses inwardly for taking such a huge risk and exposing herself in the light of day. How could she be so foolish? She was desperate for it, the sun. She craved it. The fresh air and open skies were intoxicating, numbing any sense of logic. Now that a constant sense of terror has consumed her every waking minute, she cannot fathom how she could have been so careless.

———

After three uneventful days, Maia's deep tension slowly begins to unravel. She uncurls her stiff fingers from around her knife and slides it back into its case. When Lucas comes in once again, she leaves it by her side, too tired to panic. She lays her head on the ground and watches his feet.

He stands nearer the door, three rows of crates away from her, and pulls a few boxes down, shuffling through them. After nearly six weeks of hiding, he has never once entered the last row of crates where her nook sits tucked in the back corner. She often wonders why. Maybe he knows about her, has an agreement with Davies to protect her. Or maybe her area is off-limits. This seems more likely. At least this is what she tells herself to stop from hyperventilating when it seems her capture is imminent.

Maia has memorized this Lucas's voice, the shuffle of his feet, his tattered sandals. Some days he whistles and other days, depending on the severity of the muffled voices above, he curses in a foreign tongue. Or at least this is what she imagines he does as she listens to his dark, hushed tone.

Today, as usual, Lucas's feet stay turned away from the row of crates where Maia hides. He picks up a box and grunts as he places it on a shelf. He sighs. Maia reaches for her knife as he shuffles closer. He pauses for a second, then works his way down the next aisle, and then around towards the last. He stands just around the corner, rummaging through a box in an impatient manner. His feet continue to face away from her. Despite herself, Maia keeps her head to the ground and very carefully lifts the bottom corner of her curtain.

His dark brown hair falls over his face as he rummages through a box. His hand dives deep within the crate and he looks up. She flinches, dropping her curtain.

For the first time in her life, Maia feels something she's never felt before: *drawn to him*. Curious. She lifts the corner of the curtain. He closes up the crate and places it back on top of the stack. The deep grooves of his muscles are tense on his arms, his cut yet slender body visible through his oversized sleeveless shirt.

He sighs again and surveys the room. She slowly drops the curtain. A smile slides across her face, surprising her. *Lucas.* She watches his feet as he turns and walks towards the door, latching it quietly behind him as he exits the room.

Footsteps suddenly pound down the basement stairs, startling Maia out of a deep, mindless slumber. It's late. She has already been out of her nook to use the toilet and stretch. She fumbles in the dark to close her curtain but the latch of her door has already clicked open. Bright light streams across the floor and she falls flat to her back, uncovered and holding her breath. A pair of soiled, neglected boots enter the room.

"Fucking rats!" The stranger scuffles and kicks, missing the large brown critter as it frantically scurries beneath the crates, heading straight towards Maia's face. She recoils, but the creature is unfazed and dives into her bundle of hair on the ground. Her hands snap up to her mouth as she forces herself not to move.

The man stands at the open door. The rat burrows itself deeper into Maia's hair and she heaves back a retch. Chills run up her spine. The man scuffles forward.

"Okay, where are you?" he slurs. His belt buckle clanks as he fiddles with it.

Maia's heart pounding, she keeps her eyes fixated on his feet as her hand searches the ground for her knife. He shuffles forward again, his large boots just around the corner from her aisle. One step forward and she will be found. She reaches for her curtain.

He grabs a crate and leans forward, the top of his balding, scabbed head peeking into the aisle leading to her nook. He coughs and hacks a mound of yellow mucus onto the ground. He slides forward, his belt buckle hanging below a hard, extended belly. A sour smell wafts from his body and he hacks once again to the floor.

Maia's trembling hand pulls at the blanket stuck on the slivered crate above. It won't budge. A tear rolls down her cheek.

More steps pound down the stairs and a familiar set of boots appear at the door.

His voice booms through the silence. "What the *hell* ... what are you doing?"

"Davies, you scared the shit out of me. What does it look like I'm doing?" the old man slurs. "I'm looking for the pisser."

Davies laughs nervously. "Well, you're not going to find it in here, you old drunk. Come on, you're in the storage closet." His feet slide towards the old man's.

"For fuck's sake, *whereindahell* did it go?"

Davies quickly shuffles the man out, slamming the door behind them.

Maia lurches forward. Chills race up and down her body as she squirms out from under her nook in a panic. She shakes her head and the rat races underneath the crates lining the back wall. "*Get!* Get out of here!" she whispers, stabbing her knife under the crates.

The rat scurries towards the door and squeezes underneath, leaving Maia on all fours, gasping for air.

TWENTY-SIX

"**D**arling, hurry!"

Her mother reaches out; the ominous city looming behind her is now bigger, closer, encroaching. The buildings tower into the sky and the sun glints off their vast network of metal and glass. The wind has picked up, angrily heaving surges of waves against the shore. Maia shields her face as they break at her feet, blasting a white spray into the air.

Tears glisten on Maia's cheeks as she stands alone with clenched fists, a fiery temper burning within. She inhales to scream but is silenced as a single crack travels through the ground between her feet. A menacing roar thunders through the air as the crack splits in a hundred different directions. Before she can brace herself, the earth drops out from beneath her and she plummets into the water below.

Her body once again sinks as if being pulled from the deep. She strains her hands through the sun-pierced water, reaching for her mother who stands above, shaking her head in disgust. Maia flails about, sinking as the darkness swallows her whole.

A flashing beacon from the top of a skyscraper appears, shooting waves of red light into the deep gloom. Another building appears. And another. Maia sinks lower, the brightly lit windows flowing past in greater succession until she lands softly in the middle of a busy city street.

Shielding her eyes from the bright sun, a few air bubbles escape Maia's mouth. They float up into the sky, then disappear with the surrounding water as if being sucked by a vacuum. Her hair slaps wet across her back as the weight of gravity pushes against her feet. She stumbles back, coughing and gasping for air.

Hundreds of people heading in different directions go about their days, taking no notice of her. Cars zoom past on the streets. Motors hum, cars honk, doors close, heels click … the noise coming from every direction hits her like a shockwave. She flips and twists and turns, watching as more people than she has ever seen in her entire life pass by in opposite directions.

Everyone seems to be holding conversations, laughing, talking, agreeing … with no one. They pass by, one after the other, with distant eyes, looking into something Maia cannot see. She reaches out to a young man walking by, horrified as he passes right through her.

A woman's shrill voice yells from behind. Maia turns to find her leaning against the glass of a storefront, tears glossing over her bloodshot eyes as she screams at no one. Maia reaches up to touch her but her fingers slide through as if made of air. The woman's eyes dart back and forth as if she were reading. Maia follows the woman's gaze, searching the surroundings behind her. She turns back to the woman, bewildered. The woman's fingers—they flicker into the air at her side.

"Yes, I'm looking!" she screams and Maia jumps back.

"I'm looking right now. They haven't raised the prices online. You go back in there and demand a reboot of their sales staff. They clearly haven't been updated. Stop *yelling* at me!" She pushes off the wall and heads in another direction.

Laughing. Glasses clinking.

Maia follows the noise into a building's open front doors. A flickering sign, *BAR*, looms above. She finds a large room filled with people standing at tall, circular tables with dividers extending up above their heads. Four to a table, each person divided from the next. Every person is drinking, a few eating as well. One man is taking a shot, lifting his glass to the blank partition. Laughing. Talking. Nodding his head. *With no one.*

"Aw, thank you, ladies. *Cheers!*"

Maia looks to the table closest to her. A tall, slender woman is holding up her drink and for a brief moment, Maia can see other women reflected back on her dividers, seemingly in other places like this one, holding up their drinks. Their arms all have icons lit up on their skin. The bottom of the partition reads, "*CONNECTED.*" A small rectangle is flashing in the corner with the word, "*CHARGING.*" Astonished, Maia moves closer to the screen but the women disappear. The woman standing next to her starts laughing.

Maia slowly wanders the room. The establishment opens to a handful of other rooms brimming with tables filled with people, all talking into the air. Not one person is speaking to another. Not one person is looking at another. Stairs lead the way to a second floor. The noise is deafening.

A large bar extending the length of the back wall is lined with patrons on tall stools. No dividers. Their eyes unblinking, they stare into blank space like robots. Their fingertips hover just above the wooden bar, scrolling, scrolling, scrolling. Their arms lit up like fireworks.

CONNECTED.

CHARGING.

A small child with fiery red hair shoves past, her giggle trailing behind her like dust in her wake. Maia looks after her in shock, clearly having felt the child's hands push into her side. The child's giggle travels over the noise, reaching Maia in soft waves as she weaves through the crowd. Maia strains to see past the bodies, just missing the girl's face as she stops at the doorway.

With the crowd closing in, Maia barrels her way through, slicing through the oblivious patrons like a ghost. The child runs out onto the street. Maia steals one last glance at the woman with her partition of friends, now looking intently at the empty space in front of her, nodding her head.

As Maia steps out onto the sidewalk, silence falls over the city like rain. The people, the cars, the honking ... everything disappears, leaving behind an empty, dripping, murky city. Maia glances back towards the bar, now dark and deserted. A long ribbon of seaweed hangs off the chair where the woman was just nodding her head. Water drips from its green tendril into a puddle on the floor.

Maia's mother calls out to her. Her voice reverberates against the drenched city buildings. Maia slowly wanders the empty streets. She steps over a flopping fish, its gills opening and closing as it slowly suffocates against the wet cement.

Her mother calls again. Maia turns to see her standing down an abandoned alley, smiling and motioning for her to come.

"Mum." Maia grins like a child, relieved, and runs down the alleyway towards her.

Her mother smiles tenderly, then slowly disappears as Maia approaches. Maia stops but her footsteps still echo down the narrow alley.

The small child peers out from behind the brick. She giggles, then runs across to another alley. Irresistibly drawn to her, Maia follows the sound of the child's laughter through a complicated maze of soiled brick corridors, always just missing the child's face.

Rounding another corner, Maia stops in her tracks. Situated at the end of the narrow lane is her old wooden cabin, nestled in the heart of the city. Maia gazes tenderly at her home. The little girl now stands on the front porch, reaching for the front door.

Maia's mother's face flashes before her. The child wanders inside, leaving the door open. Maia reaches out her hand as she shuffles towards the cabin, drawn like a magnet. Her mother's face flashes before her like lightning.

Maia ambles up the front steps. The old wood groans as it always has, but she pays it no mind. She keeps her eyes fixated on the open front door. The child's giggle echoes from within.

Crossing the threshold, Maia finds the young girl facing the fireplace, standing next to a man. With his back towards Maia, the man crouches next to the child and tenderly sweeps a red curl from her face. Something about him is so familiar. Maia strains her eyes but her vision blurs. He turns his head to the side as Maia's world dims into blackness.

TWENTY-SEVEN

Maia awakens to an unfamiliar noise. Grimacing, she rolls over and peers under the crates. Nothing but a network of thick cobwebs and a few dead roaches on their backs, their legs pointed towards the sky. She rubs her temples, the visions from her dream filling her head like a foreboding fog.

It smells different in here. Something is different. She peeks out from behind the curtain. A small plate of food sits around the corner. Davies never brings food in the middle of the day. Confused by how long she was sleeping, Maia looks up at the window. A hazy soup of gray clouds covers the sun. She touches the notches on the crate. Maybe Davies was feeling generous?

Maia peers out again. This plate has a few candies on it. She hasn't had anything sweet besides a few half-rotten apples. She checks again under the crates, scanning every inch of the dusty floor before cautiously sliding open her curtain. Half-asleep and curious, she crawls towards the food, her mouth salivating. She slides the plate back into her nook and pulls the drapes closed.

"I had a feeling you'd do that."

A loud *thud* shakes the floor as two feet slam to the ground. Maia's curtain is ripped open. She sits wide-eyed and shaking as they stare at each other face to face, neither one saying a word.

Lucas's face is angry, his clenched fist ready to swing, but as he takes in the sight of her, his demeanor fades to confusion. "You are the one I saw the other day..."

He surveys the state of her in her cramped nook. His skin is rough. Lines trace out from his brown eyes and his sculpted jawline is sharp under a shortly trimmed beard. His gaping mouth clenches shut and he lowers his fist. "Who *are* you?" he asks. The accentuation of his *r* is drawn and sharp.

Maia cannot speak a word, shaking and gripping the plate. Her candies one by one bounce to the ground.

"Please, please." He grabs the dish. "Stop with the shaking. I am not going to hurt you." He picks up the candies one at a time and drops them back onto the dish. He nervously eyes the door.

Maia can't stop staring at him. She hasn't looked at another human this close in what feels like a lifetime. He's *beautiful*.

Lucas turns towards her. "Listen," he bites in a hushed tone. "You *must* be more careful. You are not supposed to be down here. Do you not know how dangerous some of these men are? It will be very bad if you are caught."

"I know."

He flinches, eyeing her like an illusion. After a moment, he regains his composure. "So, it was Davies, yes? He smuggled you on board?"

"No."

"Right. *No*—I want nothing to do with this. This is

dangerous, especially for a woman. Do you have a death wish?" He thrusts the plate back at her. "*You* are the reason he put me down here. It all makes sense now. I had the perfect job diving for food until Davies threw me down here. Now I know why. It is because with one ear I cannot hear. No. I will not cover for you. I knew someone was in here, but a *woman*? No."

"Please, please don't say anything." Maia starts shaking again. "I won't leave this area again. I'm sorry."

Lucas lifts himself to his feet. He stands tall, his jaw clenched. "*Why* are you here?"

"I..." She hesitates, afraid to tell him the truth. She looks up at him, her demeanor like stone. "Why do you care?"

"I don't." He closes the curtain on her and rushes from the room. The door slams loudly behind him.

The rest of the day, Maia lies motionless on the floor —*terrified*. Every noise causes her heart to pound. Questions circle her head like winged demons. Are they coming for her? What will happen to her now? A loud bang sounds from above and she grimaces. Night falls and Davies does not bring her dinner. She keeps her head to the ground, staring at the space beneath the door, awaiting a dark fate that is sure to come.

TWENTY-EIGHT

The storage room door slowly creaks open. Maia shrinks into the corner of her nook, clutching her knife. Davies clears his throat and slides a small plate across the floor. Maia peeks out from under her curtain, seeing only his boots under the crates. She scans the floor, waiting for more feet to appear.

He clears his throat again. She rushes out, sliding her empty plate back, and he leaves immediately.

She sits on her knees, staring at the food in disbelief. *There is breakfast on this plate.* She looks up at the early morning sky through her small window. Still dark, a few sleepy stars are all that remain in the violet expanse.

Nothing happened.

She crawls back into her nook with her plate and shovels the food into her mouth. She carves another tally on the crate.

Forty-eight days.

The next week, life resumes its normal course. Once again, it takes a few days for Maia to stop jumping at every bump through the ship's old wooden floorboards, but after Davies leaves breakfast and dinner a few times over, her tension begins to ease. Lucas comes in a few times as well, and she watches his feet from the floor in her nook. She does not move or look out from behind her curtain and often hurried, he does not stay long.

Drifting in and out in a sleepless daze, Maia is startled when the door slowly creaks open. She drops her head to the floor and watches Lucas's sandals walk towards her nook. The light across the room indicates that it's most likely midday. He stops just around the corner. She listens for the sound of crates being opened but there is silence. A large folded blanket drops to the ground. Lucas exits the room just as quickly as he came in, letting the door slam loudly behind him.

Maia hesitates. She saw only one set of feet enter and one set leave ... Is this another trap? She sits frozen inside her nook for what feels like hours until the same habitual footsteps sound through the ceiling, marking the beginning of dinner. The banging cupboards, clanking dishes, and echoing voices crescendo until at last they dull into a murmur. The men are eating.

She peers out from behind her curtain. The blanket sits where Lucas left it, with an apple and a small piece of dried meat on top. She eyes it like an apparition. Straining her eyes through the quickly darkening room, she searches the tops of the crates for anyone ready to pounce. The room is empty. She knows this but is unsure of what to do.

Davies's feet pound down the stairs. She jumps out from behind her curtain and pulls the blanket into her nook just as the door swings open. An exchange of plates slide past each other and then she is alone again.

Kneeling in the dark, Maia gently runs her hands over the thick wool. *This ... is this an act of kindness? Or a trick?* She lifts the blanket onto her lap. *So thick.* Keeping it folded, she slides it under the thin, ragged blanket she has slept on for the last six weeks and crawls on top, instantly cushioning her aching bones.

A smile slides across her face and she sighs with relief. She stacks the apple and meat on top of Davies's small plate of food. She now has *two* pieces of dried meat, an apple, and a biscuit. Combined, it nearly looks like a normal dinner. She nibbles each delectable piece while enjoying her newly cushioned bed. For the first time in over a month, Maia's belly is full. She curls up on her new bedding and falls fast asleep.

A few more days of silence pass before Lucas returns. He sets a large box on the ground and shuffles through, fiddling with something metallic. A loud, crisp *snap* breaks through the quiet room, followed by more clatter. Maia keeps her cheek to the ground as he places a rattrap under the shelving of crates near the door. He opens another and sets it on the ground before placing a heap of what appears to be a batter on top. She salivates at the sight.

He is methodical in his arrangement, carefully placing a half-dozen traps throughout the room. *Why would he bother?* He slides another trap under the row of crates in front of her, his hand so close she could reach out and touch it.

Lucas seems to be taking his time and Maia cherishes the company. After so many days alone in her nook, she feels as if the brink of insanity is hovering at the edges, like an army about to ambush as soon as she drops her guard. She is losing track of time. Some mornings, she questions whether she has marked a tally and spends a great deal of her day debating whether she should carve another.

She continues her stationary exercises each morning, as well as saying her prayers, but even those are declining as she finds herself desperate to find things worthy of being grateful for. Her grandfather's face is fading. Her dreams are often blank, but when she does dream about her mother, the visions are both harsh and terrifying.

Just one row of crates away, Lucas sits on the ground, cursing in a foreign language as he assembles a rattrap. Maia places her blanket beneath her head and watches what little she can under the shelving. The mound of batter has fallen off the trap and onto the ground. He curses again.

As he sets the last trap, Maia stretches her hand beneath the crates towards him. Just hearing him breathe, watching his feet shuffle around the room, the sounds he makes when he touches things, moves things—against her better judgment, Maia finds herself craving his presence.

His visits are but a brief respite from her state of desperate desolation. Despite what was said at their first meeting, it is clear he hasn't disclosed her presence. He could have. Or he could have kept her his own little secret—even though she would have fought him with every ounce of her being, she knows she is weak and vulnerable. She despises this more than anything.

After setting the last trap, Lucas packs up the box and places it on a shelf, leaving the room without saying a word. Once again, Maia is left alone with the mind-numbing uncertainty as to how long her next bout of solitude will last. The only difference now being the random *snap* startling her in the darkness.

Maia rests her head against the back wall of her nook, completely captivated as imagined clusters of figurines dance playfully in the black velvet before her eyes. Their arms open and close, they twirl on a toe, a dancer flips another into the air. She claps at their performance. *Encore! Encore!*

A low rumble reverberates the contents of the storage room. Glass jars clink together as the roar intensifies. Flickers of light. Maia smiles at the effects. What a show.

The figurines continue to skate on a sea of nothing. Maia's head flips forward. Again. *Why does it keep doing this?* Annoyed, she leans it back against the wall. The netting holding the crates in their shelving strains, creaking and popping as it stretches against their weight.

Gravity pulls Maia forward, breaking her entranced state as she falls through the curtain of her nook. Startled, she looks around. Flashes of light flicker across the tall columns of shelving. The boat aggressively heaves her body back into her nook and then forward again, rolling her into the shelves across the room. Lightning flashes, momentarily blinding her.

One one-thousand. Two one-thousand. Three—

Another rumble. Far ... soft, then traveling across the sea it resounds a menacing roar. Maia's body is pulled forward again as the ship travels over another wave. She crawls towards her nook in a drunken, wobbly pattern, her hands slapping over each other.

181

Once inside her nook, Maia lies on her back and braces her feet against the crates, holding the netting above her head. Rain pelts the side of the boat. They travel over another surge. She holds on, nearly standing upright for a moment before the ship crashes back down. Her head smacks hard against the floor. She looks up at her window. Flashes of light stretch across the rolling black clouds of the sky.

She waits. *Please don't. Please don't.*

BOOOOONG! The ship's warning bell sounds from above. Footsteps pound the floor, and the sound of another large wave crashes on top of the boat like an explosion.

BONG! BONG! BONG!

Maia jumps up with her beloved wool blanket and grabs the netted crates as her feet slide out from under her. She chucks her blanket into a second-row box and stumbles back to her nook. Losing her footing, she rams into a stack of crates.

Bong! Bong!

Grabbing her pack from the floor, she steps onto the first shelf and heaves it as high as she can into a crate. The boat's floors tilt upward and she tumbles towards the door. Someone runs past the other side and she fumbles to crawl back to her nook. More flashes of light, followed by a loud snap of thunder. The warning bell continues to ring as the sky lights up through the basement window. Maia shoves herself back into her nook, bracing her legs and clutching the nailed-down shelving around her.

The boat groans as it rocks violently from side to side. Colossal waves batter the ship like bombs, causing buckets of water to stream down the stairs and beneath Maia's door, drenching her again and again. A few rats scurry towards her and she kicks at their shadowy silhouettes. They fight to climb on top of her and she releases her grip in a panic. The boat tosses her across the room. The men yell and pound the floors above, running back and forth as the storm repeatedly hammers at the ship.

Maia's stomach clenches and twists on itself. Her bucket is nowhere to be found. She rolls across the wet floor as they travel up another surge and she retches as her stomach drops. The ship lands hard on the raging ocean, only to get slapped with another wall-like deluge.

Shaking and chilled to her core, Maia grabs the shelves' legs as she loses her footing. A stream of seawater splashes against the opposite wall. The last of the rattraps snap and Maia vomits the precious remnants of her dinner. The towers of crates are illuminated in wild pulses as countless critters scatter through the flooded basement. They climb on top of Maia as she retches and heaves.

The ship travels up another wave. Maia loses her grip and rolls on top of a rat. It pierces her shoulder, biting hard under her weight. Tense anger surges through her as she screams in agony. The boat pummels forward as she grabs the rat from her shoulder and whips it across the room. It hits the wall with a *thud*!

Unable to cope, Maia breaks. She climbs to her feet and screams with all her might through the booming thunder. An otherworldly wail pours from her lungs and the storm is silenced. The sea calms. It feels as though their ship has been plucked from the raging waters and set afloat in the sky. The men's muffled and confused voices yell from above as rain lightly patters against the window.

Exhausted, Maia collapses to the floor, splashing into the sloshing seawater as the light rumbling of thunder fades into silence.

TWENTY-NINE

Half-dazed, Maia hunches against the wall of her nook. Her curtain remains drawn. She pulls her knees into her chest and keeps her arms wrapped around them to stay dry. Her head hangs heavy and slumped over her famished body. Empty, like a bag of hollow bones.

Another loud thump booms from the floorboards above. The men have been hard at work all morning running, hammering, repairing ... the constant banging above mirroring the *throb, throb, throb* of her pounding head.

The room is filled with an early morning light. Dim, but bright enough to see the state in which she has been left. The ship now drifts along a serenely calm ocean. In the pauses between the banging, the silence of the room is filled with water dripping from the shelves into the stagnant pool on the floor. A stench she can't quite pinpoint seems to be drifting into her nook in short, foul wisps.

She doesn't remember crawling back into her little cave. She doesn't remember much, actually, since being thrown around the storage room in the middle of the night. All she knows is that she has survived another horrific storm. What she can't figure out, however, is whether she should be grateful for it.

She now sits in about an inch of black water. Her wet clothing hangs from the bones of her sunken frame. Her mouth is parched—still saturated with the sharp, foul taste of stomach acid. A trap ensnaring a dead rat floats within reach. She gags and kicks it from her nook.

With the tip of her finger, Maia pulls back the curtain and her heart sinks. Crates hang from the shelves. Bound by netting, they are half-fallen in midair. Some have lost their contents, which now float next to dead roaches and rubbish in the grimy water. Other crates have pushed through the nets enough to reach the ground. Any crates not secured lie broken and drowned in the shallow water with their contents hollowed out like guts. Lucas had worked hard at keeping most things nailed and netted down, but there is only so much damage that can be prevented when a ship is flipped repeatedly on its side.

Maia focuses on one fallen crate in particular, immediately devastated. It must've been one of the loose crates, sitting high on a shelf. A dead rat lies facedown next to it. Submerged beneath the water below the cracked wooden frame lies her wool blanket. Her reprieve. The only thing that has helped her endure the long, tedious days crouching in a ball on the floor.

She is disintegrating. Her bones dig into the hard ground, sending a piercing ache up her back and down her legs. The pain is often followed by a general queasiness reeling about her stomach. She wraps her arms around her concave gut, her body tense from the unending shivering. A sharp pang radiates from her back. She winces as she brushes the bite just below her shoulder bone, now protruding beneath her clammy skin to an alarming degree.

She hasn't seen herself in a mirror for a long time, but she can imagine she doesn't look good. This trip has taken much longer than she had anticipated. She thought she only had to make it through a month and she'd be on solid ground again. It has been at least double that. Or has it? She has officially lost track of time.

Weak, fading, broken. The food Davies brings is keeping her alive, but it is barely enough. She is always hungry. Always cold. And dizzy. Almost delirious. She lifts her head for a moment and then lets it hang back down.

And then it becomes painfully obvious. This one devastating fact, sinking deep into her hollow gut.

She is slowly starving to death.

Lucas enters the room. Or at least she can only assume it is Lucas. His rubber boots send ripples across the putrid water.

"*Meu Deus*," he whispers. It *is* him. His heavy boots nudge floating traps and debris. Stepping over a broken crate, he carefully treads down the center aisle towards her nook. He stops around the corner. "Are you still here?" he asks after a while.

Maia keeps her head down, her eyes closed. A broken "*yes*" stumbles out from her stale mouth, her voice shattered to bits as if spitting out the last remaining pieces of her dignity.

Lucas doesn't move. Eventually, his boots tread through the water back out of the room, but he leaves the door propped open.

Maia spends the rest of the day huddled in a daze in her wretched nook as Lucas mops the water from the basement by the bucketful. The murky water slowly dissipates, leaving small puddles, their surfaces swirling with oily rainbows. In various parts of the basement, he seems to have help from others. The men work and call out to each other throughout the day as they clean the fetid mess of seawater, traps, broken crates, and dead rat carcasses.

By nightfall, Lucas is alone again, finishing his mopping near the open door. He sets up a few new traps just as the smell of dinner wafts into the room. Maia lifts her arm around a ghost-like Huck sitting next to her. She lays her head upon his shoulder as he pants, then reaches up to fix his flopped-back ear. She's always loved the velvety soft-ness of a dog's ears. She smiles as he licks her face.

The door to her storage room slams shut and Huck disappears. Her arm drops to the ground.

Lucas clears his throat. "Bathroom."

Maia's head snaps up.

"Tonight," he adds. His voice is clear as day, cutting through Maia's mental fog like a knife. He clears his throat again and adds "*late*" before opening the door and leaving her alone.

She holds her temples and shakes her head as her brain strings words into thoughts for the first time in days.

What did he just say? Bathroom?

Why? why? WHY?

And what does "late" mean?

Is this it? Now? Now, after everything she's been through, now he'll take advantage of her? Kill her? Bring her to the men of the ship?

She falls to her hands and knees and scans the newly mopped floor. Only a few cobwebs remain, laced with drops of water like pearls. And new traps too. Why save her from the affliction of rats only to treat her like one?

After it is clear the men have gone to sleep, Maia

prepares herself. She cannot fathom why Lucas would want to meet her in the bathroom, but she can only hope it is to talk and not for anything sinister. Either way, she can't risk not going. Lucas has kept her a secret, a risk he didn't have to take. So far, he hasn't shown any malevolent intention. She decides she must go. But she takes her knife—just in case.

The bathroom smells clean, the crisp tang of soap a welcome smell. She gingerly latches the door behind her and leans against it. Her eyes strain against the blackness. "Hello?" she whispers.

Only the ship's traditional nighttime chorus of creaks and bumps respond.

"Lucas?" Her hands reach out in the dark. Her sheathed knife is tucked behind the cinched waist of her baggy pants. She listens, but as far as she can tell, there is no one in this room.

She shuffles forward, running her toe into a large bucket. It's filled with water, still steaming hot. She leans in and smells the contents. It doesn't smell like anything— certainly not the cleaning solution Lucas was using earlier. Next to it, her fingers fall upon a small towel resting on top of another empty bucket, and next to that, a dry woolen blanket.

Lucas has left her something to wash herself.

She dips her fingertips. It must have been boiling when he left it, knowing she wouldn't get to it until after dinner. She falls to her knees, grasping the rim of the steaming bucket of water in disbelief. And then she holds her head in her hands and sobs.

With shivering hands, she dips the towel into the water. Chills race up her spine. She wrings the cloth and leans her head back, draping it across her face. The warmth permeates her depleted body. She inhales the steam, holding the cloth until it cools. She dips again and again, tenderly wiping her tired and aching body, praying with each swipe erasing the filth that she could erase the memories as well.

She cleans the dirt from under her nails. She wipes the grime from her feet. She leans her head over the bucket and washes her hair. Then she tiptoes back to her room and grabs her pack, which has somehow survived the storm. The dirty yet dry clothes she changes into are a small blessing. She has finally stopped shivering, leaving her aching muscles weak and depleted.

She sneaks back into her nook and uses her wet towel to wipe the area clean before placing her new wool blanket inside. She then leaves her dirty towel next to the bucket inside the bathroom.

When she returns the next night, the bucket and towel are gone.

THIRTY

Lucas stands just outside Maia's nook. A jumble of netting is piled at his feet as he readjusts and secures the crates. Maia rests quietly in her little cave, listening to him work. She reaches with a trembling hand and grabs hold of her curtain, hesitating briefly before letting go. Frustrated, she leans her head against the wall and rests her hand back in her lap. She has repeated this circus at least a half-dozen times now, grabbing the same section of curtain and working up the courage to say something to the man standing just outside and then backing out again.

A heap of rattraps sit by the open door. The rats' small, lifeless bodies dangle from the wooden slats with their necks flattened beneath the rusty brackets. Maia used to feel a small pang of guilt every time she heard a snap in the night, despite the fact that they have stolen her food, bit her, and been a general nuisance the entire time she has been down here. She grazes the tender wound on her shoulder. She'd cleaned it as best she could with the warm soapy rag, but needless to say, she doesn't feel so guilty anymore.

Before he leaves the basement, Lucas shovels the traps into a plastic bucket. A little while later, he returns, placing empty traps back beneath the shelves. Maia can hear him fiddling with something, standing just outside her nook. Her heart pounding, she grabs the blanket again and slowly peels it back. She looks up at him standing just a few feet away. His hands inside a crate, he stops what he is doing but does not return her gaze.

"Lucas," she whispers.

He glances over his shoulder, eyeing the open door in an obvious way, and then turns to her with a blatant look of disapproval. As their eyes meet, a look of pity falls over him.

Maia's eyes well in tears. "*Thank you*," she whispers.

As he stares at her, his gaze softens and his shoulders drop. He sighs. "You're welcome." He looks back at the open door. As Maia closes the curtain, he whispers, "Wait—"

She peers back out to find him looking down at her with an uncertain, almost pained look across his face. He rushes to close the door and shoves a small wooden block beneath. Plucking a step stool from between the shelves, he places it around the corner and pulls down a crate. He grabs a small rectangular package from inside and steps next to her, crouching down so they are face to face.

Maia eyes the package, then watches him, now sitting so close she could reach out and touch him.

He looks at the packaging in his hands, shaking his head. "You are going to The Old Arctic Circle," he says with concern as he looks her over.

"Yes."

"*Uh-huh*." He shakes his head. "You will never make it," he adds in his thick accent.

Her heart sinks. "Why do you say that?"

"Eat these. They are calorie-dense biscuits," he says, still eyeing her. "It's taking us a while longer ... the weather ... it is so unpredictable. No matter how many books I read, they are all outdated and irrelevant." He waves his hand as if getting off topic. "I said I wouldn't get involved. I cannot imagine why Davies would agree to smuggle a woman on board. You must have given him an offer he could not refuse."

"I didn't—"

"It does not matter. I am not involved. I won't be any part of this." He stands, handing her the package of biscuits. "I just cannot look the other way as you starve to death, knowing that these are here. *There*—" He points towards the crate he pulled them from. "They are just there. You found them *yourself*. Be careful to resecure the netting and don't eat too many at once."

He returns the crate under the netting then heads for the door.

"Lucas?" Maia crawls out from her curtain.

He stops, pausing for a moment before turning around to face her.

"I'm Maia."

He looks down and nods his head, then turns and leaves the room.

Maia huddles in the dark, contentedly eating her biscuits and a small plate of food from Davies. It's been weeks since her last conversation with Lucas. The dense biscuits made her empty stomach feel sick at first, but now she happily packs them in with her meals, two or three at a time.

After a few weeks, precious weight and vitality slowly trickle back into her system. The once protruding bones soften beneath her skin. She feels like herself again. With the strength to restart her daily routine, she takes a wild guess at how many notches she's missed and carves them into the wood. She whispers to her grandfather again and stretches in the pitch black while she says her prayers. Her biggest source of gratitude is now the very thing that initially caused her grief. *Time*. Time to put on weight. Time to prepare. Time to pull herself back together before she is on her own again.

That's the thing about the human spirit, what one can endure in the face of great hardship. She's stood at the doorway of death and has come back again with a resolve stronger than ever to make it to The Old Arctic Circle.

One morning, as Maia lay in her nook with her curtain slightly opened, she stares at the sky outside the basement window as a seagull swoops past. She saw it, didn't she? *Did* she? For the rest of that afternoon, she watches for the bird —seagulls are usually an indicator of nearby land—but she doesn't spot another. She begins to wonder whether she'd seen one at all. Seagull or not, the thought of spotting a bird rekindles her faith that hopefully, someday soon, they will be close to land. It has to be close. It *has* to be.

Sunday afternoons are a time for drinking. And generally playing cards, Maia imagines. The men often participate in something that induces long periods of silence or speaking soft enough for her to barely hear anything. But with the passage of time and alcohol, the sailors grow more and more boisterous. There are generally loud bangs and yelling, followed by cursing and laughter.

The afternoon passes as Maia listens to the men playing in the room above. She strains to pick out Lucas's accented voice. A few times she can hear him laugh alongside these criminals, and she wonders about him. Most Sundays are like this. She recognizes the men's different voices now, making up faces and names and backgrounds to go along with each.

An object in the ocean drags along the outside of the boat. The pressure from it pushing against the ship creates a loud screech, followed by sporadic thumps and bangs. Whatever is below, the boat is slowly pushing through it like sludge. This outside commotion has been happening with increasing frequency the last few days and this one is particularly loud. It starts from the front of the ship and slowly makes its way towards Maia's window. She waits in anticipation with her gaze fixated on the glass.

A long plastic rod appears, wrapped in a bright blue net hanging from it like a curtain. Trapped in the weave, along with a few plastic bags and seaweed, is a dying fish. Maia watches in horror as it hovers into view, its mouth and gills gaping as it is shoved against the glass.

Without thinking, Maia rips open her curtain and runs towards the window. She climbs the shelving and slaps her hand against the glass. She has never seen a fish so big; it must be the length of her arm. Tangled and gasping, it slowly slides past, suffocating in the open air. A dying fish. What a waste in an ocean almost completely void of them.

Then the view from the window is left unhindered, and the horror of what Maia sees washes over her.

THIRTY-ONE

The once pristine, vast blue ocean is now an endless blanket of waste. Layers of sludge drift between the infinite scraps of plastic, half-submerged buckets, doll heads, debris, netting, bins, bags, and bottles. The boat continues to shove through the mountains of rubbish like a sledge through ice, the layers so thick they blanket the water as if it were land. Maia grips the wooden shelf with one hand as her other slowly covers her mouth. A tear runs down her cheek.

She climbs up another shelf and peers over the ledge of the window. As far as she can see, massive islands of condensed trash float between a chunky soup of plastic. The thick blanket of pollution has smothered any hope of blue, leaving an endless woven expanse of gray. Rain threatens from the dark clouds. A drop splats against the window.

Birds walk along the more consolidated surfaces, picking and jabbing their beaks through the decay. With their heads lowered, they squawk and charge after one another, claiming their territory over the offal. A smaller bird stumbles and trips on top of a mound. Its leg bound by a clear ring of some sort, it drags more rubbish behind it like a ball and chain.

The ship has moved beyond the broken rod of plastic. Maia can see it extending from the trash just beyond the edge of their boat. The fish hanging from the nets has stopped moving. Anger swirls from within her gut.

"Pretty horrific, *yes*?"

Maia loses her footing and swings off the crates. Her hand grips the shelf just long enough to brace her fall and she stumbles to her feet.

Lucas stands before her, fighting back a smile. "*Maia...*"

"I'm sorry, I just..." She straightens her top. "Where *are* we?"

Lucas shoves the wooden block beneath the closed door. Maia's heart skips a beat.

"We passed the old Hawaiian Islands a few days ago." He walks up next to her. "I had a feeling we'd run into this." His voice is hushed with a hint of liquor on his breath.

She backs into a shelf. "Into ... *what*?"

"They used to call it the ... how do you say ... The Great Pacific Garbage Patch. The ocean currents were different back then—stronger. They pushed garbage that was dumped from the land into these massive piles in the middle of the ocean. A hundred years ago, it was mostly only little disintegrated pieces of plastic. Once the piled garbage became thousands of miles across, our ancestors made big programs to clean them. But they were not fast enough compared to the millions of tons of rubbish from all over the world going into the oceans every second."

"Every ... every *second*?"

He grabs the crates and steps onto the first shelf, peering out of the window. He grimaces. "Then the oceans rose. Cities all over the world slowly drowned under the incoming water and *more* garbage leaked into the ocean." He jumps back down. "And then you know the rest." He circles his hands and his head in an *on-and-on-it-goes* sort of manner. "Storm surges and tsunamis and king tides destroyed whatever coastal regions were left and the oceans were obliterated with debris. This is just what you can see; it goes as far deep as it is wide. The bottom of the ocean is covered with mountains of garbage. It just layers on top of itself. The currents are slower now, but they still pile the rubbish in the middle. Davies initially tried to sail around it, thinking it would damage his boat. But it takes too long to go around. We've tried before but it was a waste of time. It just seems to never end. So, we just slow the boat way down and *push* our way through."

Maia looks up at the window, fighting against the anger swelling within. "I've spent my whole life walking among our ancestor's decaying structures and rubbish." An incensed heat burns across her cheeks. "I *resent* it." She looks up at him. "I resent everything about it. It makes me feel deeply alone ... *abandoned*."

"Well, you are—we all are. We are the ones left behind, Maia. We are the forgotten ones." He gazes down at her and for once she can no longer see resentment or pity in his eyes, but something else entirely.

"You look..." He nods his head and a smile tugs at the corner of his mouth. "You don't look ... so bad."

A smile spreads across her face, surprising her. "I want to thank you, Lucas. Again. For everything."

He looks down at her with a kindness in his eyes she's never seen before. And then his smile fades. He backs up. "I should go. You should hide. You shouldn't be out in daylight. This is dangerous."

He turns to leave and Maia grabs his arm. "Sailing where?"

"Excuse me?" He turns to face her, standing once again within inches of her face.

She fights the urge to step back. "You said Davies sails around the garbage. Sails around ... to *where*?"

"You want to know if we are sailing to The Old Arctic Circle."

"Are you?"

He hesitates.

"Please tell me it's not a myth."

He takes a step back and grabs a shelf as he looks out the window. "No ... no, it's not a myth."

She smiles.

"Before you get excited ... we do not go to The Old Arctic Circle. Our ship is banned. People like us—people like Davies ... We are pirates, Maia."

"*Pirates*."

"We are businessmen. We follow our own rules."

"You're criminals."

He doesn't answer.

"You sure don't act like a criminal."

"How do you know?"

"You've protected me."

He winces. "No, I haven't."

"You've left me food and blankets and you set up rat—"

"I've done things."

"Have you killed anyone?"

"No."

"Raped?"

"No. But that doesn't mean—"

"Okay, well, I don't need to know. If we aren't going to The Old Arctic Circle, then where are we going?"

"Next stop is the West Coast of the United States. I assume that is where Davies will have you get off."

"Right. Close enough."

"Not really."

"Closer than I was before. That's all that matters."

He looks at her incredulously, almost amused. It seems he wants to ask her something. As she waits for his reply, her focus lingers on his lips and she suddenly realizes she wants more than just a response. *What is it about this man?* She looks into his eyes as it dawns on her that she is quite captivated by this Lucas. And by the way he is looking at her, it's possible he feels the same.

"Maia, your *eyes*..." He steps closer.

"...the *fuck*?"

Lucas and Maia whip around to find a man standing alone at the open door, the wooden block from beneath now dangling in his hand. A sinister grin spreads wide across his lips.

THIRTY-TWO

"Well, well, well ... *looky looky* what we have here," the man sings loudly. His rasping voice booms through the small storage space. As he scuffles towards them, his soiled boots flop against the ground. He looks Maia up and down, licking his lips between a mostly toothless grin.

"*Bode...*" Lucas steps between them with his hand held out. The man's robust body towers over him. "It's not what you think," Lucas says sternly.

"Like hell it's not. Here I am, coming down to *help* you and you're off fucking some little stowaway."

"I am not—*por favor*, please, let us talk about this."

"*Oooo!* She's a goodie, too. Look at her!" Bode yells.

Lucas flinches and glances back at the open door.

Bode pushes up his sleeves as he takes another step. "Oh, this is going to be fun." He kicks off his boots. "You know the rules, Lucas, we share *these* ones. Don't want to create animosity."

Maia grabs Lucas's arm and steps behind him. Her heart racing, she glances towards her nook. *Where is her knife?*

Lucas keeps his hand out towards the man. "Don't do this."

"Fuck you." Bode reaches around Lucas and snatches Maia's arm, aggressively pulling her into him.

Maia reaches for something—Lucas, a shelf, *anything*—but her toes barely touch the floor as Bode lifts her from the ground. Grabbing her by the shoulders, he lifts her up so they are face to face. "You're coming with me." His offensive breath hits her like a wrecking ball.

Lucas tries to pull her away and Bode shoves him hard against the crates. Maia drops to the ground.

Bode heaves her out of the room, sending her tumbling across the floor. She grapples to her feet and runs towards the stairs but Bode grabs her hair and yanks her back to the ground. "*C'mon* now, no use putting up a fuss." He lifts her off the floor like a rag doll.

Lucas jumps on Bode's back and wraps his arm around his neck. Bode arches back. Still holding tightly onto Maia, all three fall to the ground.

Lucas tightens his forearm around Bode's neck. "Let *go*."

Bode holds Maia's arms so tightly she fears they may break. She cries out as he gasps and spits in her ear. He releases his grip and hurls her into the wall.

Maia scrambles to her feet and runs up the steps on all fours. She briefly looks back to see Lucas lying under Bode, who is still pulling at Lucas's arm around his neck.

"Fuck *you*," Bode spits through a clenched jaw. The veins pop from his deeply reddened face.

Lucas releases his arm and shoves him off. Bode sputters on all fours.

"We don't have to do this," Lucas gasps.

Bode climbs to his feet and yells as he charges towards Maia. She runs up the stairs to the back deck where she had once enjoyed a few moments in the sun. A few drops of rain splat against her face.

Nowhere to go.

There's nowhere to go.

She turns just as Bode lunges for her and she ducks his embrace. Tripping over her feet, she stumbles to the other side of the deck. He slams into the railing and laughs as he grips the metal, half his body now hanging over the edge. He sneers at her with beads of sweat across his scarlet forehead. "I like *'em spicy!*" He smiles as he stands to face her.

Maia backs up to the railing.

"Bode!" Lucas trips up the steps. "Please, let's go back downstairs and talk about this."

"What the actual fuck, Lucas! You selfish piece of shit. We're out here on this ocean for months and you hide this hot little bird away for *yourself*? 'Member what happen to the last fucker who did that?"

"Bode! Keep your voice down!"

"Man overboard!" Bode tips his head back and throws his hands into the air.

"*Fight!*" A man leans against the railing above, pointing down at them. Another man runs up. And another. And *another.*

"And the wee lady..." Bode leers at her with a feral look in his eye. "Well, she barely survived two nights."

Bode reaches for Maia and Lucas reaches for Bode. Bode swings around and lands a punch across Lucas's jaw. Blood splatters across his face.

"Stop! *Please!*" Maia screams.

"I said, FUCK OFF!" Bode screams at Lucas.

"Hey, there's a *woman* down there!" A dozen men have gathered on the upper deck, leaning over the railing with mesmerized looks upon their faces.

"Punch him back, Lucas!"

Maia turns to see Lucas pummel Bode in the eye, and then Bode jumps on top of Lucas, punching him again in the face, then into his ribs. Bode climbs to his feet, leaving Lucas curling into a ball and gasping for air.

Panting, Bode wipes the blood from his cheek, smearing it across his face. He turns towards Maia, licking his lips. She pushes against the railing as he steps forward, a smile spreading across his face. "Now, like I was saying..." He reaches for her.

Lucas screams and charges. Bode flips around and grabs Lucas by the shoulders, running with him towards the rails of the ship. He uses their momentum to shove Lucas up and over the railing.

Maia screams as Lucas falls towards the water and collides into a mound of rubbish. She and Bode look over the railing as Lucas comes up for air, flailing about the pieces of garbage with blood streaming from his lip.

The men above deck are yelling, Lucas is thrashing in the water below, and Bode is laughing uncontrollably, but suddenly Maia can't hear a thing. Life creeps into a muted slow motion as her shortened future flashes before her.

I'd rather shoot you dead and put you out of your misery before letting them find you.

Bode continues to gawk over the railing, his face as shocked as it is delighted, while the boat of men above eye Maia like a fawn to be devoured. She turns to face the ocean and the endless rubbish disappears. Her mother stands in the middle with her white dress flowing in the breeze, calling to her.

Bode's bloody hand reaches for Maia. Without thinking, she takes a deep breath and hurls herself over the railing.

Lucas screams from the water. "Maia! *No!*"

It's the last thing she hears before slamming into the ocean.

THIRTY-THREE

Maia's body claps hard against the almost impenetrable soup of debris and the garbage closes in on her like quicksand. Pain sears through her leg, and then her back, as she plunges deeper through the thick layers of muck. She kicks with all her might as she fights to swim back to the top.

Breaking through the dense surface, she gasps wildly and pulls at the netting covering her face. Her fingers interlace the weave as she wrangles against it, inadvertently pulling it down over her head. The netting is everywhere. It wraps around her foot. She kicks harder, her screaming half-muffled by water.

"Maia! Stop pan—"

The netting pulls her beneath. She seesaws her body, thrashing against it. Objects bang into her as her hands graze through the mound of garbage. Something wraps around her other foot. Panic-stricken, she tries kicking it off. Her head shoots above the water and she sucks in another breath of air, pushing away the stinking rot.

"Stop panicking, Ma—"

She disappears below the surface as the sludge sucks her in.

Sinking deeper, she struggles to untangle the netting around her foot. The clouds open and sunlight pierces through the water above. The mass of debris slowly fills in after her and the water begins to darken. She can't separate her legs; the netting has wrapped itself around her like a boa constrictor. The water continues to darken.

So tired. She stops flailing. A rubber slipper grazes against her cheek and she swipes it away. Her mother's face flashes through the garbage. A few air bubbles escape Maia's mouth. Her mother flashes before her again, yelling, then disappears. Maia looks up through the dregs as she sinks deeper. Air bubbles stream from her open mouth and float upwards in succession.

Her grandfather appears from above and swims towards her. "No, child." He reaches out his hands. "Not yet. Fight. *Fight!*"

Maia strains to reach him, shocked by the physical force when his hands latch on to hers. He pulls her up next to him and grabs her face. They lock eyes—*it's Lucas*. He dives farther down to untangle her legs and they kick back to the surface.

Breaking through the waste, Maia desperately sucks in air. Lucas fights through the heaps of trash and grabs a large plastic board.

The sludge coats her face. "*Ah!*" She pulls at a slimy bag covering her eyes. "I can't *breathe!*"

Lucas swims over, pushing a large slab of plastic towards her. "Grab hold! Stop panicking, Maia!"

She wraps her arms across it as she heaves and coughs up seawater. The boat in the distance travels farther away from them. A dark figure stands at the back deck. Maia wipes the scum from her eyes, focusing on him. Davies watches them with his arms crossed over his belly, shaking his head. He almost looks sad. She stares back, breathing hard with a shredded bag wrapped around the top of her head.

Seagulls call from their circles above. The sun peeks out from the high cloud and a breeze travels over the stagnant waste, filling Maia's nose with a sour stench that can only come from death. She watches as her one and only hope to get to The Old Arctic Circle sails farther and farther away. Her pack and supplies ... all gone. Every last bit of hope is floating away from her. She's escaped death, only to be left in the wake of it. Davies turns from the back deck and disappears from sight.

Maia surveys the trash-filled ocean. Lucas treads water just a few feet away, holding onto his own plastic bin. His face is horrified, dazed, his eyes unblinking. His swollen and bloodstained mouth is half-open as if silently screaming. He slowly meets her gaze and they stare at each other in a state of shock.

She reaches across the rubbish, inspecting individual pieces of floating trash. An old toothbrush missing most of its bristles. A doll head with only one eye. Handfuls of plastic bags, utensils, and straws. Bottles and lighters and bins. A broken sandal coated with green slime. Half a comb with only half its prongs.

"Maia."

She looks up at Lucas. He shakes his head slowly, a stunned look still frozen across his face. "What just *happened*?"

She looks around her new fate in disbelief. "I..." She loses her grip and sinks to her chin. Wrapping her other arm around the floating slab of plastic, she hoists her upper body on top. Trembling, she looks back to Lucas, his face unresponsive. "I don't know," she answers.

His face softens, overcome with sadness. "Did you *jump*?" His voice barely escapes a whisper.

Her eyes fill with tears. She looks back to the boat, now a distant spot on the horizon.

She can't answer that.

She can't answer that.

What just happened, what she just did. What did she do? She can't answer that.

After all that time. All those terrifying nights huddling in the dark like an animal. So close. She was *so close*. Maybe if she stayed on that ship, she could have survived what they would have put her through. She's strong. She could have made it through. She could. Women from the beginning of time have survived the worst of it and have come out stronger. Then she could have still made it to The Old Arctic Circle. And she wouldn't have just lost everything ... for nothing. For death. For more wasteful, meaningless death. Left to rot with the rest of the meager life left in this squalid ocean, tangled in the dredge of an expired and decaying world.

"Oh *GOD!*" Maia cries out. A fury of tears coats her cheeks as her drawn-out cry wrings out every last drop of air from her lungs. When she finally breathes in, she unleashes a desperate, grief-stricken wail.

Lucas only closes his mouth, watching her passively with glossy, lifeless eyes.

THIRTY-FOUR

"*You are my sunshine...*" Maia lies draped across her board, half-submerged from the brimming, clunky water. Her eyes glazed over, she's secured her place on her board with one outstretched hand—white-knuckled and clutching the top ledge. "*My only sun ... shine.*"

Neither Maia nor Lucas have spoken a word to each other in hours. After emptying herself of her grief, and Lucas unresponsive in some sort of paralyzed stupor, she has laid her head on her board in defeat. She's passed the time in a daze, observing shattered bits of debris slowly gathering and swirling around her body, singing so softly to herself she barely recognizes her own voice. Far away ... like someone else whispering into her ear.

It doesn't seem that long since she's given her other hand a rest but the throbbing ache within her joints tells her otherwise. She lifts her arm out of the water, too tired to remove the black cord hanging from her wrist, and grabs the top of the board. She winces, then rests her head on top of her wet arm and drops the fatigued one beneath the surface. She stretches it among the rubbish.

She's not sure how much longer she can keep doing this routine, but it can't be long. At this point, she has no other option. Hold on until she can't any longer, then switch arms. Repeat. She's tried climbing on top of the plastic slab but only seems to capsize the board. So, she's managed to rest her upper body on top and if she stays completely still, it remains relatively easy to stay afloat.

She dips the tips of her fingers in the thick amalgam of bits, twirling them in mini whirlpools. Her eyes glaze over once again. "*You ... make...*"

Something is wrapped around her ankle, another cord or netting of some sort. She swirls her foot in one direction and then another, wrapping and unwrapping the rope. "*...me hap—py...*"

She looks up. Squinting towards the horizon, her head wobbles like a newborn. Fragments of plastic goo drip down the side of her face and she absently wipes her brow.

It's becoming one of those stunning sunsets that paint the sky in bright watercolor hues of coral and deep blue, illuminating the expanse of wreckage into a kaleidoscope of colors. Although the landscape isn't pretty, Maia can at the very least be grateful that it's calm. And warm. A few seagulls hover in the sky above, scanning the muck for food. She lays her head back down and switches sides, slowly unlatching her aching fingers and letting her hand sink below the surface.

So, this is how I die.

Swirl. Twirl. Swirl. Twirl.

"*Please don't take...*"

With the sun hovering just along the horizon, the grave threat of darkness now looms. A tear travels across the bridge of Maia's nose and drips onto her arm. "*...my sunshine...*"

"There." Lucas's voice startles her from her trance. "Maia."

Maia searches the rubbish until she finds him, still wrapped around his own floatation device. She hasn't looked in Lucas's direction for hours. A deluge of guilt crashes into her as she remembers Bode, his blows to Lucas's face—and his ribs. Lucas gasping and curling into a ball, fighting for this woman he barely knows.

And now look at him.

His left eye now suffocates beneath a swollen mass of red and purple. A deep rift above his eye is cracked open with dried blood collected along his brow and down the side of his face. His lower lip has doubled in size. Seems the tables have turned. Now it is *Maia* looking down at *him* with pity.

"Does it hurt?"

He looks confused at first, then softly grazes his eye. He winces. "A swollen face is the least of my worries," he says quietly. He checks his fingers for blood, then licks his swollen lip. "There," he says again and points to a large mountain of rubbish with a flock of seagulls resting on top. "I wonder if that island is thick enough to climb onto?"

Maia glances to the mound. It seems bigger than before —taller. Wider even? Possibly the currents have pushed more rubbish against it. Either way, it's large and dense and if it's good enough for the birds, it's good enough for her.

The seagulls eye them suspiciously.

"I'm going to check it out. Stay here." Lucas lets go of his board.

"No—take it. In case you get tangled. That stuff is like quicksand."

Lucas holds the large plastic bin across this chest and lies on his back, kicking his feet to propel himself backward.

It takes much longer than Maia would have imagined for Lucas to cross the relatively small section of garbage to the island. A few times he runs into small mounds so thick he can't seem to move them, so he has to go around. Maia grabs a long stick and levers it under a dead jellyfish floating too close for comfort, pushing it in the opposite direction.

Eventually, Lucas's head disappears within the peaks and valleys of debris. Maia strains in the dusk to locate him. She would normally be petrified of being stuck in an ocean teeming with jellyfish, especially not being able to scan the open water for them to keep her distance. But her curse is also her blessing. So far, the only jellyfish in this mess are dead ones.

A loud whistle travels across the water. Maia looks up to see a dark figure standing on the mound, waving his hands. Seagulls and birds lift in flight with a great deal of fuss.

"Maia! Here!" Lucas falls forward, circling his arms for balance. "It's not completely solid, but solid enough."

Maia levels as much of her body on top of her slab as she can and uses it like a paddleboard, making her way through the thick waste towards him. Something heavy slides down her leg towards her ankle. She panics, then relief showers over her. She grabs it just as the fabric begins to unravel and lifts the dripping blade before her in disbelief. She had forgotten. After weeks of quiet back on the ship and the imminent threat of the men diminished, she forgot she had put her knife back in its sheath and secured it under the leg of her pants.

"Maia! Grab any netting you come across!"

She kisses the knife. *Thank God.*

"Maia?"

"Yes! Got it!"

She clenches her encased knife between her teeth as she

paddles through the mire, stopping every so often to untangle some netting. She leaves behind a few segments filled with rotting birds. She finds an old cord with red and yellow copper wires hanging out and threads it through the nets to keep them together, then slowly weaves her way towards the island.

"What do you have? Is that a *knife*?"

"It was tied around my leg."

"Clever girl," he responds quietly.

The junk condenses as Maia approaches the mound, which has grown drastically in size as she's approached. The feeling of pushing through the chunky mess makes her stomach churn. So many empty bottles ... What she wouldn't give in this moment for some water. There seems to be a lot more seaweed and murk within this section of the patch, mixed in with the tiny bits of debris—like a mountain of plastic has been shoved through a wood chipper.

"Almost there, Maia. Here, hand me the nets." Lucas leans out to her, a pile of netting already layered beneath his knees. His hand sinks beneath the mound.

"This looks dangerous," Maia says with concern.

"That's why we are going to use this netting to build a better foundation. Grab my hand. It gets thicker towards the middle."

Maia reaches out and Lucas pulls her towards him. His knees drop through the mound and he sinks to his waist.

"Lucas!" Maia holds his hand, helping him climb back out of the sludge. "This is too thick," she says. "I don't like it. It's going to suck us under."

"No, it's okay. We just have to get out of this part and get to the thicker stuff." He keeps hold of his board and reaches his other hand below, slapping the mounds of netting on top. "Just don't let go of your slab. We'll inch our way through together."

Placing their boards before them, they lean forward and displace their weight across the plastic. Only their knees sink into the muck and they quickly learn that the faster they crawl, the less chance they have of falling through.

By the time they reach a part so dense it feels like land, darkness has fallen over them. They each feel out a spot among the softer bits of rubbish and lay out their netting.

"We should probably still put most of our weight on these boards. I'm not really sure what this is ... I don't trust it," Lucas says from beside her.

Lying side by side on their backs and catching their breath, exhaustion sets in. Maia stares up at the glittering sky as a shooting star burns across the expanse. This is the first time she's looked up at the open night sky in months. She sighs, relieved to be out of the water and on this island of debris.

"Lucas?"

"I'm here."

She turns towards the sound of his voice, but she can't see a thing. Despite herself, her hand searches along the soggy terrain for his.

When she finds it, she is surprised at how tightly he grabs hold.

And he does not let go.

THIRTY-FIVE

Loose scraps of rubble shuffle just beyond the black abyss of Maia's closed eyes. Sharp pains resonate from both her lower back and calf. She's contorted awkwardly; the side of her face digs into the layers of debris and sand while her lower half has twisted into the fetal position. She slides her arm out from under her hip, grimacing from more bruises, no doubt, protesting from the underside of her body. Bruises from falling into thick layers of garbage blanketing the ocean. Falling from the ship she's fought so desperately for months to stay alive on.

The ship she willfully jumped from.

More shuffling.

She has been awake for a few minutes now, reluctant to open her eyes and face the grim reality of her situation. Seagulls call from their circles in the sky and savagely squawk at one another from the heap.

Whatever is next to her face twitches again. She can't open her eyes just yet. Not yet. The early morning sun is so warm on her body. She savors the heat, trying in vain to ignore the growing threat of its intensity while still being so low in the sky.

Maia's eyes flutter open and are met with the curious glare of a small sand crab. She is momentarily stunned; she was sure these didn't exist anymore. His two seedy black eyes extend like antennae from his knobbed shell the color of pale lemon. A permanent grimace stretches across his white face. His claws rest before him on the amalgam of sand and plastic. A few pieces of debris litter his thin, almost translucent shell. A speck of sand is stuck to his left eye. *Sand*?

Maia sits up and the crab scurries off sideways in a panic. She surveys the spot she spent the night sleeping on, the netting beneath her now mostly dry. The thick layer of debris once swaying with the waves now appears solid. She grabs a small pipe and stabs it into the layers of garbage. Solid.

Shielding her eyes from the sun, she scans the gruesome scene laid out before her, feeling her heart break into more pieces than this Great Pacific Garbage Patch could ever hold. Even though she has witnessed the decaying span from both above and below, the shock from where she stands is no less deplorable. The stench of a dead bird wafts towards her and she stares at it through the blur of her tears. Its matted body decaying, its left wing is broken—wrapped in a clear plastic twine.

He was right. Her grandfather warned her about this world, but she went anyway. And now she is stuck with a stranger on an island of garbage.

Off in the distance, Lucas is stumbling around, shifting and wobbling on the uneven ground like a toddler just learning to walk. He has a black rubber boot on one foot and a faded blue sandal on the other. A small collection of shoes is piled in a netted bundle on his back. He leans over and pokes into the rubbish with a long plastic tube, pulling an old buoy from the mound. He tosses it into a pile of other buoys as he stumbles towards her.

"How are you feeling?" he asks as he approaches.

Maia quickly wipes the tears from her eyes. She gathers her hair and wraps it high into a knotted bun, her back beneath already drenched in sweat.

"I'm okay ... considering." She looks around. "Are we on *land*?"

"Looks like it. I think we're on an old flooded island somewhere around Hawaii. I *think*. A lot of islands in this area that used to be inhabited are now mostly underwater except for a few. And even some of those only exist during low tide when small slivers of land pop back out of the ocean. That would explain why last night this mound got thicker—it's sloping up the coast to a small patch of land. And why we were floating last night and now we're not. I think we stopped just in the tidal zone. It drops off again just over there.

"Here." He chucks the bundle of shoes towards her. "I've found these. Sort through and find something for your feet. Some of this rubble is sharp."

Maia surveys his finds. Some of the boots are way too big, the shoes too small, the sandals too broken. Eventually, she sorts out a large sneaker with a thick rubber bottom and something called a "Croc," according to the branded imprint, which fits her right foot perfectly. She grabs a reflective red shard and scrapes off the crustaceans stuck to the bottom and inside the sole, leaving a slimy layer she is all too happy to ignore considering she now has something to protect her feet.

She slowly stands, half-expecting to fall through. But

just as Lucas said, the ground is solid. Half-dry. She, too, seems to have mostly dried out. The only remaining dampness is on her chest and left hip where she was curled on the ground.

Shielding her eyes again, she scans the area. The rubbish moves with the ocean waves, lapping against the mound where they now stand. A few bits and pieces shift in sporadic bursts across the land, more sand crabs she can only assume. A bird coasts in the breeze above.

Maia's empty stomach roars in protest, and her mouth is dry as a bone. She looks over to Lucas. His face is somehow more alarming than it was yesterday. New hues of purple and red swirl around his swollen eye.

She flashes him a sympathetic look. "What are we going to do?"

For a while, he can only shake his head as he examines the wreckage. He lifts his hand to shield his eyes, flinching when grazing his broken brow. He notes for the first time the cuts and bruises across his knuckles. "We're alive, aren't we?" he finally mumbles without looking up.

A few seagulls rest on one leg near the shore.

"Think we could fashion something to get one of those birds?" Maia asks.

"Like what?" Lucas chucks some rope in a pile. "And cook it how? Even if we could start a fire, we'd poison ourselves from the melted plastic."

"There must be a way. There's always a way," she says while scanning the litter.

"I saw a few crabs wandering about. I tried chasing them but couldn't move fast enough on all this *shit*." He kicks a broken skeleton of a computer monitor.

Maia looks up to the sky. "We should probably think

about water. And shelter. We're definitely far from New Zealand. The day has barely begun and it's roasting."

"So, it was New Zealand, then? That's where you joined us?"

"Yes."

He nods, staring at her with blank eyes as if computing something in his head. He quickly snaps out of it. "Yes, it's going to be really hot from here on out, we've moved much closer to the equator. And it's summer season over here, versus your winter." He shakes his head. "I understand the temperatures are not always that cool where you're from, but it was so refreshing. And beautiful. Why the hell would you want to leave that?"

Maia picks up an old water bottle, covered in grime and lumps of green moss. "Considering the predicament I've landed in, I'm not so sure how to answer that right now."

"Don't bother. I've heard it all before. You want to go to *The Old Arctic Circle*." He chuckles as he shakes his head.

Maia looks at him in dismay, slighted by his blatant cockiness. "I'm not sure why you're mocking me, but I don't need your judgment right now."

He raises his hands in a gesture of truce. "I'm sorry. I don't mean to be—I'm just a bit shell-shocked right now."

Maia pulls another bottle from the sand. A large hole has broken through the top. Annoyed, she tosses it back to the ground.

"Let's start over. I'm Lucas ... you know that already. I am from Brazil. I joined the ship a few years ago."

"Why? You always wanted to be a *pirate*?"

He shrugs, ignoring her jab. "I guess I needed to start over. When I saw Davies's ship come in, I didn't know where they were going or where they came from. I didn't care. I just knew I needed to go with them."

"Sounds familiar."

"So, you were running—that's why you left?"

"Not exactly. I was alone. I guess a part of me was running ... that's another story. But I've always felt called to The Old Arctic Circle, even before I knew it existed."

"But you know nothing about it."

"I know enough."

They stand apart, staring at each other with words hovering on their tongues, unwilling to release them. She can't quite read this man, the look of frustration across his face. It's clear he's holding something back, but what, she can't figure out.

Lucas finally looks away. "Let's get our water sorted."

They search the rubble in silence, sifting through the shredded mess for any solid bottles with lids intact. Maia keeps her distance until she has an armful, careful to avoid the shoreline, a difficult task as land and sea blend into one continual expanse.

She wanders over and drops her bounty of bottles next to Lucas, who is working on cutting the bottom off a large bottle with a triangular metal shard. Maia unties her knife from her leg and offers it to him. He stops sawing at the plastic and looks at the covered blade. He flashes her a humbled smile.

She returns to her search, stopping every so often to watch him. He cuts off the bottom of each bottle and folds in the rims to form a deep lip around the inner circumference. Then he rips off the lower half of his pant legs and cuts the fabric into pieces, soaking the strips in leftover puddles of stagnant seawater and placing each inside makeshift vessels he's found around the island. After lining them up, he places the bottles carefully over the top of them. He stands and surveys the lot with a look of uncertainty across his swollen face.

He looks up to meet her gaze and his hardened demeanor softens. "With the heat of this sun, we hopefully won't have to wait long before these condense fresh water to drink. It won't be much but it'll be something."

Maia drags a tattered blue tarp over to Lucas and drapes it over her head. "We should build some sort of shelter."

"We should. I'm just not sure yet how far up this tide goes. I think we'll have some land left up there but I cannot be sure. If we lose it, we will have wasted precious energy building something the tide will come in and destroy."

Maia follows his gaze up the mound of garbage behind them. The blanket of debris slopes up the coast to what seems to be a small hill. "Well then ... maybe we should build a boat."

Lucas inspects a moss-covered buoy, then glances at her from the corner of his eye. "My thoughts exactly."

THIRTY-SIX

A nother bead of sweat glides off the tip of Lucas's nose as he whittles a piece of driftwood into nothing. Maia watches quietly from the corner of her eye. A delicate shaving of wood falls in a curl to the ground. She swipes the pile of scraps and adds them to their kindling.

He's taking it too far.

She goes back to securing a small rope through the slivered end of a plastic rod, then ties it to the other side, forming a loose bow. They have already carved a small plank from driftwood with a triangular sliver cut from the side where the spindle will sit. They have even found a clunky piece of coconut shell to protect Lucas's hand from the friction. Now that she has fastened a bow, all they need is the spindle and they can work on making a fire.

Lucas continues to carve. His face is intense, focused. His jaw clenched. His eyes are far away, like he's in another world.

"Lucas."

Carve. Carve. Carve.

More shavings fall to the ground. She bites her tongue. He's going to ruin it.

"Lucas, I think it's good."

Carve, carve, carve.

Driftwood is scarce on this island—every piece matters.

"There will be nothing left ... if you ... *Lucas!*"

The top snaps off. He drops his head, then whips the stick across the mound.

Maia stands, unimpressed. She tosses her bow into the pile.

Lucas grabs another small stick. "Were you not going to hunt for crabs?" he mumbles without looking up.

Two days have passed since they crawled onto the shoreline of this tiny island and they've been hard at work. They've assessed the borderline of the tidal zone, which has left them a small sliver of island that does not submerge beneath the water. The only way to judge the shoreline is by the movement of rubbish on top of the lapping waves, so to make it easier, they've placed pole markers into the garbage to measure high and low tide.

They've also dug out as many layers of rubbish as they could and have set up a small makeshift camp at the top of the hill. A hole dug deep into the sand is now filled with the wooden shavings from their bow drill. Behind it lies the tattered blue tarp, propped into an open tent where Lucas now huddles. An eclectic assortment of old water bottles are condensing water in the midday sun. It's a slow process but steady. They've already successfully gained a few decadent cups of water each.

A substantial pile of netting and buoys wait next to their camp, along with detergent bottles, petrol cans, a few large pieces of driftwood, slabs of plastic, deflated rubber tires—anything that could be condensed and tied together to form a raft. They've even started a pile of lids for the lidless bottles, finding that with thousands of tops around, there is sure to be one that fits. It must float, and it must seal. These are the only requirements.

Maia slides on a pair of mismatched rubber boots and grabs some netting, heading back onto the beach. Every step must be methodical. An infection from a single cut could kill. She piles a few more buoys and a jug into her netted pack and then drops the bundle to the ground. The heat is overwhelming. She wipes her forehead with the back of her arm and arches her aching back. She and Lucas lock eyes. Again. He looks away.

This has been their day, watching each other in silence. Glances, eyes meeting before one of them turns away. No words. No smiles. Last night they passed out on top of the rubble with their backs towards each other, with some sort of unspoken affliction growing between them. Mostly from Lucas, and Maia could feel it ... whatever it was, rolling off him like steam. Some sort of weird conglomeration of sadness and anger. Possibly attraction too, but she just can't read him. They've known each other for months, yet are complete strangers.

Lucas has finished his spindle. She watches him with the bow drill. The cord is tightly wrapped once around the spindle and he saws back and forth, constant and methodical. Back and forth, back and forth, back and forth, grinding the spindle into the small wedge in the plank. All he needs is a little dust to catch fire and he can drop it onto the kindling.

Maia's stomach growls. It's certainly not easy to hunt for crabs, especially as she's never done it before, but she's comfortable with the patience and stillness required. She wades out into the soggy tidal zone where she knows they are hiding.

Two antennae pop up from the rubble, next to a square container labeled "Tupperware." She shifts each boot into the layers of scraps, careful to be as quiet as she can, and makes her way closer. Now she waits. Slowly crouching down, she watches the spot where the crab hides below.

Her eyes flicker up to meet Lucas's. This time he does not look away. He looks pensive, almost sad.

The rubble moves, stealing Maia's attention. The crab sits just beneath a clear shred of a tarp. Maia moves like lightning. Grabbing the crab by its back foot, she whacks it against a large container, temporarily stunning it. She chucks it into her net. *Food.* She proudly looks up, but Lucas is no longer watching.

Within a few hours, Maia has a full net of squirming, wriggling crabs.

A large wave pushes a pile of rubbish against their high-tide marker. She picks up Lucas's broken spindle, slipping and sliding through the wreckage back up to the tarp where Lucas continues to work unsuccessfully on building a fire.

"It's high tide," Maia says as she approaches.

"I know."

"I got us some food."

"I know."

She proudly sets her bag of crabs next to him but he doesn't look up. She clears her throat. "Lucas, I never thanked you for saving my life."

Exasperated, he sets down the bow. "What are you talking about?"

She is taken aback. "On ... the boat. With that man ... *Bode.* I can't imagine how horrific that could have turned out."

Lucas doesn't speak. He picks up the bow and begins to drill again, faster and faster as Maia talks.

"And for the food. The blanket ... the hot wat—"

Lucas slams the bow back down and wipes the sweat from his brow. He looks up at her and says straight and stern, "I should have never said anything to you. I should have stayed out of it. I should have kept my head down. Now we are both going to die."

She is stunned. He's clearly angry ... and at her. "Because of me ... right? Is that what you're saying? This is all my fault?"

"I didn't mean it like that. You didn't force me to do anything. This is *my* fault. I made the decision to go down there, in the middle of the day ... to see you." Their eyes meet. "And Bode followed me." He looks back to the ground and starts to saw the bow. "If it were not for me, you would still be on that boat," he says through gritted teeth. Sweat drips off his nose onto the rubble. "No one would have ever known you were there." He looks up at her, his eyes pained. "I didn't save you, Maia. I handed you a death sentence."

"If it weren't for you, I would have slowly starved to death in that closet. Or gotten really sick. You *saved* me."

Lucas shakes his head.

Maia doesn't move. "Lucas?"

He continues shaking his head.

"Lucas—"

"And after all that ... how could you *jump* off that boat?"

"I didn't think—"

"You are right; you didn't think."

"Lucas, they would have done terrible things to me."

"At least you would still be alive."

"But I'm alive *now*."

"Not for long," Lucas mumbles under his breath.

Maia's heart begins to pound. "So that's it? I make it this far and now I get to die on some shithole trash island?"

"Maia, we are in the middle of nowhere. *Compreendo*?" He speaks slowly, patronizing her.

Despite being unfamiliar with his language, she can assume by his tone that he's asking if she understands. She puts her hand on her hip in defiance.

"Look at us!" Lucas stands, throwing the bow to the ground. "We are stranded on a mountain of trash that no boat will ever come near. We are *fucked*, Maia. We are just delaying the inevitable."

"You know what? I used to think you were so brave, fighting for me back there with that man—"

"Bode! His name was Bode. And he used to be my friend."

"Your *friend*? How could you be friends with someone like that?"

"There is a lot you don't know about me."

"Yeah, I bet there is. Well, I'm not giving up. I'll never give up. I'll find a way..." She stumbles away from him, repeating like a prayer, "There's always a way. There's always a way."

Maia trudges as far across the limited patch of land as she can until the rubbish lumps into piles from the waves. She sits down in a huff. She's used to being able to run away, leave whenever her temper flairs, but now there is nowhere to go.

She's stranded on this puny island with that asshole.

She tilts her head back and breathes deeply to calm her nerves. Time slips away as the sky swells into a deep orange before fading to a pale violet. A few early evening stars flicker along the horizon while the makeshift hills and valleys of wreckage move atop the placid ocean. Crabs sporadically scurry across the mounds. The evening ushers in a slightly cooler breeze, a relief after the scorching hot day.

A seagull calls from above as wafts of smoke drift before her. He's done it. And he also has all the food.

Dammit.

Is this all her fault? Lucas is clearly blaming himself, but surely she is equally to blame. She shouldn't have been out in daylight. She shouldn't have left that nook. She should have kept quiet. She certainly shouldn't have talked to him.

But she couldn't *not* talk to him.

Lucas slowly makes his way across the rubble behind her and four smoking crab legs lower in front of her face. "Peace offering?" he asks quietly from behind.

It takes every ounce of restraint not to rip that crab from the blackened spear and inhale it like a dog. Lucas sits next to her, silent as she devours every delectable piece. He hands her more and she takes them without speaking.

"I had a feeling there was a stowaway. I knew about you for a long time. Not *you* exactly—but someone. There were a lot of careless clues left behind. It wasn't the first time Davies had smuggled someone on board, but I am almost certain it was the first time he had smuggled a woman. He had that damn *area* blocked off and made sure we all knew it was off-limits. He put a few blankets over different crates to create a ... how do you say ... *diversion*?"

She nods.

"Anyway, it was not hard to see your area did not have a crate. I was preparing to make a deal with him to keep you a secret. I had been thinking of different negotiations. He was always a man of his word. In a world of criminals, your word is more valuable than gold. But he is also a powerful man, not one you consider threatening lightly."

"Negotiating? For what?"

"I wanted to get off the ship in South America, which is not allowed. You join the crew—you join the crew for life. Our ship is not a taxi service." He pauses, absently inspecting an empty crab shell. "But once I saw you..." He tosses it to the ground. "I cannot really explain. I wasn't sure what would happen and that was not okay anymore. Davies could surprise you sometimes." He looks at her. "I couldn't be sure you would be safe. Maybe he would negotiate—maybe he wouldn't. He could have laughed at me and gave you to the men, or thrown you overboard. He could have thrown me in, too, for trying to blackmail him. I knew those were options before we met ... but after ... it was not a risk I was willing to make.

"But then, I could not stop..." He hesitates, looking away. "I *couldn't* stop thinking about you."

She looks up at him, surprised.

He is shaking his head, gazing across the fading horizon. "I found myself drawn more and more to the basement—to *you*, despite *everything* in my gut telling me to stay away. A storm would pass through and all I would do was worry I would find you the next morning facedown under some shelving I had not secured properly. When I heard your voice after that cyclone, I was relieved. But then ... then I watched you starve. You could not see your face but I could. You were wasting away. The color of your skin, your cheekbones sticking out."

"Lucas—"

"Once I gave you food, started taking care of you, I knew I was in over my head. I was in it now. That old man who came down to your room one night..."

"I was terrified."

"It was me who tipped Davies off. I saw the man wander

down there but I did not want to make a scene. He was wasted ... he is a pretty useless human being, to be honest. I knew he wasn't looking for you but he is a hardened old man who would not have cared at all about what happened to you. He is one of the originals with Davies. I made sure not to look up from my cards and said, 'That man pisses in my basement, he's dead.' I knew Davies would jump—and he did."

Maia looks at him, captivated by his face, a face she'd memorized for months while hiding down in the basement of that boat. He rolls the colorful cord tied around his wrist between his fingertips. His shoulders slumped, it looks like a blanket of shame is anchoring him down. Despite all his attempts to prove otherwise, it's clear this man cares.

She brushes a curl away from his swollen eye. It certainly seems like the worst of it is over. "You don't look ... so bad," she says with a smirk.

He grunts and a smile spreads across his face for the first time since the ship. He looks at her fondly from the corner of his eye. "Thanks."

THIRTY-SEVEN

The intense, early morning sun hangs low in the sky, hurling rays like fire across the far-reaching wreckage. Dawn has only just awakened and the suffocating heat surrounds them like the inside of an incinerator.

Lucas shuffles up to their camp and dumps an armful of driftwood next to a squirming net of crabs. "This is the last of it, as far as I can see. We have a couple of pretty big logs in our pile of boat supplies, but I think we should save those. If we get the entire thing built and do not need them, we can always make another fire before leaving."

"I agree," Maia says as she surveys the small selection of scraps. "Okay, so this is it."

"This is it. After this, our fire goes out for good."

"Do you think there's enough to split into two lots so we can eat again tomorrow?"

Lucas nudges the pile with the tip of his boot, his face calculating. "I don't think so. By the time we cook these crabs, our fire will be bordering on embers. There is just enough to keep the momentum going for one big meal."

"So ... we feast."

"We feast."

Huddling under the tarp, nothing but the sounds of snapping crab legs, slurping, and crackling embers can be heard. The heat surrounds them like a furnace, yet Maia barely breaks a sweat anymore as dehydration kicks in. Lucas hands her the small collection bowl of water.

"Is there enough?" she asks.

"We have some more condensing over there to add. We can drink this bowl but should definitely ration the rest."

Maia takes the bowl and sips at its limited supply. "It feels like rain is coming."

Lucas smiles. "You said that yesterday."

Maia slurps another mouthful of water. She forces herself to put the container down. "I know. It's coming."

Lucas picks up the last cooked crab from their makeshift bowl. "Shall we split it?"

"I'm so full. I feel like I'm going to be sick—"

"You can do it, Maia." He cracks the legs in half, keeping two for him and handing her the rest. "Eat it."

As they sit huddled under their tarp with a bounty of shells surrounding them, they watch mournfully as the last of the fire smolders into faint whispers of smoke.

"Lucas?"

"Yes?"

"I'm sorry about Bode. I didn't realize you ... *cared* about him."

He looks at her for a long time without saying anything. "The thing is, it's easy to judge. I joined that ship and thought I could be hard and tough like the rest of them, wall myself off, not give a shit about anyone but myself. It's safer that way. But over time, I learned a lot about those men. We did not really talk about our 'feelings,' but the stories came out in bits and pieces—mostly when we were drinking. I've spent time with some of the worst people in the world, and some of them, yeah, they are animals. But they were children once. Many of them loved, some of them had children of their own. They are hardened from the atrocities of life, from having nothing left to lose. Most of us were only on that ship because the lands we left held too many ghosts."

He pulls at a loose string hanging from his ripped pant leg. Maia watches him, unsure of what to say. All she can think about is, he said, "*us*."

"Anyway, looks like we might be getting that rain after all." Lucas points to the horizon where a billow of black clouds is swelling up from the seams of the earth. Lightning flickers within the dark mass and a strong breeze rolls loose debris across the shore. "I think we are in for a big storm. We should lay out as many bins and bottles as possible to collect water. It's moving pretty fast; most storms around here come and go quickly. This could be a game changer for us, Maia."

"I told you it would rain." She smirks.

Lucas smiles as thunder growls from a distance. He nearly looks like himself again. The swelling of his lip has dissipated and the rift along his brow is closing in. Only faded patches of yellow surround his eye. "*Vamos!*" he says as he grabs her hand.

They run across the rubble gathering bottles and bins ... anything wide enough to collect as much rainwater as possible. Maia shields her face as the debris and sand pelt into her skin. The light continues to fade as ominous black clouds advance steadily across the sky. A blinding flash and piercing clack knocks Maia to her feet as the heavens and earth connect through a single blade of light.

"Are you okay?" Lucas yells over the wind.

"Fine!" she yells back as she stumbles to her feet.

"Nothing that can fly away in the wind!" Lucas shouts. "Put them close to our tarp so we can refill them as quickly as possible!"

The heavens open and pound the earth with an avalanche of rain. Lucas runs towards the tarp to secure a loose end but Maia remains in the deluge. Tilting her head back, she lifts her hands to the sky as bolts of lightning zigzag across the clouds. She opens her mouth, spinning and giggling like a child as she catches the rain on her tongue.

And then she stops.

Lucas watches her from beneath their tarp. This time he does not look away. Lightning flashes and an immediate crack of thunder collides into the earth, its boom like a sledgehammer. Maia doesn't move. She stares at Lucas through the thick haze of rain, completely captivated, and she knows. She knows from the very depths of her being that this man's life will be forever entwined within her own. It is their destiny, written in the stars. She gulps hard, her eyes flittering against the onslaught of rain. She is falling for him. She is falling for him with a fervor unlike anything she's ever known.

She stands in the downpour until another flash of lightning shatters their trance. The rain pours even heavier now and she sprints towards him under the tarp. "How exhilarating," she says as she crawls in next to him.

"Yeah," he says as his gaze fixates on her. "Let it rain."

They watch in awe as the storm crashes into their little island in relentless waves of fury. The blackened sky flickers in endless flashes of light as mammoth waves of rubbish crash against the shores. Maia sits next to Lucas. Her heart pounding, she is unable to speak.

Just like that, everything changes.

Lucas runs back out into the rain and grabs a few full containers, carefully tilting the sloshing water into larger bins before setting them back out again. "*Meu Deus!*" Lucas shrieks with his hands raised triumphantly in the air. "So much water!" He grins wide before grabbing a bottle and chugging the entire thing. He fills it up again from a large bin and races it over to Maia. "Drink!"

Sitting under the tarp, the worst of the storm has passed and the rain has settled into a patter. A dozen assorted buckets and bins of precious water are lined up before them.

"Lucas..." Maia's heart pounding, she finds it hard to find the words. "May I ask you something ... *personal*?"

"Ask me anything."

She looks to him. "You said, '*us*.'"

"What?"

"You said, 'most of *us* left because home held too many ghosts.'"

"Yes ... I did." He takes another swig of his water and they sit in silence.

A seagull walks up to their tarp, tilting its head as it looks between the two of them. It wanders away.

"I was married," Lucas finally says. "We had a son."

Maia looks at him, stunned.

He twists the fabric around his wrist. Unblinking, he stares into the sand. "We had to move from our home in Brazil. The Amazon flood lands were overtaking everything.

235

We moved down the coast and set up a new life with a small community of others. My wife wasn't so intent on leaving Brazil—traveling wasn't safe, especially with a baby—but I insisted. I wanted what was best for us, and I thought we would find that in leaving. We found a beautiful abandoned house next to the mountains. It was so peaceful." He lets go of the bracelet and now fidgets with a plastic ring between his trembling fingers.

"My son had just learned to walk." He looks up to the sky and sighs. "My wife and I were outside in the garden. We had started growing our own food. It was like ... it was like all of my dreams were coming true.

"He was sleeping inside the house when the earthquake hit. It was so violent—the shaking. We could hear things breaking. My wife ... she was running inside to get him. Neither one of us could stay on our feet. She was so much closer to the house than I was. I kept stumbling across the yard—I couldn't find my footing." He finally looks at Maia. "Our house started falling apart ... like it was nothing, like a house made of cards. I could hear my son crying inside."

Maia grabs his trembling hands, still knotting the plastic ring.

"It all came crashing down ... the bricks and the wood and the floors. I was *screaming*, running towards the house. By the time I got to it, the earthquake had stopped. And his crying..." Lucas breaks free from her grasp and wipes the tears from his eyes. "There was no more crying." He holds his breath, swallowing hard, and tears escape his closed eyes.

"Oh Lucas, I'm so sorry."

"I worked for days. The rubble..." He holds his hands wide. "Some of it I couldn't move. My hands were a bloody mess. Others tried helping. They told me I should rest, that I should eat, but I could not. I couldn't stop. I thought just maybe they will still be alive.

"It took two days until I got to her. Her body was still huddled over him, cradling him. She was hit, *hard*, in the back of her head. Her body was mangled. Her back, her clothing, sometimes it was hard to distinguish between her and the rubble. But my son under her, he did not have a scratch on him. He died in her embrace, under the weight of our new home. The home I insisted on having.

"I buried them under the monkey puzzle tree. And then I buried myself with them. The community tried taking me in, but I could not stay. I should have been stronger. I should have run faster. I should have protected them. But I was weak."

"Lucas, *no*."

He looks up at her. "I was dead inside, nothing but a shell. When Davies's ship pulled up to shore, I knew they were pirates. I knew they would probably kill me. But I had nothing to lose. I had to leave South America, dead or alive. I bared myself to them and told them to kill me or let me on. They threw me another crew member, hungry to fight. 'Kill him or die. Only one of you will get on this boat.' So, I fought him. I used all my anger and I fought hard. I wanted him to kill me, and the more I beat him, the angrier I became that he was not killing me—I was killing *him*. Eventually Davies stopped the fight. He had called me, 'fearless,' which made me even angrier, because I was not fearless. I was a coward.

"Looking back, I learned that this man and Davies were close, but Davies had to keep the respect. A week later we left that man onshore. I will never forget his face, bruised and broken, glaring at me with more hatred in his eyes than I have ever seen. Every night it haunts me still.

"So, I became a pirate. It was not easy but it was an escape. I could work hard and no one asked questions. There was booze, and sometimes there were women. I threw myself into learning English—I didn't care about anything else. For four years I was wasting away from the inside out, barely existing day to day in a used-up, decaying world." He looks up at her with grief-stricken eyes. "Until I met you."

The clouds have swept clear from the horizon, leaving a sliver of blue sky where the sun is slowly disappearing into the sea. The breeze picks up, sweeping loose strands of hair over Maia's face.

Lucas leans forward and gently brushes them back. "I have never talked about this to anyone."

"Thank you for telling me, Lucas. I am so sorry, I can't imagine."

"No, I am the one who is sorry. I'm sorry for the way I have been acting towards you. It's just ... I have not felt this way about anyone since my wife. And it has been really hard for me."

Maia looks down and Lucas tenderly lifts her chin. "You thanked me for saving you, Maia. But I didn't save you ... *you saved me*."

A distant wave of thunder rolls across the silver sky. Maia's breath catches in her chest as Lucas leans in, slowly, until his nose grazes hers. He hesitates, his breath hot against her lips. And then he pulls her to him, softly kissing her as sporadic raindrops pelt against the tarp.

THIRTY-EIGHT

In the dead of night, Maia awakens. Lucas sleeps soundly next to her. The features of his face, so often worried or focused, are at peace. His chest rises and falls as soft breaths escape his gently parted lips. In. Out. In. Out. A few dark curls hang across his face. She fights the urge to touch him.

Sitting up, Maia rests her arms on her knees and gazes out across the dark blue expanse of decay. The full moon casts stunted shadows across the shallow banks of rubbish and a blanket of twinkling stars scatter across the sky, awakening memories of her beloved glowworms back home.

Home. Seems like a lifetime ago.

Last night Lucas kissed her. He kissed her with a tenderness that took her breath away. It was her first kiss—her *only* kiss ... stranded on an island, surrounded by garbage.

And it felt like coming home.

She softly brushes her lower lip with the tip of her finger as if some part of him was still there. Something has happened; something has evolved between them that has changed everything.

Crawling out from under the tarp, she stands beneath the array of glistening stars, breathing in the soft whispers of a faint ocean breeze. Was this horrific nightmare all meant to be? Is this fate? This is certainly the first time in her life she has felt its hands so strongly molding the course of her days. Does that mean the appalling chain of events leading up to this moment was all written in the stars? Like robots, they have been programmed to a predesigned lifeline of events?

She inhales and she knows. No, she had a choice in the matter. She could have stayed in New Zealand. But, like magnets, she and Lucas gravitated towards each other, and the events fell into place as they found each other among the decay.

Tomorrow they will build a boat. Tomorrow they will work hard, all day, on leaving this little island. It's not so bad anymore. A crab scurries across the debris. She smiles to herself. Okay, it's *awful*. But somehow, in this one peaceful, drifting moment in time, it seems safer than out there.

Out there. Something still calls to her out there. Something real. Something strong. Is it her destiny? This force to be reckoned with? Maybe she didn't have a choice after all. This *something* ... whatever it is, has caused her more pain, more despair, and more loss in one short glimpse of her life than in all her days combined. All choices she has made, on her own, that could have been avoided. Choices that have now caused a ripple effect across the lives of others. She could have been home, safe, next to a fire with Huck by her side. Lucas would still be on his ship, and the battle wounds on his face would have never been broken.

"Maia?"

She turns to find Lucas sitting up under the tarp. His eyes search through the darkness for hers.

But then, they would have never met. This undeniable, unspoken connection between them would have remained a rift—an unmet void in the great expanse. Lucas would still be an empty shell, and they would have lived out their days without each other. Never knowing. Deep lines would trace between her brow from age and worry. Her hair would gray and her back would hunch. She would have lived out her days in New Zealand, safe. Alone. Ending every day looking out into the horizon with wonder.

And deep regret.

She wanders back under the tarp and curls up next to him. They lie facing each other and she sweeps a strand of hair off his face. He closes his eyes and she shifts so close to him that their foreheads meet. She puts her hand in his.

Yes, pain. So much more danger and pain.

But also ... *life*.

The following day, Maia awakens to a headache. Not knowing when rain may come, they have rationed out their water to the least amount needed each day to keep them alive.

Lucas crouches along the shore with his back towards her. She walks towards him, crushing broken plastic beneath her.

Lucas turns around. "Morning."

"Good morning." She rubs the tiredness from her eyes. "Another hot day."

"Sure is. Today is massive. Are you ready for this?"

Maia squints across the mounds of rubbish. The romantic evening has disappeared with the moon, leaving the sun to highlight the appalling wreckage in all its grotesque horror. "I am."

"I want to be gone within the next few days. Are you any good at knots?"

"I am."

"Okay, so everything we have collected to make this boat must be put together and secured with nets, triple knotted and secured again. First thing we must do is separate our stack of netting into one pile that is in great condition as is, and another for broken or frayed pieces to be taken apart for rope. Can you do that? I will go hunting."

"Yes, of course."

He holds up a hollow metal pipe. "Have you seen these before?"

"A tube? Yes, I'm familiar."

"No, the things attached to it."

She stumbles over to him and grabs the pipe. Attached to the bottom are clusters of what looks like dinosaur nails. The finger-like tubular growths extending from the metal have a long, ribbed neck the color of rust, gradually darkening to black. The ends are adorned with a sharp plated shell that looks like layers upon layers of shark teeth.

She squints at them in disgust. "I've never seen these before. They must be poisonous."

"They are not. They are called 'gooseneck barnacles.'"

Maia lightly pulls at one. It doesn't budge.

"They are normally stuck to cliffs and rocks along the shores," Lucas says. "I can only guess they are out here because a lot of this stuff used to float close to land and have drifted here. I can't imagine it's common, but it is our best shot."

"Best shot to fish?"

"Fish? Fish for what?"

"What else then?"

"We're going to eat them."

She looks at them again and her stomach churns at the sight. "I don't know."

"Yes, you do. Besides, you don't have any other options."

She pulls at the slimy appendage, grimacing. "And where will you be hunting for these ... *things*?" She pokes at the hard-shelled tip.

"They are around the sludge of this island, the parts that generally stay wet."

"You can't go out there. It will pull you under."

"Not with these floaters I've made." He proudly lifts a few buoys.

She smirks. "Cute. And how do you presume we eat these things? We don't have any spare wood to burn."

"Raw. It's safe, they were a delicacy for years. We can net them up and keep them behind the boat beneath the water so they stay alive. We will have to ration them out, but they may be our only guaranteed food source for a while."

She lifts the pipe. Jingling the appendages back and forth, they clink together like a wind chime. The corners of her mouth pull down into a grimace.

Lucas grabs her hand. "Maia, every day we stay in this rubble is another day we risk getting hurt. Even a minor cut could become infected and kill us. Every day we spend here is another day we could be drifting in the currents towards land. I think we are somewhere between the old Hawaiian Islands and North America. Getting out of this garbage patch and back to the currents is our *only* hope. Otherwise, we die here in this graveyard."

"So. Knots, then."

"Knots."

Maia sits cross-legged with mounds of netting surrounding her. Pulling, sorting, tying.

Lucas walks up with a large net full of assorted objects with barnacles attached. "I'm going to find a secure spot outside the tidal zone to keep these beneath the water. We don't want them getting distressed."

"What about taking them off the garbage to save space and weight—is that an old basketball in there?"

"Yes ... how do you know about basketballs?"

"I've read a lot of books," Maia says with a smile.

"Yes, that one is loaded with barnacles; it was my best find. But no, I do not want to take them off until we eat them. I'm not experienced at pulling them off and may kill them in the process. Don't want to do that until right before we eat them.

"I have brought you a gift," he says as he reaches into his back pocket.

"Please don't say it's a doll head. Those things are really starting to freak me out."

"Better." He pulls out a bright yellow rubber ducky.

She gasps as she snatches it from his hand. "Where did you find this!?"

"Under the rubble down there. I had to give it a good polish but she is as good as new."

"I read a children's book once about these, when I was little. I've always wanted one." She cradles it in her hands and looks up at him, beaming. "You're sweet."

Lucas heads towards the shore to secure the barnacles and Maia returns to her task. She places the yellow duck in front of her like a mascot, stopping to smile at it every so often.

After a while, Lucas sits down next to her. "You mentioned you had read about rubber ducks," he says as he grabs some netting from the pile. "So, you've been educated?"

"I have. My grandfather had just started as a university professor when The End hit. He believed very strongly in education."

"You were close? With your grandfather?"

She looks down, a wave of grief crashing over her. "Yes, we were very close." She swallows hard. "He was everything to me. It was just the two of us, and we had our moments, but it was pretty effortless."

"And your grandmother?"

"It's complicated. My grandpa wasn't actually my real grandfather. My real grandfather didn't survive The End, the same as with my grandmother. He worked with Grandpa; they were at the university together. He asked Grandpa to take his one remaining child, my mother, and leave the city. To protect her. Grandpa never had any children and his wife had passed away, very young from what I gather. They hadn't been married long.

"So, Grandpa took my mother and escaped into the mountains of the Southern Islands where he had some land as a spot for hunting. He rebuilt a life for my mother and himself. They were hiding away when The End hit." She stutters a bit, embarrassed she still doesn't know. She looks for a spark of familiarity in Lucas's eyes.

He waits for her to continue.

"My mother met my father years later. She died giving birth to me."

"I am so sorry, Maia. Is your father still alive?"

"Yes, but I never knew him. He's a drunk. He's still on the island ... it was actually him who secured my spot on your ship. He made a deal with Davies—I don't know what—and showed up at my cabin in the middle of the night to tell me. He knew I was trying to get to The Old Arctic Circle. I had twenty-four hours to pack up my life and leave."

"What did your grandfather think about that?"

"He didn't. He had already passed away."

Lucas looks down, shaking his head.

"I was all alone."

Lucas fidgets with the netting. "I am sorry, Maia. I judged you when I accused you of the sort of 'deal' you would have had to strike with Davies to come on board."

"I know."

"I'm sorry. I told myself what I had to about you to not get involved."

"I didn't ... I wouldn't."

"I know. I know that now."

There is a long silence. Maia tugs at a frayed net, trying to separate the cording.

"I am sorry to hear about your grandfather. How did he die?" Lucas asks.

"It was his lungs. I don't know what was wrong with him but it was a very slow and painful death. He was sick for a long time. I did everything I could, but in the end, there was nothing I could do but sit by his side and watch him die. I burned his body in the corner of our yard." She sighs and drops her knotted net into her lap. "And I finally got it. I finally understood what it meant when my books mentioned a 'broken' heart. That sort of pain, the kind that guts you, hollows you from the inside out ... You *will* your heart to stop beating, you think surely it can't bear another minute of the immense emptiness from loss. But somehow it beats on, unwavering and cruel. And suddenly, nothing is the same. And you know it will never be the same again."

There is a palpable sadness in Lucas's gaze, but he says nothing.

Maia stands to survey the piles of nets. "Anyway, this is it. Everything is separated and ready to go."

Lucas rises to his feet next to her. "Somehow, from all this mess, we will have a boat."

"Think it'll work?" Maia asks.

"It will. I know it will. It's just going to take a hell of a lot of netting and tying, but we can do it."

"There's always a way," she adds.

Lucas and Maia stand side by side over their collection of scraps ... the driftwood and the bins and the buoys and the wide slabs of plastic that kept them afloat on their very first day in the Great Pacific Garbage Patch. Quite possibly, the greatest adversary to lead to their demise could also be their salvation.

Lucas chuckles beside her and Maia follows his gaze. She giggles. With their hands on their hips, they marvel as a brave little sand crab lifts his claws in defiance of Maia's yellow rubber duck.

THIRTY-NINE

"I don't think I can do this," Maia says as she glares at the prehistoric barnacle sprawled out across her palm. "You can. And you must. You need all the strength you can get before we start building."

Maia holds back a retch, swallowing hard. A swell of queasiness rolls about her hollow gut. Somehow this thing has become even more grotesque since being torn from its home. It looks more like a severed limb with gangrene than a "delicacy" to be devoured. Eggshell-colored meat spills from the ribbed, leathery tube, which morphs from a reddish brown into a deadened black. The shell of layered teeth at the tip is laced with red in the middle where it opens like a mouth.

Maia's stomach churns. "So ... what do I do?"

"Hold the tip with one hand, like this." Lucas holds out a barnacle in front of him. "Then grab the sheath just under the head and sort of twist and pull down in one motion." He grimaces as he slides the sheath down, revealing a sliver of goopy meat inside. He quickly bites it off and tosses the shell. "It's only a mouthful but we have plenty. I will load our raft with everything we have and we will pick up as much as we can on our way out."

She watches him chew, then looks down at her hand.

"Go on. Don't let me eat them all," he says with a wink.

Maia holds the tip. Then, as directed, she twists the black, ribbed coat from its shell and pulls down. Seawater squirts across her face. She thrusts the barnacle away from her. "What was *that*?!"

Lucas chuckles. "Here, let me help." He tenderly wipes her cheek as her eyes flutter from the assault. "Sorry, they can do that sometimes." He swipes again, his face inches from hers. "I should have warned you."

Her eyes focus on his. He hesitates, leaving his hand on her cheek. A smile curves from the corner of his mouth. "You are up, darling." He motions at the barnacle.

Darling. That's the first time she's heard the word since her grandfather.

She wavers, unconvinced, then hastily bites into the flesh. Chewing as rapidly as she can, she swallows it down.

Lucas looks amused. "And?"

She stares at the claw.

"It won't help you to look at that. Just chuck it." He swipes it from her hand and throws it across the mound.

She swallows. "It's not bad. It tastes like the ocean."

"Good." He looks relieved. "We feast. Here are some more." He hands her a deflated basketball.

She rips a handful from the bottom. "God, *why* do they have to look like this?"

"Just close your eyes and eat up. Tomorrow is a big day."

Maia braces herself as she interlaces her fingers through the waxy weave of netting. She digs her heels into the rubbish, placing one foot behind the other.

Lucas stands across from her, mirroring her stance. "Ready?" he asks with a large grin. "Just pull as hard as you can. If your knots are strong enough, this will tighten them. If not, it will show us where the weak links are so we can retie them."

"This better work," she says as she braces herself.

"Pull!"

Together, they heave against the weave of nets. Maia arches her back, putting her weight into it.

Lucas laughs in spurts through gritted teeth. "You're stronger than you look."

The nets creak in their resistance. Maia's knots are holding.

"Stronger than you," Maia says with a flicker of playfulness.

Lucas yanks the nets with an unexpected jolt, flinging Maia into him. "*Are* you, now?" he teases as he catches her. He holds her against him and for a moment he doesn't let go. His face just inches from hers, a bead of sweat drips down his temple.

Maia recovers her footing and he lets go, flashing her a flirtatious smile.

"Nice one," Maia smirks. Dusting off her shirt, she regains her composure. "So, they're good. My knots?"

"They are *excelente*."

She smiles. "Good, I don't think my fingers can handle any more tying," she says as she wipes the sweat from her brow.

"Unfortunately, that was only the beginning. We are ready to build and the success of this thing will depend completely on our weaving skills." Lucas gathers up the nets and sets them in a heap beside their boat supplies. "Let's just start with the basics and build a frame. We will have to clear this patch of sand as best we can to have space. We have three large pieces of driftwood. I think we should lay two along the edges and one across the middle and then fill in the gaps with buoys. We have some large pieces of plastic to place on top as well. I think we can give ourselves a bit of a gap between our raft and the water by placing the floor on a square row of bins beneath us—anything large that can float can be tied together. We can assemble the rows of bins first, pack them tightly together, and then wrap them with rope and netting. Same with the raft. Then we can weave the pieces together."

"Okay, I'll start on the bins." Maia grabs a large canister and some netting.

"Maia, we are only as secure as our nets. They will be the only thing holding this raft together. To be meticulous would be an understatement."

"Don't worry, Lucas. I've got this." Maia wraps her hair in a bun and takes a swig of water. All those years working on jellyfish netting will pull through for her now. She will weave and tie like she's never tied before.

Lucas and Maia work tirelessly through the next few days, from sunrise to sundown. Resolved. Resolute. Tying. Wrapping. Weaving. Tying.

Nothing would stop them.

Only a few early morning stars remain as light seeps into the corner of the sky.

"Maia? Are you awake?"

"Yes." She sits up, looking anxiously at Lucas.

He grabs her hand. "You ready?"

She takes a deep breath. "As I'll ever be."

Last night they slept in their newly-fashioned boat, testing it in the tidal zone. Beneath them, a square row of tightly packed jugs tied together prop their raft of driftwood, sheaths of hard plastic, and buoys above the water. The entire unit has been tied and intricately woven together. Their blue tarp has been fashioned over rods for shelter and a rain collector. A few makeshift crates of goods sit in the back of the tarp next to a foam container of bottled water. Everything is tied down in multifaceted ways, including Maia's yellow rubber duck, which now sits on the front of the raft like a ship's figurehead.

"Lucas?"

"Yes?"

"Back on the ship..." She bites her lip, hesitating.

He waits for her to continue. "Yes?"

"You mentioned you didn't go to The Old Arctic Circle, but you also said it wasn't a myth."

"Right."

"So ... there *is* something up there? You've seen it?"

"I have not seen it. Like I said, our ship was banned long before I joined, but clearly there is something there with enough power to keep pirates away."

She smiles.

"What are you thinking? You think the place is some sort of haven?"

"No."

"I don't think it's everything you are making it out to be."

"How do you know what I'm making it out to be?"

"Well, why risk everything for it? People are still people, Maia. I know they are rebuilding, but that doesn't fundamentally change who we are. Doesn't mean it's not without problems."

"Like what?"

"I cannot really say. I guess I've heard rumors. But those are from bitter men who weren't allowed in for some reason or another. So, I don't think it's worth getting into."

"Look, I had a choice. Die doing something with my life, or die doing nothing. Either way, I'm still going to die ... every day that's a possibility. But staying in New Zealand would have probably killed me in a much more drawn-out and painful way. Sure, I was relatively safe there, but I was alone. I had no one. And what would my life have been? I would have died after a lifetime of just existing. What a waste."

"Were there not tribes where you were?"

She sighs. "Yes. There were. Not any I was willing to join."

He looks unconvinced.

"Anyway," she says, slapping her hand against the netted wood beneath her. "The raft made it through the night. The tide is almost completely back in. Just a little more time and we can start to paddle through this muck."

"Do you think we have everything?" Lucas searches through their containers of supplies.

"Everything we could salvage and use. Is the paddle back there?"

"Most definitely." He hands her a cracked rowing paddle, one of their most cherished finds.

She places it next to her and pats it for reassurance. It was a beautiful moment when she pulled this from the sludge. She and Lucas just stared at it, mouths gaping. They couldn't believe their luck.

They sit on the back of their small netted raft and watch the sunrise while feasting on a handful of barnacles.

Maia looks out across the clunky expanse. "How long do you think we've been stuck here?"

"I'm not sure. Not long..." Lucas chuckles. "And yet, *too* long." He looks at her with an undeniable affection in his eyes. "I just cannot believe that we're sitting on this thing."

Maia runs her hand along the layers of woven nets holding together the refuse of the world. Their only hope, their only salvation, was once their worst nightmare. This certainly isn't how she imagined getting to The Old Arctic Circle, but there was a point not so long ago when she "knew" it would never be an option. Life isn't always pretty, but it certainly has a sense of humor.

"What we could use now is a good rain," Maia says while sliding back the sheath of another barnacle.

"Any day now, I'm sure," Lucas mumbles.

They bite into the flesh in unison.

Lucas peers over the edge and sticks the paddle into the water. It disappears, hitting the ground about a foot down. "Okay, let's do this. We will head in that direction. Not as many stacked mounds to work around."

Sitting on opposite sides of the boat, Maia strokes her paddle through the murky soup while Lucas uses a half-broken plastic bowl. The raft moves forward. They smile at each other, an electrifying charge between them.

"Watch out for that stuff there. Here, I will push us around." Lucas leans over the edge and Maia hands him her paddle. He shoves it into the pile, pushing their raft around it.

They continue paddling through the clumps of debris as the morning sun climbs across the hazy sky. Maia glances back. Their island appears smaller now, blending into the expanse the way it had before they discovered it. She looks ahead and smiles.

The farther out they paddle, the less condensed the mire becomes. The tall mounds of rubbish now blend with the massive sea of waste behind them. Patches of blue ocean begin to open up between the bits and pieces.

Every stroke they take, they become further strengthened in their resolve, stealing glances and chuckles and smiles. They've made a raft from garbage. A good raft. A solid raft. How long it will last is anyone's guess, but every day they are still alive is a monumental success.

———

After four days, Maia and Lucas lie on their backs beneath the shelter of their tarp.

"Hey." Lucas grabs her hand.

Maia turns towards him but he doesn't speak. Exhausted, they only smile at one another.

They've done it.

They have paddled their way out of the Great Pacific Garbage Patch and now float serenely atop the calm ocean swells.

FORTY

Maia awakens from another muddled, blank dream. She peels herself from the layered netting, woven like cobwebs between the lopsided assortment of buoys and bins, crisscrossed driftwood and scraps of plastic. She rubs the indents on her cheek, then clutches her fingers between the top layer of ropes. These ropes ... these ropes are life. She runs her fingers across the interwoven, multicolored layers. Nothing else matters if they don't hold up.

Seawater sporadically splashes against the large plastic bins beneath, adding what will soon be another dried coating of salt across Maia's skin. The frayed end of a yellow cord sticks out just above an empty red petrol container. She quickly pulls it tight and secures it around the netting before tucking it back in, then scans the rest of the raft for any other discrepancies, running her hands over the top for reassurance. It's still holding. They are still floating. Everything is as it was before she fell asleep.

It's taken nearly a week for Maia to stop waking all hours of the day and night in an all-out panic that the raft may have come undone in the moments she wasn't watching. The overwhelming urge to want to somehow wrap herself around it to hold it together has eased, if only just slightly. All she can do now is hope. Leave her life in the hands of fate. The major deciding factor of whether they live through this nightmare or perish at sea now depends on this makeshift raft of garbage held together by a string.

———

A few days have passed since Lucas and Maia have officially paddled themselves out of the mire of the garbage patch. Initially, they were elated. The sun was high, the water calm. There was food. Even though it was limited, just knowing it was there was profoundly comforting. And there was water —two full crates secured in the back of the tarp.

They had defied logic. Escaped death. Created something from nothing. They felt like gods, arrogant in their success. They toasted their waters and shared slimy barnacles and passed the time laughing and telling stories under a relentless and menacing sun.

Now, Maia's hollow gut rumbles, almost painfully so. She crawls to the end of the raft and pulls up their empty net like a lifeless sack. It used to be so full. Maybe the large scraps the barnacles attached themselves to were misleading. Maybe they didn't have so much after all. She thought they had rationed out the barnacles for at least ten days, so how could it be empty? Although it did take them four days of paddling to find their way into blue waters. And then another few days have passed since then ... three? Maybe four? It's amazing how easy it is to lose track.

Now that their supplies have dwindled, their spirits have quickly followed suit. With neither food nor water, the days pass by in a numbing fog, the two souls sinking in and out of a mindless daze.

Where will the currents take them? Will they starve to death? Dehydrate? How long will it be before they spot land? Will this raft of rubbish actually hold? And if it doesn't ... they drown in the middle of this endless ocean. Who would go first? This is the most terrifying thought—who would be left behind. Maia can't bear the thought of it. The questions circle her mind like a cruel and merciless carnival ride. Round and round and round, faster and faster, until she finally seeks refuge through sleep.

Maia crawls over to the basket of bottles sitting in the sun outside their tarp. Only a minuscule swallow of fresh-water has condensed in each. *So thirsty* ... it's all she can think about. Lucas lies sprawled under the tarp, sleeping. She watches his belly rise and fall. A bead of sweat slowly travels down his reddened temple into his hairline. She's mesmerized by his face, now half-hidden under a thick beard and full head of curly hair.

What can she do? She is bordering on desperation—she can't just sit here. The water glimmers in its reflection and she is reminded of the sparks of light within the trees in New Zealand. The random occurrences of apparent "magic," the dreams, the bees dying, and the branches moving. She hasn't thought about any of that since leaving. Too painful. Too confusing. She didn't cause any of that to happen ... did she? No, she was just *there*. And now that she isn't there, nothing has happened. No dreams. No mother. No magic. Empty. Void. *Again*.

She sits hunched in the harsh rays of the sun. While being grateful for the calm weather, she is equally nervous, knowing the heat will eventually bring storms. Not only that, but *repeated* storms. Lucas has told her not to worry, that a storm means rainwater. But all she can think about is that a storm may also bring back the waves that almost crushed their massive ship with a large crew of men. What will happen to the two of them on this piece of tied-up garbage?

Must do something. Must think about something else. She grabs a rod she saved from the island and a ration of netting and works on tying her knife to the end.

Lucas sits up, rocking the raft. "Hey," he says, rubbing his temples. "What are you up to?"

"Spear. I need to do something or I'll go crazy."

"Have you seen anything?"

"No, but when the sun goes down a little more, I'll be able to see better. If there's anything down there, I'll be ready."

"How is our water?" he asks, still rubbing his head.

"Slow."

"Hey," he says, motioning for her to join him. "It's too hot out there. You don't want to sweat too much."

She slides next to him and works on tying her knife to the rod. "It's a long shot, but it's better than nothing."

"Can you spear with that?" He looks unsure.

"Not from the boat, the rod is too buoyant, but I can lower myself in the water and wait for any fish seeking shelter beneath our raft. I've seen a few over the last week but was unprepared. I can spear them by hand. It's tedious, but it can be done."

Without waiting for an answer, she dives into the ocean. Gliding through the waters, she plunges deeper, the cooler temperatures a relief from the steamy conditions above. Gripping the spear, she inspects the waters for life, feeling at home for the first time in months. She swims back to the surface and sucks in a big gulp of air, a smile stretching across her face. Lucas watches intently from the raft.

She dives back under, somersaulting down. The sun pierces the water in scattered beams across the surface and a few rogue jellyfish bounce and drift in opposite directions. In the vast expanse, it's not hard to steer clear of them.

The water is beautiful but Maia's energy is low. After a few dives, she swims back to the raft for a break.

Lucas reaches down. "Hand me the spear, I will have a go."

Holding onto the raft, Maia hands over the spear.

After a few rounds and the remaining daylight diminishing, they decide to take a break. The temperature has softened, leaving Maia chilled. She wrings the water from her top and they sit in silence at the edge of the raft, exhausted.

"There's nothing out there," Maia says, holding her head in her hands.

"We'll keep trying." Lucas puts his arm around her. "Maybe we should stay out of the water now. We need to start drying before nightfall."

She rests her head on his shoulder and he gently kisses her brow.

Movement below the surface catches Maia's eye. "There's something there," she says. She can almost smell it, the prey just beneath the surface. "I'm going back in." She grabs the spear but hesitates as a lone fish swims towards them. She can't jump in and scare it; she has to spear from the raft.

She slowly lowers herself to her stomach, with her arms

and head hovering over the water. Lucas holds down her legs. The fish glides closer. Gripping the spear, she holds her breath. The fish is just beneath the surface, lured by the protective shade of the raft. Maia hovers the tip of the knife along the water's edge. The blade dips in and out with the waves. The fish drifts beneath it. With every last ounce of strength she has, Maia stabs, splicing directly into the center of the fish.

She lets out her breath.

Lucas starts screaming from behind. "Oh my God! You did it!"

The raft wavers from side to side but Maia doesn't move. Gripping the spear with eyes wide, she stares in disbelief at the fish writhing beneath the surface.

They may just live another day.

Lucas leans over and grabs her spear, then helps lift her up. He holds the silver fish between them, its scales glimmering in the early evening light. It's even bigger now that its size is no longer warped by the water. They marvel at it in disbelief.

Maia pulls the fish from the knife and whacks it hard against a timber of driftwood, killing it instantly. As Lucas unties the knife from the rod, Maia holds its lifeless body in her hands. Closing her eyes, she whispers, *Thank you.*"

When she opens them again, Lucas is observing her, a soft tenderness behind his gaze.

"Ready?" he asks.

"More than."

Holding up the knife, he says, "We feast!"

After taking a swig, Lucas hands Maia a half-crumpled plastic bottle. A few mouthfuls worth of water slosh around the bottom.

"Is this the last of it?" Maia asks.

"Afraid so. Most of our condensed water was tainted from us rocking the boat."

Maia holds the battered old bottle, hesitating. "I'm sorry —that's my fault. Here, you should have the last of it."

"No. You worked really hard today. You should have it."

"We'll split it."

"Maia. Take it."

"Okay." She swallows the last swig whole, knowing this is a battle she'll never win. She resoaks a black cloth with seawater and places it in the middle of a bottle, then sets it in the crate with the others. "Fingers crossed," she whispers.

They sit with their feet dangling over the edge of their raft as the sun sets behind a thick layer of low-lying clouds in the distance. The moon hangs as a faded sliver in the light blue sky. Lucas grabs a piece of fish intestine and works it around a hook he had wrangled out of some tangled vine back on the island.

"I spent my entire childhood watching the moon come out," Maia says with a sigh. Closing one eye, she raises her arm to the sky and covers the milky-white crescent with her thumb. "I used to find it so comforting. Like knowing no matter what, the night is coming and we will rest. Tomorrow will be a new day." She slides her thumb back and forth, covering and uncovering the ghostly snippet. "No matter what uncertainty lay ahead, the moon is constant. *Safe*." She lowers her hand and looks away. "I haven't watched the moon come out in seven years."

"Seven. That's pretty specific. What stopped you?"

She bites her lip and then gazes back up to the moon. "I stopped trusting the darkness."

Lucas stops what he's doing. "What happened?"

Maia hasn't thought about this in years ... not until recently when she was faced with the very grave threat of seeing them again. "I was only thirteen," she says. "A *young* thirteen. My grandfather and I were traveling the islands searching for options for my future. He was getting older and I was getting bored. We had found one of the only large communities in New Zealand. They called themselves 'The Northern Tribe.' There were maybe seventy-five people in it. There was nothing like that anywhere around—there were either small handfuls of people or ghost towns. There seemed to be a lot of young women there, but not a lot of young men. Just *old* men." She swallows hard.

"One night, I sat out after everyone had gone to sleep. I wanted to see the moon. I needed to think; I needed to feel safe. One of the elders came out. I remember being surprised by how close he sat next to me. I inched away but he immediately moved closer. He had made me uncomfortable from the beginning, but I kept that to myself." She lifts her feet out of the water and then back in again, grappling with an overwhelming sense of anxiety rising from within, like a latent poison now seeping from her bones.

"His face was so close to mine. I could feel the hairs of his beard touching my cheek. There was a strong stench of alcohol on his breath. He reached up and started stroking my hair, telling me how beautiful I was." Chills prickle down her spine. "My heart ... I've never felt my heart pound so hard—I thought it would stop. When he put his hand on my leg, that's when I *prayed* it would stop.

"I was young and naïve, but I knew I was in serious trouble. And my voice ... my voice was stuck. Like a jagged stone had caught in my throat. My breathing was so loud, coming out in short spurts. It felt like he was suffocating me and he had only just put his hand on my leg. He had this smile on his face—I'll never forget it. His features were highlighted by the light of the moon. He sat back and watched how terrified I was—with *amusement.*"

Lucas shakes his head. "God, Maia, where was your grandfather?"

She can hear Lucas speak, but it doesn't register. It's suddenly as if she's no longer here. No longer stuck on this raft in the middle of the ocean but is thirteen again, stranded between the light of the moon and the shadow of a monster crawling out from the darkness.

"I ... I didn't do anything at first. I was frozen. I remember feeling so *betrayed.* Not only did I feel stupid for putting myself in that situation, but I was so angry that my grandfather wasn't there, this man who had spent his entire life protecting me from what seemed more like ghosts of the past than actual humans. He wasn't there! He was *sleeping.* And there I was, with an actual ghost.

"The more the man whispered to me, the more frozen I became. Like if I didn't move, maybe it wouldn't happen. Or it wouldn't hurt. Or maybe I could disappear. And then he moved real close to my ear. The magnitude of his breath was like a megaphone. His lips touched my skin and my heart nearly stopped. He whispered, 'If you say anything or fight back, I will kill your grandfather.'

"He started touching me. His hand moved up my leg." Maia looks up at the sky, the contour of the moon now blurred through her tears. "I remember thinking that it would be the end for me. That I'd end up another young girl in a commune of old men. And I'd just have to accept it. That was just the way things were now.

"He pushed me onto my back. As he was turning to lie on top of me, there was a loud thump and he went limp and fell to his side. I looked up to find another young woman, just a little older than myself. She looked as scared as I felt. She was clutching a wooden board in her hands. We stared at each other in shock. I was about to say something, *anything*, but she stopped me.

"She said to me, 'Leave, and don't come back.' Not in a malicious way, but in a *kind* way. The old man started to grumble and lift his head. She dropped her board and we ran in opposite directions. I snuck back to my sleeping grandfather and crawled back into bed beside him. The next day the elder was 'sick' in bed with a 'headache,' and I begged to go home. I never told my grandfather what happened."

Lucas looks down. "I don't know what to say."

"I'll never forget the look in her eyes—that woman who saved me. It was like the life had been sucked out of her. Her eyes were so sad ... *hollow*. And I knew I could never go back. Whatever happened to her must never happen to me."

"How could your grandfather not know? How could he not see how obviously abnormal the tribe was?"

"We see what we want to see. He was so focused on his old age and on not leaving me alone. I think he wanted to see a bunch of men like him, taking care of each other. He wanted that to be the truth more than anything. I think he noticed the oddness of the tribe's age disparity ... but he couldn't really *see*.

"The thing is, my grandfather was adamant in teaching me not to trust strangers, to always stay hidden. He reminded me almost daily that the outside world was such a dreadful place. But for some reason he had this idea, *stuck* in his head, that we could find security within a trusted community like the Northern Tribe. He was blinded by his desire to keep me safe, and in turn led me into one of the most dangerous places on the island. What is that saying again? That everything you believe to be true, the opposite is also true? That woman had nothing to gain and everything to lose. But in the end, it was a stranger who saved me."

FORTY-ONE

Lightning flickers silently in scattered bursts from a dark corner of the horizon. Maia and Lucas lie side by side on their backs, completely silent. Besides the ominous black clouds in the distance, the early evening is calm, soothing. She tries to focus on this instead of her gnawing, almost mind-numbing thirst. Or that look on Lucas's face ... his brow furrowed, eyes distant, his mind seemingly battling against the weight of the world. She knows that look by now and decides to let him be. Folding her arms beneath her head, she breathes deeply and tries to reign in her focus.

The expanse above gently cascades from a pale blue into a soft violet as the sinking sun lassos the light from the sky. A delicate breeze sweeps across their raft, carrying the scent of rain.

Eventually, as darkness falls around them like a faint whisper, the Milky Way punctures the sky with its canopy of stars. A long-tailed comet burns across the glistening expanse and disappears behind the dark wall of ascending clouds.

Lucas is the first to break their silence. "It's so strange to think we are looking out into the universe. I wonder what else lies beyond our ancestors' explorations. I bet there was still so much our dying race didn't know."

"You think the human race is dying?" Maia asks.

Lucas sighs. "*I* don't think so, no. I think this may be a new beginning. After every extinction, a small percentage of the living remained. We are the new humans, Maia. We are the one percent who will evolve from this."

There is another flicker of lightning, followed by a low rumble of thunder rolling like a wave across them. It trails off into the distance.

"When was the last time you saw electricity?" Maia asks.

"When I was a child—our village still had some."

"How big was it?"

"How big was what?"

"Your village."

"It was one of the bigger ones I've seen while traveling the world ... maybe thirty people? We were surrounded by emptiness and the elements were harsh, so we had to stick together. It seemed to give us an advantage, especially when some of us still had electricity. But one by one, the homes with 'renewable' energy sources had gone dark. It was always the 'big news' around the village—whose house had finally caved in to the shadows. I guess things can only last for so long without the resources necessary for upkeep. The last time I saw a working lightbulb was ten years ago. What about you?"

"We had electricity for special occasions, when it wanted to work, but lightbulbs were limited. My grandfather wanted to make sure our life was sustainable without them so that by the time the last lightbulb went out, we wouldn't be affected. The last time he tried switching on a light, I was around ten years old—it didn't work. I barely remember it now," Maia says quietly. She continues staring up at the stars. "But I still think about it from time to time when looking up at the sky.

"Back in New Zealand, sometimes on a full moon, I'd sneak away in the middle of the night and head to our closest city, which was always an all-night affair, but I was *fascinated* by it. I'd walk the dark, littered streets, enamored by the broken streetlights. My grandfather used to tell me the bulbs inside would shine so bright, they'd illuminate the streets like sunlight.

"I'd wander past the city's gutted shops, full of dust and weeds and half-naked mannequins, and I'd try to imagine what it was like when they were brimming with life. Back when the broken things were once held together and the city lights glowed so bright they could be seen from space. My grandfather used to tell me stories about the cities. They sounded so magical."

"You would explore this place on your own?"

"I was always on my own. There was no one left."

The raft is silent, the only sound coming from the occasional choppy wave sloshing between the bins below.

"Anyway," Maia continues. "I'd follow the old railway tracks back home, mostly hidden under weeds and bushes. But there's a particular old station I really loved. It was covered in vines but had this beautiful red brick underneath. It had an old, ornate clock on the front of the building as well, forever stopped at 2:36.

"The station had cathedral ceilings and this gorgeous tile work on the walls, although half of it was shattered on the floor, but it wasn't hard to imagine the place in its original state. There was also an old grocery store..." She smiles. "I could just see the frantic people running in to grab some bread before they missed their train. '*Wait!*'" She giggles and flails her arms about. "'*Hold that train!*' And there was this coffee shop..." Her smile fades, suddenly embarrassed by her theatrics.

"To be honest, I'm probably giving it more credit than it deserves. The entire building was full of broken glass and weeds and rats ... it was quite pathetic, actually, but it seemed like it would have been a truly grand place once upon a time. I used to sit and daydream about what it would have been like to be there back then, when the paint was fresh and the coffee hot. I'd imagine I was waiting for a train to whisk me off somewhere new ... like I was meeting a lover or heading off to explore the world with everything I owned in a single pack. My favorite daydream was that I was leaving for university. What I wouldn't give to be able to learn at a university. With the whole world at my feet, endless possibilities..." Her voice trails off.

Lucas turns towards her and reaches for her hand. He holds it within his but says nothing.

Maia swipes a tear from her cheek. "How lonely it is to sit along the tracks for a train that will never come."

The raft rocks from side to side as Lucas sits up beside her. She watches him between the flickers of light. His head is in his hands.

"Lucas?"

He doesn't speak.

"Is it the storm? Do you think we should be worried?"

"I cannot. It is not possible."

Maia sits up. "What?"

Scrunching his hair in fists, he is shaking his head. "I can't do this anymore."

She leans forward, searching the darkness for his face.

"Lucas?" She touches his shoulder and he flinches. Alarmed, she pulls back. "Lucas? What's wrong?"

His shadow turns towards her. "Maia," he says sternly, then pauses.

Lightning flashes, briefly illuminating his eyes—serious, pained. *Glassy.* Maia is taken aback. A splat of rain breaks across her shoulder. Another low growl of thunder reverberates across the sea as their raft travels over a small swell.

"Maia," he says again. "I cannot hold back anymore. I can't. I *won't*."

"Hold back?"

He grabs her hand. "Never again, Maia. You will never be lonely again. *Ever*."

Her chin quivers as she searches the dark for his eyes. A gust of wind pulls at their tarp, flapping the tattered plastic in and out. A few more drops of rain splat against Maia's cheek.

"Maia." He grasps her hands and pulls her closer to him. "I'm coming with you—to The Old Arctic Circle."

Her breath catches in her chest and she glares at him, unmoving.

Another flash of light illuminates his eyes, staring intently into hers. "I never want to be in a world where you aren't in it, Maia. I will follow you to the ends of the earth. I am in this now..." He hesitates, then says quietly, "That is, if you will have me."

She exhales, overcome with emotion. Speechless. Releasing his hand, she reaches for his face, wanting more than anything to melt into him. "*Have* you?" she finally whispers, shaking her head. "If I'll *have* you?" Her eyes flicker back tears. "You have *me*, Lucas. You always have."

Thunder rolls through the air as the sky continues to flash, the expanse of stars now devoured by the clouds. The smile on Lucas's face fades. He holds her hand against his cheek and closes his eyes. Lightning zigzags across the sky, immediately followed by a ferocious clap of thunder.

Lucas leans in and his lips softly touch hers. Grazing at first, gentle. He cups her cheek with his hand, then traces his fingertips down the side of her neck and across her collarbone.

More flickers of light.

She runs her hands through his head of curls, then without reservation, wraps them between her fingers. Pulling him into her, she kisses him passionately. Wild. He reaches up and under her shirt, stretching his hands across her back. His breathing now labored, he pulls her body closer to his, closer, kissing her harder, faster—almost ravenous.

She straddles herself over him and he wraps his arms around her. The wind picks up and swirls around them, their battered tarp beating against the gusts. More raindrops spatter against her skin.

Maia grabs the sides of Lucas's face, tugging his lower lip between her teeth. The raft rides over another swell. Lucas peels off her top and whips it under the tarp. She holds his head against her as his lips move across her chest. Clawing at his back, she tears his shirt up over his head. The warmth of his skin is hot against her as they embrace under a sudden deluge of cool rain.

She craves him, yearns for him, overwhelmed by the strength of his embrace. He kisses the skin down her neck and her head falls back, awakening something deeply primal from within.

Lightning flashes wildly as the waves continue to propel their raft up and over their crests. Lucas moves with Maia and lays her onto her back. Her dark hair lies in wet ringlets across her face as the wind and rain whip around them. He peels off her ripped pants and she reaches up to grab him. He crawls on top of her and holds her tightly as she wraps her legs around him. She unbuttons his pants and shoves them down, gasping against his kisses. Another avalanche of water smashes down on top of them.

With his naked body on top of hers, Maia can feel Lucas hard against her and her skin scatters with chills. He grabs her face, looking into her eyes as the sky fills with flashes of light. A magnificent crack of thunder seems to split open the heavens. She grabs the back of his neck, arching her body against the raft as he moves inside her. Her other hand reaches above her head, tightly gripping the nets as Lucas envelopes her beneath him.

Lightning flashes.

Thunder crashes.

The storm rages on.

FORTY-TWO

Maia awakens to rain pelting hard against the tarp. Seawater jumps between the rows of buoys and bins beneath her, licking her skin in cool, brisk bursts. Chilled, she rolls over, reaching across the empty space beside her where Lucas had fallen asleep. Her hand lays hard against a large timber of driftwood criss-crossing their raft.

She turns to find Lucas sitting topless in the rain, his body silhouetted against the early morning light. His eyes focused, he funnels the water pouring from the tarp into an empty bin. Their crate of bottles, now secured between his legs, is completely full.

She wearily pulls herself upward, gripping the netting with both hands as the raft rocks from side to side. He stops, smiling tenderly through the onslaught of rain. Without saying a word, he grabs a bottle and hands it to her.

She desperately unscrews the lid.

"Please, take your time," he says above the rain, resting his hand on her foot. "You will make yourself sick."

She nods as she gulps down the water, stopping halfway to catch her breath.

"We have an entire crate full. Try to give yourself a min—"

But Maia is already finishing the bottle. She hands it back to him to refill. He curls the end of the tarp into a funnel and sticks it through the top. Maia watches him, a new wave of concern stabbing from within. The muscles of his arms, something she had memorized during all those weeks on the ship, have deteriorated significantly. His back slightly hunched, undulating waves of ribs now emerge from beneath his goose-pimpled skin.

Why hadn't she noticed this before?

They've gotten small dregs of food here and there, but clearly, it's not enough—and it's starting to show.

As he hands her the bottle, she is taken aback as he holds her in his gaze. There is something different about the way he is looking at her. Holding her. His demeanor has been stripped bare, like the final wall between them has fallen and he is now seeing her clearly for the first time.

Water drips from his curls and slides down his temple into a full beard. He reaches out and holds the side of her face with an overwhelming affection in his eyes. She holds his frigid hand against her skin. Turning into it, she closes her eyes and kisses his palm.

Oh, dear God, please let us live through this.

After she finishes the second bottle, Lucas fills it again. Her shrunken stomach is pained from the overload of water. She fights the urge to vomit.

"Go back to sleep," he whispers. "It's okay—I have this."

She lies back down. Keeping one hand gripped beneath the netting, she folds into a ball for warmth, hugging her bottle of water. A few minutes later, Lucas crawls beneath the tarp and curls his body around hers, wrapping his arm around her like a cocoon. She smiles and slips into a mindless slumber.

———

Maia awakens with Lucas's arm under her neck. She runs her hand along his skin until she reaches his wrist, then intertwines her fingers within his. This man. This man who risked everything looking after her in the storage closet of a ship. This man who dove down and pulled her from the depths of an ocean drowning in rubbish. And then last night, this man who held her while a storm raged around them.

His fingers clasp around hers. "Good morning," he says from behind.

This hand. This hand she wants within hers. Forever. "Good morning," she whispers through her smile. She flips around and lays her head on his chest, peering through the small opening of the sagging tarp to the exposed part of the raft. She dips her toes into the warm rays of the sun. "It looks beautiful out there."

"It is a beautiful day out," he says. Then chuckling, he adds, "How did we survive that storm last night? I can't stop thinking about it." He reaches across and holds her cheek, kissing the top of her head. "Or you."

She beams. "Was it pretty bad? The storm? I ... wasn't ... paying attention." Her cheeks flush with heat.

He delicately brushes the hair from her face. "It was definitely intense," he finally says. "But as far as storms go, its bark was bigger than its bite."

Her head still resting on his chest, she wraps her arm around him. Somehow, in the course of a single evening, the stakes of living through this nightmare have become even higher. She can't be sure if that makes her feel better or worse.

———

Maia's head pops above the surface of the ocean.

"Nothing?" Lucas shouts from the raft.

"Nothing!" Maia gasps. She swims towards him with an empty knife.

"Watch to your left! Jellyfish!"

"I see them."

Despite losing an obvious amount of weight, Maia's body feels heavy. Each stroke through the water has become laborious and draining. Lucas holds out his hand and pulls her back on top of the raft. She sits on the edge and hangs her head, wiping her eyes. "I'm just so frustrated. It's been *days* since we ate that small fish."

"Shall I give it a go?"

"Sure … although it's pretty tough. There seem to be a lot of jellies moving in tonight."

"Maybe I will spear from here then." Lucas leans back and pulls some spare strands of rope from a bin. He grabs the rod from the back of the tarp and begins tying the knife to the end.

"You're making a spear?"

"I know we can't spear far, but it will at least give us a bit more depth to work with." He stands. Gripping the rod with the knife attached, he peers into the water.

A buoy slips from beneath his foot and he staggers forward. Maia grabs his arm and they steady themselves. He flashes her a relieved look, then sits down along the edge.

Maia looks across the raft, uneasy. This raft has slowly

gone from sturdy and tightly packed to a bit loose and ... wobbly.

"It's okay, the knots are just tighter, so there is slightly more wiggle room." He winks at her.

She is unconvinced.

"Hey." Lucas squeezes her hand. "Everything is still holding, okay? Don't worry." He goes back to scanning the water.

She sighs. "Lucas, we have been fishing for days. There's nothing."

"*There.* I see something."

Maia follows the direction of his pointed finger. "It's a ... *fish*?" Maia whispers, stunned.

"I'm going to try. Get back." Lucas steadies himself on his knees along the edge of the raft.

Maia watches from behind, biting her nail. The small silver fish glides closer, a little deeper than the last. Maia's mouth waters at the sight.

Lucas hovers the blade just above the water's edge. He swiftly stabs into the ocean and misses. The fish scurries off in a panic.

"*Damn*," he mumbles, and Maia's heart breaks a little more.

Lucas's head tips forward as he nods off to sleep. The light continues to slip from the sky. Maia crawls over and slides the spear from his hands, startling him.

"Oh, sorry, darling," he says groggily.

Darling. She smiles.

"I can do this, sorry ... I fell asleep." He reaches for the rod.

"No, let me try. Take a break." Staring into the water, Maia *wills* a fish to come. They've practically burned their retinas from staring into this empty ocean for days but something has to come around sometime. It has to. It *has* to. She'll be damned if she misses it.

A glimmer catches her eye as that same silver fish has looped back around, drawn once again to the shade of the raft.

Maia lowers herself to her stomach. Gripping the spear, she repositions her hold, an animal-like instinct honing in. Clear as day, the fish glides closer. Closer. Maia tucks her toes beneath the netting. Holding the spear high above her head, she thrusts it into the water.

The fish swims off untouched.

Maia's frustrated moan curdles into a scream.

"It's okay. We will keep trying," Lucas assures from behind.

"No ... it's all ... *warped*—doing this from above. I *have* to get in. I can't spear with this stupid plastic." She sits up, fidgeting with the knot of the rope holding the knife.

"There are jellyfish around. I don't think we will see another fish for ages now," Lucas says.

She focuses on the knot. She's getting in that water.

"Maia, you cannot go in there. They could surround you."

"There's not *that* many jellyfish around—"

"There are, actually. Please—it's not worth it."

"Lucas, it's *fine*. I've been doing this my entire life. I'll be fine."

The knot loosens. Almost there.

"*Por favor*—" He grabs the rod and the lax rope is ripped from Maia's grasp.

"Oh—" she freezes. The blade slips from the weave and

drops between the buoys. Maia's breath stops. The edge of the knife's handle dangles from a rope.

"*Meu Deus*," Lucas gasps.

The blade teeters for a moment as the raft rocks against the choppy waves, then twirls halfway before *bloop*! It plunges into the ocean.

"*NO!*" Maia scrambles to the edge.

Lucas grabs her by the shoulders and yanks her back down. "Maia, *no!*" He holds her down as she wrestles to break free. "Maia! The ocean is teeming with jellyfish!"

She wriggles free, hysteria brewing, and crawls frantically back to the edge. Three mammoth jellyfish hover just below the surface next to their raft. Several large clumps of them have dispersed across the vast expanse, and that's only what she can see—there'll be more.

Sickened with horror, she presses her face against the netting and shoves her fingers between the buoys to peer beneath. Her precious knife—the only reason they have survived this long...

Gone.

Her breath escaping in short spurts, she searches the water below in complete disbelief as the three colossal jellyfish float casually into view.

FORTY-THREE

Two more days have passed.

Their water reserves are dwindling and they haven't eaten anything in nearly a week. Maia sits cross-legged in a sunken groove in the floor of their raft. Frayed ends of rope keep popping from the weave like weeds, something that used to send her into a panic ... until now. Biting her nail, she glares across the sea as mammoth black clouds quietly climb on top of one another like ravenous vultures at a feed.

Dread swims about her empty gut.

Lucas sleeps soundly under the tarp with his shirt wrapped around his head as a barrier from the nets. He is curled tightly into the fetal position, his backbone protruding from his sun-blackened skin. Every day he disappears a little more, both physically and emotionally. Fading down to skin and bones. Sleeping around the clock.

Quiet.

Caving in on himself.

Another flicker of light sparks from deep within the

expanding dark mass. It's been constant—the lightning, like a silent war waging within. The sea and wind are calm— eerily so. The sky is saturated in a bizarre hue of yellow ... almost green. The color of sick. The color of dread. It's as if the earth itself were preparing for an assault.

Thunder snarls from a distance. This feels different from the last storm. How different, Maia has no way of knowing, but it doesn't look good. The hairs on the back of her neck stand on end as she glares at the wall of approaching clouds, suddenly indignant. She knew this was coming—it was only a matter of time—but she did not come this far to become a casualty of another natural disaster.

This will not be the death of her.

This will not be the death of him.

This will not be the death of them.

This will not be the death of them.

This will not be the death of them.

"Maia?"

She turns to find Lucas sitting up. Pulling his shirt back over his head, his face is alarmed as he peers over her shoulder.

She stops biting her nail. "It's pretty bad ... isn't it?"

The color drains from his face.

"Lucas, what do we do?"

His eyes wide, they dart between her and the swirling, dark clouds. The look on his face makes her heart sink.

"Lucas?"

He surveys their raft—sunken, loose, frayed. He pulls on a tattered rope and ties it tight, then looks around the raft, clearly noticing for the first time how many loose ends there are. "Hold on, Maia," he says quietly, meeting her gaze. His troubled demeanor collapses to sorrow. "We hold on."

Maia crawls over to him, an arduous task across the sunken raft. A piece of netting unravels beneath her and she sinks to her chin. Panicked, she rolls to her side and quickly pulls the ends to tie them together again. Lucas watches her with sadness in his eyes.

"This is just a storm. Right, Lucas? We've survived quite a few already, this one shouldn't be any different?"

"Maia." He slowly shakes his head. "*That* ... those clouds." He pauses, chewing on his words. "This is not just a storm," he says in defeat.

She swallows hard, gripping the netting as the raft wavers beneath them, suddenly bullied by an onslaught of waves. They look at each other for a long time without speaking.

Thunder travels across the sea and a gust of wind bowls into them. The raft flows over a small swell. Lucas grabs the flapping tarp and lowers the center rod to flatten it. The rapidly advancing clouds devour the remaining light from the sky.

The raft travels over another swell and Maia and Lucas roll forward. Alarmed, she grips the netting and her fingers twist within the weave. Lucas bolts forward to grab the sliding bin of water. They brace themselves by lowering on all fours as close to the raft as possible.

A flood of rain suddenly spills from the sky. Maia watches Lucas through the torrent. Something in his gaze shifts and his fear is replaced by anger. He releases his grip from the netting and pulls her face close to his. "No, I am not going to lose you, Maia. Not now, not ever."

An overwhelming sense of sadness swells from within and Maia begins to sob. She holds his hand against her cheek.

"Maia, this is not the end for us."

You promise? Maia silently mouths as the wind and rain howl around them.

A wave smashes on top of them, pounding Maia into the raft as if a mountain of boulders has crashed on top of them. She coughs up seawater and Lucas grabs her chin, forcing her to look into his eyes.

"I promise," he says. He pulls her into him and kisses her as a loud snap of thunder fractures the air. Lightning stretches across the swirling sky. He crawls to the crate at the back of their tarp and starts handing her bottles. "Drink!"

Maia doesn't hesitate to chug them down and Lucas does the same, one after the other, all while bracing themselves against the endless combative waves. A gust of wind clutches at the tarp and it snaps back like a sail, pulling their raft backwards up a swell.

"Hold on, Maia! *Hold on!*"

Maia drops her face to the nets. Lucas throws himself next to her as the top of the raft lifts out of the water and then slams back down. Maia pulls at the netting. It gathers loosely in her hands. The tarp angrily snaps in and out as the rain continues to monsoon on top of them.

"Lucas!" Maia grabs the back of his shirt and shows him the netting between flashes of light. "Lucas, it's falling apart!"

The raft makes its way up another swell, sliding up the towering wave like a wall of water. Maia cries out as her legs slip from underneath her. They momentarily hang from the netting before slamming down onto the other side.

Maia can feel the buoys of the raft separating. "Lucas!"

"Hold on, Maia!" Lucas yells through the deluge. "The tarp!"

Maia looks up at the tarp, taut in the blustering wind.

Lucas crawls to the corner. The raft slides down another swell and his body rolls across the boards, slamming into her. With one hand gripping the nets, she grabs his shirt as he rolls towards the edge. He clutches at the loose nets as his legs swing out over the raft. The ocean waves hurl into them like fists of water pounding into their backs.

Lucas drags himself to the tarp and works at untying it from the raft. One corner flies up into the wind ... the corner where the last of their water was secured.

Gone. Everything is gone.

Lucas kicks in the prop holding up the tarp. Lightning flickers, followed by an instant clash of thunder. Lucas and Maia cling to the raft as it sails up another mammoth swell. Their legs once again slip from beneath them. Maia cries out, struggling to dig her toes into the ropes as the raft is pushed up, up, up until it flips on top of them.

The raging storm is muffled as the weight of the ocean envelopes her. Maia reaches for the tarp dragging beneath their raft and kicks ferociously towards the surface. Pushing her hand between the loose buoys, she clutches at the netting stretching across the exposed bins on top and gasps for air.

"Maia!" Lucas yells from the other side of the raft.

She takes a deep breath and sinks beneath the water, fumbling her way across the bottom of the raft to the other side. Breaking the surface, she gasps.

"Climb on top!" Lucas yells, clinging to the raft as unrelenting waves crash into him.

"The containers are too big!"

"Climb the netting!"

The upside-down raft sails over wave after wave as Maia struggles to lift herself out of the water. She grapples over the large plastic jugs that once sat below them. Lucas pushes her from below and she drops to the other side, splashing into the loose netting between the containers, now half-submerged beneath the water. Her foot slips between the nets and lands on a board of driftwood still secured underneath.

"Lucas!" She secures her foot on the plank and stands out of the water. Reaching over the large container, she finds Lucas still gripping the netting off the side of the raft. She pulls at his arm as they sail over another swell, thunder crashing around them like the air itself is splitting to pieces. Lucas rounds the top of a container. Maia screams as she uses all her strength to haul him over and he splashes to the nets below.

Lucas grabs her face and they focus on each other through the flashes of light.

They are still alive. Somehow, they are still alive. They travel over another swell, but the bins around them now provide a barrier from falling out. The raft is more stable upside down, although the sagging floor they now crouch on leaves them half-submerged in water.

Maia tries to keep her focus on Lucas as they brace themselves against the onslaught of elements. *This will all be over soon. Just hang on. Don't let go.*

Something catches her eye over Lucas's shoulder. A white dress appears from within the darkness. She squints through the thick haze of rain as her mother appears on the ocean, her white gown flowing in the wind.

Smiling, Maia reaches out her hand. "Mum?"

No—not her mother. It's *Maia*, that same vision of herself from her dreams. She is majestic, with fire-red, wild curls. Crystalline eyes. Her face fierce. Her skin porcelain. The water beneath her glimmers with bright blue embers and a peculiar grin spreads wide across her face.

Maia's heart begins to pound. To her horror, the water she sits in now also glistens with the same bright blue energy. Sparks fly out from the deep. Her tattered clothes have been replaced by the same white gown.

It's happening—that power. That power she's tried so hard to leave behind. That power she's spent months convincing herself was the land of New Zealand. But it wasn't New Zealand. It wasn't the trees or the bees or the whispers within the wind ... it was *her*.

The chaotic world around her dims into silence as she becomes acutely aware of the vibrant, universal life swarming around her. From the countless minuscule creatures in every drop of water on her skin to the surge of power and electricity blasting through the atmosphere, life streams through her as if there were no actual barriers of skin and water and sky.

Her wet auburn hair drenched across her face curls into corkscrews, transforming into bright red—*NO!* She scrunches her eyes shut. Lucas can't see her like this. This can't be happening. This isn't *happening*!

A familiar euphoric current surges from within. Bubbling up from the tip of her toes, it courses through her legs and up across her chest. Her skin tingling, icy-hot, burning from the inside.

Maia keeps her eyes closed, pleading for it to stop, that Lucas is not watching her at this very moment as her entire world unravels. What would he think? Her world would be over. He would know she was a monster, and how could anyone love a monster?

Maia focuses on harnessing this power and wrangling it down. Back. In. Down. Back. In. Like forcing an army of savages away from the gates. The visions slowly fade and her tingling fingers once again feel the cool, wet netting beneath them. Her world becomes loud and the wind once again batters her from all angles. Gripping the ropes around the containers, she focuses on breathing between the constant barrage of waves.

And Lucas's face. That puzzled look on Lucas's face.

FORTY-FOUR

Maia's head hangs shackled like dead weight from her bony frame. She reluctantly scrunches one eye open, and then the other, flinching from the intense glare of the sun. Lucas still sits hunched in front of her. Propped against the bins, he nods in and out of a daze.

His shoulders are burning.

They've been so diligent up until now in guarding against the sun, but their tarp—if it's still attached—will be trailing behind them beneath the water. They sit half-submerged on the loose and torn netting, hanging between an open square of large containers that once floated beneath them. Two pieces of driftwood still remain, along with a few clusters of buoys, but the raft as a whole has been destroyed.

And Maia's beloved rubber ducky is gone.

The bins that once propped their raft above the water are intact on three sides, but the fourth wall has torn from the middle and they've lost half its containers. Now, it will only be a matter of time before they lose the entire side. Their sunken floor of netting is the only thing keeping this whole thing together. Once that lets go, it will be the end for them.

The placid ocean sits peacefully around them. Lucas lifts his wobbling head and surveys the raft. When his eyes eventually meet hers, the devastated look across his face is unbearable. Maia looks away, fighting back tears. And so, they sit, neither one saying a word.

"Maia."

She awakens to Lucas's hand wrapping around hers. "Was it only a dream?" she asks, her voice cracking.

"We are still alive. That in itself is a miracle."

Opening her eyes, her heart breaks all over again. It wasn't a dream. "What now?" she finally asks.

"We have to get out of this water. I think we could try to maneuver the pieces of driftwood from the netting below and line them across our remaining three floating walls. We can tie them against the middle row, which will give us a wider ledge to rest on out of this water. We can drag the tarp back up as well—get out of this sun."

"Will it last through another—"

"No ... but it's all we have."

"Is there any way we can flip the raft back over?" Maia asks.

"I have thought about it, but it would be next to impossible to flip something this big in the water and with the ropes as torn as they are, it will only make them tear more. Not to mention we are losing that wall of bins there..." His voice trails off. "So, no," he says quietly. "There is no way to flip this raft."

She knows he's right. She knew before asking, but she

thought maybe it isn't as hopeless as it appears. They could untie the netted floor from the bottom of the floating bins and secure it along the top, turning their battered square frame into a triangle. But the weave is layered and intricately tied through the *top* of the containers—for easy maintenance—which is now underwater. They complicated the hell out of it on purpose, to give it more stability. The amount of work to untie it would take days and a vast amount of energy. Energy they don't have.

So, for now, their living space will dwindle down to the width of two logs of driftwood.

Maia chokes back tears.

"Maia, don't you dare."

"This is all my fault." She buries her head in her pruning hands. "I was warned ... over and over and over again. But I went anyway and then I took you down with me. Now look at us, Lucas! This raft is disintegrating—*we're* disintegrating. We're going to die out here ... and it's all my fault."

"What happened to my girl? What happened to 'there is always a way'? Don't do this, Maia."

She lifts her hand from the water and reaches for him as she quietly sobs. He gently kisses her palm before placing it against his sunken chest.

This beautiful human. She's done nothing but bring him pain and destruction. How could she be so naïve? For so long she thought she would find life out here ... she *knew* she'd find it. But she was wrong. And this world is destroying them.

"I've waited my entire life to meet you," she says quietly. "I just can't believe it's already over."

"It's not over." Lucas clutches at her hand. "Maia, look at me."

She refuses, holding her head in her other hand.

"The currents are pushing us, every minute of every day. Just a little while longer—"

"And this will all be over," she chokes in response. "Yes, I know."

Lucas dives under first. He doesn't stay submerged for long before coming up, gasping for air.

"What's wrong?" Maia calls from the raft, straddling a row of containers.

"It's just ... this is harder than it used to be," he yells breathlessly. He sucks in a deep breath of air and disappears beneath the glassy surface.

They spend the afternoon taking turns swimming beneath the upside-down raft, eventually separating the driftwood from within its weave and re-tying any swaying loose ends dangling along the bottom. Lucas climbs back over the barrels and they heave the large planks of drift-wood against the middle row of bins. With one next to the other, they now have a small shelf to lie on above the water. The width of the raft was designed to be based on the length of these logs—they were the sturdiest part—so they sit perfectly supported by the wall of containers on either side.

When they are finished, Lucas and Maia huddle next to each other beneath a dripping-wet tarp.

"Maia?" Lucas bites his lip.

"Yes?"

"Last night..." He shakes his head. "No, forget about it ... I must have been hallucinating."

Last night. Memories of the storm come flooding back to her. The glimmering water, the electric stream of power coursing through her, the world warping around her as the mirror image of her ... *smiled.*

"It's just..." he begins again.

Her heart pounds. She looks up at him as she grips the driftwood with trembling hands.

"For a minute, you looked ... *different*," he says.

Her heart hammers beneath her chest. "Different?"

"Yeah ... you did not look ... you looked..." He's stumbling on his words—something's wrong. "Back on the ship, we had this ... how do you say ... this *myth*. Well, a haunting, actually."

"A haunting."

"Our ship was ... haunted—by a *siren*."

Maia's mouth dries. "A siren."

He looks out across the ocean. "I know it sounds crazy, but the men swore by it. Quite a few of them saw her; some dreamed of her. She was absolutely stunning, alarmingly so, with bright red curls and a white dress." He looks directly at Maia. "And two different-colored eyes."

"Did you ... had you ... seen her?" Panicked, the skin on Maia's face begins to prickle.

"No. Although I thought I had ... on the afternoon you escaped your room in the middle of the day. Obviously, I was confused, as your hair is not the same, no white dress ... but I had no other way of explaining it. I just saw you for a brief second from the corner of my eye. But last night, during that storm in the flashes of light ... I swear to God, you looked *just* like her. Your eyes and your hair, even the dress. Just for a moment, I thought she was sitting across from me." His eyes search hers. "That's crazy, *yes*? Tell me I'm crazy."

"Yeah," she says, forcing a smile. "You're crazy."

Now would be the time to tell him. Tell him what,

though? *She* doesn't even understand. Up until last night, she had completely convinced herself it was all an illusion, something she was a spectator of versus the possible origin.

But maybe she could talk about it ... maybe she doesn't have to hold it in the way she has her entire life. Lucas saw her. Her grandfather never saw her, even when strange things were happening right in front of his face.

But Lucas *saw* her.

"Lucas—"

He waits for her to continue. That face, those kind eyes ... what she wouldn't give in this moment to protect him from any more harm. She would give her life.

"What is it, Maia?"

The words are right there. Just tell him he's not crazy.

But then, he may never look at her the same way again. This beautiful man. This one person in the entire world she loves more than anything would know she was a monster. He called their siren *alarming*. It would change everything. No, telling him would only hurt him. He could never love her knowing the truth. She would lose him—she would lose everything—all over again.

A fate worse than death.

"Nothing." She forces a smile, then softly kisses him beneath the protective shadow of the tarp.

He never has to know.

Days pass as Lucas and Maia float numbly on their tattered raft in the middle of the ocean. Their broken wall has finally lost its containers, so they now lie on a u-shaped line of bins connected by a half-torn, sagging net.

To protect herself from the heavy assault of the sun,

Maia has ripped off the bottom of her shirt and has it wrapped around her head. She sits hunched over in a daze, squinting across the endless ocean. Her head is pounding and her mouth is dry as a bone. Lucas's sunken belly rises and falls as he sleeps soundly next to her.

Her leg cramps again. She grimaces as she rubs the muscle. Eventually it relaxes and she lies onto her back, exhausted. Dizzy. Shivering cold despite the heat. "Lucas?"

His face slowly turns towards her but he does not open his eyes. His reddened cheekbones protrude above his beard, and his pale lips are cracked and peeling.

"Lucas? Are we going to die?" she whispers.

He peels one eye open and looks at her. His face is overcome with sadness, but he does not say a word.

———

"*So* thirsty..." Maia giggles as she flips her head from side to side. "So thir—Huck! *Stop*." She giggles again, lifting her foot up and down, up and down. "*Soooo thirsty*."

She opens and closes her mouth, clacking her tongue and grimacing from the taste. "Huck! Seriously? You're really starting to annoy me." She flips her head away as Huck playfully licks the bottom of her foot. "HUCK!" She kicks her leg down. *Hard*.

Intense, white-hot electricity sears up Maia's leg. She sits up, screaming in agony.

So confused. *Where*—

Somehow, she has wandered away from the safe driftwood ledge next to Lucas and is now on top of a low-lying barrel. Agonizing pain pierces through her body and she thrashes back, lifting her leg from the water.

Scanning across the horizon, panic sets in.

A bloom.

They are surrounded by thousands of jellyfish, tightly stacking on top of each other as if they had swallowed up the sea.

Swollen red lines trace around her ankle and calf. Gasping for air, an otherworldly howl pours from her mouth. Her stomach cramps violently and she doubles over. Gasping, wheezing—clutching her throat. Clutching the nets. *Writhing* in pain.

Lucas jumps across the netting. His voice rolls across her in waves. "*Maaaaaa—*"

Muffled.

Blurry.

Spinning.

FORTY-FIVE

A twig snaps from under Maia's foot. As she treads carefully down the familiar wooded path, the dead leaves beneath her shatter like glass. Countless chirping birds dance across the swaying branches above, flooding the sky with their song. Closing her eyes, she inhales the scent of rich, wet earth.

The smell of heaven.

The smell of *home*.

Overwhelmed with relief, she feels almost weightless from the sudden absence of *thirst*. Cruel and relentless, it's been a burden for months. Stretching her arms overhead, she gazes across the ancient pine and pōhutukawa trees. She knows this bush, this path in particular—she's walked it a thousand times. Her fingertips brush along an overhanging branch of a fern. The dew drips like rain from its tendril.

Entering a large clearing, her breath hangs in brief clouds in the cool mountain air. With an outstretched hand, she steps forward, her tears overflowing with each unbelieving flutter of her eyes.

Their same two wooden chairs sit on the cabin's old

sagging porch, with a cup of steaming tea resting on the table between them. Smoke pours from the chimney. Maia's mouth waters as the delectable smell of frying onions drifts across the yard.

A wheelbarrow full of chopped wood waits outside the cabin's slightly ajar front door, ready to be taken in. That door—the door she had closed and locked and held her head against as she said her tearful goodbyes, waiting for Huck.

She looks around the yard. Is Huck here? No—but neither is the grave in the corner. There are no char marks on the tree. It all looks ... untouched.

Maia watches in disbelief as her little black fantail lands on the cabin's mossy wooden fence. It flips forward and back, fanning its black and white tail.

"Hello, old friend," she whispers.

The bird stops and watches her with its head cocked to one side. A tūī swoops overhead. It dives below the tree line before disappearing down the path.

Behind her, the cabin's front door slowly groans open. A creak sounds from the wooden porch. Maia freezes, her heart pounding. A puff of smoke wafts past, lingering on the wind. Her breath escapes in short bursts.

Can't be.

She must be dreaming—but everything is all so real: the cool, damp earth beneath her feet; the intense, almost over-whelming sound of birds; the delicate warmth from the morning sun sieving through the trees. Another cloud of smoke drifts overhead and she inhales the nostalgic smell of pipe.

Slowly turning towards the cabin, her hand flies up to her mouth.

Maia's grandfather stands on the porch, watching her

through tear-soaked eyes. He's regained his weight but his gentle, weathered face is still the same. He smiles with a quivering chin and a tear slowly tumbles down his cheek. "Hello ... my darling," his voice cracks.

She bursts forward.

Her grandfather rushes down the steps as she runs across the yard. Extending his arms, he grunts as Maia slams into him. Her mouth gapes but not a single sound escapes. Her tears soak into his shirt. With a deep gasp, she wails a deep and solemn cry.

"Oh, my sweet child." Sobbing, her grandfather holds her head against his shaking chest. "My sweet, sweet child."

"Grandpa, I thought you died! I burned your body..." She looks up at him, tears streaming down her cheeks.

"I know, child."

"I never thought I'd see you again." She buries her face into his chest. "I've missed you *so much*."

"I'm right here, darling. I've never left you."

She keeps her arms wrapped around his body, no longer frail but sturdy. Strong. The way it was for so long until the end. "Grandpa ... please let me stay with you. *Please*? If even just for a night?"

"I wish you could," he chokes. "More than anything."

"Grandpa?" She looks up at him. "Where am I?"

His face saddened, he shakes his head. "Somewhere you are not meant to be," he says.

"What do you mean?"

"Child, this place is not meant for you."

Her eyes cast down. "It's really bad, isn't it?"

"Don't give up, Maia. Fight!" His voice is suddenly quiet —far away.

"Grandpa?!" Panicked, Maia clutches at his fading shirt. "*NO*! Don't leave me!" she screeches as her grandfather slowly disappears before her. "No, please! *Please*! I'll do anything!"

"I am always with you."

She throws herself upon him but falls to the ground. Pounding her fists into the earth, water splashes back at her. Startled, she opens her eyes to find herself lying atop a calm blue ocean, the familiar abandoned skyscrapers towering beneath her. A white dress flows across her clenched fists.

"Hello, Maia." Her mother holds out her hand.

Maia stands, unsteady, and gazes across the large body of water surrounding them. The cool water laps the top of her feet.

"Maia."

Stunned, she turns towards her mother. "Am I ... am I *dead*?"

Her mother smiles and tenderly brushes Maia's cheek. Closing her eyes, she brings their foreheads together.

Maia gasps as her entire life flashes before her. She and Lucas huddled together on a raft made of garbage as an onslaught of waves crash on top of them. Shivering alone in the dark basement of a ship. Kneeling before her grandfather's burning pyre as a fury of ashes fall around her. Tending tomatoes on a wobbling wooden stool, her grandfather observing from over her shoulder. Giggles floating down an ancient trail as she runs through the bush as a young girl.

"No, child." Her mother touches their foreheads together again. "*Remember*."

Maia's eyes burst open, but her mother no longer stands before her. She sees herself as a child, giggling as dozens of birds land across her outstretched arms, her grandfather watching in shock from the front porch. As an adolescent, she sits cross-legged in the yard, mesmerized as the blades of grass bend and move under her hovering hand. Tripping over a tree trunk, a branch swipes across her chest to catch her. Flashes of shimmering energy coursing through her from the veins of the earth. Waking at dawn under a thick weave of branches protecting her from the previous night's storm. Slamming her fists into the ground and the entire earth quaking in response.

Maia returns to herself, huddling in a quivering ball on top of the ocean. New lights shine forth from the city below and the tower's beacons flash across the dark haze of the sea. Maia holds her breath, bracing herself for the floor to shatter, plunging her once again into the darkness.

"Come," her mother says, still standing before her, but Maia doesn't move. "Maia, why are you so afraid to acknowledge who you are?" Her mother reaches down and helps her to her feet.

"What is this?" Maia whispers, peering into the submerged city below.

"*This* is your destiny..." Maia's mother lifts her chin.

"I don't understand."

Her mother brushes the tear from Maia's cheek. "You've spent your entire life being afraid of your power, always ignoring or pushing it down. But *you* ... you were made this way ... *on purpose*. This is who you are. Continuing to deny it will only cause you more pain. You've escaped into the stories of your books, wanting more than anything to be like everyone else. But you are not like anyone else. Trying to be anyone other than yourself is squandering your own magnificence."

Her mother steps aside, revealing the reflection of Maia behind her. Terrified, Maia cowers back.

"You don't have to be afraid, Maia," her mother says sternly. "She is only a reflection. This entire world and everything in it is only a reflection of what lies *within.* Once you finally understand this, you will know what it is like to be truly free."

Reaching out a single trembling hand, Maia softly grazes her reflection's face. Her hair is different, curled tightly into delicate ribbons of red, but her eyes are the same. Her reflection stares blankly ahead as if she were made of porcelain, and for the first time, Maia no longer sees a monster standing before her but a creature of exquisite beauty.

Her mother stands aside as Maia gazes into her own eyes and her entire world reflects back to her. Her childhood. Her fears. Her hopes and every soul-crushing dream. Everything she is and everything she ever has been echoes from deep within her eyes.

"Your life is divinely inspired, Maia. You have risen from the depths of the earth and have a power unlike anything this world has ever seen. You have finally found your voice. *Use it.*"

Maia turns towards her mother. "What do you mean? *Who am I?*"

"You are the reincarnation of a living Earth, long forsaken. You are *her.* You are the soul of the trees, the heartbeat of each crawling ant, the breath of every humming bee. You are the music of the babbling brook and the pulse of each undulating wave. You are the spotted clouds of deep red sunsets and every reflective crystal of white mountaintops. You are the delicate drop of rain and the crushing avalanche of ice. You are all of it."

As her mother's voice fades, a dark world appears before her. The world as it is now—violated, flooded, void of life, *abandoned.* And then the world of their ancestors—fast-paced and brimming with life. The earth like a plane of fractured glass, buckling under the pressure from billions of hungry people always demanding more.

A sharp pain resonates from deep within Maia's chest, and then another at her back, her head, her lungs—as if being stabbed repeatedly across her body. She doubles over as the ache of the world devours her from the inside out. Terrifying visions flash mercilessly before her. Oceans swelling, crawling inland, overtaking barriers and devouring cities. Unprecedented weather events rising up across the world, slamming against the earth repeatedly with relentless, indignant fists. Mass migrations of billions. Wars over land rising up from the dead. Social structures fracturing under the weight of unfounded chaos. Limited food supplies from over-burdened soil, flooded land, pillaged oceans.

And then there it is, the proverbial straw, falling like a feather on a plane of splintered glass; a single mutation from a creature long forgotten. And for the first time in hundreds of years, nature's decree of checks and balances is restored.

In the end, there is silence.

Heaving for breath, tears coat her cheeks. It all makes sense now. The faded red Xs on doors. The ghostly quarantine buildings. Her grandfather's horrified face and refusal to speak. She can see it all, catastrophic and swift.

Then, relief showers over her as the world before their ancestors reveals itself. An oasis. Life growing and thriving. Then an ice age. Mass extinction. Oasis. Ice age. Extinction. Like a beating heart, life sprouting from the earth and then retreating back. The same life force traveling throughout all living beings, burgeoning since the dawn of time, born from a single exploding moment.

Maia opens her crystalline eyes. Her long white gown

flows into the ocean as a shimmering, expansive energy streaming through every living thing surges from the depths of the earth and up through her veins.

Delighted, her mother watches from a distance. Maia laughs and lifts her hands to the heavens as a vortex of ocean swirls around her and into the sky.

"You hold within you exquisite power, Maia, both nurturing and destructive. You are still young; you need time yet to harness your energy. Trust the journey, trust the gut pull you feel and follow it above all else, whether it's deemed logical or not. This will not be easy. Soft at first, your intuition will strengthen as you use it.

"And Maia, you *must* guard against your temper. As you become more powerful, so will it. Do not be fooled by what your eyes see; you are more than the skin that binds you and the bones beneath your chest. You are not who you think you are—you are so much *more*."

Maia gasps, and the entire world flashes before her.

FORTY-SIX

I nhaling deeply, a foreign air swirls around Maia's lungs. Extending her legs into a gloriously long stretch, she curls and uncurls her toes and reaches her arms with fingers wide beneath the sheets, unfurling as if she were filling the hollow bones of a body long vacated.

The earth below her sways back and forth, telling her that wherever she is, there are still waves beneath her. She flutters open her heavy eyes to a strange room blanketed in a bizarre light. Dozens of stacked boxes line the walls across from her bed. A small, rectangular window above them displays the blue horizon, slowly see-sawing back and forth as the ship coasts along the wide ocean crests. A large oval mirror hangs above a weathered hutch in the other corner of the crowded room. The cot laying at its feet is piled with a stack of crumpled blankets.

Maia turns towards an object on the small bedside table to her left, her eyes wide in awe. *A lit lamp*, shining away. She reaches up to touch it but is tethered by a cord extending from the vein of her right hand. A crisscross of tape is holding it in place. The cord attaches to a clear bag of liquid hanging on a metal hook next to her bed. She has clearly been cared for, and for a while, as she notes her skin is no longer blistered, her stomach no longer suctioned to her bones.

Something moves at Maia's feet. She sits up and a wave of relief steals her breath away.

Lucas.

Draped across the foot of her bed, he sleeps with his head nestled on top of his folded arms. His long, sun-bleached curls have been trimmed away; his thick beard shaved down to stubble. His lips, gently parted as he sleeps, are no longer cracked and peeling, and his sharp cheek-bones hide once again beneath his cheeks. The tattered rags she last saw him in have been replaced by new clothing.

She smiles. He looks like the Lucas she first laid eyes upon not so long ago in the musty basement of a ship. Back when they were strangers to each other. Back when it could never have occurred to her that in facing this journey, she would be stripped bare, forced to her knees to the brink of death. That every long-held dream and every deep-set fear would simultaneously collide, shattering her from the inside out. Like some sort of exploding supernovae, she would be made anew, discovering hidden deep within the folds of her worst nightmare was everything she was always meant to be.

And now, everything has changed. She has had a glimpse of who she really is, although she doesn't fully understand yet what that means. She holds her hands out before her, fighting the urge to rip the needle from her vein. She's still human; this is for certain. Yet, she is more than that ... a reincarnation born from the soul of the earth.

It all makes sense now. The unimaginable force of nature she could harness when her emotions ran wild. The constant visions of her true self, desperate to break free from the fear that has for so long kept her shackled within.

All she knows in this moment is that her destiny—stronger than ever—still calls her to The Old Arctic Circle. Her mother told her the answers will be found on the journey and to trust her instincts, even when rendering no reason.

Lucas stirs but does not wake. She knows she must tell him the truth and in doing so, she may lose him, a fate she fears worse than death. But she has no choice. He deserves to know, and she cannot hide anymore.

Lucas opens his eyes, drawing a sharp breath as he focuses on her sitting before him. He stumbles over himself as he rushes to her side. "Maia," he sighs. Holding the sides of her face, his eyes are wide and glassy. "You are awake, oh my God—" He tenderly kisses her. "*Meu Deus*," he whispers as he kisses her lips, her cheeks, the tip of her nose. "*Thank you, thank you, thank you.*"

Maia is overcome as she is engulfed within Lucas's warm embrace, yearning more than anything for this single moment to last forever. She places her palm against his cheek, her heart breaking a little more as his tears crash into her.

"You have no idea how worried I've been," Lucas whispers. He lays his head on her chest. "Your poor heart is beating so fast."

Maia runs her fingers through his soft curls as she stares up at the ceiling, clutching for the last dregs of her rapidly crumbling composure. "You've cut your hair," she says finally, her voice hoarse and broken.

Lucas sits back, snorting through his tears, and they share a smile. "Yes, darling," he says as he wipes his eyes. "I finally decided to get a haircut." He pulls his chair closer to her and they stare at each other for a few quiet moments as the ship softly groans around them.

"Lucas, where are we?"

Clasping her hand within his, he kisses her fingers. Then he looks up at her, grinning like a child. "A boat picked us up. *A boat,* Maia. Sometime after..." The smile slips from his face. He sits back into his chair, his eyes searching hers.

She swallows hard. "After ... *what*?"

His brow furrowed, that familiar look of worry returns to his face. He shakes his head. "No," he says. "You should rest. We can talk later."

"Please, Lucas, let's talk now. Explain ... all of this." She sweeps her arm across the room, once again distracted by the cord still tethered to her hand. She pulls at a curled end of the tape.

"Maia—leave it. You still need fluids."

Exasperated, she drops her hands into her lap. "Lucas. *Explain.*"

He sucks in his lips and sighs, running his hand through his hair. "Maia," he says somberly. "What do you remember?"

Flashbacks of their tattered raft flash before her. The crushing heat. Overwhelming thirst. Lucas's burned and sunken cheeks. Searing pain. Gasping for air. *The jellyfish.* "There was a bloom ... I was stung?"

"Yes. You remember that?"

"Of course."

"And?" Lucas leans across her bed, grabbing her hand.

Her eyes well as she recalls her grandfather's tear-soaked face, their cabin, the smell of smoke, and the crisp grass below her feet. And then there was her *mother.* And then ... and then there was... "I'm..." she chokes. "I'm not sure." She can't. Not yet—*please not yet.*

Lucas sits back with his head in his hand. He takes a deep breath to speak, his brown eyes gazing into hers. Hesitating, his lips part but the words remain trapped.

There is silence.

"Lucas?"

"I keep thinking I must have been dreaming," he says finally. "I *must have.* We were so close to dying. I slept a lot, I know this. Everything was a blur towards the end ... but I will never forget you being stung. Never. I remember it clear as day. I know it happened ... but your leg—there is *nothing* now."

Maia's brow knits together. "What do you mean, *nothing*?" She whips back the sheets, exposing her legs extending from beneath a plain nightgown. No scabs, no scars, not a single trace of a sting. Confused, she looks up at him. "Lucas, I was stung."

"Maia..." The color drains from his face and he leans closer. Grasping her hands between his own, his eyes well with tears. "*You died.*"

"*What?*" she whispers.

"You died," he repeats quietly, his breathing now labored. "I know it sounds crazy, but I will be haunted by it for the rest of my life. You were *seizing* in my arms. I was using all my strength to keep you from falling off the raft. Your skin," his voice cracks. "You started turning blue. And then—"

His face is horrified as the words slowly fall from his mouth. "You stopped breathing. I was holding your head, giving you mouth-to-mouth. I was shaking you, *screaming* at you. You were not breathing!" He stops and looks at her like he doesn't recognize her anymore. "And then your *eyes.* You opened your eyes and they were ... they were like crystal. I nearly dropped you. Your hair ... your hair turned bright red and spiraled into a million curls right in *front* of me!" Anger flickers across his face. "You were the *exact same woman* I saw the night of the storm." He shakes his head. "And then you suddenly gasped this deep breath and..." He falls silent. His hand is in a fist at his mouth and his glassy eyes quiver.

"Lucas?" *This isn't happening.*

"When you breathed out, every *single* jellyfish surrounding us died. The entire bloom just ... *floated* to the surface."

Suddenly lightheaded, Maia's heart pounds beneath her chest.

"And then you fell unconscious. I swear I stared at you for hours. Even now, I still think I must've been dreaming. I *must* have been. But the jellyfish? And your leg? Every day I think about it, every day I try to convince myself that it must have been some sort of hallucination brought on by exhaustion or dehydration. People see all sorts of crazy things when they are starving to death. But what about your leg, Maia? A sting like that, if it doesn't kill you, would take *months* to heal, you would scar for life ... but it was like it never happened."

Maia gazes across her legs.

"Maia, I am going to ask you again. Did I hallucinate?"

She sits in silence, staring at her legs. *This is it.* She has to tell him—no more lies. She looks up at Lucas and his beautiful face blurs through her tears. "You didn't hallucinate."

"I didn't. I *know* I didn't." He sits back in disbelief. "What *was* that, Maia?" A twinge of indignation taints his voice.

She can't speak. He's fading before her eyes; she can feel it. The walls are rising between them once again as he sinks back into the shell of the man she first met on the ship.

"That stuff doesn't happen in real life, Maia. Books, yes —not real life."

"I wanted to tell you, Lucas, I've wanted to tell you for so long. I've experienced glimpses of it before, but I just didn't understand."

He looks at her with equal tones of fear and confusion.

"*Lucas.*" She reaches for him but he's cold as ice. She pulls back. "Lucas, I'm still the same girl. I just ... sometimes..."

"Well, hello there." A petite young woman has peeked her head into the room. Her black hair is neatly tied into a bun, her spectacles pristine. "Oh, thank *goodness*. I was really starting to worry about you."

"Maia, this is Claire. She's been caring for you," Lucas says. His voice is flat, void of emotion. He adds, "She is the only reason either one of us is still alive."

Maia shakes Claire's hand. "Thank you. Thank you *so* much."

"Of course. I'm just glad we found you when we did."

Maia glances back and forth between Claire and Lucas. "So, where are we?"

"We found you, both passed out, floating on a half-sunken raft about five hundred miles off the West Coast of the United States. Lucas woke as we were hoisting him on board," Claire says.

Lucas glares at Maia as Claire talks. Maia flashes him a pleading look and his face softens.

"We were on our way back from South America," Claire adds. "We were picking up people and supplies from our old village."

"Back?" Maia asks.

"Maia," Lucas says softly. "They are from The Old Arctic Circle."

Maia looks up at Claire. "*What*?"

Claire smiles tenderly. "We live up in The Old Arctic, dear. We are more than happy to take you with us if you'd like."

Maia looks at Lucas and he nods reassuringly.

Claire puts her hand on Maia's shoulder. "Lucas has told us about your journey. You have come a long way. Please rest. I'll make you some soup." She latches the door as she exits.

Maia stares at Lucas, wide-eyed. Speechless.

His hardened demeanor fades and he sighs, placing his hand on top of hers. "You can talk to me, Maia. I am not sure what happened that day or the night of the storm, but I have had a lot of time to think about it. There is nothing you can say that will make me stop..." He falters, his face suddenly flushed. "You can talk to me," he says.

"I will, Lucas. I promise I will. I just..." Her chin begins to quiver as she battles against an onslaught of tears. "I just need a minute. This is all *so much*."

"Okay. I'm sorry. Please rest. But Maia—" He lifts her chin so they are eye to eye. "I am here. *Okay*? I'm not going anywhere."

Overcome with relief, her head drops into her hands and she collapses to her side. Her body trembles as she sobs.

Lucas rests on the edge of her bed and gently lifts her by the shoulders. She falls into him. Laying her head against his chest, an ocean of tears permeates his shirt as he gently rocks her back and forth.

FORTY-SEVEN

Gazing out of the small cabin window, tiny glittering stars tiptoe across the early evening expanse. Her breath racing across the glass in undulating waves, Maia cranes her neck, searching for a glimpse of the moon. She finds it low in a faraway corner, like a cratered bow caught in the fabric of the sky. She sighs, tightly grasping her mother's jade necklace in a fist at her chest. They're safe. They're on their way. They're going to be okay.

This is all so *surreal* ... she can't wrap her brain around it. It seems like only a moment ago they were slowly dying, drifting on a half-sunken raft in the middle of the Pacific Ocean. And now? They are on a ship headed to The Old Arctic Circle.

She had died, both physically and metaphorically. She has seen the beginning and the end, stretched her fingers wide across the breadth of the heavens as the soul of the earth surged through her veins. Water streamed from the depths of the oceans, enveloping her like a cocoon as it curled and twisted into the abandoned hollows of her bones, leaving her born anew. Something inside her has shifted. It feels like she has been reunited with a long-lost love, and for the first time in her entire life, she is no longer afraid.

Laughter once again erupts from down the hall, with both men and women's muffled voices intermingling into a messy jumble of sounds.

Maia quietly slips back into her bed and pulls the crisp blankets up to her neck, relieved to finally be free of the needle in her hand. She smiles, basking in the glorious comfort of the plush mattress and inhaling the scent of freshly washed sheets. After sleeping for months on a cold floor in the musty basement of a ship, a rotting island made of plastic, and a netted bundle of bins and driftwood, she can rightly admit—never has a bed been more comfortable.

A sliver of light streams in from beneath her door, along with wafts of roasting meat. Her mouth waters. She reaches out to touch the cool metal of the bedside lamp beside her and a harsh, artificial light bursts forward. Shielding her eyes, she swipes at the lamp's base until she is once again blanketed in darkness.

Peeling back the sheets, she slides out of bed and plucks Lucas's sweater from the end of the cot. She pulls it over her gown and heads for the door.

Following the scent of roasting meat, she shuffles towards the end of the narrow corridor. She slides the pocket door open. A dozen strangers huddled around a crowded kitchen table simultaneously look up at her.

"Maia, hello," Claire says warmly.

The man next to her stands, his enthusiasm similar to the men of the Northern Tribe. Maia fights the urge to recoil.

As Lucas stands from the opposite end of the long table,

the legs of his chair screech against the tile floor. He walks over and wraps his arm around her. "It is nice to see you awake," he says softly. "Are you okay? I was going to bring you a plate."

"No, it's okay—I'm fine," she whispers, taken aback as the entire table stares at her. It's been years since she's seen this many people at the same time. "I thought it would be nice to join you."

"Great!" The man standing beside Claire motions Maia towards the table. His smile is wide and greedy. "Come. *Sit*. I'm Jake." Slightly older than Lucas, he has a light speckling of gray through his hair. He is undeniably attractive with a haughty air of arrogance. Something about him makes Maia immediately uncomfortable.

Another young man leaves his seat next to Lucas's empty chair and grabs a spot across the table. He nods with a smile and introduces himself as Mario as he takes his new seat.

Lucas grabs a plate and piles it with mashed potatoes, steamed beans, and a leg of roast chicken. He places it before Maia and kisses the top of her head. After days of nothing but soup, she has to restrain herself from diving into the plate headfirst and shoveling the food in with her hands.

"Maia, we've heard so much about you," Claire starts. "Maybe we'll go around the table and introduce ourselves."

"I'd love that," Maia says as she scoops a heaping spoonful of mashed potatoes into her mouth.

"I'm Claire. I'm one of only two doctors in the village where Jake and I are from. He came back for me so I could be properly trained at the university up north. I'll have to work for my schooling, so I probably won't go back home for another five years, but once that's finished, I plan on starting my own clinic and medical school."

"Uni—" Maia chokes on her words. "*University*?"

"Pardon?" Claire leans in.

"There's a university?" Maia asks again, tears surfacing.

Claire smiles. "There is. It's small ... well, the campus is massive but there are apparently only a few people to run it. They're still building it up. Once we get it all going again and I have the right team in place, the technology should be close to where it was before The End."

Maia looks down at her food, now blurred through her tears. There's a *university* there. An *actual* university.

Lucas rubs her back.

"Is she okay?" someone whispers across the table.

"She just needs a minute," Lucas responds, leaving his hand on the small of her back.

As Maia devours her meal, she discovers the eclectic group of people around her are mostly orphans as well, in search of a better life. A few people are already from The Old Arctic Circle, crew members to accompany Jake in his journey. He is a representative for his village in search of a more sustainable community. He had traveled up a year ago with Mario.

"So, what's it like up there?" Maia asks as she cleans her piece of chicken down to the bone.

"They're rebuilding," Jake is quick to answer. "They've named the city Leucothea."

"Leucothea ... like the Greek Goddess who protects sailors?" Lucas asks.

"I suppose so." Jake shrugs. "It was originally founded by some hippies, so the name is a bit romantic, if you ask me. But it's run by a new government now. They call it *The New System*. The city has this massive wall around it."

Maia stops cutting her beans. "A wall? Why would they need that?"

"Just want to have more control about who is coming and going. It's still pretty rabid out there. But everything is relatively new and a lot of special systems have been put in place considering ... and there's still snow in the winter. That's pretty epic. It's exciting but I wouldn't say it's magical." Jake chews on a piece of meat.

"I disagree," Claire interrupts. "I think at a time like this, to see people coming in from all over the world to gather together *is* magical. It's magical that we are even here at all."

"*Nah* ... humans are resilient. *Strong.* We'll make it out of this, thriving like never before," Jake says, winking at Maia.

Maia glares at him. "As long as we don't 'thrive' like we used to, I think we'll be okay."

Jake's eyebrows raise and an amused smile curves up from his lips.

"So, what is it like then, this *New System*?" Lucas asks.

Maia tears apart a bread roll, shoving a large piece into her mouth.

"I think it's best to discover it for yourself, to form your own conclusions," Jake says. "That's what I've told everyone here. Leucothea may not be for everyone, but they still have renewable energy sources. It's pretty amazing to see a touch of the life our ancestors used to live."

"And you traveled up by foot?" Lucas asks.

"And boat."

"What was that like?" Maia dips her bread into the potatoes and shovels it in despite her quickly filling belly.

"I guess a little bit of everything," Jake answers while eyeing her. "Land near the equator is unimaginably hot and barren. We tried to sail past it but a storm hit and our boat didn't make it. We were prepared, stuck close to shore and had a small lifeboat that got us to land. That was about halfway up the West Coast of North America, so it was still pretty hot. It was a long, *long* journey."

"You stuck close to shore you say?" Lucas chimes in. "What did you do about pirates? They love those areas."

Maia looks down at her plate and cuts her last few pieces of food.

"We have more, Maia," Claire whispers.

Maia's head snaps up. "*More*?"

"Maybe give it a minute. You haven't eaten much in a while." Lucas rubs her back.

"Honestly, I feel fine!" Maia excuses herself from the table, stumbling to grab another roll.

"We ran into them once or twice," Jake says.

"Once or twice," Lucas repeats flatly, a hint of suspicion in his voice.

"Yeah," Jake replies.

The two men eye each other and an awkward silence ensues.

"The world out there was pretty rough," Mario says with a sigh. "There were some real dangers, some crazies too ... especially around the condensed areas like the West Coast of the United States. But there were good bits too."

"Rare," Jake scoffs.

"Lucas ... *Lucas*. Every time I hear that name, I think of that crazy man we met in the United States," Mario continues.

"*Hmph*," Jake snorts. He leans back with his hands behind his head. "Which one?"

A few chuckles resound around the table.

"The one that broke his leg and never left. And he wasn't actually *crazy*." Mario absently pushes a few beans around his plate. "He wasn't." He gazes up at the ceiling. "He's the oldest *young* man I've ever met." He turns towards Lucas.

"He kept going on and on about his brother, *Lucas*. 'Must wait for him. He's coming. I know he's coming.' We kept telling him, 'Mate, your brother's dead.' But he wouldn't hear a word of it."

"What did you say his name was?" Lucas asks.

"We didn't. Never told us," Mario says.

"He did," Jake interrupts. "Marty or Michael ... *Miguel*. I think it was Miguel."

"He was South American?" Claire asks.

"Brazilian," Jake says.

Maia stops chewing.

Lucas's eyes are fixed intently on Jake. His jaw clenched, a light dew of perspiration has gathered across his forehead. "What else did he say?" Lucas asks.

Jake shrugs. "Lucas, Lucas, Lucas." He leans on his elbows. "Apparently Miguel's brother lost his wife and kid in an earthquake. Some village by the Chilean border. Watched them get buried alive inside their home and then spent days digging them out."

Lucas drops his fork. It clinks loudly as it falls to the edge of his plate and flips to the ground.

Maia leans towards Lucas. "You didn't tell..."

"No. I didn't," he says quietly.

"Apparently, Miguel's brother ran off in the middle of the night." Jake shakes his head as he cuts his soggy beans without looking up. "Left Miguel without saying a word," he chuckles. "I almost admire his tenacity."

Lucas pounds his fists against the table, clinking the crammed flatware together.

"What the *fuck*?" Jake looks up from his food.

"*Lucas...*" Claire reaches across the table. "Did you lose your family in an earthquake?"

"Where is he?" Lucas asks.

"Who? The crazy man?" Jake smiles.

"Please stop calling him that," Mario interjects.

"Don't know," Jake says, going back to cutting his vegetables. "Somewhere in the mountains outside of LA. We took the back roads to stay away from thieves and kooks."

"I can draw you a map," Mario chimes in. "I remember it plain as day."

"What happened to him?" Lucas's voice is steady, quiet.

"He was with his family," Mario answers.

"*Was?*"

"Yeah. I don't ... I don't know the extent of it, but it's just him now. He broke his leg," Mario continues.

"Did they just *leave* him?!" Lucas raises his voice.

Mario rubs the back of his neck. "No, they..."

"They died," Jake interjects, baiting Lucas for another reaction. "They were attacked by a mob. Pretty gruesome from what I heard."

"*Jake.*" Claire backhands his arm.

"It's the truth." Jake shrugs, still watching Lucas from the corner of his eye.

"Anyway," Mario continues. "He found this cabin in the woods to heal and never left. I think whatever happened really scarred him. So, he's up there alone. We really owe him. I'd be happy to help you find him."

Maia watches Lucas. His breathing strained, the worried look behind his eyes is fading. Calculating. "I have to get off," he states as a matter-of-fact.

"*Lucas?*" Maia clutches at his arm as he stands from the table.

Jake's face lights up. "There *ya* go, man. Go save your little bro!"

"Who do I have to speak with to get off?"

"The captain," Claire answers quietly. "He's upstairs."

Lucas shoves his chair away.

"I'll draw you a map," Mario says, standing to join him.

"Lucas?" Maia whispers, panic swelling from within. She reaches for his hand but he is already out of reach.

"Thank you, I really appreciate it," Lucas says as he heads for the door with Mario trailing behind him. He pauses for a moment, briefly turning towards Maia. She *wills* him to look at her but he turns away. Sliding open the pocket door, he disappears into the darkness.

FORTY-EIGHT

Maia's legs dangle over the edge of the giant sleeping boat. The moon's reflection scatters across the ocean, flickering in sporadic bursts as tiny waves jump up in a race to kiss the sky. A gentle sea breeze brushes against her skin, tousling her hair from her shoulders. She sighs and gazes up at the velvety black sky, placing her thumb over a bright crescent moon cracked open on its side.

Behind her, the deck's door slowly creaks open and then latches closed with a loud, metallic *click*. Footsteps sound behind her, followed by a disheartened sigh. She drops her hand into her lap, turning her head towards him in acknowledgment.

Lucas sits down next to her and flips his legs over the edge. Her heart suddenly pounding, she cannot find the strength to look at him.

"I'm sorry," he says quietly.

She doesn't respond, afraid that should she speak a word, she may shatter into pieces like the moonlight across the sea.

"I'm sorry I didn't tell you. I just wasn't ready to show you that side of me."

"Yes, well..." She swipes at a runaway tear. "I suppose that makes two of us holding back."

There is a long silence as the ocean gently laps the side of their boat.

"Maia." The pain behind Lucas's voice is agonizing.

She looks at him.

"What am I supposed to do?" he asks her with pleading eyes.

She looks away, her heart and head waging a fierce battle. She should say something to him, something to ease his pain. She must—but she can't. She closes her eyes and holds her breath as she fights back tears.

"Maia—" He grabs her hand and she swipes it away.

"Please don't," her voice cracks.

"Okay," he sighs. "I will tell you everything. My father left us for The Old Arctic Circle when I was very young." He leans across the boat's railing and peers up at the stars. "He left us for something he knew *nothing* about."

Maia nods her head in response. It's all making sense now.

Lucas continues. "I saw him leave in the middle of the night. I ran out screaming in a panic as he tiptoed into the darkness outside our tin hut. He didn't come back into the light for a few minutes—I was sure he was gone. But then he came back and crouched down so we were face to face. He told me not to worry and to take care of my mother and Miguel, that I was the man of the house until he came back. I was seven years old. We never saw him again."

"I'm sorry, Lucas. I had no idea."

"We did all right. My mother was young, but she was fierce. She never let us see her feelings about my dad leaving, but I overheard her crying most nights for what seemed like a very long time. We were left with nothing.

"My younger brother and I were the only survivors of nine children. We lived next to an abandoned library. When my brother was out foraging, I was in the library, studying English, studying everything I could get my hands on. He gave me a hard time about it for years but as we grew older, we started to realize how much we needed each other."

"Your brother, Miguel?"

"Yes, he became my best friend. Then my mother got sick. She just needed antibiotics. I was sure of it. If we could just find her some antibiotics, she would get better. Miguel and I searched for weeks as she got sicker and sicker. There was a powerful gang in the next village that we heard may have some. Antibiotics ... they were like gold. We decided to barter with them, said I could fix their solar panels. They were the last people in the area with working electricity but it was fading from something faulty within the lines ... or the panels themselves. They were beginning to panic, so they were quick to agree.

"I worked for days and all hours of the night. As I grew tired, some of the men started to harass me, telling me I was wasting their time. Tensions were high. Miguel got into a fight with one of the men after seeing him slap me on the back of my head. Miguel was badly beaten. It took us all day and night to hobble back home.

"Once I got Miguel settled, I went back. Begged them to let me in. I continued working for weeks for a solution to their problem. When I finally figured it out, I ran home with the pills. I ran like I've never run in my life—panicked, nearly mad with desperation. When I arrived, Miguel was digging our mother's grave."

Lucas swallows hard, blinking fast. "It was just the two of

us after that and things were different. I had failed my family. I couldn't save my mother and my little brother was angry. He had looked up to me, he depended on me, and I had failed him. He did not look at me the same after that, and I was young and guilt-ridden and thought it would be best if I left. So, I left. Just like my father. In the middle of the night. Without saying a word."

He shakes his head, his eyes burdened with tears. "Jake had the story wrong. My brother was not there when I left my village after my wife and son died. He must have shown up afterward in search of me. He would have seen that I was a coward when I was younger and I am still a coward."

"You're not a coward, Lucas. You're the most incredible person I've ever met."

He grunts. "You haven't met that many people."

"You should stop being so hard on yourself," she whispers.

He turns away, toying once again with the braided bracelet around his wrist. It's one of the first things Maia noticed about him back on the ship. He stops and looks up at her. "It's from Miguel. He made it for me when we were young but I never wore it. I brought it with me when I left him and carried it around for years. I tied it on when I left South America. It was always my intention to find him again. I looked for him in every port on the small chance he was out looking for me too. I have thought about him every single day of my life."

Maia looks out across the ocean. She knows what is coming, and she knows there is nothing she can do to stop it.

"Maia, this is something I have to do. He is the only family I have left, and he is up there all alone." His voice breaks. "And it is all my fault."

"Lucas—"

"I cannot *stand* the thought of him up there in those woods alone, waiting for me. It's *killing* me. I let him and my mother down. I was weak. I left him. And now he has no one." He turns towards her, grabbing her hand. "Maia, please."

She glances at him briefly, then looks away. "I know, Lucas."

"You are safe here. These are good people. They will take you up to The Old Arctic Circle. I will find my brother and then we will come for you."

"I know." Facing him, she brushes a curl from his eyes. "I know this is something you have to do. As much as it hurts me, I understand. I could never ask you to stay. You wouldn't be you if you continued north knowing he was all alone in those mountains."

Lucas holds her face in his hands. "I will not stop until I am by your side again, Maia. You are my life. You are my *everything*. I will find my brother, and we will come for you. Okay? Nothing can stop that."

Tears stream down her face. "I don't want to live without you, Lucas."

"We will be right behind you."

"But it's dangerous out there. What if something happens to you?"

"It won't."

"You don't know that."

"It will be okay, Maia. It will be okay because it *has* to be. I will carry him on my back if I have to."

"Lucas."

"I will do whatever it takes to be right back next to you. This boat will take you to safety. You can find us a good home, and I will be right behind you."

"I could come with you?"

"Absolutely not." Shaking his head, his face is resolute and stern. "I knew you would say that. No, it's too dangerous."

She looks up at him. "How long?"

"What?"

"How long? How long will you have to travel now by foot?"

"We are currently just outside the old United States. They are going to sail in a little and send me out on a small raft."

"A *raft*?"

"It's okay. I won't be too far from land. I have a map and supplies. I will find Miguel and then we will head up to The Old Arctic Circle."

"How long, Lucas?"

"I am not sure ... maybe a year."

"*Lucas*—" She drops her head in her hands.

He wraps his arms around her as she sobs. "I just don't feel I have a choice. Please understand, Miguel is my family. I cannot fail him again. I could never start a new life with you up north knowing ... please understand."

Maia pulls away. "Find your brother," she says. "Find him and come back to me. Promise me you'll come back to me. *Promise me*."

"I promise. I promise you with every last beat of my heart." He kisses her and then he pulls away. Gazing down at her, he whispers, "I love you, Maia."

She closes her eyes. A fate worse than death. She felt losing him would be a fate worse than death, and she was right. "I love you too, Lucas." She places her forehead against his. "I'll love you forever," she whispers. "And I will wait for you."

FORTY-NINE

Maia gazes into her reflection across the antique oval mirror on the wall. She smiles, sweeping away a red curl from her face. Reaching out a single hand to the glass, she traces the mirror image of scattered freckles across her cheeks, the curvature of her nose, her shimmering blue eye and then the green.

As she pulls her hair off her shoulders, her jade necklace catches on a curl, then falls across her neck. She loosely braids her thick hair off to the side, then leans towards the mirror.

The last time she stared at the reflection of her carving, she was sitting on the edge of her floating dock back in New Zealand, waiting impatiently for a fish that would never come. Huck, of course, stood watching from the shore. She had spent her entire life hiding from the light emanating behind her eyes, the same light reflecting back to her now. Never could she have imagined the journey that lay ahead. Never could she have imagined who she truly was. Not just a young woman from a small secluded island at the ends of the earth.

No—more.

So much more.

A knock sounds from the other side of the door. Her curls fall and the light dims from her eyes just as Lucas peeks in.

"Hi." He smiles and closes the door behind him.

"Is it time?" she asks nervously.

"Not yet."

"Good. Lucas, I wanted to talk to you about what you saw ... *on the raft.*" She sits on the edge of her bed.

"Okay." He settles next to her.

Her cheeks prickle in anxiety and she pauses, wringing her hands. "I'm not really sure how to say this."

Lucas grabs her hand. "Maia, I saw everything. *Everything.*" He lifts her chin. "And I am still here. There is nothing you can say that will change how I feel about you."

She stands to face him. "Lucas, I am not who you think I am."

He smiles. "Okay then, who are you?"

"I think ... I might be ... the soul of the earth—*reincarnated.*" Her cheeks flush.

His eyes narrow. "What, like ... *Mother Nature*? Or some sort of Earth goddess?"

"No. Like ... *Maia.*"

"I don't understand."

"I don't believe there has ever been anyone like me, although there have been myths. I think I have come to give a voice to all that have lived in silence. I am here to make a stand."

Lucas watches her through narrow eyes, his mouth slightly agape. "A ... *stand...*"

"I know it sounds crazy. I *know.*" She stares at her feet as the silence of the room closes in on her. "Please say something," she finally manages to breathe.

He rubs the back of his neck. "Okay, so ... you are an 'incarnation' of the earth. And you have powers? Clearly, you do."

"I have ... power over..." She stumbles on her words. "I *think* I may have power over the elements of the earth, but I've only experienced glimpses. I don't fully understand it yet, but I'll figure it out as I go. That's all I know."

"Are you ... *human*?"

"Yes, I'm human. I'm still me, Lucas. I can still get hurt and I can still die. I still feel embarrassed and vulnerable and afraid. I still love." She smiles. "My life is still my own."

Unblinking, Lucas glares at the ground. Their long silence is broken as footsteps pound across the floors above. The boat begins to slow.

Lucas stands and walks over to her, wrapping his arms around her waist. "I *see* you. As crazy as this sounds, nothing you have said surprises me. I was there. I saw your power. I saw everything. I have had a lot of time to come to terms with this when I wasn't sure you would ever wake. I have told you before and I will tell you again—I love you, Maia. I am in this now."

Running her hands through his curls, she smiles through her tears. "You have me, Lucas. You always will."

The morning sun pours through the window of the small room. Lucas lifts her off her feet and she wraps her legs around him, kissing him tenderly as he carries her to bed.

A knock sounds from the door. "Lucas?"

"Yes, we are here!" Lucas yells.

Maia's head is on his chest. She closes her eyes in dread.

"Come upstairs. There is something you should see."

Maia and Lucas quickly dress and head down the hall towards the stairs. He holds open the door at the top.

As Maia steps onto the sun-drenched deck, the horror of their foreign surroundings steals the breath from her lungs.

The boat is slowly weaving its way between a dense forest of half-submerged skyscrapers, rising like skeletons from a dark and stagnant ocean. The blinding sun glints off their glass and a black and green slime creeps up the buildings from the murky depths below. A seagull soars beneath a tangle of low-hanging vines, draped between the buildings like cobwebs.

"*Lucas.* Where—"

"We are in the United States," Lucas says quietly. "They used to call this place 'Los Angeles.'"

"This is *America*?"

Maia gazes across the jungle of flooded high rises. Any abandoned floors not submerged beneath the water have been consumed by bushes and weeds. A few dark souls peer down at them from obscure corners behind busted windows. They flinch back like savage cavemen when seen.

"There are people up there," Maia whispers.

"Don't make eye contact."

As they continue to sail down the narrow corridors, the boat's crew members scramble to clean the litter from tearing through endless draped vines. Jake leans over the railing to push their encroaching bow away from another building's rusted antennae. A seagull lands on a moss-covered cross emerging from its church beneath the sea.

On the deck below, a few crew members have been preparing Lucas's raft. Claire carries over a large pack filled with supplies and drops it inside. Mario tosses a rolled-up blanket on top.

"My whole life, I've dreamed about The Old Arctic Circle ... *Leucothea* ... before I even knew it existed," Maia turns to Lucas. "It's all I've ever wanted, and we are *so close*. And now you're leaving. It doesn't seem right to continue on without you, Lucas. It just doesn't feel ... *right*."

"*Maia—*" Lucas grabs her hands. His lips parted, it seems he wants to say something. He hesitates.

Jake calls out, "Lucas! We can't go any farther."

Lucas squeezes Maia's hands. He glances back to his raft and the crew members waiting to help. Swallowing hard, he turns towards her. "I guess it is time," he says.

Maia nods her head, unable to look at him. Her vision blurs around the edges and a tear slides down her face.

"Maia." Lucas lifts her chin. "I *promise*—"

She throws herself around him.

"*Lucas!*" Jake calls from below.

Lucas grabs her face, kissing her one last time. She wipes the tears from his cheeks. "*Okay*," is all she can manage to gasp.

Lucas opens his mouth to speak. Then shaking his head, he wipes the tears from his eyes before walking away.

Trembling, Maia stumbles to the railing of the upper deck as Lucas runs to meet the crew below. Jake puts his arm across Lucas's shoulder and they shake hands, exchanging a few last words.

Maia grips the cold metal railing, feeling as if she is going to be sick. Lucas and Jake each grab an end of the raft and drag it towards the edge of the ship. With the help of a few others, they drop it overboard.

Maia gasps as she sobs. *A fate worse than death.*

Lucas glances up at her one last time. Stepping over the railing, he climbs down the ladder and disappears over the ship's edge.

FIFTY

Maia remains frozen on the top deck of the ship. The wind picks up, whipping her hair across her face as her trembling hands grip the railing. She keeps her gaze fixated on the water below the front corner of the boat, gasping when his raft finally appears.

Heaving the paddles back and forth, Lucas rows farther and farther away, his weary eyes never once leaving hers.

Her hand covering her mouth as she sobs, she watches as her love travels deeper into a foreign and dangerous land. This could be the last time she'll ever see him. She could grow old up north, never knowing where he is—never hearing his laugh again, or listening to the beat of his heart as she lays her head on his chest. She may never know if he found Miguel. Or if he's lying in a ditch somewhere, alone and in need of help.

An intense, instinctive pull tugs deep within her gut. Calling her. Battering her from within like a frantic caged bird. It's the same pull she felt when deciding to leave the safety of New Zealand for a treacherous journey across the unknown. The same strong impulse that urged her to jump from a pirate ship into an ocean of garbage. The same intuition her mother instructed she must listen to, whether logical or not.

Trust the gut pull you feel and follow it above all else.

And she knows.

Her heart pounds so rapidly in response, it nearly bursts from its seams to scream at her face to face. *You must go with him.*

She needs to yell out, tell them to stop the ship, get Lucas's attention to turn around.

Maia remains frozen. Get off this ship? This ship that will be delivering her safely to The Old Arctic Circle within the week? She has always known that is where she belongs. She *knows* that is where she must go. How could she possibly get off? No, Lucas will rescue his brother and they will come for her. She can make a home up north and wait for them.

The thought of this crushes her. *Wait?* How could she possibly sit and *wait* for him? She came all this way to be a part of something far greater than herself. To find others like her and to join a community. To connect and build something from the midst of ashes and decay. A life was calling out to her, and it was her duty to find it.

And find it she will. But what would any of it mean without love? She could go north and create a beautiful home, attend university, join this community where she would thrive ... but what would any of that matter without Lucas by her side?

His raft appears smaller now.

The crew on the boat have hoisted the sails and the ship slowly moves back out of the drowned city. Maia rushes to the other end of the deck, keeping Lucas in her sight as the ship continues its full turnabout.

Her gut is screaming at her. *Screaming.*

"Stop," she says quietly, taken aback as the words leave her mouth. Looking around, panic suddenly overtakes her.

Jake yells orders at the crew and they pull at the ropes. The ship picks up speed from its grand white sails.

"Stop," Maia says again, a little louder this time. The ship turns a bend and Lucas disappears from her view. "*STOP!*" Maia screeches. "Stop! I have to get off!"

The ship's bewildered crew members glance between each other but the ship forges ahead. Maia races down the outside steps connecting the upper and lower decks. Turning the corner, she runs into Jake.

"Maia!" He seizes her by the shoulders. "It's okay," he says, his face inches from hers. "Lucas will be okay. He'll meet us up north. You're safe here."

His greedy smile causes chills to run up Maia's spine. She struggles to break free but his grip is too tight. Claire runs up to them.

"Claire! I need a raft! Where is another raft?!"

"There are no more rafts, Maia." Claire's face concerned; she reaches out her hand. "Come. You're understandably upset. Let's make you a cup of tea."

Horrified, every minute Maia spends on this boat is another minute Lucas rows away from her. "Let me go, *please!*"

More crew members gather around them, whispering about this sudden hysterical woman they've taken on board. Claire and Jake grab Maia's arms and lead her towards the cabins.

"No," Maia whispers. "No, no—this is wrong. This is WRONG!" Her world begins to spin and her legs give out.

"She's about to hyperventilate. Someone grab me a bag?!" Claire shouts.

Maia frantically twists around, arching her back as Claire and Jake drag her towards the door leading downstairs to her cabin. "*No*. I have to go with him!"

"Maia—"

"You're not *listening* to me!" An indignant anger burns from within. Maia digs in her heels and turns towards Jake. "Let. Me. *Go*," she says through a clenched jaw.

Jake turns with a smile but his face breaks with alarm. He releases his grip and stumbles back. "What the *fuck*?"

Claire follows suit. "Jake? What—"

Maia doesn't waste a second. She rushes back to the railing, spotting Lucas's raft gliding past the old church. She can still catch up. She turns back towards Jake and Claire. "I need another ra—"

She stops. Jake's face is now angry as he whispers to a worried-looking Claire. She nods her head and they slowly walk towards her, holding out their arms as if corralling a wild animal. "Maia, it's okay. Let's sit you down," Claire sings in her most soothing voice.

Maia twists where she stands. "*Lucas*! *Wait*!"

But Lucas is too far away; he can't hear her anymore. Her heart pounding, she grips the railings and steps over to the other side. Her toes jutting over the edge, the sheer drop below causes her head to spin.

"Maia, *don't*!" Claire screams from behind her.

Maia breathes deeply, electricity surging through her veins. Whispers of *yes!* surround her and she releases her grip. Falling forward, she dives headfirst into the foreign waters below.

Kicking to the surface, she gasps for air and a wild smile spreads across her face. She looks back to the ship in astonishment. The crew members run to the railings in alarm. Claire is yelling out to her but Maia turns her focus to

337

Lucas. She places one arm in front of the other and begins to swim.

Claire continues yelling, "Maia! Please, Maia, stop—"

Maia dives beneath the surface. Gliding through the water, she opens her eyes to the submerged city below. This city ... *so familiar.*

This *city...*

She stops. Her eyes dart back and forth as she scans the otherworldly scene: rusted-out cars piled in the streets, an overturned school bus ravaged by seaweed, a small school of fish swimming past ghostly cafés. The fire hydrants and parking meters and yellow dashes of street paint peeking out from the swirled layers of sand.

This is the city from her dreams.

Maia has spent her entire life walking these underwater streets despite never having been here. It was always *Los Angeles.* She has come full circle. She is *exactly* where she is meant to be.

As Maia comes up for air, a loud horn sounds repeatedly from the ship behind her. She looks towards Lucas, now standing on his raft and shielding his eyes. He quickly sits down and turns his raft around, rowing back towards her. She dives beneath the ocean once more and kicks with all her might, spinning through the waters above the city from her dreams.

She has a distance to go, but she has always been a strong swimmer. The buildings' antennae beneath the water begin to flash like beacons, steadfastly guiding her through the darkness. Every stroke she takes only strengthens her resolve.

Just keep kicking.

Don't stop kicking.

FIFTY-ONE

Coming up for air, Maia gasps as the commotion she's caused assaults her from every angle. Lucas calls out from his raft, rowing towards her as frantically as she is swimming towards him. Behind them, Claire is still yelling. The boat's horn blasts out another deafening blow.

Maia sinks below the water's glassy surface and glides down the drowned streets of Los Angeles. It is so peaceful down here. Away from the noise of the boat, she can hear herself think. Streetlamps flicker as she passes and she twirls through the water, propelled by some great unknowable force. She swims back to the surface, swallowing a mammoth gulp of oxygen before flipping her feet into the air and sinking back down.

The outline of Lucas's raft is so close. His oars lift from the water and he yells out for her.

Maia kicks back to the surface. "Lucas!"

Lucas stands on his raft, shielding the sun from his eyes. He spots her and picks up his oars once again.

Paddling over a streetlamp blanketed in seaweed, an

overgrown tendril wraps itself around Maia's foot. Her startled screams echo off the mossy towers.

"Maia!" Lucas's panicked voice travels across the water. He dives off his raft.

She flips to her back and kicks the green ribbon from her ankle. "Lucas! I'm okay!" she calls out breathlessly.

"Maia!" Lucas yells as he swims towards her. He is so close. So close.

"Oh Lucas, I couldn't. I just couldn't!" she sobs as he approaches.

He grabs her outstretched hand. Pulling her to him, he kisses her as they tread the water. "Are you okay?! What happened back there?"

"I'm coming with you," she pants.

He looks shocked. He glances back to the ship as he catches his breath. "Come on, let's get you to the raft," he says.

Lucas hoists himself on board, then reaches for Maia's arm. He pulls her up and she falls on top of him. Grabbing his face, she kisses him, her wet arms folding him into her embrace.

"Oh, Maia, I am so sorry. Rowing away from you was one of the hardest things I have ever had to do."

The ship's horn blows out another menacing blast behind them.

She lifts off him. "You have to start rowing, Lucas. Row away so they know I'm not coming back."

His face conflicted, he sits up, glancing between the ship and Maia. "You are not going back? No, this is too dangerous. I could never..."

"*You* didn't—I did. This was *my* choice."

He looks at her, shaking his head. "Maia ... are you *sure*?"

"More than anything."

He peers behind her to the dark and tangled terrain awaiting them. "What if something were to happen to you, Maia? I could never live with myself."

"Safety is an illusion, Lucas. Something could happen to me at any time. All that matters in this moment is that we are together. We can do *anything* together. I know this now."

Lucas's head falls into his hands and they sit in silence on their small raft. When he finally looks up at her, he smiles, surprising her. "Okay, my love," he says. "Okay, yes. We do this together."

The horn sounds again in three long calls. Maia turns to see the ship sailing away. Relief showers over her.

"Maia ... what happened?"

She looks at Lucas. "I jumped," she responds nervously.

He leans back. Clutching his head with both hands, he gapes at her with equal tones of shock and amusement. "Oh my God. Honestly, Maia, you have *got* to stop doing that."

She twists her hair to the side, wringing out the water. "I just suddenly realized, with all the danger and the uncertainty that lie ahead on this journey, that there are two things I know without a *shadow* of a doubt."

Lucas stops rowing. "Okay..."

"The Old Arctic Circle is my destiny."

"Okay."

"And so are *you*."

His eyes glassy, he looks away. "Maia, if anything were to happen to you..."

"Nothing will happen to me," she says sternly. "We will make it to The Old Arctic Circle. I *know* it."

He looks at her for a long while before responding. Leaning across the raft, he tenderly brushes a tear from her chin. "Okay, yes. We do this together," he says with a smile. "But can you promise me one thing?"

"What's that?"

"From here on out, no more jumping off ships."

She smiles. "If you jump, I jump."

His eyes narrow. "Okay," he says as he begins to row. "But to be fair, *I* never jumped."

Maia bites her lip. "Touché."

Lucas slowly paddles through the drowned city streets. Now outside the cluster of skyscrapers, the smaller buildings remain mostly submerged, opening the expanse of water ahead of them. They pass by what seems to be an unending, crumbling brick warehouse covered in moss and a thick web of vines.

A small shirtless boy with his thumb in his mouth watches them from behind a half-destroyed brick column. Dirt is smeared across his face and his brown eyes are wide and curious.

Maia begins to say something and Lucas rushes to cover her mouth. "That boy won't be alone," he whispers. "*Don't say a word.*"

When Maia glances back, the boy is gone.

The water begins to shallow into streams. Fallen road signs unearthed from soggy street corners slump on top of rusted vehicles. One- and two-story derelict buildings stretch along the bloated streets, with massive holes like puncture wounds collapsing in from their decomposing roofs.

"Okay, I think this is where we walk," Lucas says quietly. "Take this." He holds out a sheathed knife. "Now we each have one. Place it somewhere out of sight but easy to grab."

"Thank you." She tucks the knife into her back waistband beneath her shirt.

Lucas steps out of the raft and the water rises to his shins. Maia hands him his pack and he throws it on his back before helping her over.

"You nervous?" she asks as she dips her foot into the water.

"A little." He shrugs. "You?"

"A little."

They quietly wade through the swampy streets, taking each step as deliberately as possible to avoid attracting any unwanted attention. The city is eerily quiet, the only sound coming from a seagull calling from above.

Ahead of them, the water recedes, revealing dampened soil and a partly hidden trail leading up to a wooded hill.

"Shall we check this out?" Lucas whispers. "I need to get my bearings."

"Let's do it."

They trudge through the marshy bank onto drier land where rotted-out tree trunks litter the trails and old vines cloak the trees like netting.

"Doesn't look like anyone has been up here in ages," Lucas says while tearing down a vine.

"Should we still go up?"

"We won't go too far—I just need to get a visual of the city to make sense of the map Mario gave me."

Hiking the overgrown trail, Maia's heart skips a beat. An animal-like instinct takes over and the hairs on the back of her neck stand on end. She slows her stride and scans the trail behind her.

Lucas stops. "Maia?"

"Yeah ... I just ... it feels like someone is following us."

"What did you see?"

343

"Nothing." There are eyes on her, she can feel them. "I just ... have a feeling."

Lucas backs up, step by step, until he is standing next to her. He slowly pulls out his knife. They stand motionless and search their surroundings.

A few branches break in the distance and Maia releases her knife from its sheath. An eagle flies through the trees, disappearing above the canopy. They both let out their breath, laughing nervously.

"Okay," Lucas whispers. "We should keep moving."

He leads the way down the path, crawling over downed trees and pulling vines as they go. Every step they take, that ghostly feeling that they are not alone follows her. Turning a corner, they come across an abandoned shed.

"Stay here, I will go see if there is anything we can use from inside." Lucas slinks from view to the front of the shed.

All the hairs on Maia's body rise. She doesn't know how, but she knows whoever has been following them is still lurking, and she knows he's a male. Carefully grasping her knife, she holds it before her as she scans the ruined forest, listening for movement.

As her instincts continue to kick in, her sense of hearing and smell intensify. The crystalline energy of the earth appears, flowing through the trees in streams. Her hair draping across her face spirals into a dark red before her eyes.

The intruder creeps up from behind, breathing shallow, nervous breaths. His eyes focus on her and he crouches down. She slowly turns on her heels with her hand outstretched and the foliage bends to her command.

Then she stops, releasing the vegetation. The trees groan as they return to their upright stance.

She steps towards him, still anxiously cowering behind a

cluster of bushes. An intense maternal love washes over her and she drops her knife to the dusty ground. She shoves back the prickly twigs.

Cowering before her, his head lowers to the ground and his ears pin back. He whimpers as his piercing yellow eyes take in the sight of her and he sniffs in her direction.

Maia stands frozen before the adolescent tiger. "My God," she breathes.

A gust of wind swirls through the battered forest and a peculiar grin spreads wide across her face.

Read on for an excerpt from
The Burn of a Thousand Suns
The Forgotten Ones Book Two

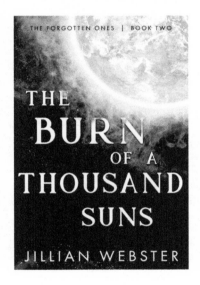

Available August 2021

PROLOGUE

A cloud of dust billows from Maia's feet.

Like everything else around these parts, the gravel has shriveled up. Caved in. Crumbled to dust like hollow bones of the earth.

A mirage of water hovers along the horizon in a tsunami-like, metallic wave. The hot air blowing across them is like the inside of a furnace, the heat so intense it nears suffocating. Every step is a struggle. It's as if Maia's legs have been wrapped in lead, weighing each foot down to the ground the moment she lifts it.

A scorpion scurries across the road.

The endless desert highway they now roam has been swallowed in oscillating mounds of sand; the scorched earth cracked open like a gaping spider's web. Any cement left exposed to the elements has been ruptured by the crooked arms of barren shrubs, desperately clawing from beneath the rubble.

Maia casts a glance at Lucas. A red cloth is wrapped across his nose and mouth like a mask, a thin layer of sand glued to the areas wet with condensation. His tired eyes squint against the early evening sun, hovering like a demonic orb suspended in the brown haze of sky.

Another gust of sand hurls across them.

Maia motions her hand to catch Lucas's attention. He nods and she tosses him her staff. He hands her a small rag. They've been switching the two items every few miles. The staff doubles nicely as a walking stick. And with just a flick of the wrist, the rag can swat away the relentless black flies, frantic for the moisture of their skin and eyes.

Maia's face is also wrapped with a bandana, now matted and drenched across the bridge of her nose. Her auburn hair has been tied into a thick bun on top of her head, which not only keeps her cooler but also protects her scalp from the harsh rays of the sun.

A black shadow flickers across them as another circling vulture curls on a wing. The birds have been tracking them for miles, ready to swoop the moment one of them crumbles to the ground.

Maia reaches for her steel canister, secured with rope against the side of her pack. She brings the hot metal to her lips, delicately sipping the warm water and swirling it around the taut skin of her mouth. Her teeth crunch on a piece of sand before swallowing it down.

The vulture circles around again.

This California desert road has felt endless, but the wide-open expanse—albeit harsh—has been a blessing. It takes a tremendous amount of energy to constantly be on guard, and out here, they've got none to spare.

But the harsh terrain also filters out the crazies, so they don't have to worry as much about malicious bandits taking something they hold dear. There are no half-breeds —*bounders*—hiding behind seemingly innocent, rotted-out vehicles abandoned on the side of the road.

Like that one car back in LA, with the juvenile cotton-wood exploding from the hood.

With every skeleton of a vehicle they approach, they each take a side, splitting around it with a wide and cautious stance. So far, there has only been one body found out here and he was far from alive. The only threats on this road seem to be the scorpions and the rattlesnakes—and even *they* want nothing to do with the lethargic, shuffling humans.

A rusted sign on the side of the road lies crooked and covered in layers of sand. Lucas swats the dust from the faded green metal.

Seattle 994 Miles.

Nine hundred and ninety-four miles. Maia's heart sinks. Having grown up with kilometers, she's not as familiar with the unit of distance, but she knows the number isn't good. They've been in America for over two months … and they've only traveled less than a hundred miles.

Of course, most of that time was spent hiding within the treacherous streets of Los Angeles, preparing for their four-thousand-mile journey up the new North American West Coast. Every day they would scavenge the crumbling, deserted homes and eerie, waterlogged streets in search of the right supplies. They planned for every possible danger, packed for every harsh and foreboding terrain. They knew they were using precious time staying in LA, but every minute was desperately needed.

Even still, after all that, she feels like nothing could have prepared her for any of this. Sitting around a fire in a deserted home *talking* about what to expect doesn't shield one from the numbing pain of swollen feet, open blisters and a merciless desert sun. Or the bee stings, the slithering things, and the icy-cold evenings.

But, one foot in front of the other—they've discussed this. They've made a pact. There is no room for negative thinking, which, especially when out in the elements, can prove equally as fatal.

Just keep moving.

Lucas turns from the sign and his face drops.

Maia's seen this face before, back when they were stuck on a collapsing raft of garbage in the middle of the Pacific Ocean and a storm was heading their way. Her heart plummets to her gut as Lucas slowly pulls the bandana from his gaping mouth, his eyes wide in horror as he scans the horizon behind her. He mouths something. She cannot hear him but she knows exactly what he's saying. She reluctantly follows his gaze and her rag drops to the dust.

"*Meu Deus,*" she repeats as Lucas steps next to her.

They stand frozen before the swiftly approaching, mammoth wall of sand.

Lucas turns towards Maia and yells through the barrage of dust suddenly pelting the side of their sun-scorched cheeks, but she can no longer hear him.

Every possible danger.

Every imaginable terrain.

The billowing cloud mushrooms from the horizon, quickly choking out the last remnants of the sun. They should be running for their lives, but Maia is paralyzed by her thoughts.

What she wouldn't give to be back in the hellish streets of LA.

CHAPTER 1

The once stagnant layers of grime now swirl along the surface of the murky waters. Maia nudges a floating teddy bear with the tip of her finger. Drowned facedown, his fur is matted with thick layers of dust. Lucas is ahead of her, slowly wading through the flooded mall's thigh-high waters.

They crane their necks as they scour the massive lobby for a map. Heavy layers of black mold sprawl across the cathedral ceiling windows, interrupted only by the occasional beam of light streaming through its broken glass. Rows of suspicious murmuring pigeons perched along the ceiling's high ledges glare down upon them through the crisscrossing of vines. Lucas and Maia carefully maneuver around another rusted grocery cart tipped on its side.

"Careful around these escalators." Lucas's whispers echo across the lobby. "Lots of broken glass around the railings."

"Escalators?" Maia whispers back.

"Yes, the stairs here." He points towards the steps leading down from the floor above. "They are called 'escalators.' They used to move so people didn't have to walk down them."

Maia studies the corrugated metal steps. "Move ... and go where?"

Lucas smiles, shaking his head. "I'll explain later. We need to keep moving."

They quietly shuffle past a row of submerged benches engulfed in clumps of weeds. Maia's foot slips beneath the black water. She sinks to her chin and her hands slide along the gritty tiles below.

"You okay?" Lucas wades back towards her.

She gains her footing and lifts herself out of the muck. Dripping wet, she nervously scans her palms.

Lucas grabs her hands, flipping them front to back. "*Nada*?" he whispers.

"Nothing."

"Good. A cut is the last thing we need." Lucas looks around. "Okay, back on the ship, Mario told me there would be maps in open areas like this. Look for some sort of framed glass, something that would have information on it."

Maia glances around. They are in the middle of something called a "mall," in a lobby of some sort. Dark halls extend in every direction while four different escalators descend from the floor above, circling around them with tarnished metal railings. In the middle of the room, a grand Romanesque statue of a man emerges from the water. His marble fingers reach to the ceiling as if in a desperate plea for help.

Nestled against one of the back walls is a large glass frame supported by a stand.

"Lucas."

He stops in a beam of light and turns towards her. His long curls are tied off his face, half-hidden once again under a thick beard. He looks at her with that same serious Lucas face, the face she has probably seen far too much of these last few weeks living in LA. Always worried. Always on guard.

Maia tilts her head, smiling at him, and his features soften.

"You okay?" he whispers.

She nods towards the sign. "Could that be what we're looking for?" she asks.

He twists in the water, following her gaze. "Could be."

They carefully wade towards the sign. Slowly. Methodically. Their feet search beneath the black waters for sure footing before taking each step.

Maia tears the vines from the glass while Lucas scoops water between his cupped hands, splashing it against the cracked pane. The water rolls down in tiny balls across the heavy layers of dust. Lucas wipes the sign with the back of his fist, revealing a diagram of multicolored boxes.

He sighs in relief. "Okay, Mario said that our best hope to find supplies would be from places most out of reach. Difficult places." He glances at Maia from the corner of his eye. "*Dangerous* places."

She nods.

He looks back at the map. "There should be a shop here that used to sell hunting equipment. Mario mentioned it will be at the end of one of the dark corridors and will have many floors. The most coveted supplies will be underwater on the lowest levels."

Lucas continues to wipe the frame. Along the far edge is an index. He drags his finger along the glass. "Here, I think this is it." He looks up, scanning the massive space for the correct entryway. "There. It will be down there."

They both look in the direction he points—a gaping

black hole leading down a long corridor. A curtain of vines hangs from the opening like fangs. A green *Emergency Exit* sign dangles between them. Half-unhinged from its post, it is slowly being pulled from its grip by a vine's leafy tendrils.

Lucas looks down at Maia, his eyes plagued with doubt.

She grabs his hand. "Lucas, we've got to do this. We need more supplies before we try to find your brother and this city is *tragically* picked over."

"Yes, okay," he sighs. "Let's just get this over with."

Together, they wade across the expansive foyer to the corridor and push their way through the vines. Lucas reaches into his pack and pulls out a small flashlight. Flicking it on, a white beam cuts through the blackness.

The ceiling appears to be pulsing. He flicks his light upwards, revealing hundreds of sleeping bats.

"Oh, *God*," Maia whispers.

"It's okay. They won't bother us if we don't bother them."

"I guess that would explain the smell," Maia says with a grimace. "No wonder this water is so dark."

"Try not to think about it."

Lucas sweeps the torch back and forth across the flooded corridor, guiding their path in bursts of light as they continue to navigate their way deeper and deeper down the dark passageway. There are much smaller shops down here, their busted-out storefronts tattooed with graffiti, thick weeds, and a lacework of vines. Lucas shines his light inside each but only briefly. One by one they are all the same, their insides long gutted from years of looting.

"That torch is amazing," Maia whispers. "I can't believe Jake would ever part with it."

Lucas is quiet. "Yes, well," he finally says without looking at her. "They had a few. They were very kind to me with their supplies."

Maia's foot rams into something beneath the water. "Lucas?" she whispers.

"What is it?" He shines the torch into the murky water, but the light only reflects back at him.

"I don't know, but it's not completely solid. Do I step over it?" Maia asks.

"Go around."

She nudges the mound with the tip of her foot, slowly inching towards Lucas. A metal shelf sticking out from the water slides off the submerged bulk, sending small waves in every direction. Lucas continues to shine his light where Maia now stands. A few air bubbles break along the surface of the water, and a bloated body of a man emerges.

Maia recoils, her hand to her mouth. The back of his matted head has been gravely injured, his skull caving in at the site of the wound.

"He's not that old, Lucas. People have been down here."

"Let's keep moving."

Lucas continues to sweep the light of his torch across the corridor, stopping every so often to listen for noise. It is eerily quiet, save for the occasional flutter above. His light pauses on a row of vending machines looming before them, a perfect place to hide. He holds his hand up, telling Maia without words to *stop*. Pulling his knife from its sheath, Lucas takes a wide angle around the machines, searching the surroundings with his torch. He stops, then glances back at Maia. "All clear."

Finally reaching the end of the corridor, they are met with a large wall of busted glass doors. Lucas's flashlight skims the rusted letters sprawled above them.

Outdoor World.

"This is it."

They carefully step through the doorways of broken

glass. Once inside, they wade past lane after lane of small black screens, the drawers below them open and emptied. It's a scene Maia has come across her entire life. Those drawers used to hold papers and coins inside that held all the power in the world—a power now as useless as the papers. She wades past the closest lane. Its empty drawer sits on the countertop, untouched and covered in dust. A few paper bills still float beneath it.

Lucas and Maia reach the railings of another set of escalator stairs peeking out from the water, leading down into a gaping black hole.

"I think this is it," Lucas says.

They stare down into the murky depths. Maia unzips her pack and pulls out a bundled rope.

"Let me go first," Lucas whispers.

"But I'm the stronger swimmer."

He takes the rope from her hands. "Maia, this is a fight you will never win."

Maia sighs. Snatching the torch from his hand, she shines the light on him as he unravels the end of the bundle. He ties it around his waist and knots it a few times, then hooks the rest of the rope around his shoulder. Fumbling below the water, he unties his shoes, then hands the dripping sneakers to Maia. She sets them on the counter behind her, then turns to grab his shoulders.

"Okay, start packing your lungs like we've practiced— we'll do the first round together." She holds up her pack and he loops his arms through the straps. "As soon as you dive, I'll start counting," she continues. "After thirty seconds, I'll tug the rope, and unless you give three sharp tugs back, I will start pulling to help you get up as fast as possible. If you need me to pull at any time, just tug the rope once."

Maia holds up one finger. In unison, they take a deep

breath and hold it. She uncurls a second finger, and they fill their puffed cheeks with more oxygen and push it down into their lungs. Lucas nods and turns towards the escalators. Without hesitating, he dives into the black hole leading to the lower level.

Maia releases her breath as Lucas's tiny beam of light disappears beneath the murk, leaving her blanketed in complete darkness. She grips the end of the rope as the water sloshes against the shelving.

One one-thousand, two one-thousand, three one-thousand.

After thirty seconds, Maia tugs hard on the rope. No response. She pulls hard, one hand over the other, grunting from the weight. Her feet sliding beneath her, she props them against the bottom of the escalator railings for leverage.

Just when she is about to panic, the light of the torch cuts through the blackness and Lucas breaks the surface with a desperate gasp. Maia holds the escalator railing and pulls him to shallow water. She takes the torch from his hand and surveys his body for cuts. Searching his face, she whispers, "Are you okay?"

Lucas looks up at her but can only respond in gasps.

She lifts the pack from his back and he wriggles his arms out. "What's it like down there?"

"There's not much," Lucas says as he catches his breath, "but we'll keep diving. It's hard at first not to panic and vision is limited." He unties the knot around his waist, then hands Maia the rope and takes the torch from her. As she works on tying it around herself, Lucas clears his throat. "Any chance you can use any of those powers of yours to hold your breath longer?"

Maia looks up at him, unsure. "I wouldn't know how. But

I can hold my breath for a long time. I've been diving my entire life."

"I have too, Maia, but it's pretty unsettling down there."

"Where shall I go? No point scouring the same area."

"Yes, dive straight to the back. There seems to be a lot more the farther back you go. Looks like hunting supplies back there."

Maia smiles.

Lucas grabs her hand. "Be careful. Don't let your rope get caught on anything. It's a mess down there. Keep it wrapped like this." He hands her the bundle. "And let it unravel as you swim."

"Okay."

"Don't forget to keep track of time. The farther back you go, the longer I have to pull you out and the more dangerous this becomes."

"I know, Lucas. I can do this." Maia places her shoes next to his on the counter.

"Don't be stubborn! Listen to your body—"

"Lucas, *I've got this.*"

He grabs the sides of her face and kisses her. "Yes. Okay," he finally says. "Just please be careful."

Maia takes the torch from his hand and wades to the end of the stairs. Her toes totter along the edge of the first step. She works through packing her lungs and then dives down. The water is disturbingly warm. She places the torch between her teeth, and the light cuts through the darkness in a small beam. She kicks farther down, gliding above the long trail of escalator stairs as the rope unravels around her arm.

Once at the bottom, her light trips over layers of toppled shelving covered in a thick blanket of sand. The endless mountains of rubbish seem to blend in one muted mess.

She sweeps her light across the clutter until she sees the back wall.

She's only just arrived and can already feel the strain on her lungs, like a balloon about to pop. Panic sets in but she pushes it down, kicking deeper through the chaos of half-floating boxes, shreds of clothing, and endless bits of debris.

The darkness and the wreckage seem to close in on her. Lightheaded and disorientated, Maia twists within the water. Which way are the escalators? She traces the trail of rope beneath her with her torch. Reassured, she flips towards the back wall again, scanning its contents with her light.

And that's when she sees them.

Still encased in flooded glass are what appears to be a selection of carbon hunting bows. Made with a system of cables and pulleys, they give the hunter a power and speed unmatched by any handmade bow.

Maia's lungs thrash beneath her chest. She is out of time. The rope begins to unravel around her arm and she grabs hold as Lucas pulls from above. Kicking ferociously, she swims up the escalators, desperate to take a breath.

She gasps as she breaks the surface and swims towards Lucas's open arms. "I didn't ... didn't ... get anything."

"It's okay. Take a rest, and I'll try again."

"Back wall. Go..."

"Yes, I've got it." He unties the knot from her waist and winds the rope around his arm, then dives back under.

Maia stands gasping in the dark, beginning her count-down once again.

When Lucas comes back up, it's sooner than before. "I'm out of practice," he says as he coughs up seawater. "I needed to turn around before I reached the back wall."

Maia is more determined than ever. She can do this. She

has held her breath many times diving for food. But then again, there was an endless ocean above her. And light. And she wasn't in a flooded mall in the middle of Los Angeles with danger lurking around every corner.

That back wall. That back wall has everything they need. She must get to that back wall.

Plunging beneath the water, Maia follows the same path as before. Her tired lungs begin to ache but she keeps kicking, gliding over the mountains of refuse and bins and shelving. Her light sweeps over the back wall while she fights to ignore her panicked lungs.

Reaching the bows, she bangs at the glass with the back of the torch. Air bubbles escape her pressed lips. She hammers again—nothing. She scans her light around for anything sharp to break it.

Breathe. Need to breathe. Can't breathe.

More air bubbles escape.

She's waited too long. She tugs at the rope and holds on tight as it drags her along. Grimacing, she covers her nose and mouth. The pressure from her burning lungs feels like it's ripping her from the inside out.

Can't ... breathe...

She is on the verge of passing out. The rope tightens around her waist and Lucas tears her from the water.

"*Maia!*" he screams at her. "That was too long!"

Wheezing and coughing, she falls across Lucas's arms. "I..." she finally manages to mutter. "I ... made it ... to the ... back wall. There are bows down there, Lucas."

He sighs, holding her until her breathing calms. "Maia, what good is a bow if you're not here to shoot it?" he asks quietly.

Maia pushes away from him. "I have to go back down."

"No."

She laughs. "*No?*"

"It's too dangerous, Maia." He gazes down at her. Then shaking his head, he adds, "I don't trust you."

"I can hold my breath longer than you. I'm the only one between the two of us that can make it that far." She coughs again. "Those bows ... just *one* of those bows will make all the difference in the world for our journey. It will allow us to hunt and protect ourselves in a way that *far* exceeds any homemade bow. And they're *right there*. I just need to break the glass. Give me your knife."

Lucas reluctantly hands her his knife, and she tucks it into a zipper on the outside of her pack. He glares at her as he winds up the rope, then lassos it around her arm and hooks it over her shoulder. "This is the last time, Maia. I won't lose you over a bow," he says dryly.

"You won't. I'll get it this time." Maia doesn't wait for a response. She fills her lungs and dives down. Gliding through the water, she is focused. Resolute. Her lungs begin to panic but she is already at the glass. She keeps her flashlight between her teeth and pulls the knife from her pack, driving it hard into the case. Nothing. She stabs again. And again.

Fractures splinter across the glass. Her lungs burn. Panicked, she continues to bang. Hard, *harder*. Desperate for air, her chest feels like it'll burst.

This is all in her mind. She needs to calm her mind. There is plenty of oxygen in her blood. She'll be okay—she knows this.

The glass is fractured but it won't break. The pressure from the water must be holding it in place. This is her last shot; she can't come down here again. She closes her eyes and focuses on the energy of the water surrounding her. Hovering her hand just outside the case, she pushes the weight of the ocean against it. She opens her eyes, watching in awe as the glass splinters further.

She rips her hand back and the glass shatters across the gloom.

Maia's rope tugs hard and without a second's notice begins to pull her from the bows. She reaches for the wall but Lucas has already pulled her too far. She twists within the water and grabs the rope, tugging back three times. The rope slacks and she kicks back through the floating layers of shattered glass.

Grasping the bow with both hands, she places her feet against the wall and rips the contraption from its mount. She swims farther down and grabs a container of arrows. The rope around her waist tightens once again. She wraps her arms around the glorious carbon as Lucas drags her across the ceiling of the enormous warehouse and up the escalator stairs.

Breaking the surface, Maia thrashes as Lucas shouts. Grabbing her pack, he yanks her from the flooded stairwell and holds her until she finds her footing.

Embracing her brand-new bow, Maia catches her breath, peering up at an unimpressed-looking Lucas with a smile.

CHAPTER 2

E ndless rows of dust-covered cars line the deserted streets of LA. Lucas and Maia walk side by side down the middle of the crumbling road, stepping around small patches of bushes flourishing between the cracks.

Constantly scanning their surroundings, their pace is hurried. Quiet. Their time is limited. With the light around them already beginning to fade, they must get back to their home base before dark.

Maia's beloved new bow is strapped across her chest. She holds it close to her side. Their mission in the flooded mall was dangerous but necessary. The streets of LA have been completely destroyed and scavenged over the years, but there are still treasures to be found. They just have to know where to look. It's been a process, but with thousands of miles ahead of them, they must take full advantage of their current location to find what's left.

A stray dog growls from the shadows. A few more wander alongside them, curious and sniffing with their noses in the air.

Maia smiles at Lucas with his dripping sack of new supplies, but she does not say a word. It is imperative that they travel as quietly as possible. Do not attract attention; no speaking allowed. Maia waves her hand to grab Lucas's attention. When he glances at her, she points to her eye. He smirks and points to his heart. She points back at him and he nods with a grin.

The sun disappears beneath the hill behind them and they pick up their pace. Fireflies flicker in small clusters and right on time, the endless hordes of crickets begin their nightly symphony. Maia has never heard so many crickets in her entire life; the sound is nothing short of magnificent. If it weren't for the looming and near-constant threat of danger from walking the city streets, she might actually enjoy being here.

There is beauty to be found in the simplicity of nature slowly devouring the ugliness left behind. Green weeds and brush are swallowing up the roads. Dust and dirt are tackling the slow and steady transition from man-made rot back into earth. It will take a long time, but it will be just as Grandpa said. It will be like humans were never here.

Maia and Lucas approach an intersection with an enormous yellow traffic light smashed in the middle. They quickly skirt around it and continue across. A decaying car on the other side catches Maia's eye. The tires have been stripped and the windows broken, but this car has a small tree bursting from its hollowed-out hood. She wonders what sort of tree it is. A cottonwood, maybe? Do those grow here?

Something moves from behind the car, and Maia's heart skips a beat. Another stray dog? They're everywhere.

No—not right. Something isn't right.

The hairs on the back of her neck rise. The tranquil beauty of their surroundings fades, and Maia's world becomes eerily quiet. She slows her pace, holding her hand up wide in the air. Lucas glances in her direction.

Stop.

She listens for movement, her heart pounding. Lucas waves his hand, trying to steal her attention.

A dark figure pops up from behind the rusted car. Lucas and Maia stop in the middle of the intersection. A man steps out into the street. Shuffling his feet along the sandy cement, torn strips of his baggy pants drag behind him. He smiles a haggardly black grin, and his crusted skin wrinkles into folds around his eyes.

Another figure wanders out just a little farther behind him. He is also smiling. A little younger than the first man, he wears thick leather boots. His bony hands tremble at his side.

Maia can't help but wonder how old these men actually are—it is impossible to say. They are cloaked in the harshness of their surroundings. Small scabs cover their faces. Their long hair grows sparsely around clusters of scaly, blood-crusted bald patches.

Bounders. Despite being mostly deserted, this city is overrun with them, making Maia and Lucas's short time here a living hell. The smiles slide from the men's faces as they slowly approach.

"Stop right there," Lucas says to the older man.

The man cocks his head to one side, never once taking his eyes off Maia. A smile curves from his cracked lips. "What is that you have there?" he sneers.

Maia slides the bow behind her as if her petite frame could possibly shield the large weapon from view.

The man steps closer to Maia and Lucas lifts his hand towards him. "I said—"

JILLIAN WEBSTER

The man pulls out a gun and points it at Maia. He glares at Lucas. "I heard ya."

"What do you want?" Maia asks. Her voice is low and cold as ice as she grips her bow behind her. She knows exactly what he wants.

"That's an intriguing question you ask," the man says, turning towards her. His cheek twitches as he looks Maia up and down, a gesture she has grown tired of seeing since leaving her cabin back in New Zealand. "Is that—" His face twitches again and he stops, picking at a scab on his cheek. Smiling, he flicks the crusted skin in her direction.

Refusing to react, Maia lifts her chin.

"Is that a *bowgun* you got there?" the man asks.

"We were just passing through. We'll be on our way now," Lucas says, keeping his hand lifted.

The man looks at Lucas in annoyance and pivots his gun towards him. "I said, I *heard* ya." Keeping his weapon pointed at Lucas, he walks towards Maia.

She steps back.

"*Ah-ah* ... don't move a muscle," he warns.

The younger man behind him approaches, laughing and covering his mouth in excitement. "Boss, she's a demon! Look! She got one blue eye and one green! *Demon!*"

The older man tilts his head to the side. "*Nah*, she's not a demon ... she's just a *freak*."

Maia glares at him.

"I think..." He pauses, rubbing his chin with his other hand. "Yes, I think you should hand that bow over to me."

Maia tightens her grip. He veers his gun towards her, pressing the cool metal against her forehead.

He's bluffing. Surely. There are a lot of crazies around here, a lot of old guns. Never ammunition.

At least not yet.

"Lady! He's going to *shoot* you!" the young man yells, jumping up and down.

"I'll shoot the both of ya if you don't hand over that bow."

He's bluffing. He would have done it by now.

"Hold him," the older man barks.

The young man marches over to Lucas, now holding his knife before him.

"Throw the knife to the ground," the older man yells. He keeps his gun against Maia's head, never once taking his eyes off hers. "Do it now or I'll shoot her."

"Don't do it, Lucas," Maia says through gritted teeth. There's no ammunition in that gun. She doesn't know how, but she's sure of it.

The man gives her an amused look. "You have a death wish, girl?"

"Maia?" Lucas yells and she glances towards him.

The man pummels his fist into her ribs and she doubles over, gasping for air. The metallic sound of Lucas's knife skids across the cement. The younger man swipes it from the ground, then stomps up to Lucas, punching him hard across his chin. Maia flinches, struggling to keep a straight face. Lucas falls to the road, and the young man kicks his side with the tip of his boot. Lucas cries out, arching backward against the ground.

"*Stop!*" Maia shrieks.

The younger man drags Lucas up by his hair and places the knife against his throat.

"This is your last chance," the old man says. He wraps his hand around the back of Maia's neck, pressing the pistol deeper into her skin. "Hand it over or die."

"Maia!" Lucas pleads from the ground.

Maia continues to glare at the man.

"No?" He releases her neck and steps back, still keeping the gun pointed at her head. He shrugs. "Okay, then. Better step away, this'll be messy."

"No, *please!*" Lucas yells.

He pulls the trigger.

Click.

She knew it.

"What the—" He looks to the other man, confused.

"Shit, boss, I *told you*—"

Maia glances at Lucas and he nods. Reaching for the young man's hand with the knife, Lucas twists it behind him and kicks him hard into a car. Maia grips her bow and without hesitating, arches back and swings it around, bashing it across the older man's face. He stumbles back. Screaming and holding his cheek, blood pours between his fingers.

"*Run*, Maia!" Lucas yells.

They race back up the street, bursting through clouds of fireflies. The younger man advances behind Maia, panting loudly as his boots hit the pavement. She keeps the bow held out in front of her, slowing her stride. The man lurches forward. Clutching the bottom of her shirt, he rips the lower half away. She wavers but maintains her footing. Lucas continues running ahead of her. Their precious pack of supplies has been left behind.

A pack of stray dogs race alongside them, barking and nipping at their heels. The young man cries out from behind and pounces on top of Maia. They fly into the sandy cement. The dogs surround them, barking and growling and revealing their teeth. The man straddles her, grunting as he fumbles with the strap of the bow around her neck.

"No!" Maia screams into the dust. She flips to face him, clutching at the strap. "No, *please!*"

"Just give us ... the ... *bow!*" he spits through his gasps. He wraps his hands around her neck, placing all his weight on top.

Maia releases the strap. Clutching at his hands, her feet kick against the pavement. Lucas runs to her side. Tearing the man off her, he throws him to the ground and kicks him in his ribs. Maia crawls away on all fours, gasping for air, her bow dragging against the cement.

The older man walks up with their pack on his back and grabs Maia by her hair, dragging her up from the ground. He steps behind her and holds her against him, wrapping his arm around her neck. Still gasping for air, Maia clutches her bow.

"Stop. *Now*," the older man says.

Lucas looks up and releases his grip from the younger man's shirt. The man wipes the blood from his nose, then pounds Lucas hard in the gut. Lucas doubles over and drops to his knees.

"Okay," the older man huffs. "So, you called our bluff— no bullets. But *here's* something new, my buddy here left your knife for me." He waves the blade in front of Maia's face. "And I've grown *tired* of this fighting."

Lucas holds up his hands in a sign of truce.

"Such a beautiful lady," the man whispers into Maia's ear.

She closes her eyes, fighting her rage rising within.

"Maia! Just *give* it to him!" Lucas yells from the ground.

The man yanks her hair back, forcing her chin to the sky. "Can you feel *that*?" A sharp pain digs into the side of her throat.

"Maia, *please!*" Lucas begs.

"Okay!" Maia cries out. "*Okay*." She holds out her hands, leaving her bow hanging across her chest.

The man pushes her away, pulling the strap of her bow out from around her. He holds it in the air, then howls in laughter with rattled lungs. The pack of dogs around them continues to bark.

"Look at this *beauty*!" he proclaims with wide, twitching eyes, the blood still oozing from the gash ripped across his cheek and nose. "We're done here," he says with a nod. "Now, don't move until you can no longer see us." He wraps the strap of the bow across his chest and spits at Maia's feet. "Ya hear me? Or I'll kill the both of ya." He wags the bloody knife in her face.

The men back up slowly. Maia doesn't break her glare, her cheeks hot with indignation. A stray German shepherd barks at the older man and he swipes at it with the bow, barely missing its head. The men continue to walk backward up the street until they are out of sight. Their cheers echo off the buildings.

Maia falls to her knees next to Lucas, grimacing as he rubs his back. They gaze at each other for a long while without speaking.

Something trickles down Maia's neck. She swipes at it. Her fingertips are coated in blood.

Lucas leans over, scrutinizing the cut. "We need to get you home."

"How badly are you hurt?" Maia asks him.

"Not bad," he says, opening and closing his jaw. He eyes her, shaking his head. "You are the most *stubborn* woman I have *ever*—"

"I knew they were bluffing," she whispers.

Lucas stares at her neck. She covers it with her hand.

"You didn't know that," Lucas finally responds.

"They would have shot us in the beginning, surely."

"No, not *surely*. Not if they were smart. They would have

tried to hold on to their bullets unless it was an emergency. But I promise you, taking our bow would have been worth a bullet," Lucas says, hanging his head between his knees.

Maia looks up the street, a small hill shadowed by a barely lit sky. The silhouettes of a few dogs sit at the top. Another one scampers across.

"They took my bow," Maia whispers, her eyes unblinking.

"They took everything," Lucas mumbles.

"*Everything* can be replaced. And we have backups at home base. They *took* my *bow*." Maia fights back tears. "I nearly died getting that bow."

"You nearly died for keeping it too."

Maia hangs her head.

"Can't you just make one?" Lucas quietly asks.

"Not like that. Not anything *near* close to that. Having a bow of that caliber could mean the difference between life and death for us."

"Well..." Lucas shakes his head. "It's gone now."

A fiery anger burns inside her. After everything they've just been through. All that risk. All that time diving and endangering their lives for that bow, and just like that ... *it's gone.*

"This can't happen again," she mutters between gritted teeth.

"What are you thinking?" he asks.

"Combat training," she says definitively. "At home base. We don't leave LA until we can seriously fight and defend ourselves."

Lucas looks at her a long while before answering.

"I know what you're thinking, Lucas. But it has to be done."

"I could never fight you."

"You can. And you will." Her voice breaks. "You *must*."

He sighs, staring at the small cut on her neck. He lifts a single finger to his eye. Then his heart.

A muggy darkness falls over them.

"I love you too," Maia whispers.

To be continued...

Be the first to know when the next book is released by signing up for the author's newsletter at:

www.jillianwebster.com.

THE WEIGHT OF A THOUSAND OCEANS BOOK CLUB QUESTIONS

PLEASE NOTE: In order to provide reading groups with the most thought-provoking questions, it is necessary to reveal important aspects of the story. If you have not finished reading *The Weight of a Thousand Oceans*, please consider refraining from reviewing these questions.

1. The story begins with Maia asking her grandfather about what happened before The End, and despite having clues scattered throughout the book, the author never discloses exact events. Do you think this has any effect on the overall storyline? The author writes, "And then there it is, the proverbial straw, falling like a feather on a plane of splintered glass; a single mutation from a creature long forgotten. And for the first time in hundreds of years, nature's decree of checks and balances is restored.

In the end, there is silence.

Heaving for breath, tears coat her cheeks. It all makes sense now. The faded red *X*s on doors. The ghostly quarantine buildings. Her grandfather's horrified face and refusal to speak. She can see it all, catastrophic and swift."

What do you believe this is alluding to?

2. Maia's foreboding dreams often involve her facing an image of herself that terrifies her. The dreams often take place on the ocean. Maia wears a white dress. There's a dark city looming behind Maia's mother. Do you believe these features are symbolic? In what way?

3. When Maia's grandfather is dying, she thinks a lot about her ancestors and the life they lived. She likens them to a virus. "A force to be reckoned with." How do you feel about this? Do you agree? Why or why not?

4. Grandpa fights very hard in the beginning to keep Maia in New Zealand, despite knowing how deeply unhappy this makes her. Why do you think he does this? What would you do if your child or loved one had a dream for their life that could put them at risk? Would you support them or try to stop them?

5. Maia's power is speckled throughout the story but she doesn't understand what it means until the very end. What were your thoughts on this as you read? Did you gather who she was before she did?

6. When Maia is spreading her grandfather's ashes, she has a flashback where they are cleaning out the rubbish from a river. Her grandfather tells her that every little thing they do makes a difference. Do you agree? Why or why not?

7. Maia's father negotiated with a known criminal to get her smuggled on board a ship of pirates. He warned Maia that should she get caught, she could be killed, "or worse." Do

you think this was a *selfless* or *selfish* act? Do you believe he went out of his way just to help her or was it possible he was only doing it to relieve his own guilt for being an absent father?

8. Maia's story is filled with both beautiful and devastating scenery. Which scene stands out the most to you and why?

9. In a post-apocalyptic world, Grandpa says that the people left behind have been thrown back into the Stone Age. Humans may still go extinct, so therefore it is Maia's "duty" to procreate. After the steps taken to free women of this stereotype, how do you feel about this?

10. If you were in Maia's position and had a choice to stay home safe but spend your entire life alone, or go out into a dangerous world to find a new life that may or may not exist, what would *you* do?

11. When Maia dreams about walking through the city streets of her ancestors, most of the people she sees have become one with their phones. "Connected" and "Charging" are displayed on their arms. Maia wanders into an establishment where people are lined along a bar. "Their eyes unblinking, they stare into blank space like robots. Their fingertips hover just above the wooden bar, scrolling, scrolling, scrolling. Their arms lit up like fireworks." Some would say this is not far off from where we are now. Do you agree? Would you consider this to be a good or a bad thing?

12. The story ends with Maia discovering an adolescent tiger. What are your predictions for the next book?

ACKNOWLEDGMENTS

First and foremost, I would like to give immense gratitude to my husband, Rich, for not only supporting me as I pursued my dream of writing this book, but for believing in it as much as I did. Thank you for being my biggest cheerleader, my toughest critic, my sounding board and my partner. You are the first person to whom I wrote, "I will love you forever, and when forever is over, I will still keep loving you." Thank you for letting Grandpa and Maia borrow it.

They say it takes a village to raise a child. I would say the same goes for publishing a book. I'm not good at asking for help, but I set that aside when it came to writing this novel. To all the people I reached out to who helped me out of the kindness of their hearts, I owe you my most heartfelt thanks: Sophia Ling, Christine Ling, Heather Applegate, Melanie Segur, Jen Page, Lisa Feder, and my dearest Elizabeth Packman. You've all played a part in making this book what it is and I thank you for that.

All the love in the world goes out to my biggest supporters: my family and my closest friends. You guys are my rock.

And to my grandfather, who I unexpectedly lost while writing this book, I hope I've made you proud.

To my cover designer, Murphy Rae, I am beyond grateful I found you. I am madly in love with this cover and can't wait to see what magic you whip up for the next books.

To my editors, Amanda Hughes at Haint Blue Publishing and Madeleine Collinge at Madeleine Collinge Publishing Services: the thought, detail, and attention you put into my manuscript blew me away. From the bottom of my heart, I thank you.

BIBLIOGRAPHY

The following materials were useful to me in writing this book:

Beeson, Chris. *The Handbook of Survival at Sea.* Lewis Intl Inc., 2003.

Flannery, Tim. *The Weather Makers: The History and Future Impact of Climate Change.* The Text Publishing Company, 2008.

Flannery, Tim. *Here on Earth: A New Beginning.* Allen Lane/Penguin Press, 2010.

Goodenough, Ursula. *The Sacred Depths of Nature.* Oxford University Press, 1998.

Harari, Yuval Noah. *Sapiens: A Brief History of Mankind.* Harper Perennial; Reprint edition, 2018.

Johnson, Elizabeth A. *Ask the Beasts: Darwin and the God of Love.* Bloomsbury Continuum, 2014.

Lovelock, James. *The Revenge of Gaia: Earth's Climate Crisis and the Fate of Humanity.* Basic Books, 2007.

Mancuso, Stefano, and Alessandra Viola. *Brilliant Green: The Surprising History and Science of Plant Intelligence.* Island Press, 2018.

Maslin, Mark. *The Coming Storm: The True Causes of Freak Weather – and Why It's Going to Get Worse.* Barron's Educational Series, 2002.

Pollan, Michael. *The Botany of Desire: A Plant's-eye View of the World.* Random House, 2001.

Shubin, Neil. *Your Inner Fish: A Journey into the 3.5-Billion-year History of the Human Body.* Pantheon, 2008.

Shubin, Neil. *The Universe Within: A Scientific Adventure.* Penguin Books, 2013.

Weisman, Alan. *The World Without Us.* Picador/Thomas Dunne Books, 2008.

There is a wealth of information on the Intergovernmental Panel on Climate Change. I gleaned most of my information from this source. With 195 members and thousands of contributors, the information given by this Nobel Peace Prize-winning organization should be a mandatory read by anyone wanting to educate themselves on the state of our planet. Please see ipcc.ch for more information.

ABOUT THE AUTHOR

Jillian Webster is the author of *Scared to Life: A Memoir* and has also written for *Access Magazine*. Originally from Michigan, Jillian now lives in New Zealand with her husband and dog, a rescue collie-mix named Biggie. When she's not writing, she enjoys nature walks, yoga, and cooking.

The Weight of a Thousand Oceans is her first work of fiction and is the first book in *The Forgotten Ones* trilogy.

Stay connected:

www.jillianwebster.com

facebook.com/websterjillian
instagram.com/authorjillianwebster